In 1991 Joe Donnelly was awarded Scottish Reporter of the Year for his investigative writing on child abuse cases, and for the feature that resulted from his being first on the scene after the Shotts Prison riot. Currently writing for the *Sunday Mail*, he has worked for various newspapers and travelled extensively. He is the author of three subsequent chillers, STONE, THE SHEE and STILL LIFE, and lives in Dumbarton with his family.

By the same author

STONE

THE SHEE

STILL LIFE

BANE

Joe Donnelly

ARROW

Arrow Books Limited
20 Vauxhall Bridge Road, London SW1V 2SA

A division of Random House UK Ltd

London Melbourne Sydney Auckland
Johannesburg and agencies throughout
the world

First published in Great Britain
by Barrie & Jenkins Ltd 1989

This edition published in 1993 by Arrow Books

5 7 9 10 8 6 4

Printed and bound by Firmin-Didot (France),
Group Herissey. No d'impression : 27748.

ISBN 0 09 970300 9

FOR
MARY, MARTIN, NICK AND ALAN

ONE

The road I travelled skirted the firth. At every second bend I could see that flat expanse of blue-grey stretching far out. If I'd looked hard enough I could have seen the smudge on the horizon where the Gantocks poked out its long finger almost as far as the shipping lane, but if I'd done that I'd probably never have made it home.

Home. I suppose I could call Arden that. More than any place else, I reckon. When I'm far away, that's how I think of it. But the closer I got – and if I was on the Kilcreggan Road, then I was pretty damned close; no turning back now – the less sure I was. Oh, I'd travelled this road plenty of times, but those times were a while back. This was *now* and that is always fraught with uncertainty. The picture in my mind always gets rosier in direct relation to the distance from the place I usually call home.

When I was a kid, we'd go on holiday to Devon or Yorkshire, and even once to France where I was sick for a week after drinking a bottle of wine and told I had nobody to blame but myself. Holidays were fine. It was the coming back that sent those cold fingers of apprehension trailing up my spine. Would our *home* be there? Would Arden still be the *same*? I would always be in the back seat, with my carrier bag filled with books and puzzles to keep me amused as the Morris or the Austin, or whatever old car my father's salary as a teacher would run to, ate up the miles. My father would drive with his head back, that straight pipe jutting out, humming some classical tune just a shade louder than the engine. My mother would be asleep, curled on her seat, feet tucked up. All I'd see would be a mess of light brown curls, and maybe the glint of her tiny gold – real gold – earring.

Going home for them was easy. For a six year old in the

1

back seat, looking out at the unfamiliar territory out there, it was a matter of mounting concern. And when we got on to the Kilcreggan Road, when my father would nudge my mother awake, it *was* different. Familiar, but different. Not in a menacing way, but as if it had to be re-affixed in my memory. The house always looked smaller, the garden larger, at least for those first few moments before *home* was impressed again on a young mind.

Now I had that same feeling, and it wasn't just a fortnight or three weeks that had passed. This was a homecoming, a prodigal returning. A lot of water had passed under Strowan's Bridge since I had last seen Arden. I'd come back once or twice for the compulsory wedding or two and funerals. The latter (two in quick succession were those of my parents) were in every case occasions of numbing depression from which I had to flee as quickly as decently possible.

No, it was ten years, more like twelve, since I had last thought casually, warmly, of Arden as home.

On tape, another one had stopped biting the dust. Old Freddy Mercury and his band were the champions. I cut him off in mid champ. Two more bends, first a right, then a left, then the boundary welcome. No?

No. Four more bends. That memory again. The road hadn't changed. The sign was still there, black on white, though, instead of blue. It seemed smaller. On over the bridge, with its sharp right at the bottom, and there I was, in Arden, coming in from the east.

It had changed, although the fabric was essentially the same. There was nothing substantial to the change, just a different feel. It was smaller. Or I was bigger. It seemed to me the roads were narrower, the houses set closer to it, the trees that bit more shady. It didn't have the feel of home.

Please, a small voice whispered inside my head. Let them just smile and say hello, long time no see, how is it going, have a drink.

Some hot-shot, hard-bitten ace reporter is Nicky Ryan. Nicky Ryan's a little bit scared.

And that was only the half of it. I was coming back to start all over again. I'd made the break. I'd made up my mind that twelve years chasing stories all over the world with a foot in somebody else's door were no longer for me. I'd grabbed my books and all those half-filled notebooks with the half-chewed plots and story lines, the novels I'd promised myself I'd write one of these days, and said: 'Do it. Do it *now*.'

This was now. This was me coming home. This was me going hell for leather to get up there beside Forsyth and Ludlum and King.

And what was really bothering me was that I didn't know if I could write more than ten paragraphs without putting in a shock, a horror or a drama.

I didn't know if the old home town had changed, or whether I could.

Let me tell you a little bit about Arden.

It's not a big town even by local standards. A large village would probably give you the picture, housing maybe three thousand people. But as I've said, it's old. Until the government started fooling about with the structure of local government and amalgamated lots of small individual towns into a great amorphous region, Arden was quite happy to trundle on alone. Officially, and the tiny council which loosely ran the place was fond of reminding you, it was known as The Royal Burgh of the Parish of Arden. A mouthful for a place its size.

Somewhere along the line, not long after William the Conqueror started his book-keeping operation, one of the Scottish kings granted the harbour town royal status, which was a bigger deal in those days than it is now. Being a Royal Burgh meant that Arden could have its own town council and make by-laws. It had a court and a sheriff who was the local judge and a provost who was a kind of country sheriff. They could jail people, and they could hang people, and if you didn't go to church on a Sunday they had all sorts of painful ways of saving your soul.

Bruce died near here of what the history books reckon

3

was leprosy, but now I'm not so sure.

Until only a few years ago, nobody knew that the mound around the Ardhmor peninsula was a Roman wall, built at the same time they were building the big one from Old Kilpatrick right across the country to the Forth. There's some standing stones poking out of the soil in a few places which make Stonehenge look like a new building project, and in the mud flats at the east of the town they once dug up a dugout canoe which was thousands of years old. Inside that were some bones which were said to be near enough human as to make no difference, and others positively identified as mammoth.

It's an old place, and probably hasn't changed all that much in a long time. The parish council allotted some land at the Milligs at the turn of the century for workers' housing, and later on some of the rich traders put up some sandstone mansions on the slope above the harbour where they could overlook Westbay, which held the bulk of the town's population. Then, as now, you had three classes of people, easily identified by their location in the town. Milligs was poor, Westbay was middle, and Upper Arden was pools-win territory. Looking back, I remember the feeling of awe when I considered that these people had gardeners, and maids. In my mind's eye they were royalty. My perspective has changed, but that feeling of being not among the *Upper* Arden dwellers is something that still sits uneasily in those shady corners below conscious thought. Then Upper Arden was Rovers, Westbay was Morris travellers, Milligs was pedestrian only. So what has changed? Ah, the internal combustion engine has reached the Milligs. The town's scrap yard is down there, and the sons of pedestrians drive beat-up Ford Cortinas with dented bumpers and the grey camouflage patching of fibreglass fill. Not too many road tax discs, or working sidelights, but Milligs has been emancipated into the era of road transport.

Westbay is where most of the people live. It merges with Milligs from the east and crowds round the harbour

4

in the west where the old Royal Burgh peters out to good farming on the shore side, and some low jagged cliffs north of the main road. Westbay now is new Cortinas and Fiestas. The people live in sandstone cottages and semi-detached and terrace houses one or two storeys high, or in those white rough cast boxes builders are throwing up all over the country in the few areas in Arden where they've found an acre or two to cram them on.

Upper Arden is still leafy and winding, the imposing homes set well back from the roads in well-tended gardens where rhododendron and azalea flank long pebbled or tarmac drives. There are bay windows, multi-chimneyed roofs. Here it is Range Rover country. It is Volvo estates with daytime sidelights. It is Barbour coats and green rubber boots, Pringle sweaters. Here is the tennis club, the dinner party, the barbecue, the pony paddock. Here is the wealth that shouts down the hill at those below. We've made it. We've got it. And we always will.

Past the sign there's a stand of trees on either side of the road, followed by a couple of smallholdings, and then the first houses, again flanking the Kilcreggan Road which veers away from the shore sharply. The Milligs. Even here you have a sub-division of class or wealth. The shore side, with its scrap yard and the town dump and the great gun-barrel of the main sewage pipe stretching far out on to the flats, is tougher and rougher and more raggedy than the other side of the street. Shore side has shacks and pigeon huts.

It has a couple of dog pounds where no doubt live the many times great-grandsons of those huge German shepherds that scared the shit out of me when I went exploring the dangerous, exciting side of town. On the far side of the road, the council housing was plain but solid enough under the peeling paint and the dirty grey roughcast. There is a section of allotments where people grew potatoes and onions, and a couple raised a chicken or two. No rhododendrons here. There was a corner store and a hardware store that used to be run by old Mr Smollett who'd sell us

5

milbro slingshots – the kind with the thumbprint grip that give you a black nail every second shot – then threatened us with a severe kick up the arse if he ever saw us playing with them near his shop. I was wondering if he was still alive when I passed by, slowing down to ten miles an hour, and I was pleasantly surprised – no *enormously* surprised and pleased when there he was, still wearing that old striped butcher's apron with the big pockets on the front, still wearing that close cropped grey moustache. He was coming out of the shop, preceded by two small boys, bending low to tell them something. I could swear that if I could lip read I'd make out what he was saying: 'There y'are now, and if you fire that thing near my window you'll get a toe up your arses. All the *way* up.'

On the right, still on the far side, I saw my first change. Ronnie Scott's garage had disappeared, to be replaced by one of those glass and steel beam carport filling stations with a tyre bay and an accessory shop. Ah, that was a loss. I teamed about at school with Ronnie's son Alan who was set to become a fair mechanic. We used to hang about in the workshop, among all those old, oily tools, camshafts, crankshafts and a huge lifting jack that took the two of us to pump, and then we'd stand on its lifter for that delicious moment when the other would twist the grip and float us gently to the ground. The big asbestos shack always smelled of old rubber and rust and oil. It was a place where we could use the grindstone to whittle down broken hack-saw blades into arrowheads and daggers, where we could sit in the cabs of smelly diesel trucks, or maybe in the front seat of a Jaguar from up the hill and roar around the Monza circuit. Alan's dad used to wink at us from under whichever car he'd be, or from the depths of his mechanics pit, occasionally yelling at us to mind we don't get mucky footprints on Doctor MacGregor's seat, or not to let off the handbrake of the big yellow caterpillar tractor. That was a garage. What I was pulling into was a filling station with a modern steel and concrete iron bay behind it.

My backside was sore and my accelerator foot was stiff

6

after all the miles the Subaru had rolled since I had left London late on the previous afternoon. I climbed down from the high seat and unhooked the nozzle from the pump. Four star burbled into the tank and I let it run, trying to stretch and arch my back with only one hand free. The big tank took twelve gallons before the automatic cut-off. I flipped the cap, jangled the nozzle back into its place and crossed over to the cash desk.

Passing by the pumps I realised what was really so different about the yard. It wasn't just new motorway modern. It was bigger, and set further back from the road, and the workshop and small glass-fronted showroom stood where the Scotts' tiny little cottage and garden had been the last time I'd seen it. I reckoned maybe his father had given up trying to make the small operation work, although he always seemed to be busy whenever we hung about on the rainy afternoons. Alan was determined to be a mechanic just like him, a wizard of the machine, who could get any engine chugging back to life. But I assumed with the recession he'd probably sold up to the petrol company and got out of Arden.

In at the cash desk a young girl of about sixteen with wavy brown short hair and a smattering of freckles flashed me a quick glimpse of a really perfect range of teeth. I asked for a couple of packets of cigarettes which brought the bill up to enough to give me one and a third coffee mugs. The smile vanished when I brought out my accordion of credit cards. For a second she looked at them blankly, then smiled that pretty way again and said: 'I'm sorry, we don't take them.'

'What, none of them?' I asked. 'Not even Access?'

'I'm afraid not. The boss says it's cash or cheque. We don't have one of the machines to work these cards.'

Normally I would have grumbled about the inconvenience, but she was only a girl doing a boring job, and the last thing I wanted on my first day back was an argument.

'That's OK,' I said, reaching inside my bomber jacket, before I halted. I'd just remembered using my last cheque

7

in a similar service station outside of Watford. Worse still, I only had about five pounds and small change in the pocket of my jeans.

I stood and stared at her for a moment, then the silliness of the situation overcame me and I burst out laughing. She started laughing too. 'You're not going to believe this, but I haven't enough money. I thought everybody took credit cards these days, but I'm wrong. So what do I do now?'

'I'd better get the boss,' she said, still smiling, and pressed the button on a bell which rang faintly somewhere in the other building. She left it a while and I nosed around among the oil cans and rows of replacement wiper blades.

She pressed the buzzer again, and there was a muffled reply from the workshop: 'All right Janey, I'm coming.' This, I assumed, was the boss, so I pretended to read the de-icer cans left over from winter while mentally composing how I was going to tell a complete stranger that he'd have to trust me until the next day for his cash.

'Well sir, what seems to be the problem?' A voice which said, 'This explanation had better be good' without actually saying the words.

I turned around to see a tall, slim-built man with a shock of jet-black hair falling over his forehead. His eyes widened in instant recognition just as the thought flicked through my mind that that hank of hair was just like his father's.

'I don't believe it,' he said, starting to smile as he crossed the couple of yards to grasp my hand and pump it vigorously.

'Nicky Ryan skint. I never thought I'd live to see the day.'

'Flat broke and up the creek without a paddle, Alan,' I said, returning his handshake. 'I can give you a fiver down payment on account if you'll trust me till tomorrow.'

'Ha. Trust you. *You*? A washed-up old hack? Are you kidding?'

He didn't wait for a reply. 'Credit cards? We don't take them any more. I quit about six months ago because it was taking too long to get the cash back. And with the by-pass it's hardly worth my while.'

Before I could say anything, Alan gestured around his forecourt and said:

'What do you think of this then? A big change from the old place.'

'That's what I thought when I pulled in. I thought there was something wrong with the place. It's too neat. Not like it was when it was a going concern.'

'Going concern? It's been great. I tell you, I haven't looked back since I got the franchise.'

'Oh? You got a dealership then? I thought maybe your dad had sold up?'

'No,' Alan said, still beaming proudly. 'I got the Caterpillar deal for the whole district. Everything from tractors to farm machinery . . . plus Leyland spares and repairs.'

I looked him up and down, taking in the neat tweed jacket and well-cut slacks, clean hands and a white collar.

'You've not been spending too much time under trucks,' I said. 'Got a whole team doing the dog work for you? I thought you always wanted to be the best mechanic in the world.'

'But I am, I am. I just found a way to do it without lying on my back under a sump all day. I took over seven years ago, but I didn't want to rely on just the village trade. And I *am* the best anyway.'

'Alan, that's terrific,' I said, and I meant it. 'But, I tell you, just when I came round that corner I was thinking of us playing about in the old shed, and sharing your mother's soup in the cottage. Don't you miss the old place?'

'No, I needed the space. My dad works for me, doing the books. He's better at that than he was at fixing cars. He's got a house only a couple of doors down from your grandfather's old place, and guess where I'm living now?'

The look on his face was so proud that I knew at that moment that one of the Milligs boys had made it, at long last.

'Down the shore side,' I volunteered.

9

'Don't be such an arse.'

'OK, OK, I'll have another guess. Bayview Wynd?'

'Close enough. Harbour Avenue. Just round the corner.'

I could see Alan was getting enormous pleasure telling me of his good fortune. It gave me a pleasant buzz too.

'Upper Arden. Why fan mah brow, mastah,' I said, dredging up a catch phrase we'd used on each other as boys.

'Just moved in last year. It's the old Erskine place, just on the corner.'

I couldn't place it yet, but I nodded anyway.

'I suppose you've got maids and gardeners too?'

'Don't be daft. Just a man who cuts the grass once in a while, and my wife looks after the house. She's happier than a pig in shit to tell you the truth.'

'I'll bet she is. Who is she anyway?'

'She's my wife.'

'Yes. No. I mean who did you marry? Do I know her?'

'I don't know. Maybe you do. Janet McCrossan. She was a couple of years younger than us. Came from Shandon.'

I had the vaguest recollection of a small girl with a fair pony tail and a bright smile that could have been her, but I wasn't sure.

'You probably never met her,' Alan said before I could reply, 'but if you stay around you'll have to come up and see the place. And meet Janet too.'

I could feel Alan was dying to show off his big house, and frankly, I was keen to see it. Alan seemed pleased when I told him I'd be staying around for quite a while and that I'd love to come and see his mansion in the sky as soon as I'd got my own things sorted out. He assured me there was no rush for the cash I owed him, and I could tell he meant it. As I left his filling station he asked: 'And how have you been going? You don't seem to have changed that much.'

'Only a bit older and a bit wiser, and still the best with a slingshot.'

As I adjusted my seatbelt and jiggled my backside into the position it had kept for the last four hundred miles I caught a glimpse of Alan's face in the offside mirror. He was shaking his head and smiling as if he didn't believe me.

I clicked off the steering lock and nosed the car out on to the Kilcreggan Road again. I waved a casual hand out of the window, pleased that it had been Alan and not some pompous service manager who would have made a big song and dance about not getting the cash.

The road took me over Strowan's Bridge which effectively marks the boundary between the east and west of town, an old stone hump-back, just wide enough to take two-way traffic as long as each way isn't a twenty tonner. Strowan's Water, which runs below, is a clear stream which starts way up on the moorland at Cardross Hill, neatly bisects the town and forks east and west to empty into the firth on each side of Ardhmor, that big hunk of tree-covered rock that juts out into the grey water to the south.

On the down-slope of the bridge the road continued, past another couple of smallholdings and the beginning of Westbay, the solid middle-area of Arden with its tight sprawl of cottages and two-storey buildings, its neat shopping centre, the town hall and little cinema, the library and the school-house. At first glance, and from a speed that had slowed to ten miles an hour as I eased the Subaru along while searching for a parking space, the changes had not been too drastic. The grocery store had been converted into that type of mini-market that has sprung up, breeding like rabbits, all over this country and just about everywhere else. McKay's had been a family concern then, one of those old-fashioned places where the potatoes come dirty from burlap sacks, and huge jars of boiled sweets are kept well out of reach of small hands. Now there would be rows of canned food, trolleys, and spotty girls with uniforms, kneeling in the aisles, risking the wheels of the laden trolleys, click, click clicking with their price guns.

I found a space in the little car park they'd carved out

behind the new store. I planned to pick up a few provisions, maybe some beer, before going down the harbour road to the cottage. My aunt, who'd looked after my grandfather for a decade or so – not that that old salt needed much looking after – had been living there since she'd sub-let grandad's place, and had found this a convenient time to visit *her* aunt, my Great aunt Jean. Knowing Aunt Martha's habits, I reckoned the place would be pretty shipshape. Strangely when I thought back, I seem to remember thinking of grandad's place more as home, a place where I spent a lot of fascinating hours, weekends and evenings, never tiring of the old travelling tales of the old travelling man.

Holly's bar was still there, the first place I ever had a drink with the real men when I was only sixteen. Big John Hollinger, a great bear of a man with a ruddy, laughing face behind a big highlander's beard, had known exactly how old I was, but he'd let me buy a Guinness anyway. I hadn't a clue what I was drinking, and I still cringe with embarrassment when I remember how he'd stared me in the eye until I'd drunk every last drop of the thick, creamy beer. I hadn't the taste for it then, but that was a while ago, and I planned, in the very near future, to head up to Holly's for a refresher course.

Mary Baker's, the most aptly named shop in town, still displayed its small loaves and tea cakes in the front window, but the shop next door had changed. I recalled it as a small clothing store where mothers would drag their reluctant children on the last few days of the summer vacation to have them fitted out with the school uniform. Now the shop was some sort of arty-crafty souvenir place with shells and tartan rugs, odd-looking home-made candles and grotesque little pottery representations of the Loch Ness monster, who, if he looks anything like he's depicted in these tawdry tourist shops in every west coast village, should pray for extinction.

Mary Baker – the second that is – her mother having passed on even before I'd hightailed it for the big time,

12

was essentially the same. Those glass display cases were still filled with delightful confections that she had been baking since five o'clock that morning. The danish pastry was thick and light; the brown loaves were solid, and roughcast with pure grain which always came from one of the local mills, mostly the little granary up at the Abbey seminary where the trainee priests practised self-sufficiency to help them get along with their upcoming vows of poverty, chastity and obedience. Mary recognised me right away and flashed me a big smile from behind those huge bottle-end glasses. I could have been there for an hour or so, if I'd stayed to answer all her questions. As it was it took me half an hour to buy a couple of spicy buns and a thick farmhouse loaf which I intended to savour.

In the supermarket I found everything as expected. I loaded up a trolley with tins and packets and a dozen cans of what had always been my favourite lager, although the girls depicted on the outside of each can, while pretty enough, lacked the older woman allure of the mid-sixties models. I added a bottle of whisky and another of vodka, having first checked to find out whether the store accepted credit cards. I made a mental note to get to the bank on the following day anyway, but the little supermarket was keen to take almost any kind of plastic I threw at it.

All the provisions were crammed in two garish da-glo plastic bags in the back of the Jap, precariously balanced on my boxes and travelling bags.

The cottage looked tiny as I drove round the right-angled turn into the avenue. Tiny, a bit shabby, as if it had been left to lie, forgotten, for a while. I stood back from the Subaru and had a good look at the front of the building, and noticed patches where the sandstone had worn; and a couple of slates missing from the roof were angled up in the gutter to which they'd slipped from higher up. The paint around the sash windows was old and grey-mired, but the glass was clean. No doubt aunt Martha had been whizzing around with her duster, her substantial backside bustling briskly around the overstuffed armchairs,

13

as she flicked here and there with the duster. My old key opened the Yale lock easily and the door, which used to squeak, didn't. Inside smelled of air freshener and bleach, so I knew aunt Martha had been busy, but it was dark in the living room, a kind of depressing shade, and quiet too, as if the room was sleeping, not really expecting a caller. The window let in little light, but outside it was overcast, and the old dark green curtains were designed to keep the outside out. The first thing I did was pull them apart to their greatest extent, and tie them back with the faded braids. The room looked a little brighter, but not much. I dumped the groceries on the sofa and sat down on the easy chair that had once been my father's. I sat on the edge, feeling almost that I shouldn't be sitting there. The place was empty, except for me and a million memories. A sprinkling of tiny dust motes caught a stray patch of light that must have slipped through the clouds, and sparkled lazily in the air. This was the room where I'd spent a huge chunk of my life with my mother and father. Now there was just me.

Just me and a whole crowd of memories that jostled and swirled like half-recognised faces at a busy party. I nodded briefly to them all as they came and paused before moving back into the swirl. Just me and the girls on the cans of lager which plinked and fizzed steadily. I was on good terms with Sharon and Leslie and I had Shona twice in the space of a couple of hours. I knew I would regret the acquaintance later, but what the hell, I just sat in my father's old chair with its high back, within easy reach of the bookshelves and the mantelpiece beside the sighing gas fire and got into the girls one after another.

Sharon and Leslie and two satisfying sessions with Shona was enough for me. I'd toyed with the idea of a shot of vodka, but it wouldn't have sat well down there where the girls were already complaining of the crush. Those snatches of memory loomed in and faded out before I could grab a hold of them. It was a disorientating feeling because my mind couldn't settle. I decided to go to bed.

Up the narrow staircase the walls shifted just a little, letting me know I should have given Shona a gentlemanly break. Strangely, I instinctively put my foot on the inside edge of the seventh stair, the one that had always creaked. After all those years, that just came back to me out of the cobwebs in the back of my head, and it wasn't until I reached the top landing that I realised I'd done it. When I was very small I used to sneak down those stairs in the early mornings of summer, tip-toeing slowly, my little hand reaching up to hold the smooth wood of the banister, heading into that pool of light the early morning summer sun would shoot through the kitchen window. It was always quiet, except for the low rumbling snore from my parents' room, and maybe a couple of early birds out in the back yard. I knew that if I stood on that creak on the seventh stair then one of them would wake up and order me to get back to bed. If I made it downstairs, I could grab a biscuit and a drink of milk and gingerly snap back the old mortice lock on the back door and out into the morning. Not creaking on the seventh step had become one of those fixed-in rules that *never* got broken.

I grinned when I realised I'd kept the rule.

My bed was still the same, but the room like the house and everything in it, seemed smaller. Otherwise it hadn't changed. My old pictures were still on the walls. Me and my grandad out shooting duck down on the mud flats. Me being prepared and looking solemn in the scouts. Old Jimmi Hendrix still looking as if the wires on his guitar had shorted out and he'd got most of the shock. (He did later, didn't he?) Paul Simon looking a little sensitive and thoughtful and a bit hurt, just the image I'd hoped to project after my spell of wanting to be as mean as old Jimmi. I knew if I opened the drawer next to the bed I'd still find the bits of string, the old penknives with their smooth-worn handles, and probably a lot of unsent letters to a few half-remembered girls.

I shucked off my jeans and my Treks and threw my shorts over the chair by the window, before pulling back the goose-down duvet and crawling into bed.

The last thing I remember is thinking of my mother hanging out my father's white shirts on the washing line where the sunlight shone right through them. I don't know where that picture came from, probably somewhere down deep, but she was looking over her shoulder at me as she clipped the clothespegs into place and was smiling at me.

I dimly remember smiling back at her, but I must have fallen asleep pretty quickly, for there was nothing after that until . . .

TWO

. . . The phone rang.

Loud and clear, like 'a stuttering firebell. I awoke with alarm, suddenly sitting up in the single bed, with my heart thumping like a triphammer inside my ribs.

A dream's aftershock washed through me like a black, oily wave leaving a bitter, soiled taste in my head. I'd been somewhere, in a cave, or a tunnel that was dark and dank with rotting slime. I had been wading through water that was cold and sluggish and slicked around my calves, and from up ahead came the dreadful beating sound that shook the walls and batted echoes all around me and the people I was with (who were they?) and the hairs on the back of my neck crawled, because there was something ahead of me in that darkness, something that moved with dreadful ponderous intent towards us. And in the dark tunnel of my dream I had seen the pale green glow ahead, the two pallid circles that were a yard wide and a yard apart, the great dead eyes of the thing that was bearing down on me like a mad train. There was a scream that rose high until I felt my body vibrate, and I knew it was a scream of rage, and I was screaming too because I was running, splashing through the slimy water, running towards the thing with the eyes that wanted to eat me. . . .

The phone rang again and the jangling sound shook me out of the aftershock, and the insistent ringing hauled me, shivering in the cold air of the night out of bed.

Down the stairs, into the living room. I almost fell across the other chair in my haste to grab the receiver and shouted 'Hello.'

Nothing. Not a sound, unless you can call an echoey silence a sound. Inside the phone was like a deep cave –

like the one I'd been running through in the dream – and there was an ambience that made no sound, but gave the impression of big, dark spaces.

'Hello. Hello!'

I waited for an answer. Somebody was playing a joke. There was still a silence accentuated by the faintest whispering hiss of electrons in the line. I was just about to slam the receiver back down when I heard something just at the lowest edge of my hearing. It was a muted thud that was so low it was almost a feeling. It came again. A little louder, a little deeper. And again, and again. A slow, pulsing beat that expanded and grew in power, like the thumping of an immense heart. And behind that beat came a low moan that started to rise in pitch, rapidly edging up the scale until, within seconds, the sound was blasting out of the earpiece and was tearing at the inside of my head. It was the sound I had heard in the dream.

It was just exactly the scream I had heard as I ran towards those huge eyes. The fright this realisation gave me was a jolt that made me slam the receiver down on its cradle. It made a solitary tinkling sound.

I stood there in the dark living room, breathing heavily, and feeling the sweat on my back like a cold trail. Gingerly I picked up the phone again, and slowly brought it to my ear, expecting that sluggish pulse, and that ear-splitting scream. But there was only the low burr of the dialling tone.

I put it back and watched it for a second or two, waiting for it to ring. It didn't. I shivered in the cold and decided to get back to bed. I headed up the stairs.

And for some reason, maybe because I was shaken, I broke the rule. The seventh step gave slightly under my foot and let out a sharp two-toned creak. Cree-eak. Suddenly my heart was jackhammering again, higher up this time, somewhere near my throat. I can't say why, but standing on that step hit me with a weird feeling of despair. As if I'd gone and done it. As if I was going to get *caught* going and doing it.

I lumbered up the stairs, two at a time, and into my room. When I awoke again, it was still night, but it wasn't the phone. It was the rain, drumming hard and fast on the breast of a hard westerly wind right on to the window. The rain came down in solid rods against the glass. From somewhere up in the roof I could hear the gurgle of water pouring from the slates into the gutter and down the drainpipe. Peeling back the curtains, I looked out into the black night. Rivulets raced down the pane as the wind rose higher, blasting more hard water in from the west, up the mouth of the firth, and splatting it all on Arden. Peering out, I could make out the shapes of the other houses, and beyond them a belt of trees, then a dark mass of grey-black cloud that seemed to swirl right down to water level, boiling like the contents of a witch's cauldron. The wind rose higher, from a dull roar to a shriek that caught the telephone wires and sent them swinging.

I wasn't tired any more, so I just sat for a while, after pulling on all my crumpled clothes again, watching the big storm boil up into a real Armageddon. From somewhere further up on the roof I heard a piece of tin flashing rip off and jangle metallically. In the next day or two I was going to have to get one of the men from Milligs up on the slates to nail on a new piece.

Out on the firth a foghorn sounded out, like a huge beast in its death throes. A minute later it went off again, bellowing out of the night. It wasn't foggy here, but the rain must have brought visibility down to twenty yards clear, and out there on the heaving water the clouds would be scraping decks. It wasn't a night to be out on a boat.

At about four in the morning, after I'd sat there for an hour or so and smoked a couple of filter tips in the darkness, the horn reached out again, this time much closer, sending out a vibration that shook the glass.

Much closer? I remember that thought jumping into my head. That big bellowing horn sounded *awfully* close, and I suddenly had a crazy mental picture of a huge, sharp bow bearing down relentlessly, crashing through that stand of sycamores, crushing through the houses and slicing through the wall of the bedroom.

The black marker buoys that edged off the shipping lane were more than two miles out on the wide firth. And that horn was nowhere near two miles away. It was *too* close in. Too near Arden and its little sheltered harbour.

Just as I thought it, an eerie orange flash blossomed out there in the turbulent sky. Another flash of orange went up just as the first one was dying slowly, floating below the rooftops and out of sight.

It must have been the second flare that got me moving. I had watched the first one like a spectator at a fireworks display. When the second one burst I spun round and downstairs to the phone. When I picked it up there was none of the echoing silence of before, just the normal burr. I dialed 999 and asked for the police because I didn't know if the emergency service could call out the lifeboat.

I rattled out what I'd seen and the officer at the other end calmly started asking me for some details, and my name and address and that kind of life-saving information that they always seem to need when you think there's not a second to lose. I hid my frustration as well as I could and gave him the whole picture and he said: 'Thank you sir, we'll get on to it right away,' and I hung up.

It took me several minutes to find my oiled cotton coat and a pair of boots and a big Shetland sweater I'd inherited from old seafaring grandad. I pulled the hood tight and popped the studs in under my chin and headed for the door. Just before I went out, I noticed a couple of walking sticks in the holder at the base of the bentwood hatstand. I hefted one out, and instantly recognised its natural hawthorn-root handle. I'd cut that stick myself for my grandad the time he'd sprained his ankle the day he'd slipped on the rocks trying to tie our dinghy to an anchor ring. I'd gone up by Strowan's Burn and cut him a walking stick, and I'd worked the handle, following the lines of the wood, into a smooth grip.

The old man had laughed when I'd presented it to him

and had immediately thrown the smooth walking stick he'd been given at the little Hermitage Cottage Hospital into a corner.

'Now there's a cromach,' he said. 'A real walking stick. A shillelagh no less,' and he'd laughed again and ruffled my hair while I beamed up at him. He'd used that stick while his ankle had healed, and then he'd gone on using it when he went on his long walks up on the Cardross Moor or down along the Havock Shore, swinging it up with every stride like a natty boulevardier, and occasionally lopping off the heads of thistles at the side of hedgerows. And he never seemed to tire of boasting to his cronies down at the boatyard how his grandson had gone and cut him a *real fine* walking stick.

I got a buzz of warm pleasure even then and I lifted the old shiny hawthorn breach with its knotted handle, and yanked open the door and into one of the worse nights I care to recall.

There wasn't much to see. Down at the harbour there was a knot of people in yellow oilskins huddled together and pointing out into the rolling grey.

When I joined them, a couple of them nodded to me and turned back to look out to the firth where nobody could see a damned thing except the whitened tops of waves and a dark tumble of cloud. One of the men turned round and I saw recognition in his face, but I couldn't put a name to him although his face was familiar.

'Nicky Ryan, right?'

'Yes, that's me,' I replied, trying to smile through the blasting rain driven in on at least a force niner.

'Thought it was you,' the man said. His name just came to me then – Bill Finlayson, who ran a little chandlery shop for the summer sailors who used the harbour during the holidays.

'Haven't seen you in a long time, except on the telly,' he said, and grinned or grimaced against the downpour, I couldn't tell.

'No, I just got back yesterday afternoon.'

21

'Good time for it. This one's blowing up to be a belter. Looks like sixty-one all over again. That was a bad one.'

'I saw a flare and called the police. They say they'll get the inshore lifeboat out.'

'Dare say they will. Don't fancy being out in that, though. It looks pretty pissy out there.'

'Anybody know what's happening yet?' I had to shout over the high whistle of the wind and the crash of waves on the storm wall of the harbour. Great fountains of spume were being whipped up and over the capstans and into the quay.

'Some ship's ran aground out about there.' He pointed out due south which was roughly where I'd seen the flares go up, and I nodded.

'Brian Bailley heard it on his short-wave. Big sugar boat I think, heading for Greenock. It's way off course if it's on this side of the water.'

Another flare lit up the clouds again, just where he'd pointed. It only seemed about a mile away. On the far side of the harbour a couple of cars had arrived and a handful of men were leaping out and into the inshore lifeboat shed.

Bill leaned over, pulling the sleeve of my coat to yell in my ear.

'It's a bit heavy for the inshore, don't you think?'

'Yeah. Why don't they send for the big one from Kirkland, or over at the Holy Loch?'

Just then one of the other men shouted something which was carried away on the wind. Bill pulled me over to the rest of the huddled group. One of the men had a big FM tucked inside his coat. It crackled like the riggings of the toy dinghies. He turned and shouted. We had to crowd close to hear.

'They've put out boats. The ship's aground just off Ardhmor, maybe a mile, maybe less.'

'If it's not sunk, there's not much good in putting out when the water's like that,' another of the group said.

'No, by Christ. I'd stay on.'

On the quayside, a square of light flared as the inshore

22

bay doors were flung open and the orange figures of the lifeboatmen – their suits just the same colour as the flare – dragged out their matching inflatable. I've been on these little scudders before. They're fast and light and strong. But you can bet a month's pay you wouldn't have got me out in one that night. I could tell from the other guys' faces that they were thinking along those lines too.

One of the team started up the big double Evinrudes as soon as the craft slapped into the water. The rest were in, and over the sound of the storm the boat roared into a tight turn through the narrow storm gap and out into the night.

On foot the rest of us followed out on the wall where the salt spray lashed us. The sea out there looked murderous. The inflatable bobbed up then disappeared behind huge waves, looked as if it had been swallowed, then miraculously appeared on the crest again. After it had gone a hundred yards, the roar of the big outboards was lost, drowned out in the big roar from the water and the hard lash of the rain against our hoods.

'Not much we can do around here,' somebody said.

'Y'right, my son,' a big voice boomed out. It was big John Hollinger, who ran the bar.

'We might as well go up for a warmer. What d'y say?'

'Aye,' came several replies at once, making the scene sound like a comic pirate sketch.

'All right, I'll open up. I don't suppose you'd mind Murdo?' he said, turning to another big man in flapping yellows standing at his shoulder. Murdo Morrison, the sergeant of Arden's small police station (he was the one with the FM band radio), looked at Holly as if he'd lost a few marbles.

'Mind? On a night like this I'd be more likely to throw you in jail for refusing.'

He grinned, shoving the radio further into the shelter of his ample armpit.

'We'll come back down later and see what's doing. But I'm for a whisky to get the cold out of my bones. Come on then, let's go.'

I joined the crowd, accepting a tacit invitation, and we trudged back along the cobbles with the wind at our necks. I could feel that patch of my jeans, below my coat and above my gumboots, damp and rasping the back of my legs. Holly opened the back door of the bar and we skirted around the stack of aluminium casks and into the warmth.

Holly went behind the bar, still in his oilskin, and started lining up whisky glasses. He reached for a bottle of malt and started to pour deftly. Large ones. His huge hand dwarfed his drink, which must have had about four measures. He lofted the whisky and boomed: 'Cheers.'

The rest of us stamped over, still dripping rain on to the worn wooden floor, and the rest of the lined-up drinks were quickly hauled off the bar. I reached for mine when Holly noticed me.

'Ah, Nicky, how are you my boy,' he had a voice like that foghorn I'd heard earlier. 'By God, you newspapermen are quick off the mark. How d'you get here so soon?'

A large slug of whisky burned down my throat and hit the bottom of my stomach just then. I started to cough and couldn't stop for an embarrassingly long time. Somebody banged me lustily between my shoulder blades and my eyes watered. I wiped them with a knuckle.

'I've been here since yesterday,' I said weakly, still trying to clear my throat.

'Well, you must have a nose for news,' he said, and winked. 'If I'd known you were coming I'd have poured you a Guinness.'

'Not tonight, Holly,' I said, picking up the wink he flashed to Murdo Morrison. 'This is going down just a treat.'

'It is that,' the policeman said, lifting his glass to the light and gazing lovingly at the amber. He took a large gulp, throwing it about a yard past his tonsils and let out a long sigh.

Murdo had been a constable in the Sheriff court when I worked in the *Kirkland Times* as a trainee reporter. Now he was sergeant for the town and he looked like the best kind to have in a small place like Arden; big, bluff, and not too hot on the formalities.

Just then there was a hiss of static from under Murdo's coat, and what sounded like a hacking cough from the region of his armpit. The sergeant opened the flap of his windbreaker and moved over to the corner of the room, with his head tucked under his arm like some big yellow bird. There were a few more coughs and splutters and Murdo put a couple of quick-fire questions into his police transmitter. He turned back to the rest of us.

'The inshore boat's on its way back,' he said. 'They've turned out the lifeboat from Kirkland and they've picked up one of the boats from the *Cassandra*.'

'How many came off her?' one of the men asked. I think his name was Kenny Smith, but at that time I was still trying to put names to faces.

'They think two. They've got the captain and about fourteen of the crew. I'm not sure yet, but we'd best get back down to the harbour because they've decided to put in here. It's quicker, and some of those poor buggers might need to go up to the Hermitage.'

Murdo snapped over the wide collar on his waterproofs and pulled the hood down to eye level.

'Right, thanks for the dram Holly. You might as well keep the place open a while yet. I'll probably need another one later on.'

We followed him into the night, leaving Holly behind the bar, and were instantly buffeted by a head-on wind that lashed the freezing rain straight at us. Down at the quayside there were a few more men all wrapped up in heavy weather gear, who hadn't been there before. Out at the breakwater, where the waves still lashed up the curve and over the top into the harbour somebody had switched on a big spotlight to guide the inshore inflatable in. Just beyond that, on the steep basalt rocks that formed a natural harbour entrance, two red lights, set into the stone, winked. I thought they wouldn't be much use to the men in the dinghy, for even from this close range they were just

25

smudges of light. From any distance out there they would be invisible. It was cold and miserable out there on the sea wall, but a whole lot better than being out in that mucky sea in a little boat.

It took more than half an hour for the sturdy inflatable to make it back from the *Cassandra*. They followed it on the spotlight beam, and from where we were standing it looked as if they were having a tough time, even though the wind was at their backs. Once they were in the shelter of the harbour, they steered the boat to the far ramp. Just before they hit the concrete, the steersman at the back flipped up the twin props and the boat scooted right out of the water.

The crew quickly stowed the boat and then they all made their way round to the east side of the harbour where we still huddled, peering out uselessly into the dark firth. The cox, an Englishman I'd never met, was a man called Dave King, a tall, skinny fellow with a lined and weatherbeaten face.

He and his men came over to us and the leader went straight to Murdo Morrison.

'They're coming over this way, but they'll have to make two runs, I reckon. The lifeboat picked up one of the ship's boats, but they've lost sight of the other. I gather it was getting driven off towards the peninsula, so they could even have made landfall. Ardhmor's a lot closer than here.'

All this came out in a clipped, educated voice, all in a rush, like a major making a field report. Right away I got the impression that the inshore cox was a pretty straight guy.

'I'd suggest you take a few men and go round there anyway to see if anything can be done. I'll wait here for the lifeboat if you like.'

Murdo nodded and called a few of the men over.

'There's a chance one of the boats is going on to Ardhmor. I need a few men to go round with me right now.'

A couple of men joined him from the group and then a

further four separated from the huddle and came across. Murdo asked them if they had torches and most of them said they had. He cocked his head in my direction and said: 'You want to come along, Nick?'

Frankly I could have done without it. I was cold and a bit tired and that belt of whisky was drilling an auger hole in my gut, but it was my first day back home, so I thought I might as well show willing.

'I can get everybody in my jeep, if you like,' I said.

'Well that's handy. I can't get more than four in my Panda, so I'll lead the way and you can catch me up down at the Swanson place. That's as far as the road goes and we can walk it from there.'

Down at Swanson's farm I pulled the Subaru into the yard where a beam of light shone from a downstairs window on to the hard-packed earth. Murdo was coming out of the building with the farmer, Willie Swanson, a short, sturdy man in a baggy tweed jacket that had seen plenty of better days. Under his arm he carried a walking stick just like the one I'd thrown in the back of the jeep. The farmer went across to an outhouse and emerged moments later with a great ankle-length waterproof coat heavily smeared with what I assumed was cow shit. Uncharitably, I was glad he wouldn't have to be travelling in my car. We joined Murdo and the farmer and headed down the narrow path beside the hedgerow that would take us down to the peninsula.

Ardhmor is a great hunk of basalt rock that hangs down from the north shore of the firth. It's connected to the Arden shore by a narrow neck, below which its mass dangles out into the Clyde. There's an old pathway from the farm that goes over the old dyke that's built in a bracket shape around the neck of the peninsula, and that's the way we went, torches flashing at our feet as we stumbled over the ruts and occasionally into deep holes in the mud made by Swanson's cattle. Ahead of us Ardhmor Rock hunched like a giant beast of prey ready to pounce. It was covered in a jungle-like coat of beech and birch. At its westerly side

27

there's a stand of old Scots pine that are gnarled and bent away from the wind like a crowd of old men protecting themselves from a storm. I knew the trees would be taking a beating this night.

I'd slipped and fallen a couple of times on the rutted track, and once when I went down I put my hand smack into a large cowpat. I could feel the horrid stuff covering my fingers and swore softly but sincerely under my breath.

Don't go to Ardhmor. It's a bad place. A BAD place.

Where did that come from? I didn't know, but at that moment when I looked ahead into the gloom and saw the black mass of that tree-covered rock looming over me – even darker than the storm-whipped sky – I knew it was true. I felt a shiver go right through me, and all of a sudden the dripping green cowpat I had been trying to wipe off my cold fingers was the least of my problems.

Have you ever been afraid? Really afraid? Not just wary, or apprehensive like the kind of shakes you get when you know somebody is going to punch you in the eye, or when your brakes fail and you can feel your car head straight for a wall. That's natural self-preservation fear. We all get it.

But this was a different kind of fear. It was a numbing terror that drilled its way right inside me. An unnatural fear. The kind of fear a hard-drinking man will get when he wakes up in a nest of giant ants because his brain is all screwed up and running wild. That's where I was right at that moment, and what was worse, there wasn't a damned thing I could do about it. I didn't know what it was, the psychotic terror, but I just wanted to back away down that muddy track, at a fast gallop.

But I didn't. Behind me, in the dark, one of the men following barged into my back with a thump that shook the wind from him in an explosive whoof.

'What the fuck . . . ?'

'Sorry,' I said, as if to a passer-by in a busy street whose path I'd blocked.

'Move on, move on,' said the disembodied voice. And I

28

did. Because there were other men with me.

I swear that the biggest fear in the world is the fear of people's opinion. I missed out on the big war, and the two in Asia, thank God, but I've seen many a skirmish on a border in not a few of the more heated spots on the globe. I've seen men mess their pants and still charge the barricades, and I know that every one of them *knew* that he was the only one with a disgusting secret. They may be scared out of their minds to go a step further and face whatever instant death is flying at them, but they're even *more* terrified of *not* going, because of what their friends will think.

That's what moved me along. The jitters didn't leave me. They came right along on my back on that squelchy track. But I put one foot in front of another and walked. It felt like I was walking into the jaws of death. If what happened in Arden that year hadn't happened, I reckon I would have considered seeing a shrink about this irrational fear, but I didn't get around to that, because as it turned out it was not irrational. My antennae were out on extended stalks and I was picking up messages from Christ knows where, only I didn't realise then that I had antennae. I was just in danger of making a mess in my jeans.

The path took us through a stand of beech trees which groaned under the weight of the wind. Up above, their branches crashed against each other, the fresh growth of leaves being whipped about. They sounded just like the waves that were being beaten on to the storm wall. Past the trees we skirted the low basalt cliff on a track that was scoured bare by the hooves of countless cattle, but the going was rocky so there was less mud for me or anybody else to fall about in. Here we were more exposed to the gale that was screaming in straight from the west, and I gripped the handle of that old walking stick as if my life depended on it. The black rock loomed up thirty feet above my left shoulder, and from the overhang, the rivulets of rain water that were pouring down the age-worn stone were being blown right back up again. I still had that feeling of oppression, as if I had no right to be in this place, at this time. A few yards ahead in the murk I could hear a couple of voices yelling at each other over the roar of the storm. Somebody was pointing directions and we kept going, slipping and stumbling on the smooth stone until we were past the face and heading down towards the shore.

If the scene at the harbour wall was bad, this was worse, for even right at the seafront where the jetty was built in a curve to take the force of the waves, there is still some shelter from the main thrust. Here there was none. The mighty waves that were being stoked up miles out there in the firth had been building up, backed by the huge force of the blow, and were running in on a frontal attack on the rocks at Ardhmor. All around was noise and water.

Murdo Morrison turned and motioned us all into a huddle. When we were all in a circle around him, he still had to shout to make himself heard.

'This is about where they were coming aground,' he said, jerking his thumb over his shoulder at the water pounding on the shingles. There was so much whip-spray that visibility was only twenty yards or so, even with the torches.

'The lifeboat couldn't come any closer, but the ship's crew said they were blown out of the lee and straight for here. The water's a bit rough, but they should have been able to beach here. We might as well look at both ends. I don't imagine they'll be too far away.'

We split into two roughly equal small groups and went trudging along the slippery shore line. The rocks were rounded and water-polished. As I walked, I could hear that polishing action going on as it had done for thousands of years. The rumble and crash of a big wave, then the rattling, susurrant sound of pebbles running back in the undertow. Every now and again, an even bigger wave would come lashing up the beach, tugging at our boots. The pull of the back-flow was incredible, and I was glad I had that stick with me as an extra balance, otherwise there were a couple of occasions when I'd have been floundering in the firth.

We walked that beach for more than an hour, searching up past the jagged rocks, and back from the water where the huge stones that had calved from the volcanic basalt lay in tumbles, each the size of a fair house, and under which there were warrens of cave-like shelters. There was nothing. Not a sign.

Murdo Morrison assured us that the men from the stricken ship had to be around here.

'There's nowhere else they can be,' he said, when we were huddled around him again.

'The boat must have come ashore here. Let's have another look.'

We did. The rain didn't stop, and the storm kept up its pressure. We searched high and low on the west shore of the peninsula. We shone our torchlights into every nook and cranny, and despite that feeling of anxiety never lessening, I looked in every rock cave, almost congratulating myself that I actually had the nerve to *go* into the dark places. We searched the trees and the water's edge for debris.

And we found nothing.

The first glimmer of dawn was lightening up the stage behind the roiling clouds when the big police sergeant called off the search. It must have been about seven thirty in the morning when he gathered us together again, puzzlement evident on his wide face.

'I can't understand it, lads,' he said, still yelling to beat the wind. 'Unless the boat crew made a mistake. There's just not a sign of them.'

There wasn't a sign. Not a hair, nor a scrap of cloth. Not even a spar from their lifeboat. Nothing.

When Murdo called off the search and we headed back along the track, past the overhang, through the beeches and alongside the hedge that bordered the muddy cow track, I found that I was last in the line. The dark was just beginning to lift and the further away from the firth we got,

31

the more the storm seemed to abate, but there was still a good wind blowing through the tops of the trees behind me.

When I realised that I was keeping up the rear, with no-one else at my back, that intense feeling of fear came roaring back inside me. In that instant I felt like the small boy again who is tangled in the blankets in a dark and empty room, who struggles to get free.

I almost slipped on my face when the panic jolted me forward in an instinctive attempt to get myself closer to other living beings, no matter who they were. Around me, the briars and brambles bordering the track seemed much closer in. They tugged at my coat and scratched at my wrist as I wrestled them away. Then at a bend in the track, when the others ahead of me were out of sight, the thicket really closed in, forcing me to brush past the tangle of branches. It was then that one of the spiky brambles snaked out lazily and wrapped itself around my arm. I wrenched away, trying to pull free, my mind refusing to believe what my eyes had seen, and as I was tugging at the bramble runner, I felt something coil itself around my boot. A small grunt of pure panic escaped me as I heaved myself to the right, pulling hand and foot away, and almost crashing headlong into a thick jungle of briar on the flanking side.

The thought of *that* scenario gave me a jolt of adrenalin like a tight white line straight into a vein. Suddenly my mind pictured me being overcome by writhing thorny branches, being slowly dragged in from the path. It was too much! I almost fainted from overload, but the adrenalin directed otherwise. Thorns ripped into the skin of my wrists as I wrenched back from the clutching tendril and I heard a jagged rip as I kicked my foot back. Something gave, I thought probably a root, but my boot was free and my hand, though stinging, was not caught. My right hand came up and lashed at the crowding brambles, the hawthorn stick like a sword, hacking and slashing at the leaves and branches. It seemed they drew back at the onslaught, just enough to let me race through the gap and along the track. I came through the gap in the old dyke like a rat out of a trap and sprinted up towards the group ahead who were heading for the farm. But just as I was going through the gap I heard the rustling of a million leaves and branches behind me, whipped up in the fury of the storm (at least I took it then to be the storm's anger) and over that roar I heard, as clear as anything, a low, rumbling chuckle of laughter. It was the kind of creepy laugh you only hear in gothic horror films, but it was worse than that because I was hearing it, and in that moment I knew it was laughing at me.

I almost fell on my backside again when I reached the men.

'What's the rush?' Murdo asked.

'He just wants to get back for another whisky,' somebody said and there was a ripple of tired laughter.

I didn't say anything. We all went back to the cars and drove up the farm lane towards Arden. I dropped off my crew at the harbour where most of them planned to go back to Holly's bar for a drink to dispel the cold. I decided to give it a miss. The pub that is. When I got back to the house I stoked up the fire and took off my coat. It was an expensive oiled cotton thornproof, or it should have been thornproof. But there were dozens of rips on the left-hand side. And it hadn't been a root that had ripped out of the ground. On the instep of my boot, there was a great jagged gash where a section of thick rubber looked as if it had been chewed. If it had not been for that, I would have thought I'd imagined the whole thing. I got the bottle of vodka from the box in the kitchen and poured myself about a half pint. No orange. Just straight.

In the morning after breakfast, I'd just about convinced myself that it had been imagination. After all, if you go wading through brambles, you're bound to get a scratch or two. By lunchtime, my head had stopped pounding and I was certain I'd dreamed the whole thing. I rationalised it all away.

Extract of Report by W.H. Mailley, Clyde Port Authority.
Statements were taken from Captain Elliertsen, First Mate
Cristos and several surviving crew members.

Only Captain Elliertsen and Mr Cristos were on the bridge
when the Cassandra went aground on a sandbank 1.3 miles due
west of Ardhmor peninsula, Arden, April 27 1983.

Both senior ships officers insist that they followed Clyde
navigation and marine navigation regulations to the letter. Both
have made sworn affidavits through the Company lawyer that the
Cassandra was in the port side of the shipping lane according to the
markers and confirmed by radar.

Lloyd's insurance investigators have made technical checks on
the marker buoy lights and the radar and sonar equipment of the
Cassandra. They have so far ascertained no fault.

What is clear is that the vessel (Liberian Registered, Greek
Owned) was some two miles off the shipping lane on a course
directly towards the peninsula when it struck a sandbank.

While the Captain and the First Mate insist that they believed
themselves to be in the deep channel, I can find no reason for them
to hold such a belief.

The whereabouts of the twelve crew members in the first lifeboat have not yet been ascertained. Royal Navy diving teams have
failed to locate any wreckage.

Based on discussions with Captain and crew, I can only assume
that there must have been some system failure, whether human or
mechanical. I intend to submit this report to the Glasgow office of
the Department of Trade who may be able to take the issue further.

THREE

The big storm blew itself out on the morning of April 28 leaving a trail of broken branches, a couple of deadfalls here and there, and enough roof-work to keep a team working for a month. Out on the firth the wreck of the *Cassandra* and her twelve thousand tons of unrefined sugar from Central America settled on to the sandbank, the hulk humping out of the water like a dead behemoth.

After such a filthy night, the day was remarkably clear and warm. My first breath of salt air felt terrific as I stepped out of the front door, lanced by the dappled green fire that shot through the battlemented chestnut trees that lined the street. The garden was in not too bad shape, maybe a bit overgrown, and I made a mental note to get out the old petrol-driven mower soon, as well as getting up on the roof to inspect the storm damage. I stretched in the sunlight and slung my leather jacket over a shoulder. As I left the house, I almost automatically picked up my grand-father's stick from the hat-stand by the door, but on second thoughts left it where it was. It had felt *good* in my hands in the faraway last night, but perhaps I wasn't ready to be a boulevardier about town yet.

In the main street, a few people I remembered nodded hello and I nodded back and smiled and was feeling a whole lot better by the time I got to Holly's bar.

Inside it was dark and warm, already quite busy despite the fact that it was just past lunchtime.

Up at the bar, a friendly-looking barmaid, with dark hair and brown eyes flashed me a quick smile and went on pulling a pint for somebody else.

'Be with you in just a minute,' she said, and levelled off the dark flow of beer, pushing the tap back to let the brew

35

gain a satisfying head.

She took the money and slung it in the cash register, then turned to me. Just then, her name came back to me. Linda. Linda something or other. Linda Milne. She was about twenty-three or so, fairly tall and solidly but attractively built. She had lived a few doors along from me when I last lived in Arden.

'Yes sir, what would you like?' she asked, still obviously recognising me from somewhere, but not yet sure.

'Just a Coke, Linda. It is Linda, isn't it?'

'Yes, how did you know? Have we met before?'

'Plenty of times. I'm Nick Ryan, I used to stay just . . .'

'Oh, I thought I recognised you. You look much different in real life,' she interrupted. 'We saw you on the television.'

'I hope I look better than that.'

'Yes, but you look taller, and younger as well,' she said.

'You've just made my day,' I replied, and she blushed a bit.

'You certainly look older. You must have been about ten the last time I saw you. How's your big brother doing?'

'Very well. He's in computers with British Airways. He's married with two wee boys . . . my nephews. And how about you? Worked here long?'

'Oh no. I'm on holiday from university. I just work here part time. I'm doing languages up at Glasgow. I just missed a chance at Cambridge, but really it's much handier.'

We chatted for a bit and I nursed my Coke, promising myself to stay away from vodka for a while. My constitution was definitely not up to the hammering I'd given it last night. The cool drink went down easily and the bubbles scoured me out like steel wool. It felt good.

Linda the academic barmaid brought me fairly up to date on who's who in town. She accepted a drink from me and surprised me by just having a fresh orange juice. After an hour of Arden's recent history, in which she was as well versed as any woman in a small town, she rang the bell and shouted time. I told her I'd only dropped by to see Holly

36

and she explained that he was still in his bed after being out all night after the wreck. I didn't explain that I'd been there too. I told Linda I'd see her again, hopefully, and went out into the street, deciding what to do next.

There were a couple of people I had planned to visit, but this was not the day for it. I'd also promised to go and see Alan Scott's dream house in Upper Arden, but that could wait. I stood outside Holly's, squinting in the sunlight, trying to make up my mind what I had actually planned to do. Nothing sprung to mind, so I just set off strolling down the Main Street, which was actually a section of the Kilcreggan Road which came into town from the east, became Main Street for the whole length of its passage through Arden, and became Kilcreggan Road again on the other side. I stopped off at the newsagent for some cigarettes and chewing gum – the latter a bolster for my attempts to cut down on the former – and carried on east along the street to the break where a couple of smallholdings and paddocks formed a short green belt before the start of Milligs. This had always been a favourite playing area. One of the fields was covered in bare patches where brown earth showed through the short worn grass. Kids had played football in this field since time immemorial.

The old pitch looked the same as it had done in my childhood, especially on a day like this, a high spring day with the sun higher and the bees buzzing about the flourish on the hedgerows, the daisies and clover bright asterisks against the green on the touchlines where the grass remained intact.

Along the far side there was a farm path, a good solid road that was well maintained by the passage of tractors and cars, hard and dry. On either side it was bordered by strong hawthorn and privet, lined with black knapweed, cow parsley and docken. I turned into the path and strolled in the sunlight.

Mr Bennett, who ran the smallholding and never seemed to mind the hordes of kids ruining his field, was in the yard next to his cottage as I passed by.

He was tinkering with some sort of cannister, and as I approached he put on an odd-shaped hat with a wide brim that came over his eyes. Just as I stopped, he looked up and raised a hand to ward off the sun.

'Hello Mr Bennett,' I said.

'Huh?' he grunted, just as smoke started belching from the cannister.

'Damn thing,' he muttered and reached to cover the spout with a small plastic cone.

'Do you need a hand?' I hadn't a clue what he was doing, but thought I might offer anyway.

'No, s'alright. Got the bloody thing now.' He looked me up again, straining against the sunlight to get a look at me.

'Oh, it's young Ryan isn't it?'

'Yessir.'

'Haven't seen you in a while,' he said, easing to his feet, a small, wiry man in dungarees. 'What're you up to, then?'

'Just going for a walk. Checking out the place. Seemed like a nice day for it.'

Old Mr Bennett lifted a scrawny arm and pushed the hat back on his head. It dawned on me that the thing was a beekeeper's headgear, for the fine protective gauze was rolled up behind the crown and tied with two neat laces.

'Want to come and watch?' he said. I nodded and he opened the peeling green gate that led on to a path between well-tended, just-budding rose bushes. 'It's a bit early for a swarm. Mostly July, but there must have been something wrong with the queen.'

We went round to the back of the cottage and across a patch of ground where vegetables were sprouting in straight lines. Beyond this there was a small field, bordered with ash and sycamore. There in the corner stood a dozen or so hives, white boxes against the green.

The old man pointed to a thick bush twenty yards away from the hives.

'There's the swarm. Lucky for me I noticed them before they all took off.'

I could hear, even from that distance, the soft hum of the bees. All around the bush there seemed to be a faint, dark cloud that waxed and waned in time with the buzzing.

'Come on. I'll see if this thing works. I borrowed it from Bert McFall last summer, but never got round to using it.' Old Mr Bennett pushed the single strang of wire of the fence down just enough to get his leg over it and held it down until I passed by and we made our way over the swarm. The buzzing got louder as we approached and soon I could make out the individual dots of the bees. They sounded angry, and I said so.

'Oh no, that's just the noise they always make. They hardly ever swarm, so people don't know what a whole pile of bees sounds like.'

'I've seen you doing this before years ago,' I said. 'You used a watering can.'

'That's right,' he nodded. 'I always have done. But McFall says this is easier. Quietens them down quicker, and it saves me lugging two gallons of water about every time I try to catch 'em.'

He started unrolling the netting and tucked the gauze in around his neck under his chambray shirt. With a motion of his hand he gestured me to stay back. He uncapped the cannister and smoke started billowing out all around him, white clouds that drifted lazily in the calm air. Walking towards the bush he held out the smoke gun and started spraying the fumes into the heart of the swarm. I couldn't see what was happening, but I'd watched him before, and I could picture the seething brown mass, like a huge gobbet of molasses clinging to the forked branch of the bush, thousands of bees snuggled round their new queen. The noise was ascending up into the high register as the out-runners, the scouts sent out to seek out a new hive milled about like tiny fighters. From inside the dense cloud, Mr Bennett coughed as he breathed in the white fumes. I hoped they were harmless. After about five minutes, the buzzing started to diminish and there were less scouts fly-ing out from the swarm. The returning bees flew into the cloud and most of them stayed there. Soon there was hardly a hum from the somnolent swarm.

'Hey, young Ryan. Hand me over that box,' his voice called from the dissipating cloud. I bent and picked up the carton which had previously held one of fifty-seven varieties in the supermarket and moved in to the thick bush.

'There they are. This thing does work. Look at them. Sleeping like babies,' he said.

I gave him the box and he opened the flaps at the top and wedged it in under the brown mass.

When it was directly under the swarm, he reached out and grabbed the branch, above where the bees were massed, and gave it a firm shake. A large part of the swarm broke off the main body and fell into the box with a thud. He did this a couple of times, and then the whole swarm slid down. A couple of bees dizzily flew out of the carton and banged into leaves and branches and the old man's legs. He deftly flipped the four top flaps one over the other so that they locked.

'That's us. We've got most of them. The stragglers should follow on.' He reached over with box. 'Here, you take this and I'll get the smoker.' The box was surprisingly heavy. I'd never thought bees would weigh so much. The old man directed me to the far corner where the hives were and told me to put the box down on the one second from the end.

'That's been empty since last year,' he said. 'I've fixed it up so it should take this lot.'

He took the box from me and opened the top and laid it on its side, using his hat to fan fresh air into the mass of insects which were just beginning to come out of their torpor.

'Watch this. The scouts'll fly out and some of them will check out the hive. They'll bring back word to the rest and they'll bring the queen in if they're happy. Sometimes they're not, and I've got to try another hive.'

Everything went exactly as he said. The outrunners crawled out of the box and steadied themselves before

40

taking off. Some of them looked as if they were jet lagged, but there were plenty of them and it didn't take long for them to find the hive entrance. As the old man had said, the scouts started coming back and did their little dance which encouraged more of their sisters to follow until there was a sizable advance party crawling all over the new hive. After about ten minutes, they must have been satisfied with their new piece of real estate for the whole hive started to crawl up the plank that acted as a makeshift ramp.

'There she is, that's the queen,' Mr Bennett said, leaning forward and jabbing his finger into the seething ball of insects. She was much bigger than the other bees and all around her the small workers were pulling and hauling at the big furry body, dragging it ever closer to the hive.

'Don't you ever get stung?' I asked.

'Used to a while back, but not any more,' he said. 'When I first started doing this I was always too quick. Gets them excited. Used to spend half my time pulling stings and putting vinegar on them. But I got immune after that, so the stings don't bother me, and now I don't seem to upset them at all.'

He lifted off the odd-shaped hat and spun it round in his hand. 'Still wear the old bee helmet though, just in case. I might be immune, but one of those little buggers could put my eye out.'

He plopped the hat back on his head and patted it into place, then nodded back towards his cottage.

'Come on and I'll put the kettle on and we'll have ourselves a cup.'

The tea was good, hot and strong, brewed in a big kettle on one of these old-fashioned kitchen ranges, and poured into a couple of big chipped mugs that must have held nearly a pint each.

'I haven't been up this way for years,' I ventured, after a hot mouthful. 'I just got home yesterday, then I was out last night with Murdo Morrison and John Hollinger down at the quay.'

'Filthy night, eh?'

'Too true. Murdo said there was a boat off the ship heading in towards Ardhmor, so a few of us went down there at the shore but there was nothing there.'

'Ardhmor, eh? That's no place to be wandering out at night in a storm. Wouldn't catch me there,' he said, and seemed to give a shudder. Suddenly I got a twinge of the feeling I had had the night before.

'Why not?'

'It's a wrong place. Everybody knows that.'

'Well Murdo didn't seem to bother.'

'Ach, what would he know? He's not been around as long as me. All I'm saying is it's not the place to be at night. Never has been.'

He drank more of his tea, and looked over the rim of his cup at me. 'You ask your friend Jimmy Allison. He'll tell you.'

'Tell me what?'

'He knows all about this place. He's been telling me about you and what you've been up to. Me and him and the major get together down in the Chandler of a night. If anybody knows about Arden it's old Jimmy.'

'Who's the major?' I asked. 'I can't place him.'

'Oh he's one of the incomers. Used to be in the Argylls before he mustered out. Still gets called the major. He's fitted in with us old timers. Good hand at the fishing too.'

'He'd have to be good to get accepted among you lot down at the Chandler.'

'Och aye,' he said, parodying an island accent. 'He's from up in Lewis. A teuchter. Good man on a boat and good with the stories an' all. He's done about as much in his lifetime as old Allison has.'

'That's saying something. I didn't think anybody had been about as much as old Jimmy.'

'Have you been to see him yet?'

'No. I just got in yesterday, so I thought I'd get settled first and then go along and make a night of it. How's he doing anyway? I haven't written to him in a month or so. I can't even remember if I told him I was coming back.'

'He's doing all right. Bothered with the arthritis a lot over the winter, but he still manages the organ on a Sunday, and if this hot weather keeps up he'll manage a day out for the mackerel later on.'

Old Jimmy Allison. Pushing seventy, and maybe the best friend I ever had.

Jimmy was the sub-editor on the *Kirkland Herald* when I was in my teens and faced with the decision of going to university and the unnerving prospect of becoming the teacher my father wanted me to be. Grandad knew this was the last thing on my mind, and Jimmy said he'd get me into newspapers. Grandad worked behind the scenes through my mother and she got to dad and I did the rest when I point-blank refused to go for further education. We had a couple of wild nights and black arguments and I was maybe throwing my whole future away, but Jimmy Allison got me a job as a trainee reporter in the local paper and after a while everything settled down.

Jimmy Allison was one of the most knowledgeable men I ever knew. He was big and old and rugged, and even then his hands were beginning to pain him as the arthritis started setting its teeth.

He knew newspapers inside out and had worked on them all. I thought he'd been a newspaperman all his life, but I was wrong. He'd done just about everything there is to do. The old man had run away from home at fourteen to work the fishing boats up in the Western Isles, then he'd been in the merchant navy, and he'd done a stint of fighting in somebody's army. After that he'd gone to Australia and made some money in the opal fields, then he tried his hand at sheep farming and a lot more besides.

A lot of what I am today, and I'm not too ashamed of most of it, is down to a few people in my life, and a big influence was Jimmy Allison.

Mr Bennett – it was going to be a while before I got round to calling him by his first name – poured me another cup of tea and made us both a sandwich of bacon.

The tea was just as good as the first cup and the bacon was smoked and strongly salted.

'Are you still curing your own?' I asked. I remembered he used to have a couple of sows in a pen up near the trees, always surrounded by vast wriggling litters of pink sausages, and in a separate, strongly fenced half-acre which was thickly covered in broom there was an immense old boar, a great hump-backed black and tan beast with ragged ears that used to flap about, occasionally revealing a mean little beady eye. Old Grunt used to use those tusks of his to shovel through the roots like a ploughshare, and nobody *ever* went into his pen. When we were kids, Mr Bennett never raised an eyebrow when teams used to run riot in his front field, but if he caught anybody near Old Grunt's yard he'd raise hell.

Mr Bennett told me he'd given up keeping the pigs when his wife had died some eight years ago. 'Went quick in the end. Cancer. They opened her up and had a look and said there was nothing they could do. The doctor at Levenford just sewed her back up again and a week later she was gone.

'After that the pigs were just too much for me, and anyway I could never cure the stuff just as well as Maggie. Old Grunt was just about on his last legs, so I sold him and the sows to McFall.' The old man took a gulp of his tea to wash down a giant-sized bite of his bacon sandwich, and laughed. 'If you thought that old pig of mine was a mean one, you want to see his son. Now that's an evil one for you.'

'Worse than Old Grunt? That's hard to believe. Everybody I knew was scared of him,' I said.

'Well the young one grew even bigger. A couple of years ago he got out of the paddock and went haring up into the trees. McFall and me and a couple of others got the dogs out. It was at night. We got it up in the gully near the seminary and it ripped the belly out of two of the dogs. And one of them was a pit bull terrier that had been trained up by one of Jack Ruine's boys down at the far end

44

of Milligs. That was a right bad-tempered bitch, but it didn't have a chance against McFall's pig.'

He took another bite and another swig, and laughed that short rasp again. 'Ha. Even McFall was shaking in his boots. We finally got a rope around it. I was all for shooting the bugger, but McFall said no, so we lassoed the thing like cowboys and managed to get its legs together. It took five of us to drag it down the hill to his pen. Then when we got it inside, McFall says to us to stand back and he goes in to cut the rope. He took one slice and that big bugger was on its feet like lightning and McFall almost gelded himself jumping over the fence. That boar took a snap at his boot just as he was going over and he landed right smack on the crossbar. He let out such a squeal it sounded just like the pig, and after that he showed us his boot. There was a rip the length of your hand right down the sole. Looked like it was razor cut, and they were no shop-bought boots neither. McFall said he got them at McKenzie's at Balloch, who does the farmers' boots and the soles were nigh-on an inch thick.'

'He was lucky,' I said.

'Sure he was. That animal could have taken his leg off in one go. And he's even bigger than Old Grunt. I'm as sure as hell glad I don't have that to worry about. I've still got the goats and the Jersey. Them and the bees and what I grow here's just enough for me.'

He stopped for a moment, then went on.

'I reckon you've been away quite a while. There'll be a lot about this place that you'll have forgotten about and then it'll jump back up and hit you smack in the face. Good things too, I don't doubt. I hope you get settled back in quick. What is it you plan to do with yourself?'

'I'm giving myself a break from newspapers. I've always promised myself I'd write books, so I'm going to give it a try and see if I can. If not I'll go back into journalism again.'

'Jim seems to have a lot of faith in you, so I reckon you'll give it a fair go,' he said.

'I'll have to take that as a compliment.'

'You do that, young Nicky. And come back any time.'

'That's a promise. I'll do that.'

'Go and see Jimmy soon as you can.'

'OK, that's another promise,' I said, needlessly, because I had already decided to go see him the following day.

'Oh, and don't forget to come up to the Chandler any night. You'll like the major.'

I made a third promise and thanked him for the tea and the sandwich and left the cottage. He came to the door and waved me off before turning down the path and round the back of his little house to whichever of the million and one jobs his life as a smallholder required.

I walked down the path from Mr Bennett's and was about to take the right turn to get back on to the main road when on a whim I turned left up the main path where, a few hundred yards along, McFall's small farm stood.

I was curious about that pig. I approached the farm and skirted the yard on the pebble track that took me behind the byre and into the field beyond. There was the pig pen. I could see the pink shapes of the sows moving about and adjacent to that was a thick wooden fence – not just thick, it was made of solid pine logs – which was obviously the boar's domain. As I neared the pen I could hear the snuffling grunt of the big animal, and the squelching, sucking noise as it pulled each trotter out of the mud.

Mr Bennett had been right. This thing was huge. I stood and leaned against the chest-high spar and looked over. The movement must have caught the boar's eye, for it twisted its head in a snapping gesture of annoyance, then turned and looked at me.

Old Grunt had been a big beast. This one was massive. It stood and looked at me from under those big flapping ears in that truculent, heavy-jawed way that pigs have, its little eyes glaring at me while it snuffled air in and out of its upturned snout rapidly like a pair of bellows. A trickle of saliva dripped from the corner of its mouth as it continued chewing whatever it had rooted up, and with every movement of the mandible I could see those glistening white tusks like razors move up and down.

'Hey mister,' a high-pitched voice shouted behind me. 'Hey mister, watch out for the pig.'

I turned and two small boys, who turned out to be the younger members of McFall's sizable brood came running towards me.

'It's all right. I was just having a look. It's a big pig.'

'He's a big bad pig, my daddy says,' the smaller of the boys told me. 'Boot, we call him, 'cos he bit off my daddy's boot.'

'Yes, he's big all right. I knew *his* daddy a long time ago, when I was your age.'

'Pigs don't have daddies. They're just pigs.'

I wasn't prepared to get into an argument. I nodded and smiled, and turned to go.

'D'you need any eggs, mister?' one of the boys asked. 'And we've got milk as well.'

'Not today, but I'll come back again another time.'

'All right then, but my dad says nobody is allowed near the pig.'

'Don't worry, I won't go near Boot. Honest.'

'OK mister. That's all right.'

As I walked away across the field I heard a crunch from behind me. I turned to look and the big boar was up against the pine fence, gnawing at the logs. Great jagged splinters were peeling off the wood under the enormous force of those teeth.

Jimmy Allison welcomed me with a huge smile on his broad face when I arrived on his doorstep the next day. I had bought a bottle of Glenlivet ten year old in a presentation box and went to the bank for a new cheque-book and some cash. It only took five minutes to saunter round past the harbour to west Westbay and along Kirkland Avenue with its rows of pollarded lime trees to the two-storey end house where Jimmy Allison had lived since I could remember.

'Not a phone call, and not a letter,' he said, his rich,

deep voice booming out of the porch. 'Not even a post-card to tell me you were coming back.'

'Nonsense, I told you months ago,' I countered.

'Probably you did, but I can't be expected to read all the letters you write.' He grinned and held out one of his big hands to take mine. His grip was firm, but I almost winced in sympathy when I felt the distorted knuckles under my thumb. He'd told me in his letters, and the rare telephone conversation, that the arthritis had been getting worse, and he was still undecided about my recommendations for him to get the silicone injections.

'Come in, come in,' he boomed, clapping his other hand on my shoulder, almost causing me to drop his Glenlivet.

'Here, I brought you some medicine,' I said, handing over the package. He knew what it was, of course, but pretended not to as he always did.

'For me? That's nice. What is it?'

'Sun-tan lotion, for use during the heat wave,' I said.

He winked, and beamed broadly again, his grizzled face creasing into parentheses, and let me inside.

'You'll have one, huh?' he asked, holding the bottle aloft to admire the amber in the light streaming in through his kitchen window.

'Too early for me,' I said, 'but you go ahead.'

'Well, just a wee one,' and he poured himself a tiny measure and sipped from a faceted Edinburgh crystal glass.

'I suppose I can forgive the lack of correspondence just for that,' he said, smacking his lips.

'You've not been too hot in that department either,' I countered. 'Don't tell me you can't afford a stamp.'

'Always the same, Nick. Just like your grandfather. He was a cheeky devil himself. You stick the kettle on, and then come into the room.' He finished off the small whisky and set the glass down before wandering into the room at the back of the house that was his own, personal domain. It had an old, oak desk topped with a finely worked leather that was smooth with age. Every wall was lined with bookshelves that were packed with hardbacks and paperbacks and magazines, and on every horizontal surface stood mementoes of his nearly seventy years of travelling.

The desk was littered with sheets of paper and note-books, as I noticed when I returned with two cups of coffee and some biscuits.

'You've been busy then?' I asked, indicating the clutter.

'Never a dull moment,' he said.

'Still working on the history?'

'As ever. I've had some help though, especially from the university after the dig.'

'What dig was that?'

'Down past the Roman wall, beyond the stream – Strowan's Burn. There's another wall, much older. Professor Sannholm had a team of students down last summer and came up with a lot of interesting stuff. Pre-Pict they think. I'm certain it is.'

If Jimmy Allison thought any ancient remains were from pre-Pictish times, I was inclined to believe him. The history of old Arden – and its recent history – fascinated him. He kept the most amazingly comprehensive records culled from old books and burgh records, and folders stacked with cuttings from the *Kirkland Herald*, and its pre-decessor, the *Post*, which dated back almost two hundred years.

It was due to Jimmy's records and observations and his deductions that, twenty years or so before, they had dis-covered that the bracket-shaped mound around Ardhmor peninsula's neck was the remains of a Roman dyke and ditch fortification. The arguments for and against the idea had raged in the august pages of the *Glasgow Herald* for months before the university had started a dig which dis-covered it to be true. What had puzzled the old man was the reason for the fortification. Ardhmor Rock itself would have been an ideal defensive position with a fort on top and the wall at one side and the sea at the other for added protection. But there were no remains, Roman or otherwise, on the peninsula itself.

Jimmy pulled out a large-scale map he'd drawn of the area, filled with old place names, most of them in Gaelic, based on maps dating from around the granting of the Burgh charter and beyond.

'Look here,' he said, 'just south of the dyke. I noticed these mounds when I saw some pictures taken from a helicopter going up to the base. They are well inside the wall, but they run parallel to it from one side to the other. It's as if there are *two* walls.'

'Maybe the Picts thought the rock was a good fort too.'

'That's what you would think. But Professor Sannholm has found old Pictish relics all over the mud flats and in the fields surrounding Ardhmor. But there's never been anything discovered on Ardhmor itself.'

I looked at the map. The mounds were definitely parallel to the more recent fortification which itself was paralleled by the stream of Strowan's Burn which forked behind the farm and sent its waters east and west into the bays on either side of the peninsula.

'I remember the first time you told me about Strowan's Burn,' I said, looking over the old map which Jimmy had re-drawn a dozen times in the past twenty years. 'I'd never thought about it until you told me it was Saint Rowan's Burn.'

'Not a lot of people know that still,' Jimmy said. 'But I don't think he was a saint. The name Rowan is really ancient. If there had been a monk or a hermit around here, it would have been somewhere in the records. Most of them were canonised, at least by the local folk, but you've got to remember that most of them lived before Christianity arrived in these parts. Maybe they were the equivalent of sorcerers. Mumbo-jumbo men, or even just warriors.'

'But there was a legend about St Rowan,' I said. 'I remember you told me years ago.'

'Yes, I found it in a translated version of a field report of one of Columba's people from Iona who came down this way to convert the tribes. They had a pretty good organisation, even then. They'd send out their monks to make an impression and dig out the folk culture so they could change it around to suit the Christian message. The St Rowan story is just like Old Moses, you know.'

'I remember,' I said. 'He was supposed to have struck the rock with his rowan spear to bring the water of life to the people.'

'That's it. And that's where Strowan's Burn is supposed to have come from, although why he should have bothered in a place like this I can't imagine. We've got more streams and rivers than we need.

'Anyway the professor found a wicker fence and a few other odds and ends last year just before the start of winter, but they're arranging a proper dig in a couple of weeks.'

'Will you be there?' I asked.

'Oh, I suppose I'll go down and potter around, but I don't get involved in any of the heavy work. I just like to chew the fat with the professor. We see eye to eye on a lot of things.'

'And are you planning to get any fishing done? Mr Bennett was telling me the hands are giving you a bad time.'

'Yes, he said he'd seen you. Word gets around quick here.'

'And you were always the first to know. I know that. I got more stories from your contacts here than I've had ever since,' I said.

'I wouldn't say that. You've been doing quite well. You shouldn't undersell yourself, but I gather you'll be working on a book just now.'

'Yes, once I settle in, although I've hardly had a chance yet. I was down at the shore the first night I got back, looking for the men off that boat.'

'Yes, I heard that too. Murdo was saying there wasn't a sign of the lifeboat.'

'No, we searched around for a couple of hours. It was a terrible night down there, but there was nothing at all. I don't think they could have come ashore there.'

51

'I don't know, it's a strange place.'

'How do you mean, strange?'

'Oh, nothing,' Jimmy said, and started rolling up the big map.

'No, go on,' I insisted. 'What's funny about Ardhmor?'

Jimmy turned to look at me, then looked away, shaking his head. I reached across and grabbed his sleeve.

'What is it?'

'You'll think I'm rambling,' he said. 'And I don't want you to think the old man's getting senile.'

'That'll never happen to you. But really, I'm interested in why you say it's a strange place, because something strange happened to me when we were down looking for that boat.'

Jimmy turned suddenly and looked directly at me. There was something in his eyes, maybe concern, maybe surprise.

'What happened?'

'I'm not sure. But just when we got past the old dyke . . .'

'The Roman wall,' he corrected me.

'Yes, the wall. We had just gone back there when I started getting scared. I mean really shaky scared. As if I was being threatened. But there was no reason for it. I was in a panic the whole time, but none of the others seemed to be bothered. Then, when I was coming back with the others, I was last in line on the track up to the farm and I got caught in the brambles at the edge of the path. But at the time, I was in such a state that I thought the trailers were actually trying to *grab* me for Christ's sake. It was weird.' I looked at him, and laughed. 'Now you'll think I'm rambling.'

'No,' he said, and his voice was deadly serious. 'I don't think that at all. I've had that feeling myself. Once a long time ago, and the other only a week ago. As if I wasn't wanted there.'

'That's exactly how I felt. But that's nonsense. How can you feel not wanted in a *place*?'

'That's what I've been trying to find out for years. It's a *wrong* place.'

'Mr Bennett said that yesterday. He said Ardhmor's a wrong place, and he said everybody knew that.'

'Well, I think he's right. But not everybody knows it.'

'I remember as a kid, my mother used to threaten me with all sorts of hard times if she ever caught me down there. That was after the accident, remember?'

'I remember that night all right, though I'm surprised you do. You were unconscious for a week.'

'You remember more than me. I can't recall a thing about it, only what my dad and grandad told me.'

'You'd been missing for a couple of days. You and a couple of your friends. Then old man Swanson found a jacket in the bushes at the edge of his farm and there was a big search all over that rock. That's where we found the three of you, under a rockfall. You and the girl and that poor boy who's never been the same since. Nobody knew how you got there or why you *were* there, but you were in bad shape by the time we got you out.'

'Yeah, I gather I was out of it for a long time, but surely it was just an accident. I mean, I was always a bit wild as a kid, always climbing and falling out of trees.'

'Oh, sure, that's what everybody said. But what I'm saying is that in the spring of that year, after they'd done the dig on the Roman wall, I was down in Ardhmor one night looking for something I'd lost, and I got a dose of the scaries. I came out of that place like a bat out of hell, and I was no youngster then, but I swear I would have passed Roger Bannister on the straight.'

'I often wonder what had happened then,' I said. 'But I suppose we'll never know.'

'No, I suppose not, but that was a bad summer here in Arden, a *right* bad summer. That was the year Henson down at Kilmalid Farm fell under his plough and got his hands near torn off. Then there were the bull terriers they were using for the fights down at the sewer pipe tore up that fellow that was breeding them. Forget his name now, but the sergeant, Jack Bruce it was in those days, said it was the worst thing he ever saw. Those beasts ate the man alive.

'Funny thing was, after all the things that happened that year, they stopped just after the end of summer, just about the time we pulled you out from under the rocks. I remember your grandad at the time. He was worried out of his head, 'cause he was saying you were the latest victims.

'I remember asking him what he meant, and he just said "This cursed place has taken them." But it happened, although for a while it was touch and go.'

'What do you think he meant?'

'I don't think. I *know* what he meant. There's some people around here with long memories, and there have been bad years before. Years when some terrible things have happened.'

'How do you mean?' I asked.

Jimmy finished off his coffee in one gulp. He put the cup down between the mementoes that crowded the little table beside his chair, then turned to me again.

'What I mean is that there were fourteen people died that summer,' he said. 'And it wasn't the first time. In 1906 there was another bad year when there were thirty deaths – and I mean killings. It was in the papers at the time. They thought the whole town had gone mad. They thought people had gone crazy in the heat. Apparently it was the hottest summer in living memory then.

'And before that in 1720 there was the massacre at the priory where the seminary is now, and they had to send a sheriff down from Glasgow with an armed militia. This goes way back. There's no rhyme nor reason to it, and I bet if the records were clearer we'd find more bad years going down through the ages.'

'But can you say it's abnormal? I mean every town's got a history of tragedy,' I said.

'That's true, but Arden's history is updated every now and again, like a catalogue of disaster. I know, for I've been through the records, even the old parish ones that go back for centuries and a lot of old dusty books besides. I told you about the legend of St Rowan, but there's other ones too. I'll dig them out for you some time, but I can assure you that some of the old Gaelic writings show that the old folk believed there was something wrong with this place. With Ardhmor. They called it the Sleeping Rock, and they had an idea it woke up every now and again.

'Anyway,' Jimmy said. 'Enough of this. Come on and I'll make us a decent coffee this time, and you can tell me all about what you've been up to. . . . And I want to hear about this book you're planning to write.'

FOUR

For a week I was like a caricature of a novelist, spasmodically ripping out half-typed sheets and crumpling them up into tight little balls which steadily mounted in the wastebasket and overflowed on to the floor. I just couldn't shake out those ideas that had been burbling along just under the surface, only needing to be keyed in and run together. I'd tried to work on a plot, but the more I wrote out the draft, the more complex and unbelievable it got. Instead, I just started typing along a rough guideline, and every time I looked at what I had written I was ashamed. It was wooden, stilted, the dialogue unbelievably bad.

I'd promised Jimmy Allison and old Mr Bennett that I'd meet them along in the Chandler, but I didn't make it. On the Sunday I'd sat down and sorted out all my paper and put the filter coffee maker on heat. Then I'd started writing garbage.

I wasn't sleeping properly either. At nights, I'd drag myself upstairs and throw myself into bed and toss and turn until the early hours, wondering where I was going wrong.

There was another reason of course, which I didn't realise at the time. I spent a lot of time at nights just trying to get to sleep, and when I finally did I had dreams that would shock me awake with the same drained and horrified feeling I'd had on the night when I stepped on the seventh stair. I would be running with sweat and a couple of times I had to change the sheets because they were so damp.

Sometimes I'd awake with no recollection of what I'd been dreaming about. I'd just have an overwhelming feeling of threat and dread, and although the substance of the nightmare might have vanished as I leapt with a harsh scream of pent-up terror almost bursting from my throat, the aftershock would leave me trembling.

There were other nights though, when I did remember. Not the whole story, but glimpses of the picture, sections of nightmare that were still vividly careening across my imagination. Sometimes those scenes not only left me with the feeling of fear, but shook me so badly I felt I needed to throw up. I'd had the tunnel scene a couple of times, and it didn't get better with familiarity. But there were others.

One which really did have me crying out in the darkness was an appalling dream where I was crawling in mud that was thick with blood. Behind me I could hear a slavering, grunting growl of whatever monster was after me, and my feet kept slipping while the rending teeth of the thing snapped and crunched behind me, and I knew that it was going to eat me up because there was no possibility of escape. As I slipped and slithered in the red-streaked mud I saw a small shoe lying there, embedded in a gory puddle. There were little strips of flesh hanging from it, and I knew that what was going to eat me had done this, and my feeling of terror was so great that just before those enormous jaws closed upon me, I awakened from sheer terror, panting for breath. Panting for life.

After dreams like that – and there were many of them – I'd lie in the darkness and stare at the shadows on the walls. I'd smoke a cigarette held in a shaky hand. And sometimes I'd wonder what the hell was wrong with me. In the mornings I felt slugged and dopey. The feeling of fear and oppression might have ebbed during the night, when finally I'd got back to sleep, but there was still an underlying apprehension that maybe I was having some kind of breakdown.

On the following Sunday I decided to give myself a break. What the hell. I'd enough money to last me a long time, and if it took a long time, I'd still do it. I told myself I just wasn't ready for it yet.

Holly's bar was warm and smoky and welcomingly busy

when I stepped off the street and through the smoothly polished wooden door into the light. I had to push past a couple of regulars who sat in a group playing dominoes, and made my way up to the bar. Big John was at the far end and I caught his eye. He waved. Linda, the barmaid, was nearest me and I ordered a pint of Guinness which she poured in the usual slow manner, letting the head separate from the black stout and form a creamy lid on the surface.

I turned and leaned against the bar, with my elbows propped on the surface, and had a look around. Very little had changed in the past decade. Probably in the last fifty years. Maybe a lick of paint here and there, and some new upholstery on the bench seats that lined the walls, but essentially Holly's bar was the same as ever. Holly had resisted the space invaders infiltration, and there was no pin-ball machine or juke-box. Up in a far corner there was a television for watching football on Saturdays and replays on Sundays, but that was it. It was a bar, plain and simple. A meeting place for a fair percentage of Arden's adult population. The faces hadn't changed here either. As I looked around, I recognised most of them, and there were some youngsters who would still have been in short trousers when I took off for pastures new, but they were the sons of people I knew. If I couldn't put a first name to them I could at least identify them with a family tag. No doubt that history had repeated itself down the years as the pub had been handed down through the Hollinger family. In fact, while its official name, in green paint above the door, proclaimed it to be the Arden Inn, and the old building dated back nigh on two hundred years, it had been known as Holly's for as long as anyone could remember.

I turned around when Holly tapped me on the shoulder, and thanked him for the drink which was on the house. I had just started sipping it and the big landlord had gone off to serve somebody else when a crowd of men came in and jostled past the old men at the table as they made their way to the bar. There were four of them, in their early twenties, dressed in jeans and fashionable zipper blousons.

One of them bumped into me as they crowded the bar in the space between me and the other customers.

'Three of heavy and a big Whitbread, sunshine,' one of them called out to Linda. 'Make it quick and I'll give you a big kiss.'

The girl rolled her eyes to the ceiling as she continued pouring for someone else, and the man who had called the order, the one who had bumped my drinking arm, drummed his fingers on the bar top with impatience. Eventually she came across and started working the beer tap with the order. She set the drinks on the bar and the customer handed over a fiver which he whipped back just as her fingers were about to close on the money.

'How about the kiss, sunshine?' he asked, turning to his friends, who laughed. The man was small and wiry, his brown hair swept back from his forehead, and when he grinned he displayed a set of strong, slightly misshapen teeth.

'That'll be the day, Billy,' the girl said. 'You've no chance.'

One of his friends, a tall, skinny youngster with a long, horse-like face, laughed uproariously. 'You tell him, Linda. Saving yourself for me, aren't you?'

The girl shot him a look as if to say she'd sooner kiss a snake, and quickly reached out and grabbed the money from the first man's hand.

'Better luck next time,' said horse-face, and the thin, wiry one told him to piss off.

The four of them made their way to a free table in the corner, talking loudly as they went, and pulled up the bentwood chairs as they sat in a huddle. On my left side, someone said hello to me and I turned round and went through the same half-second of disorientation that I would experience time and again over the next few weeks before the name spung from memory.

'Hi Tucker,' I said. Tommy O'Neil was the town's postman, as I discovered. He and I chewed the fat for a while, and I savoured my beer. We swapped stories about what I'd been doing and what had been happening in Arden over the piece, which wasn't much more than small-town small talk, but it was pleasant anyway. While we were talking, the pub door opened a couple of times as people came and went, but I didn't bother looking round to see who the new arrivals were until I heard one of the four sitting at the table let out a yell.

'Badger, you big daft bastard.'

Right away, I knew who was at the receiving end of that. I turned round and saw him and my stomach gave that quick lurch of sadness or pity or conscience whenever I'm faced with one of life's unfortunates. You know what I mean if you've ever been in a handicapped children's hospital, or seen mutilated beggars in the streets of Bangladesh, or the swollen bellies of stick-insect children in Ethiopia.

Badger Blackwood was one of them. And the feeling that made my insides drag was coupled with the knowledge that he hadn't always been the way he was. Badger. . . .

Colin Blackwood had been my best friend once. He was that 'poor boy who's never been the same since' that Jimmy Allison had been talking about. He'd been with me and the girl that night they pulled us out of the rockfall at Ardhmor, but while Barbara and I recovered – I was delirious for a week – Colin did not. He was damaged, brain damaged. They'd kept him in the hospital for months while the terrible injuries in his head healed over, and the scars, two great wounds that had ripped his scalp from the crown to his forehead, had left their mark. The two lines of hair had grown in white against the glossy black, and ever since he was let out of hospital he'd carried the mark. The children had started calling him Badger, and the name had stuck. God knows, he didn't have the capacity to care one way or another about his new name, for the damage inside his head had left him slow and dull, and he'd stayed that way ever since. I found out later that he was a regular in Holly's bar, where he'd be allowed a couple of shandies with hardly any beer, and he'd sit for hours watching the old men play dominoes, smiling at them all with that vacant, gut-wrenching look on his face. It was the saddest thing you ever saw, but I suppose whatever the rocks had knocked out of Colin's head had killed off any memory of what he had been like before.

'Jesus Christ, you big ape,' said the wiry youth who'd bumped into me at the bar. 'You've spilled my fuckin' beer.'

Badger just stood there, next to the complainer, his big, dark eyes bewildered and apologetic.

'I-I'm sorry Billy,' he said slowly. 'I d-didn't mean it.'

Billy had jumped up from the table and started frantically wiping spilled beer from his jeans.

'Why don't you watch where you're going?' he grated, and shoved at Badger, slamming his shoulder with the heel of his hand. Badger lurched back, and as he did so the shandy he was carrying slipped right out of his hand and fell against the small man, covering his jeans properly this time.

'Jesus! Look what you've done now,' yelled Billy, as his three
companions pushed themselves rapidly away from the table in a futile bid to avoid the deluge. The glass tumbled to the floor but for some reason remained intact.

'I-I-I . . . ' the bewildered Badger started to stammer. I could hear panic rise in his voice.

'You fucking cabbage,' Billy yelled again, and grabbed Badger by the lapel of his jacket, dragging the slow face up close to his, and shaking Badger back and forth.

'You're going to pay for that,' he almost screeched. 'Look at the state of these jeans.'

'Leave him alone,' I said, walking forward and gripping the man's arm at the wrist. 'It wasn't his fault.'

'Who the hell are you?' he hissed, rounding on me. His eyes were glaring in fury.

'It doesn't matter,' I said as calmly as possible. Inside I was seething. 'Just leave him alone and pick on somebody else.' One of his friends sniggered. I saw what was coming a mile away. Billy pushed Badger away from him – the lumbering figure cartwheeled his arms as he fought to retain his balance – and Billy's head lunged towards mine in the classic Glasgow kiss, his forehead angling down to catch the bridge of my nose. As I said, I saw it coming and had already started to move back, bringing the heel of my hand upwards as fast and as hard as I could, squashing it right into the front of his face, and my left hand came whipping round, the knuckles twisting hard, to take him solidly just under the ribs.

Billy yelled and it was his turn to look like a windmill as he staggered back, crashing into a chair which overturned, and into the arms of one of his mates.

'Oh by fugging dose,' he moaned. 'Jesus fugging *Christ*.'

The whole bar had gone quiet. From the corner of my eye, I could see the bulk of John Hollinger come through the bar-flap.

'Right. You, you and you, out. You're barred. All of you,' he boomed. 'And you, Billy. Get yourself out of here and don't come back until you learn to behave.'

Billy still had his hands clapped to the front of his face, but there was no mistaking the venom in his eyes as he lurched towards the door.

'I'll get you for this, you bastard,' he screeched from behind his hands, almost unintelligibly, but there was no mistaking what he said.

Badger just stood there with his hands at his sides, looking as bewildered as ever.

'Right. What's going on here?' Holly said. Badger started to mumble a reply, but it was beyond him.

'That one was giving him a bad time. He knocked the drink out of his hand, and then blamed Badger for it,' I said. 'He was going to hit him, so I stopped him.'

'I saw that bit. I was down in the cellar for the rest of it. That was a quick bit of hitting there, from what I saw. Billy's a mean little bastard if there ever was one.'

'I gathered that.'

'But I don't like violence here. If anybody's going to do

the hitting, it's me. It's my licence,' he said.

'Sorry, Holly. I thought I was doing the right thing,' I said, as we both walked to the corner of the bar, Badger in tow.

'You were, lad, you were. That was just for the benefit of the rest of them. Anyway, I saw the good bit. I didn't realise you were a fighting man. I wish I had an action replay of that one-two. Have you been training?'

'A couple of nights a week I do this karate stuff just to keep fit. I've never had a chance to use it before.'

'Looked pretty good to me. But watch out for that Billy. He and the rest of them are worth the watching. I had to throw them out last year for smoking whacky baccy. They're nothing but trouble.'

Holly didn't throw me out. I bought another pint for me and a shandy for Badger who was looking at me as if I was a hero.

When his drink came, Badger thanked me shyly. 'Are you all right now, Colin?' I asked.

'Yes mister,' he said, after drinking a big mouthful. He hadn't a clue who I was. I could have wept, looking at his bland, child-like face, for I remembered when we had played about the trees as youngsters, Colin bright and fast and full of fun. Destined to go places, always full of enthusiasm. Destined to lose all that under the rockfall at Ardhmor. Destined for nothing.

'You don't remember me, do you?'

He looked at me, examining my face with those dull, dark eyes, then shook his head.

'It doesn't matter,' I told him. 'I'm Nicky Ryan. I used to live here. I was in the same class as you at school.'

He smiled brightly, and nodded. I could see him puzzling over that, but he still smiled. It didn't mean a thing to him. The pub had gone back to its usual busy hubbub, as always happens within minutes of any brawling, and Badger and I sat together. He told me he worked up at the Renfrew stables where the better-off kids from all over came for pony trekking in the summer. Colin could have been anything he wanted to be. Badger mucked out stables. Behind my feelings of sadness at that waste, I'm sure there was the certain knowledge that this could have been me. I hadn't a clue how Colin and Barbara and myself had ended up getting clobbered with rocks in the old fumarole on the Sleeping Rock, but Babs and I had come out alive. Only part of Badger had.

Would somebody have stood up for me?

The nickname was maybe cruel, but apposite. The two white-grey lines on Colin's hair really *did* give him the appearance of a badger, and he answered to the name quite readily. He didn't see anything wrong with it, and in fact, before the end of the night, I found myself calling him that myself. Everybody did. It was just one of those accepted things.

I walked Badger home. It only took a few minutes to get to his house which was a two-up, two-down on the north side of Main Street on Broadmeadow Road which lay in the lea of the hill that led up to High Arden, or Upper Arden as the residents called it.

There wasn't much conversation. Badger was big and shy and talking to him was like having a conversation with a small child. Every now and again, he'd look over his shoulder to make sure Billy and his pals weren't following us, and occasionally he'd sneak a glance at me which read pure hero worship. I could have done without that.

His mother was peering through a crack in the curtains and came bustling out as soon as we reached the gate.

'Colin? *Colin!* Is that you?'

'Uhuh,' he said.

She came down the flagstones that led from the wrought-iron, waist-height gate to the square of light that came through the front door.

'Who's that?' she started to say as she walked the dozen or so steps. 'Who are you with?'

A small, grey-haired woman with a drawn face, and a pair of reading glasses dangling from a thong round her neck, she came up and peered at me. Her dark eyes were a match for her son's except that hers were quick and alert.

'Oh. It's you.' She looked me up and down, then looked at her son. I'd seen that look before, the one she directed at me. Ever since the doctors had told her that Colin wasn't going to recover, I'd seen that look on her face. Maybe she didn't consciously think it, but even at ten years of age I *knew* what it meant: 'Why *my* boy? Why not *you*?' I didn't know why then. Hell, I hadn't a clue even about *what* had happened. It was as if a handful of days of my life had been plucked out and never happened. Except that they had happened, and Badger was the living, enduring evidence.

'Hello, Mrs Blackwood. I just walked Colin home.' I was careful not to use the nickname in her presence.

'That's right mom.' Badger nodded, smiling. 'Mr . . . Mr . . . Nicky. He did it. He hit Billy Ruine.'

Ruine. That name rang a bell. One of Jack Ruine's boys from down the south side of Milligs. I knew the family well. His big brother Mick had been the terror of our generation, a whip-thin youth with a tight smile and ready fists. A fighting man among the fighting men on the far side of town. The whole family were wild.

'What's that?' Badger's mother snapped. 'What happened?'

Badger started to stammer an explanation that was beyond him. I broke in and said: 'It was nothing much, Mrs Blackwood. A couple of guys were causing a bit of trouble down at Holly's and B . . . ' I just managed to catch myself in time . . . 'Colin got caught in the passing. I just got him out of the road.'

'I don't like you going down there, Colin. You've got no business going and getting in fights.'

'No mum,' said her son, kicking his boot toe into the edge of the low wall, his hands jammed in the pockets of his jacket. He did look like a big foolish child. Mrs Blackwood looked at me, and there wasn't a lot of friendliness in her gaze. I had been a memory that maybe for her sake should never have come back to Arden.

'Right, Colin. In you go and get your tea.'

'Yes mum,' he said and shambled up the path, turning to look back at me with a big, shy smile, before going inside.

'Well, Nicky Ryan. I suppose I should thank you for getting Colin out of trouble.'

'No, it's no trouble. Anybody would.'

'I can't stop him going there. He's just a big baby, God help him. And look at you, looking after him.' I knew what she meant, and it made me feel indescribably *sad*. What she meant was that *I* shouldn't have to look after *him*.

'But thanks for bringing him home,' was what she did say. 'He doesn't know how to take care of himself, the big lump.'

'Any time, Mrs Blackwood. The Ruine boy and his pals are just loud-mouths. If I'm in Holly's again, I'll make sure they leave him alone.

She nodded, and quickly said goodnight, and bustled up the path. The door closed quickly.

I didn't go straight home, but wandered round the old harbour to the side where the lifeboat shed stood, to the left of the small crowd of boats tied up at the white-plank moorings. It was a cool, calm night, and this time the masts of the dinghies were hardly moving. I stayed watching the boats for a while, smoking a cigarette, then walked back the way I'd come and down the street towards the house. It was warm when I got in. I'd left the gas fire on, and the room's heat quickly got rid of the evening chill. I thought about trying to write, but didn't bother. Instead, I turned on the television and watched an old movie until quite late, and then just went to bed.

At two in the morning, I was wide awake again. One of those dreams had slammed me awake, and as I sat up in the dark a shaky hand groping for my cigarettes, I could feel the force of it drain away. I couldn't quite remember what it was about, but an image of something big and terrible that was after me, snapping at me with huge slavering jaws, was somewhere in the dark recesses of my mind.

I lit the cigarette and inhaled deeply, letting it all trail out again slowly. My heart was still pounding in my chest, but gradually it diminished as I became more awake. I didn't understand this. I'd come back to Arden and I'd been scared rigid on my first night, and even worse on the morning after down at Ardhmor. Now I was having a spate of nightmares about God knows what. Was there something wrong with me? Was I beginning to flip?

The thought of being a candidate for the funny farm was almost as scary as the feeling I had when I woke up. I put *that* straight out of my mind.

FIVE

Jimmy Allison insisted on me joining him along at the Chandler on the west side of the harbour. As he pulled on his overcoat, he asked me how the work was going.

'I just can't get into it,' I explained as we strode along the road. A slight smirr of rain, more a heavy mist, was blowing in from the firth, and we bent out heads to keep it out of our eyes. The night was still warm as the day had been, so the fine spray was not unpleasant on our faces. 'I just can't seem to get a start on it. I'll have to go into Levenford for a stack more paper. There's enough crumpled in the basket to start a bonfire.'

'I wouldn't worry about it. Any author will tell you that books have a hard time being born.'

'It's the conception, not the birth, I'm having difficulty with. Coitus is interruptus, you might say.'

'You'll make it. Give yourself some time.'

The Chandler is not like Holly's bar. It's more modern for a start, at least inside, although the building is easily as old as the Arden Inn. It's been a sailors' bar for decades, since the days when the deep-bellied fishing boats used to go out on the firth and up by the Mull of Kintyre after the herring. Now the sailors were the weekend sort, and the Chandler did a roaring trade in the summer. The bar was where the local boys, the men who worked on the boats and helped repair and refit the small craft, came to do their drinking. This was where my grandfather had spent a lot of the time when he was home from the sea, although to tell you the truth, he did a power of drinking at Holly's bar as well. I imagine he got round most of the bars in the area, and everybody who was anybody in Arden knew old Nick Westford.

The major was a short man with a moon face and sharp blue eyes and a thick head of iron-grey hair that was cut short and neatly parted.

When I was introduced to him he shook my hand strongly and warmly and told me he'd heard a lot about me.

'All good, I assume,' I said, trying to return his grip just as firmly and probably failing.

'Well, I suppose so,' he said, in a deep, lilting island accent, that pleasant slow speech that makes everybody think that the people of the islands are just as slow as they sound. Most of them find out too late. 'I suppose so, if you can believe a word of anything this old storyteller says, which none of us do, at all.'

I laughed along with Jimmy, and stuck up a round for the three of us. Both men had a taste for the dark malts, and I stuck to half pints.

'You're not a whisky man yourself?' the major asked.

'No, I don't really like it. Just at weddings and funerals. That's my stretch.'

'Oh, it's a pity that. I wouldn't myself like to be drinking that stuff,' he said, indicating my beer, 'it's just like cold tea.'

The major was one of these slow-moving, slow-talking men who give an outward appearance of being placid, and maybe a bit soft. But he was as hard as nails. I discovered he'd been to Oxford University, then Aldershot and then almost every trouble zone you care to mention. According to Jimmy he'd a list of decorations as long as your arm. Another thing I discovered later was that his rank was really brigadier, but he'd been in one of the special regiments which nobody really knows anything about and was quite content with the rank everybody else seemed to think he had.

'I've been telling the lad he should think about writing a book about this place,' Jimmy told him.

'Maybe he should at that,' the major mused. 'Then again, nobody would believe a word of it.'

'You mean the history?' I asked.

'Aye, the history.' He nodded. 'It's as strange as any-where. You know, my people came from here. I should have been born in Arden, but my father moved up to the islands when the fishing went bad, and that's where I was born. But I've always thought of this place as home. When they pensioned me off, this is where I wanted to stay. But as Jimmy will tell you, it's a strange place.'

'Donald's been helping me with the Gaelic,' Jimmy said. 'It's the one language I never picked up.'

'Aye, and it's a beautiful tongue for the singing, the Gaelic. I'll be going up to the islands in a week or so in the boat. Maybe you would like to come along with me and hear the singing for yourself? I've a nephew who's getting married, and you know what the weddings are like. Probably last most of the week, I shouldn't wonder.'

I told him I'd love to come. The idea of a sail up through the Crinan Canal and across the Hebrides sounded pretty good to me, and I reckoned I'd enjoy sailing with the major. He and I took to each other at first sight.

It must have been after midnight when the smart-looking owner of the Chandler – an Englishman, but none the worse for that – called time and we had to leave. We all went back to Jimmy's where he and the major polished off the bottle of malt the old man had broached before, and I had a can of beer.

Sometime in the early hours of the morning the major went home, walking steady as a rock despite what to me would have been enough to have me talking to the vitreous china again. I slept fully clothed on top of the spare bed and didn't dream. In the morning I had no hangover and felt good. Jimmy woke me with a cup of tea and toast which went down a treat. He looked worse for wear. He had coffee. Thick and black.

From the Kirkland Herald: 1906.
Mystery of Missing Trawler
   Arden fishermen and the tugboat association from Greenock

have discontinued their week-long search for the crew of the Herring Gull *which went missing off Ardhmor Point last Tuesday.*

The Herring Gull, *a Clyde-built trawler, disappeared in thick fog while netting for herring in the firth with two other Arden boats, the* Sea Spray *and* Otter, *all three owned by the Arden Fishermen's Association.*

The mystery of the Herring Gull's *disappearance is unexplained; the captains of both boats maintained that the three boats were fishing in calm water only three miles out from the home harbour in an unseasonal, but welcome shoal, when the* Herring Gull *drifted into a fog-bank.*

Such was the success of the catch that the absence of the Herring Gull *was not noted by the other boats for more than an hour, and due to the calmness of the firth, the alarm was not raised until six hours later when the boat failed to arrive to unload in Arden.*

Boatmen from north and south of the firth have spent many hours dragging the coves around Ardhmor, but no trace of survivors or their boats have been found.

Association Chairman Mr Walter Wood, having taken advice from Sergeant MacIntyre of Levenford Station, has allowed his boats to discontinue the search.

Mr Wood said he was unable to explain the mystery. He told the Post: *'Captain Mellow and his crew have fished these waters for two decades without incident.*

'I can only assume that their vessel became lost in the fog and drifted on the firth into open water. I have no doubt whatsoever that it will be recovered in due course. The absence of wreckage gives us all hope that the captain and the seven members of the crew are safe and well.'

The Clyde Pilot, Mr J. J. Thomas, said that to his knowledge the Herring Gull *had neither been sighted, nor put into any of the western ports.*

'And it never did show up,' Jimmy Allison said as he took the old newspaper clipping out of my hand. 'I heard an old story that months later they found bits and pieces of that boat all over the rock, hundreds of yards from the high-tide line. But there was nothing in the papers about *that*. There was too much going on here by then.'

'So when is this supposed to have happened?'

'Not supposed to. *Did*. In 1906, a vintage year for Arden. I was thinking about it last week when you were telling me about the sugar boat. I *knew* I remembered something similar.'

'It's hardly the same, though, is it? I mean, the *Cassandra* went down in a storm. Even then, it didn't sink, just rolled over on a sandbank. And half the crew were none the worse for wear except a couple of cracked skulls,' I said.

'For all we know, the crew of the fishing boat just took off for new fishing grounds. They were part of the Arden Association, weren't they?' Jimmy nodded and I went on. 'So there was nothing to stop them taking off and starting somewhere else where they would get a full share of the catch.'

'That's true enough. But there would have been word of it. Some rumour even. But they weren't even sighted by anyone, and you know what a clannish lot those old fishermen were. Everybody knew everybody else's business from the Minch down to the Irish Sea.

'That's not the point,' he continued. 'The point is that they went missing off Ardhmor, and they were *never* seen again. That boat from the *Cassandra* went missing off Ardhmor, and that hasn't been seen since, either.'

'But it's only been a week.'

'Come off it, Nick,' Jimmy said, putting the clipping down on a substantial pile of papers and old notes. 'You know as well as I do that if a boat goes down anywhere on the firth there's always some trace. I mean, it's not the open sea with a clear run straight out into the Atlantic, is it? That boat disappeared. And I tell you it's gone for good.'

'What makes you think that?'

'Because it's too like the first time. Or even that might not have been the first time for all I know. But it's the same, and remember what I told you – it was 1906 and that was a bad year. The disappearance of the *Herring Gull* was just the first in a whole series of strange happenings in and around this town.'

'Like what?'

'I'll tell you like what . . . next week, when I've got the whole lot looked out from this mess. Listen. I'll do a deal with you. If they don't find anything down at that rock by the weekend, which they won't, you can buy me another bottle of malt and read all the notes I've got.'

Somehow I knew he was going to win. On the following Sunday, I would have my nose buried in a mass of old and yellowing paper, culled from the old *Post*, the *Herald* and the big broadsheets from Glasgow.

But it wasn't just the fact that the boat from the *Cassandra* never turned up. Not a stick of the lifeboat was ever found. But there were one or two things that happened in the following days that made me think Jimmy Allison might have a point. I was just at the prologue to a story, and it wasn't any fairy story either. I was just at the 'once upon a time' stage, not really interested, and not really interesting. It had to get to the big bad wolf bit before I would sit up and take a bit of notice.

I was slowly sinking into a dream, the kind of fuzzy dream that was going to take a little hitch somewhere along the line and the rules to get bent right out of shape before I was going to plunge down into a black nightmare. You know the kind of dream I mean, where things just begin to change a little and you keep right on dreaming because it's only a dream, and while things do look a little bit strange, it's not yet time to wake up because you can *handle* it. So hey ho, on we go. At this stage, I reckon I didn't even know the story had started, but it had, and I was in it and even then things were beginning to take their sideways hitch out of true, but only Jimmy Allison knew more than me. He'd been around longer. He'd been places and seen things. And right soon, I was going to be seeing some of those things. And worse.

I didn't give much of a thought to what had happened

to the men on that old fishing boat that disappeared into the fog way back when my grandad was just a boy. Nor did I concern myself overmuch about the fate of the men from the lifeboat. At that time, it wasn't a *mystery*. A tragedy, maybe, in newspaper terms, and certainly a tragedy for the families of those men who were not coming back.

The reason I wasn't dwelling on that – and my agreement with Jimmy – was that on the afternoon that I'd read the old clipping, the sun came out from behind a cloud and beamed down on me. Life took an upward flip and I was looking good, feeling *fine*.

And the reason for that was that I met a girl.

Not any old girl. A very special one.

And in meeting her, all the prime characters were in place to get this story out of the prologue and into the main tract. In some ways it might have been better if I'd never met her, but I reckon it had to be. It was *meant*.

She was standing at the side of the supermarket where the sun bounced off the yellow brick wall. Her arms were tanned brown and smooth and moving quickly as she threw the two rubber balls down to bounce them on the concrete and catch them on the upward rebound from the wall. I could hear the rhythmic child-jive nonsense chanted in time to the sound of the bouncing balls. I was passing by the girl and had edged away just enough to avoid getting in her way when she mis-caught one of the balls and it bounced high over her head. I was just in the right place to reach out and snatch it out of the air.

'Good catch, mister,' she said, in a high voice which had more than a hint of an East Coast American accent. She was maybe seven years old.

'No, it was a *great* catch,' I said, turning away from the sun which was right in my eyes, to look at her.

When I looked down, my heart gave a jolt, and suddenly I was a boy again. It was like walking into a time-warp, a memory so vivid that you can hear it and smell it.

Barbara Foster squinted up at me, the hand with the ball shielding her eyes from the glare, and the other one outstretched for its companion. She was standing hip-shot in the same pair of faded jeans and white tee-shirt, wearing the same big smile and those pretty freckles over her snub nose.

I had last seen her like that more than twenty years before, and there she was, ever the tomboy, my best pal in the whole world, and she'd stayed just the same.

'Barbara?' I blurted out without thinking. If I had thought, I would have known it was utterly impossible, but just seeing her had thrown me right off balance.

'No, I'm Paddy,' she said, smiling brightly. 'Can I get my ball back mister?'

I looked at the ball in my hand. It was just the same as the balls you could buy in the ironmongers for sixpence then. Soft and spongy, a good bouncer, just made for small agile hands to juggle. I squeezed it in my hand, feeling the familiar give.

'Please?' the girl said.

'Oh, sure, here,' I said, and handed it over. She reached up and grasped it and threw it up in the air in a quick juggling motion. I'd seen her do that before too, except it hadn't been her.

'You called me Barbara,' she said, still grinning.

'Well, you look very much like somebody I used to know. She was called Barbara,' I said, and smiled back at her. The resemblance, as they say in all books, good and bad, was uncanny.

'What did you say your name is?'

'Paddy. It's for Patricia, but I hate that. It's a cissie name.'

'Nothing wrong with Patricia,' I said, 'but Paddy's nice. It suits you.'

I bent down and extended my hand. 'I'm Nicholas. But I hate that. It's a cissie name too. I like Nick, but my friends call me Nicky.'

The little girl smiled. We had something in common. She transferred the ball into the other hand which now held two of the sixpenny bouncers and took mine, shaking it manfully.

'Pleased to meetcha, Nicky.'

I was still taken aback with her appearance. The resemblance was striking, and I was about to say something else when I heard a shout from behind one of the cars in the park.

'Paddy! Patricia. Come here at once,' a woman's voice came loud and sharp. I heard the click, click of heels on the concrete and turned to see a tall, fair-haired woman striding towards me.

'Paddy. What are you doing?' she demanded, but she was looking at me, not the child. Her eyes were flashing angrily.

'Nothing mummy. I was just saying hello.'

The mother threw me another stinker of a look, and right then I felt lost for words. I could see how it looked. A strange man talking to a little pretty girl behind the supermarket.

'What have you been *told* about speaking to strangers,' her mother said, grabbing her roughly by the arm and preparing to haul her off.

'I'm sorry. It was my fault entirely,' I started to say.

'You bet, buster,' she grated, and prepared to turn away.

'He called me Barbara, mummy. He said I looked like his friend.'

'I'll bet he did,' the woman said in a stage whisper that made me feel about two inches high. Then she stopped in mid-stride. 'He called you what?' she asked, and started to turn round, and in that moment everything fell right into place.

Barbara Foster, the *real* Barbara Foster, turned her blue eyes on me, the hostility battling with uncertainty. She stared at my face in that intent way of someone with a glimmer of recognition, trying to bring it into focus.

'I'm sorry Babs, it wasn't Paddy's fault. I made all the running.' I grinned, and even as I did so I realised how stupid that would look. 'For a minute, I kind of thought she was *you*.'

'Do I know you, mister?' Her eyes weren't so frosty now, but she wasn't yet ready to be nice to the stranger who'd buttonholed her daughter.

'His name's Nicholas, but he hates that,' the little girl piped up. 'His friends call him Nicky,' she said, matter of factly.

'Nicky.' A statement.

'Nicky Ryan,' I offered. 'I know it's been a long time, but I thought at least you would have remembered.'

'Nicky Ryan?' A question. Then: 'Nicky Ryan. Dear God, Nicky Ryan, I don't *believe* it.'

'The one and only,' I said. 'The original one and only.'

'Only the lonely one and only,' she said, and started to laugh, then stopped to think of what had come tripping off her tongue, our chant from way back then. She laughed again.

'It really is you, Nicky. Oh dear, it must be . . . . '

'At least twenty years,' I completed for her. She was still staring at my face, trying to see where the boy had gone.

'Well how *are* you?' I said, offering my hand, which she took with a cool, firm one of her own and shook warmly.

'Great, just great. You've changed.'

'Now there's a surprise. I was four feet tall the last time you saw me.'

'No, I mean, you're not how I thought you'd be. God, I can't believe *meeting* you after all these years. I didn't think you lived here any more.'

'I don't. Well, I do now. I mean I've just moved back again.'

'Me too. Last week.'

'That's a coincidence. So did I.'

I looked her over. She was tall and slim and well shaped, obviously a woman who kept herself fit. Her honey-blonde hair fell in waves to her shoulders, and her deep blue eyes sparkled in a face that was heart-shaped with a well-chiselled nose and a strong, feminine chin.

'You've changed too,' I said, then looked at the girl. 'But she's still the same. She's exactly like you when you were

77

her age. It gave me a jolt when I turned round the corner and saw her. I thought I'd gone back in time.'

'Well, I can't deny maternity there,' Barbara said, and ruffled her daughter's tousled hair.

I stepped back for a real look, at both of them. Barbara had changed indeed, as could only be expected in two decades, but there was still something of the girl I knew – the third one and only – that brought a series of pictures right into my head, like fast-forward re-runs of old movies. The tomboy had evolved into a head-turner, and the new version was a clone of her mother.

We both started to say something, and stopped to allow the other verbal right of way. Barbara laughed and I said: 'Let's go for a coffee.'

'Coffee would be just great. There are one or two things I've got to pick up, but they can wait. Is there somewhere around here that does anything decent?'

'Your guess is as good as mine. Remember I'm the new boy here, but I reckon Mary Baker's tearoom is still going strong. Let's try there.'

It wasn't far along the main street and we walked in the sunshine, a little awkwardly asking questions of each other, framing them politely like two strangers – which in a sense we were. But there was a feeling of unreality about that because, despite the fact that Barbara and I had not set eyes on each other for nearly twenty years, there was a feeling between us that's hard to explain. She and I and the other one and only had been as close as any three kids could be until something happened that blew it all apart.

In Mary Baker's back pantry, as the tearoom had been known since anybody could remember, the coffee was thick and strong, and the cream even thicker. Paddy ignored her mother's warnings over the sugar on the pastry, then Barbara ignored them too and demolished one in a few big bites.

'Mmm, they're delicious,' she said, or at least that's a fair translation of how it sounded through a mouthful of light Danish pastry. 'I'll put on *pounds*,' she added when she had washed it down with the coffee. 'I haven't tasted one of these since God knows when, and they're still *exactly* the same.' Over several cups of coffee, we exchanged bits and pieces of life history, while Paddy worked her way through a mountain of calories and listened intently to every word we said.

'You're *that* Nick Ryan? I must have read about you a million times.'

'None other,' I said.

'The name never clicked. I mean I must have seen you on TV and all, but I never thought for a minute.'

'I wasn't looking my best,' I said. 'Anyway, what about you? What have you been up to for most of my life?'

I discovered that Barbara had grown up near Boston, in between bouts of schooling in England which had helped merge the Scottish and English accents into a well-rounded, pleasant one. She had married at twenty, had had Paddy within a year and something went wrong with her tubes and she couldn't have any more – another one and only, she said, nodding in her daughter's direction. Her husband, a doctor called Hartford, had been killed in a car crash five years ago and when her father, who had been the surgeon at Levenford General, retired, and decided to come back to Arden, Barbara had followed him home.

'I felt it was the best thing for Paddy. I mean, Arden's a better place for a girl than anywhere in the States. It was OK for me then, but things have changed, and they're getting worse.'

'So what do you plan to do?' I asked.

'There's no rush. John's insurance – that's my husband – his insurance was pretty comprehensive, so everything's OK there. I was a qualified physiotherapist in the States, so I might go back to that if the papers are worth anything here.'

Barbara told me her father had bought back the old family house in Upper Arden and spent most of his time re-planning the extensive gardens. Barbara had spent the past week just settling into the old town. Paddy had fallen in love with the place immediately, and her mother felt she had made a good move.

Sitting in Mary Baker's tearoom brought back a whole stack of memories one after another, that just came slotting into place like records in a juke-box. The way she looked, the way she turned her head, and even the way she sat would trigger off another far-off hazy memory that would come zooming into focus like a delicious aftertaste. We stayed there for almost two hours, until we couldn't face another coffee, and Paddy had got past the stage of being interested in the pastries. Barbara said she would bring her daughter down to visit me, and I agreed I'd go up to Upper Arden and say hello to her father. He had never been that keen on me as a youngster, but I expected him to have mellowed. We parted in the car park, standing once again in the bright sunlight, and instead of shaking my hand Barbara gave me a feather soft kiss on the cheek.

As I walked away, I heard the little girl ask: 'What's a one and only?'

I was feeling warm and light-hearted after my chance meeting with Barbara. It didn't last. While we'd been in the tearoom, an ambulance had shot past on the main street, siren ululating urgently. Just as I was heading towards the jeep, the town's police car screeched to a halt beside me. Murdo Morrison leaned out of the open window, his big face red and sweaty looking.

'Has that thing got a tow-bar?' he asked, pointing at my wheels.

I said that it had and Murdo just said: 'Right. Follow me. I need you.' He drove off and turned right at the car park entrance. I was puzzled, but I jumped in the jeep right away and the engine roared at the first turn of the key. I took off after him, along Main Street, heading west, and right again half-way to Milligs. We got to the end of the row of houses on Elm Street and Murdo, his blue light still flashing wanly in the bright sunlight, took a left down a tarmacked single track. We had gone about a quarter of a mile when he stopped at a five-bar gate that gave on to a large pasture. The ambulance was parked just outside the gate, and I could see why. At the corner, where two hedgerows met at right angles, the ground had been churned into mud by the cattle. From the tracks, I could see that the ambulance had tried to get through it and failed. Murdo leapt from his Panda and swung open the gate, his trousers were slick with brown mud up to the knees, and he jammed the heavy wooden spars against the hedge. He came dashing back and opened the passenger door and hauled himself it.

'Right through, Nick. It's Andy Gillon. He's under a tree, by God. He's in a terrible way, and the fire engine's been called out to Levenford.'

We hared across the field, scattering browsing cows to the corner where the dark green of reeds showed that the land was marshy. The four-wheel drive took me through that as easily as it had gone through the mud at the gate, and as we neared the end of the field, I could see why they needed my jeep.

A big oak tree had snapped off about three feet up from the base, and underneath it, pinned into the mud, I could see a pair of boots twitching and jerking. I hauled the Subaru into a tight turn and Murdo and I got out. There were a couple of other men, one of them kneeling beside the farmhand who was caught under the deadfall, and an ambulanceman was holding a distraught woman in the way that men do when they think that whatever the woman wants to see is something she had better not.

Andy Gillon was conscious when I got there, but he was stuck fast under a ton of oak which had squished him into the mud. Further along the edge of the field, I saw his bright red Leyland tractor angled against the ground. It looked like the axle had snapped.

Murdo started bellowing orders and organised a team to rig the rope on to the jeep while he fixed up an ingenious lever and fulcrum of logs, wedging them under the fallen oak. He lashed the tow rope on to the biggest log and told me to take it away when he gave me the call. The other farmhands and the ambulanceman started putting their weight against their levers as I inched forward.

I had to hand it to Murdo. That big tree groaned and lifted, and coupled with the pull of my wheels and the leverage of the straining backs, it came up into the air, moved in an arc and crashed back to earth a clear six feet away. I stopped the engine and hopped out of the cab. The ambulanceman holding Andy Gillon's wife let her go and she came running over to where Doctor Brant was kneeling over the still twitching man.

Then she let out a scream like I'd never heard before. It started off high and went soaring upwards until it sounded like an overheated jet engine. Then it just cut out and the woman toppled straight back and fell on the marshy ground. She was out of it in a dead faint. When I got up to where the doctor knelt, I almost joined her. Andy Gillon was still alive, still conscious then. But the look on his face showed that he knew it wasn't going to be long.

He should have been alive. Maybe bruised and battered. Maybe a couple of cracked ribs or even a strained spine. That's what should have happened when that old oak had come crashing down and pinned him in the mud. Except that where Andy Gillon had fallen, it wasn't just mud. He'd been downed on to the only spot in that whole acre of marshy land where a rock had been dumped. And Andy had come between the rock and the tree. When that old oak had been rolled away, half of Andy Gillon's guts had come away with it. The rest of them were like mashed meat, like the drums of offal you see down at the slaughterhouse on a Tuesday afternoon.

There was nothing left of him from the navel to his groin. Nothing that hadn't been put through a blender and scraped all over the reeds he lay in.

I was nearly sick, with horror and disgust. I could feel the coffee and pastries trying to make a bolt for it. *I* wanted to make a bolt for it.

You know what it's like when you come across something that shocks you rigid. Everything seems to go in slow motion. I remember clearly looking down at Mrs Gillon, who was lying there in the marsh, all by herself, her eyes wide open but only showing the whites. Doc Brant turned away from the mess. His face had gone the colour of putty. Murdo Morrison's face was still red from exhaustion. He stood like a statue, then, strangely, for the good Presbyterian that he was, he brought his hand up and crossed himself like a devout Catholic. A bunch of dung flies buzzed up in a cloud from a still-steaming cowpat, and half a field away a cow was lowing loudly. There was a buzzing in my ears that I think was just internal pressure. Like everything had been stretched way beyond its elasticity inside me. Then I looked down at Andy Gillon as he lay there, his head facing right up, and his legs still twitching in their boots although there was nothing much more than strips of mashed rags holding them on to the rest of him. His eyes locked on to mine, great wide, terror-filled eyes, rimmed with watery blood that ran down each side of his face, and I looked into hell.

Andy Gillon's gaze held on to mine and didn't let go. We stared into each other's eyes, both of us in horror and fear. I didn't know, and I still don't know, how much pain he was in, but there was no mistaking that he knew what the score was. I could read it in his eyes. His chest was working up and down in short, quick motions, and it rasped in his throat and the movement made little gurgling noises down where his belly had popped open and the glistening, torn ropes were pulsing out blood and bile and God knows what else. A white, jagged piece of bone, probably from his pulverised pelvis, shone whitely through the red at his hips. And between where his hipbones should have been there was nothing but a pulp. The old oak trunk had been punctuated with bumps and burrs and one of them had been in the right place at the wrong time and had smashed everything that Andy Gillon had had between his legs into an obscenity.

The crushed man seemed to look at me for ever, his eyes staring right through me, right into the back of my head, as if there was something important, some meaning, something that would explain how he'd come to be lying with his guts draining into the sphagnum and duckweed on a sunny day like today. His mouth was moving and there was a sound coming out of those swollen lips along with the trickle of blood. I moved in close to where Doc Brant, the young resident at the Hermitage Cottage Hospital, knelt beside him. His face was grey.

The doctor pulled his bag closer towards him and snapped open the catch with a click and pulled out a little cylindrical bottle. He jammed it into a silver syringe which he adroitly jabbed right into a vein in the man's neck. The doctor looked sick.

I don't know what I expected from that injection, but it didn't work quickly enough for me. Andy Gillon was still conscious and as I hunched down closer to the doctor – I don't even know why I did that – I could hear the burbling whisper.

'Jumped.' The breath bubbled and rattled deep in his throat. 'Jumped on me. Tree jumped.' Like a hoarse, catching litany. He was telling *me*. His eyes were bright and shockingly sane.

'What did you give him?' I said to the doctor.

'Morphine.'

'Give him some more, will you?'

'I gave him a lot. It should be working now.'

But the dying man, who knew he was dying, still locked me with those terrible eyes that glittered in the sun.

'Please, doc,' I said, 'give him anything. Just put him out of this.'

The young man turned to me. There was a great streak of bloodstained mud down the side of his face, and his expression was torture.

'I've given him *enough*. Do you understand?'

Gillon still stared at me and still dribbled the words out along with the rest of the goo that was trickling out of both corners of his mouth.

'Tree. Jumped. Jumped.'

'It's not working,' I said, and grabbed the doctor's tweed lapel. 'Put him out of it, will you? Please?'

'There's nothing else I can do. Nothing.'

'Well I can,' I told him and got to my feet and scrambled to the bole of the tree where a tangle of broken branches was strewn. I dragged out a heavy bough about five feet long and strode back, squelching through the wet. I locked eyes with Andy Gillon again. He was dying there in his field right in front of me. His insides were squashed into the mud and his eyes were on mine and he was asking me to do something. It was a plea I understood instinctively and I agreed. I hefted the heavy branch right up over my head and braced myself to swing it down with all my strength and Murdo Morrison reached up and yanked it right out of my hand. He shook his head slowly, then chucked my death-giver over the hedge. Afterwards he never said a thing about it, and never charged me with attempted murder or anything like that. Then he just looked away, away from me, from the doctor, and the woman still out for a very long count, and away from the man whose life was packing up and moving out only two yards away.

I couldn't *not* look. It was like a compulsion. I didn't even *know* the man. As far as I knew, I had never set eyes on him in my life before. But here I was, attending at his death, and he was looking at me as if I was the most important thing in his universe. He was holding on to me for that big crossover, and his litany was for *me*.

The mumbling stopped suddenly, and the man gave a grunt. He put his elbows down beside him and, still staring into my eyes, he levered himself up a few inches, his body making a slight sucking sound. With the movement, a whole gobbet of intestine blurped out of the mush below his ribs.

'Jumped. It . . . jumped.' Then a gout of thick blood mixed in with anything else he was going to say and he slumped back. The light went out of his eyes, and he was dead.

His dead eyes continued to stare at me for a long time until I turned away.

Murdo got the ambulancemen over with their stretcher and one of them vomited quickly and efficiently into the reeds when he saw the mess, and wiped his mouth with the back of his hand and carried on. They covered the body with a grey blanket and put it on the green canvas of their stretcher while the doctor attended to the still-unconscious woman.

Murdo Morrison came over to me, still shaking his head. He was a big, tough man, but there was a glint of tears at the corner of his eyes.

'Terrible thing,' he said, shaking his head. 'Terrible.'

'I'm sorry about that, Murdo. I don't know why I did that. I think I . . . . '

'I know,' Murdo interrupted. 'I know what you mean. But it's best to leave these things to the medical men.' He clapped his big hand on my shoulder in a fatherly way.

'He said the tree jumped.'

'Oh, was that what it was?' Murdo turned round and looked at the bole of the old dead oak which stood on a mound of grass, the result of centuries of old hedgerow. He and I looked back at where the old tractor was down on its haunches forty yards away. Through the grass you could see the still-flattened parallel lines where its big treads had run. And there was another line, the last passage of Andy Gillon where he had walked through the reeds towards the place where his life had been squashed out of him. The track followed a roughly straight, faint line, for the reeds were already beginning to straighten into their original positions, but you could make out his track, following the hedge, about twenty feet away from the close-cut bushes.

Murdo and I looked at each other, and back at the tracks. Then simultaneously we looked at the spot where Andy Gillon had been splattered.

The oak tree had broken off about two or three feet from the ground. The rest of the massive trunk must have been twenty feet long, knobbled and gnarled. Its outline was clearly imprinted on the soft marsh where it had fallen. The outline started about five yards from the base of the tree and continued out, past the red and green and purple patch that looked like the bottom of a wine-treader's vat, and out a few yards more, pointing to the centre of the field where the brown and white cows were browsing unconcernedly.

Murdo stared at that indentation for a long time, then he looked back at me.

'That's strange,' he said, through his teeth. 'That's very strange. And there's not a breath of wind.'

In my mind I could hear the dying man's mumbled chant. 'It jumped. The tree jumped.'

There wasn't a breath of wind, as Murdo said. Not there. Not in that sunny field. But a cold breath went right through me, right into my bones. Murdo's face looked bleak.

And in Arden, a very bad summer began to happen.

SIX

Summer 1961.

'That's what my mum says anyway,' the girl said, looking down from the fork in the sycamore tree. 'I'm her one and only. I'm special.'

'I can't see anthing special about you. You've got freckles.'

'Well they're special freckles,' the girl said, and stuck out her tongue.

'They're not freckles. They're the black spot,' a voice came from further up in the tree, the speaker hidden by the thick broad-leaved foliage.

'They are not spots,' the girl slung back.

'Not spots. The black spot. If you get one of them, you're dead. Pirates come and cut you up with cutlases.'

'My mum says they're freckles. They're a sign of beauty.'

'Beauty? Ha!' The boy at the bottom of the tree was busily carving his initials into the dark green, moss-covered bark on the shadow side of the tree. His tongue was sticking out on one side of his mouth as he worked carefully and intently.

'Anyway, I'm my mum's one and only,' the boy said as he leaned back to admire his handiwork. 'So you're not the only one.'

'Not the only one and only. Hey, that's poetry.' From the fork in the tree high above, Nicky Ryan held on with both hands, arcing his body back and forward, making the leaves shimmer and shake.

He let out a yell that was supposed to sound like Johnny Weissmuller, but just sounded like a small boy yelling.

'Oh stop that racket,' Barbara Foster said. She too sat in a fork, the place where a large, thick bough stuck out almost straight from the trunk. 'My dad'll hear you.'

'Oh, then there'll be big trouble. Heap big trouble,' Colin Blackwood said from his base position, still working his Sheffield penknife into the bark.

88

'I'm not supposed to be just the one,' Nicky Ryan said. He was starting to climb down the tree, moving carefully. 'I mean, my mum was supposed to have more. But they died. Before they were born.'

'Miscarried,' the girl said, knowledgeably. 'That's what they call it when a baby dies before it's born. That's what my dad says. Mrs Bell had a miscarriage, and my dad says she should try for another one as soon as possible. I heard him telling my mum.'

'How do you try for another one?' Colin asked. 'I thought you just got them.'

Barbara started to laugh, a high-pitched peal of tinkly laughter that almost shook her off her perch.

'Don't be so daft. Where do you think they come from?'

'From heaven, of course. My mum says that's where all babies come from, and you get a guardian angel sent down with you to look after you.'

Barbara started quaking with laughter again. Up above, Nicky Ryan called down: 'What's so funny?'

'He thinks babies come from heaven.'

'Well, where do you think they come from?' Colin called up from below.

'Inside your mum's belly. That's where.'

'How do they get in there, then?'

'Your dad puts you in there, stupid.'

'Well, where does my dad get me from, smartypants?'

Nicky had reached Barbara's forked seat. She rolled her eyes up in exasperation.

'It's sex. They have to do sex.'

'What the hell is sex?'

'Don't say hell. It's a bad word, my mum says,' Barbara scolded. 'Sex is like mating.'

'What like cows and bulls?'

'Something like that. It's all in one of my dad's books. The man puts his penis into the woman's virginia.'

'What's a penis?' Colin yelled up from below.

'What's a virginia?' Nicky said from beside her.

'Don't you boys know anything?'

Nicky looked blackly at her. She giggled. 'It's your thingy,' she said.

'My thingy? A virginia?'

'No, a penis. A woman's got a virginia.'

Nicky could feel himself beginning to blush in his ignorance.

'Why do they call it that?'

'It's just a name, stupid. A medical name.'

'Hey, why's it called a penis?' Colin shouted up at the top of his voice.

'Ssh,' Barbara hissed down. 'My dad'll hear you and I'll get called in.'

'Well, why is it called that?'

'Because you pee with it,' Barbara said briskly.

'I don't believe all that,' Colin said. 'My mum says I come from heaven.'

'Well, I wouldn't have been an only child if my mother hadn't whatchyacalled it.'

'Miscarried.'

'Right. She said they would have been boys. Big brothers. That would have been great. Huh? No getting duffed up by Fraser Ballantyne and Charlie Beaton. Great stuff.'

'Well, we're all one and onlies,' Colin said. 'The only one and onlies.' His voice broke out of speech into song: 'Only the lonelies, the one and the onlies,' badly imitating a song that had been in the charts that summer.

'Oh shut up Collie,' Nick said, sliding down the trunk, his bumpers making little scrape marks on the thin covering of moss.

'Look. I've done my name,' Colin said proudly, grinning. 'That'll be there forever.'

'Nah, it's not deep enough. That'll grow over. You've got to go right through the bark.'

'It's all right. I'll betchya a pound it'll still be here next year.'

'Right, you're on, sucker,' Nick licked his thumb and Colin did the same and they rubbed the spit together, sealing the bet.

'Hey, do you believe all that?' Colin asked.

'All what?'

'All that stuff about babies?'

'I dunno.'

'Do you think your dad would do that?'

Nick had never thought about it. He'd heard some of the older

90

boys talking about that sort of thing, but they called it by another word. A word worse than hell, *even worse than* bloody *and that was a no-pocket-money-for-a-week-my-lad word.* In a small town like Arden, that sort of thing was only a playground rumour that nobody knew too much about. Everybody knew about cows and bulls. But they were animals.

He thought about it for a bit, trying to imagine the mechanics of it, and thought about the problem of getting it into a virginia, of which he had only a half-glimpsed impression gleaned from an infant at school who'd lifted her skirt and dropped her panties and wee'd behind the tree at the far end of the small playground. Nick had done a double-take when he saw what was missing, and eventually came to the carefully thought-out conclusion that this was the big difference.

'No, I don't think so.'

'Mine neither,' Colin said. 'Especially my mum. Even if she catches me scratching down there she gives me a clip round the ear.'

Babs came swinging lightly down from the lowest branch, the one that was worn smooth from the hands and feet that had been climbing it all summer and the summer before that. She wiped her forearm across her snub nose boyishly and grinned at them, standing at ease in her jeans with the big patch on the knee, her feet planted wide apart. Her hair was a short-cut, fair tangle, and her eyes sparkled from their welter of freckles.

'Well, it's true. That's how they do it. Everybody. Just you ask if you don't believe me.'

'Not me,' Colin said. 'My mum would leather me. She doesn't like that kind of talk.'

'I've just had a thought,' Babs said. 'There's only three of us in the class.'

'What's that got to do with it?' Nick asked. He was just a week past his tenth birthday, small and lightly built, with straight brown hair that fell in a fringe over his eyes. His jeans were those dark blue denims that were just miniature replicas of men's working jeans, even down to the ruler pocket on the leg, where Nick kept his own penknife, even though it took ages to get the thing out once it had slipped down the long pocket and banged against his knee.

'I'm not talking about that, silly,' Babs said. 'I mean, only children, there's only the three of us in our class. Everybody else has brothers and sisters.'

'Lucky us,' Colin said sincerely. 'Billy Kerr's got three big sisters and they're always bossing him about.'

'I would have liked big brothers,' Nick said, with a touch of wistfulness.

'Sisters!' Colin stuck to his theme. 'Who needs sisters? They're just girls. All they want to do is dress up and play with stupid dolls.'

'I'm not stupid, stupid,' Babs rounded on him, and Colin took a step back.

'I didn't mean you, Babs, honestly,' Colin said earnestly. 'You're not a girl.'

Nick laughed out loud.

Colin's face went red: 'Well, you are a girl, but you're not like a girl.'

Barbara almost visibly swelled with pride at this.

'You're one of us, Babs,' Colin assured her.

'One of the one and onlies,' Nicky chipped in. 'The only one and onlies.'

'That's what we are. Who needs brothers and sisters?'

'Not me,' Colin said, stoutly.

'Nor me,' Nicky said, although he had always wondered what those missing big brothers – those miscarried big brothers – would have been like.

'And me neither,' Barbara concluded, grabbing their hands and placing them on top of hers.

'We're special.'

SEVEN

From the Kirkland Herald.
Double Shooting Death
Mother and Son Killed

A mother and son died in a gun horror in an Arden farmhouse last night.

Mrs Margaret Henson and her 24-year-old son Edward, of Kilmalid Farm, were found dead in their living-room after a series of gunshots.

Farmworker James McGrath raised the alarm after finding the bodies in a pool of blood. Mrs Henson suffered shotgun wounds to the head. Her son had been shot in the chest.

The tragedy comes only a week after an accident at Kilmalid Farm when Mr Henson, who took over the running of the homestead five years ago, was badly injured by farm machinery.

Mr Henson had been rushed to Glasgow's Western Infirmary for emergency surgery after his hands were badly damaged by a cattlefeed mixer.

The young man had been allowed home on Friday morning to recuperate, while doctors waited for a series of tests to ascertain whether he would have the use of his hands again.

Police inquiries into the double tragedy are continuing, a spokesman told the Herald.

It didn't take a great deal of effort on anybody's part to read between the lines of the report on the front page of the local newspaper. The story even made the dailies, but just as another shooting. Here in Arden it was a story as big as, even bigger than, the shocking death of Andrew Gillon who farmed the neighbouring acres. As the subsequent police and forensic examination showed, Mrs Henson, the farmer's widow had got the old double-barrel twelve bore

93

down from the rack, loaded in two hy-max, and given one of them to her son as he sat defenceless on an overstuffed armchair in their living room. One barrel for him, which blew out his chest and embroidered it into the chintz, and another for her, which she took in the mouth, stretching down to get her thumb hooked over the trigger. It spread the crown of her head and all its contents on the ceiling plaster.

Her reasons were not too hard to figure out either. She was mad with grief over the tragedy that was all set to ruin her son's life. History was repeating itself for Mrs Henson, and she'd decided to get in there quick and take the needle out of the groove. Maybe it was for the best.

The microsurgeons at the Western had done a wonderful job of getting Eddie Henson's hands firmly fixed on to the ends of his arms. They'd hooked up blood vessels and muscle and ligament, but those hands were never going to do anything much more than lift a forkful of food to his mouth on a good day, even if the fingers could move enough to twist themselves around the handle.

Nobody knows how Eddie Henson managed to get his hands stuck in the feed mixer. It wasn't even a mixer. It was an old Seagull outboard motor that he'd hooked on to a fifty-gallon oil drum in the byre. It worked just as well for mixing feed as it did in shoving his fourteen footer around the west bay fishing for dabs and cod. It did a good job on both, and it did a terrific job on his hands. The fact that he still had something resembling hands was a tribute to the miracles of modern microsurgery. But they weren't hands that were going to work a farm, and his mother knew it.

Her sure knowledge was easy to understand too. For twenty-three years she'd worked that farm by the sweat of her brow, scrimping and scraping and breaking her back and doing a man's work, while her husband sat at home, helpless to do otherwise.

For in 1961, the summer of 1961, Hugh Henson had tumbled off the back of his tractor when he was ploughing in the shaws of his early potatoes. Some said he'd fainted, nobody, not even him, knew exactly what had happened.

But everybody knew about his hands. For whatever reason, Hugh Henson was lying on the field and the tractor was trundling on and the ploughshare went over his wrists and nearly cut his hands right off. The bones were smashed and the muscles torn to shreds. When Hugh Henson came to, he picked himself up and walked home, dangling his hands in front of him.

No miracles of microsurgery then. The doctors saved what they could which left him with twisted talons that had no feeling in them, and Hugh Henson was helpless for the rest of his life, which he chose to end five years before his wife ended hers, except he pressed the starter button with his elbow, and let the carbon monoxide build up. Up until then he was a broken, bitter, shell of a man. Hugh Henson's young wife had given him a baby boy at the start of that year and she lived through it all, taking care of her son and doing everything for her husband until the boy was old enough to take some of the strain. She worked that farm as good as any man, everybody said, and it was a struggle. Then her husband had taken the easy way out after doing it the hard way for all those years and Maggie Henson had mourned her grief and was pleased for him that he'd gone and done it, and by this time her son was a strapping lad and an able farmer, well taught by his mother, who could work like a horse and make Kilmalid pay.

If ever a mother was proud of her son, it was Maggie Henson – the care-worn and callous-handed old woman of forty-five, bent before her time.

And when her boy had come back from the Western Infirmary, with his hands encased in two big plaster of Paris sleeves that were supported on metal stalks on his hips, and forced him to hold them out like a mildly boastful angler, she saw it all coming again, and nobody could expect her to take it.

Maggie Henson had watched her young husband

become an old man, a shadow of himself, indrawn and withdrawn. A victim of the bad summer of 1961. She was faced with the kind of decision no woman should have to make. At least not twice.

There was no way she was prepared to watch her big, smiling, willing son get like that.

She gave him the easy way out.

'That bloody by-pass is going to kill me,' Alan Scott said, swilling his drink around in a stubby tumbler, 'just when I was getting it all together.'

'I'm not with you,' I said, taking a light sip of cool lager. Out on the lawn, through the bay window, Alan's three kids, two girls and a boy, were playing a game of catch.

'The big opening's set for June seven. Next week, and from then on I'll lose the passing trade. All the traffic from Kirkland and up the Gareloch will just go zooming past, missing Arden altogether.'

'But you'll still get plenty of people coming through.'

'Maybe in the summer, but they won't be wanting petrol. At least not enough to keep my forecourt going. And nobody from the west is going to bother using that coast road when they've got three lanes each way and only twenty minutes to Glasgow.'

He paused and looked miserably out of the window. The meal had been large and satisfying. Alan was on his fourth Scotch after several glasses of wine.

'It's these Ministry of Defence bastards,' he said, and Janet, his wife, a pretty brown-haired and slightly built woman, frowned at him but said nothing.

'Yes, they call it the Trident Road, don't they?'

'Not just content with killing us all with the bloody A-bomb,' Alan complained, 'but they're strangling us in Arden too. And for what? Huh? Just so the Yanks can feel a bit safer knowing we're going to get hit first?'

Feeling was running high all through Arden, and indeed the whole district, about the Trident base which was being built into the solid granite of the Kilcreggan peninsula at a cost which would have bought a couple of British colonies back, or settled the national debt with a handshake. Billions of pounds sterling were being poured into the area which was set to become *the* major ballistic missile centre in Western Europe. So guess who was going to get struck first in a first strike? The local and daily papers had shown graphic artists' impressions of where the fall-out would go, and where the footprint of a ground strike would be, and at what radius the flash would kill unprotected humans, and where the firestorm would burn everything up. Pictures of gloom and doom. In the event, you could forget Kirkland, and Arden and Levenford, and even Glasgow. And the Kilcreggan peninsula, a long narrow neck of land that poked down from Garelochhead to Cove and Clynder would go the way of Krakatoa. Straight down.

Oh, there had been local and national protests. The District Council had declared themselves a nuclear-free zone, and that did a whole pile of good. They wore badges at meetings and joined marches, and gave hippies rent-free caravans to picket the site.

But in this neck of the woods, nobody beats the Ministry of Defence. Naturally they don't want the first strike to be anywhere near them. That's why all the silos and dumps are way out in the backwoods, rolling hills and blue lochs, little realising that there are enough highly unstable transuranic elements stored under them thar hills to wipe the breathtaking scenery off the face of the map. Think about it. Even the power stations are nowhere near the places where most people live. The big power lobbies and the nuclear lobbies say they're safe as houses. Except their houses are nowhere near them, are they?

OK, enough of the political lecture. But you've got to understand, at least I hope you do, that I'm an Arden man, going back dozens of generations – at least on my mother's side – and no matter how far I've wandered, there's no place like home, even if there are some pretty strange things going on at the time I'm talking about.

The new by-pass was going to hurt Alan Scott. Arden

was going to do him a lot of damage. There he was, having pulled his old dad's business out of the dirt and oil puddles and into the black in a big way for a small place like this, and it looked like hard times were on the way. He was right. Nobody was going to bother with the Kilcreggan Road that wound along the firth shore when they had a fast smooth dual carriageway to zip them past. Everybody knew the road was needed for the vast construction job that would be going on over the next seven years, and then it would be ideal for getting those big ominous trailers with the big ominous pointy things covered in tarpaulin, and even sheet steel, sitting on their backs, into the new base. But it was a road, and the quickest way between two points was a straight line and the quickest way was not through Arden.

'What do you plan to do?' I asked.

'I'm thinking about moving. Just when I've got it going right.'

'What, closer to Glasgow?'

He nodded. 'Harry Watkinson's place in Levenford would be just right. I'm told he'll be retiring in a couple of years, so maybe I can buy him out.'

'And still live here?'

'If I can. I love this place. I've always wanted to stay up on this hill ever since we were boys. It meant everything to me, and now I've got here, I don't want to move.'

He took a swig of his drink, and I saw his wife look at him again, one of those quick woman's looks which let you know you're doing something she'd rather you didn't, which, in Alan's case, was doing any more drinking. But he wasn't drunk.

'The problem is, if it's going to get as bad as I think it might, then there might be no option. The mortgage I've got on this place would buckle your knees, I swear to God. And there's the bloody rates and everything else. The sooner they bring in this community tax the better. I'm out about a hundred and twenty a month. A month for Christsake.'

The look he got then told me Janet didn't like blasphemy either, but Alan didn't notice it, or chose to ignore it.

'I'm sure it won't get as bad as that. You've got all the summer sailors, plus the people in town, and you've got the franchises as well,' Janet said, obviously in a bid to shake his gloom.

'We're luckier than most, I'll grant you, dear,' Alan said. 'But we need everything that's going, especially the petrol, and I've got to hold on to the car sales too.'

'Yes, dear,' Janet said, more soothingly. 'But I'm sure it will be all right. And if not, I don't mind moving. I really don't. The children are young enough to fit in anywhere.'

'I just hope it won't come to that, love,' he said, and smiled across at her. She was an artful woman who knew her man. 'I'm sure you're right.'

But I knew he wasn't sure, and he knew it too. And if I'm any judge of character, Janet Scott was also aware.

'Terrible thing down at the farm,' Alan said, charging the subject.

'Which one?'

'The shooting. Damned tragedy. That young Henson was a nice bloke. His mother was a bit of a battleaxe though. Dad and I used to fix her machinery for her and she knew just about as much as we did, down to the last nut and bolt. I swear she could tell to the penny exactly what any job was going to cost, right down to the ten per cent cash discount.'

'She must have been some woman,' I said. 'Ran the farm on her own after her husband got mangled.' From the corner of my eye, I could see Janet give a brief shudder.

'Poor woman,' she said. 'Imagine that happening twice. Father and son. No wonder she went crazy.'

'The other one was pretty gruesome, I understand.'

'Yes, it was. I was there.'

'I heard that. Must have been rough.'

'Frankly it was terrible. I had a hard time getting to sleep for nights afterward.'

In fact, getting to sleep was almost impossible for the first couple of nights after Andy Gillon got squashed. I kept seeing his face in those patterns on the wallpaper, and in the small hours of the night, when I'd be tossing and turning and trying to get below the consciousness threshold, I'd hear his voice.

'The tree jumped. Jumped.'

I kept seeing those eyes staring at me out of the walls. Pleading with me to do something to get him out of there. As I said, it was hard to sleep with that.

'It must have been awful. That poor woman, seeing him crushed like that.'

'Damned strange thing to happen,' Alan said. 'Weird.'

I nodded. I didn't really want to talk about it, but I didn't have to, for the short pause of silence was broken by the roar of a motorbike outside. Alan stood up and looked out of the window, and I joined him. Up the gravel path at a fast clip came a big shiny silver Honda, roaring up the gravel bend, with a black figure astride it.

The Honda's engine revved and I could see the rider twisting the handle, feeding more juice into the four big cylinders. The machine came to an abrupt sideways halt, spraying the smooth stones in a shower into the air. The children had stopped playing catch and were gleefully racing towards the black figure on the bike. The sun glinted on the smooth dome of his visored helmet.

'Who the hell's that?' I asked.

Alan chuckled. 'Gospel Rock.'

'Huh?'

'The piston-driven priest. He's one of the lecturers up at the seminary. He's mad keen on bikes. Thinks he's a caped crusader or something and he's always getting me to fix new bits on to that bloody bike of his. Nice enough, though. You'll like him.'

Father Gerald O'Connor was a tall, slim young man with black eyes and black Irish hair that went down a treat with his all-black leathers, and, as I discovered, his priestly clothes as well. He had a ready smile and a fund of jokes that would shock the sailors down at the Chandler's bar, but he had an Irish charm that he used like a spanner to screw funds out of every women's group in the area.

'Meet heaven's angel,' was how Alan introduced him to me. 'Father, meet my old school friend, Nick Ryan.'

The young priest flashed an easy grin as he leaned forward to give my hand a firm shake.

'Nice to meet you, Nick,' he said as he started to unzip the tight leather jacket. Street priest, I thought, taking in his longish hair and the open-necked shirt. Probably a medallion down there, rather than a medal.

'So you were in school with the mechanical wizard? He's worked miracles with my machine,' he said. Outside, Alan's brood were all sitting astraddle the parked Honda. 'It's running like a dream. I had it at a hundred and twenty up on the new road. Terrific.'

'And illegal,' Alan said.

'Only when it's open to traffic.'

'And it's the traffic that's on it which bothers us all,' Alan said sourly. 'Megatons of instant death back and forth, and meanwhile a slow death for anybody with a business in Arden.'

'I know the problems, Alan,' Father Gerald said. 'But my little run on my bike isn't going to make it any worse. Anyway, there's little we can do about it now except pray. It's a pity you're not one of my bunch, you know. We could do a quick service right here and now. Father Gerry's fast faith service. Spiels on wheels.'

Janet giggled, and even Alan had to smile at the young priest's quick-fire.

'You'd make a terrific car salesman, Gerry, honest to God. Here, what'll you have?' Alan asked, indicating his well-stocked bar.

'Never touch a drop before morning prayers. A whisky'll be fine. Not too much water in it either.'

Alan poured and the priest accepted the glass and sipped.

'Nice stuff. There must be something to the car trade if

you can afford this kind of thing. Either that or I'm on the wrong side.'

'I don't think anybody knows what side you're on, Gerry,' Janet said.

'You go about looking like a rocker on that bike of yours, and your spend all your time with those drug addicts. Old Father Maguire would turn in his grave.'

'Just as well he's in the dear arms o' Jesus,' the priest said in a thick Ulster accent. Janet shot him a mock frown of disapproval.

'He'd never have understood progress. I've been mad about bikes since I was knee high, and I've been ordered to work with our mainlining brethren, which in any case is fascinating work. When I start shooting up myself, old Father Maguire can start spinning.'

'Gerry works up at the drug rehabilitation place in Kirkland,' Alan said.

'I didn't even now there was one. I never thought there was a drug problem here.'

'There isn't,' the priest came in. 'At least not yet. The people at Shandon House are from all over, but mostly from Glasgow. They're brought down here to get away from their normal environment. We've done some good.'

'In between times he breaks all the women's hearts in town, tries to break his neck on that machine, and must have broken every rule in the book at the seminary,' Alan said.

'I'm not as bad as I'm painted,' the priest said with a smile that was supposed to make you think that he *was*. 'Just because I wear the collar doesn't mean I can't have any fun. Anyway, they've decided I'm not Satan in disguise. They think I'm just a hyperactive kid with more energy than sense, so they've decided to make me work for my money.'

He finished off the small whisky and smacked his lips appreciatively, as he set the glass down on a small table by the window.

'That's what I've come to see you about,' he said.

'They've put me in charge of the parade for the harvest festival. I'm hoping you'll give me a hand with the transport.'

'No problem,' Alan told him. 'I'll get the truck cleaned up like last year.'

'I'll need a driver too.'

'What day is it?'

'The thirteenth.'

'OK, I'll have to drive it myself.'

While they were talking, my thoughts flew back to the harvest festivals we'd had in Arden years ago. I hadn't really thought about them in years, but they were great fun, and no matter how I tried, I couldn't remember one when the sun hadn't been splitting the sky. It was the one day in the year when the whole town was together, the folk from Milligs rubbing shoulders with the rich of Upper Arden. The priests and the ministers getting together, no doubt over glasses of altar wine. A harvest festival isn't common in Scotland, mainly because the harvest isn't much to speak of in most places unless you count the annual increase in sheep flocks. But in Arden we've had the big day for centuries, maybe even millenniums. Oh, I don't doubt that the format has changed a bit since they sacrificed blood and corn in the ringstones up on Carman Hill, but it's always been a day for fun and games and feasting. In recent times, and when I say that I mean as far as written records go back (and that's just a blink of the eye by comparison with real history), the festival has been organised by the seminary, the priory, whichever name it had in all the centuries.

As I said, the seminary held its unique place in the harvest festival. In times gone by no doubt the self-sufficient monks, who owned vast stretches of the land around here, supplied the produce and kept that loyalty they couldn't gain from the fear of God through the barter system. Today, the seminary is still self-sufficient and was when I was small. They've got fields of corn and potato, a watermill for grinding corn, sheep, pigs, bees and whatever, plus an orchard where they grow just about every fruit, as every kid in town knows.

At the harvest festival, most of the food is supplied by the seminary and padded out by donations from the shopkeepers and smallholders and the farmers who still get their corn ground at the mill. Everybody is supposed to give something, then they all try to get it back again in one afternoon's binge. It's tradition.

Alan agreed to give over his truck and drive it himself and the priest seemed delighted to have that off his hands. He shook hands all round before he went and insisted I must come up and see him and have a blether. Outside, he ruffled the kids' hair and reached into a pocket of his leathers and brought out a bag of sweets and dished them around before swinging a leg over his big machine and taking off with a roar and a crunch of gravel on the bend.

'Decent chap,' Alan ventured.

'Works on his image,' I said.

'Don't let that fool you. He might be young, but they rate him at the seminary. He's got about half a dozen degrees in things I've never even heard of and he speaks a handful of languages. And he's as rich as sin too. His father owns a string of pubs in Glasgow, but despite that he's really pretty down to earth. He does a lot of work for the kids here.'

Dinner at Alan's place was hearty and as noisy as the kids could make it. Janet laid on a fine roast with new potatoes in their jackets and a stack of greens fresh from their garden. Alan didn't say any more about the by-pass and he didn't drink any more either. I reckoned he'd just been on a downer, and from the way Janet had looked at him I thought that might be a regular occurrence. He'd worked himself hard to get out of the poor side of town and up here on the hill, and that ten-mile stretch of shiny new blacktop was getting set to shove him back down again. When they finished the road that would sweep past Arden, the town would become yet another sleepy hollow, sacrificed in the name of progress and megaton capability. Oh it would be great for the summer tourists and the yachting set, but for a thriving business like Alan's it meant the difference between staying afloat and going under.

At dinner, though, we talked about the old days, school and such-like. It was nice and easy and Janet was an excellent hostess and the kids were well mannered and boisterous. I had a good time and when it came to the bit when I had to go back down the hill again I meant it when I pecked Janet on the cheek under the proud gaze of her husband and promised I'd be back again for more of the same.

The walk of half a mile or so down to Westbay helped ease the strain on my belt that the dinner had caused. It was a mild evening at the end of July and the sun was throwing pink off the edges of the high clouds giving the promise of mellow days to come. I sauntered down the tree-shaded roads listening to the evening chatter of chaffinches and starlings in the branches overhead and the screeching of swifts as they tumbled through the evening air in squadrons on the hunt.

Back at the house I tried to write a few ideas, and while the big Silver Reed hummed eagerly my mind couldn't fit things together. I gave up in disgust, had a can of beer and went to bed early. I needn't have bothered. In the early hours I woke up drenched with sweat and hauling for breath.

I'd been in the cave where things crawled out of the stone and where dead men were still alive and their hoarse screams echoed through my mind. I was propelled by some invisible and malignant force towards the pit in the middle of the cave where the thing waited for me, its hate boiling out of the hole like a festering disease. I saw it rise from that pit that went beyond the centre of the earth and felt its mind probing for mine and I knew that it would lock itself on to me and I would be swallowed up and become one of those screaming dead men.

The thing turned, and I saw its eyes, pallid and loathsome. They had no pupils but I could sense them focus on me, pinning me down with the hate. I couldn't stop myself from being dragged on unwilling feet across the cave and into the sick light that pulsed out of those eyes, and I knew my soul would be torn apart.

The dream broke up in fragments when I was thrown out of sleep again. It took me hours before I could relax enough to get some fitful slumber before the dawn.

EIGHT

On the east side of Arden harbour there's a shore path that winds its way round the rocks and shingle and past the beech trees that form a windbreak for most of Westbay. Further along the path there's some rough grass near the point that juts out into the firth and on that flat area there's a big standing stone of smooth basalt. It's been pounded by the wind and the salt spray and, on the south-west side that takes the brunt, the stone is almost as smooth as glass. It's said to be about five thousand years old. It looks as if it has been standing there pointing at the sky since the beginning of time. I couldn't remember the last time I'd been down this way. Y@ ars at least.

It was a couple of days after the dinner with Alan and his family, and since then I'd tried to write with the usual lack of success and that was sapping my confidence. I'd visited Jimmy Allison and he'd handed me a cardboard box filled with papers and books and demanded that I have a good look through them if I was short of ideas. I hadn't got around to them yet, although I did later, and I'll tell you about that further on. I'd called Barbara Foster – I should say Hartford, but I won't because she'll always be Foster to me – and arranged to go over to Loch Lomond for a picnic the following day with her look-alike daughter. For some reason, I felt elated about that. I know it sounds like something out of a romantic novel, but I'd found myself thinking about Babs in a way I had never thought about her before, which is hardly surprising since I was only ten at the time. It wasn't as strong as the thunderbolt of Puzo's Sicily, but I really wanted to see her again, and not just to talk over old times.

I stood with my back to the ancient mass of the monolith, thinking about when I'd seen Babs' daughter in the car park. Today the sky was just as clear and I had to narrow my eyes against the glare of reflection spearing up from the firth. From where I stood, I could see for miles. Due west the firth disappeared in a heat haze down past the Gantocks where it took its dog leg for the open sea. Closer in, the bulk of the *Cassandra*, lying on its side out on the sandbank, was like a great dead whale, black and ugly in the clear blue. To the east there was the curved sand shore pushing out from the marsh of Ardhmor bay, then a line of silver where Strowan's Water flowed down its runnel to the bay. Beyond that, the massive bulk of Ardhmor stood like some castle in Tolkein. Even on that clear, sunny day it looked dark and ponderous. Foreboding. I know that sounds melodramatic, but that's the way it looked. I stood there, looking at the rock and remembering the scare I'd got on the night the *Cassandra* went down, and my thoughts seemed to get on a weird track. I started thinking about things that had happened since I'd come back to Arden. The two dead farmers, the night on the rock, my bad dreams and my inability to put one word after another on paper.

That dark mass drew my eyes and held them. Ardhmor Rock. It was just a rock: some said it was a volcanic plug and I guess that was so, since most of it was pure basalt spewed up from the bowls of the earth before the dinosaurs. That great towering core of magma had cooled and solidified long before the continental drift had swept Arden and the rest of Scotland out of the tropics and into the ice ages, and then the great spear of stone that had been born in the heat at the core of the earth started the long battle with the wind and the rain and the rivers of ice that whittled and rubbed and wore it down to a fraction of its former splendour. Still it was an impressive piece of the earth's handiwork, for successive rivers of ice and storms and tides had tried to wipe it from the face of the earth and failed. Ardhmor stood like a Colossus right on the highland fault line where the old red sandstone was heaved up and folded into mountain. Even the tremendous forces that had raised the Cobbler and Ben Lomond and the Western Highlands had so far been unsuccessful in shifting the rock.

I stood with my back to the standing stone, staring out across the bay. Some gannets were wheeling in the air over the deep water, stalling on still air and sweeping their wings back to plunge like arrows into the firth. Their shrill cries carried the distance.

A hand grasped the sleeve of my windcheater and I leapt about six feet into the air.

I turned and saw an old woman. Tall, lean and weather-beaten with startling blue eyes and grizzled fair hair. Her gnarled hand was still wound round my cotton sleeve.

'Jeesus,' I gasped. 'You nearly gave me a heart attack.'

'You've come back,' she stated, staring right into my eyes. I was still trying to catch my breath and my heart was still doing a Ginger Baker solo on my ribs. She kept holding on and kept staring.

'I knew you would come back.'

Somewhere in the depths of my memory the old woman's face came back to me. Kitty or Katy something. MacPhee? MacPherson? One of the tinker folk who scoured the foreshores and stayed in corrugated shacks all along the west coast. Displaced crofters from the bad old days of the highland clearances, descendants of outlaws from the time of Rob Roy Macgregor. The old woman had lived in her driftwood hut on the point since anyone could remember. As kids we were a bit scared of her tongue which would clip a good going hedge on any day of the week. She was ancient then. How old must she be now?

The old woman's eyes held mine for a long time.

'Ach, I've scared the living daylights out of you, Mr Nicholas Ryan,' she said, and let out a huge laugh. 'And here I was thinking all the travelling would have taught you a thing of two about surprises.'

She let go the sleeve and looked me up and down, like a farmer's wife checking out the stock.

'You've grown big enough,' she said appraisingly, 'though it's not surprising, the height your mother's father was.'

'You knew my grandfather?'

'Yes, I knew Nick Westwood. Sure, I knew his father too.'

That was hard to believe. My grandfather had died well into his seventies, close on eighties. She must have noticed my mental calculations and laughed again disparagingly.

'I'm eighty-three years old, if you must know,' she said. There was a twinkle in those piercing blue eyes that were set in a leathery skin and surrounded by a fine corona of wrinkles.

'And I'm exactly fifty years older than yourself,' she said with a matter-of-fact nod. The old woman swivelled, a bit awkwardly, giving me a look at her profile. She had a strong nose, almost hooked, but finely chiselled, and a good jaw and high cheekbones. Old Celtic stock. Despite the years, I could tell she had been a stunner in her day. She moved away from me, and I saw what had made her turn awkwardly. Her right leg was bound in a splint that locked her ankle, calf and thigh in a rigid line. Her armpit clamped the seat of a crutch that looked home-made and was tightly whipped with baling twine.

Over her shoulder, as she retreated with a crablike scutter towards her hut, she called: 'The kettle's boiled. You'll have a cup of tea.' Curious, I followed.

Her hut was a scrupulously clean beachcomber's den filled with odd bits of furniture, some of which had been made from wood that had been thrown up on the flood tides, and it was crammed to the ceiling with pots and pans and dried plants. There were odd-shaped pieces of polished driftwood, and smooth stones of different hue from the shore. On a brick and iron hearth, a big, black kettle steamed enthusiastically. In minutes the old woman had made two scalding cups of strong tea. She gestured me to sit down and lowered herself gingerly into a similar but unmatched one, easing her rigid leg out in front of her under a rough-hewn table. The tea was good.

'Midsummer's day in the year nineteen hundred,' she said abruptly after taking a sip of her brew. 'That's when I was born. And you came half a century later on the same day. June the twenty first, nineteen fifty.'

'How do you know that?' I asked, feeling a bit stupid as I did.

'Don't ask how I know. It's what I know that is the most important. I am Catriona O'MacConnor MacBeatha. And my people have lived on this land since forever.'

She nodded her head over the enamel mug and across the cropped grass to the standing stone.

'My people put that there as their marker.'

There was something in the way she came out with that astounding statement that just made it seem true.

'There's a lot I know about you. Maybe even more than you know your own self. And some things I've got to tell you too.'

She stopped and looked out of the open door, way out across the bay. 'There's things I've got to say. I knew you would be coming down here, you know.' Kate MacBeth looked up sharply. 'And before you think I'm an old widow woman just talking for the sake of it, I'm not saying I know everything. But I reckoned you would come down to the point sooner or later. We've got a lot in common, you and me.'

She drank some of her cooling tea. 'Them at the town, they think I'm a witch, or maybe just a mad old fool. Ha. They don't know. They know I've been here a long time. But they don't know I've been away, just like you. And I had to come back, because I'm the last, you know. The last of the long line of the O'Connors and the MacBeths.

'And I'll tell you something else, young Nicky Ryan. On your mother's side you've the same blood in your veins as I have in mine. That's how I know about you.'

'You mean we're related?' I asked.

She nodded, again matter of factly. 'Yes, but I'll tell you about that later on. It goes back long before my time. Long

111

back. I know you were conceived on the night of the equinox in forty-nine. I know that because I knew your mother. What's more, the other two were special too. All born or conceived at the midsummer or on half-night day.

'You all were special.' She looked at me over the mug of tea with a half smile. Inviting the question.

'Who were special?'

'You all were. The three of you. And you still are,' she said. Then she paused and looked down into the cup, frowning a little.

'This ground is going to need you again, and soon.'

'I'm not sure I know what you are talking about,' I said. In fact I hadn't a clue.

'You will, Master Nicholas. There's a lot I could tell you, and there's some I will tell you, if you've a mind to listen. It won't matter anyhow, because the time is surely coming when you'll be needed again, and there's nothing I can do to stop it.'

Again she stopped and frowned into the dregs of her tea. Mine was almost done, barely a half inch of the thick, hot liquid swirling at the bottom of the mug. I wondered what the hell I was doing here in a plankwood hut down at the foreshore listening to an ancient old lady rambling on about God knows what. I suppose in my line of business I've got along fine because I've always had that ability just to sit and listen. It was doing no harm anyway, I suppose, and if it wasn't achieving anything, it was probably less frustrating than sitting over a barren typewriter.

'You won the last time, you know,' she said at last. 'When I found you under the rocks. Whatever you did, you sent it away, and it has stayed away for these twenty years and more. But it's stirring now. I can feel it. And there's going to be worse than just a handful of people buried on the hill.' Her voice was soft, but strong. There was no sign of the quaver that old women develop. 'Ah, there's madness coming, I can smell it in the air. And the walls no longer can hold it back. It comes like the tide and my time here is not long enough.'

'What's coming, Miss MacBeth?' I asked.

'I am Catriona O'MacConnor MacBeatha, of the Connors of the west and the Sons of Life – if you know your Gaelic, young Ryan, as you should. You can call me Kitty like everybody else did, before I became an old hag,' she said, with a laugh, her eyes dancing in my direction.

'I'll tell you what's coming. I'll tell you in a little while, when you start to believe and when you start to remember. I'll help your memory, boy, because it's there.' She raised up a strong hand and lightly touched her finger to my temple.

As soon as she touched me I jumped, almost spilling the dregs of the tea on to my jeans. It felt like the crackle of electricity along the side of my scalp, and a tingle right down the back of my spine.

She laughed again. 'That's the touch of Kitty the Witch, so they'd say. But it's not. It's in you my boy, and the others too. You should listen to what that old wanderer Seumas Allison tells you. He knows more than most and less than he ought.'

'Jimmy Allison?'

'The same. You pay heed to him, for he's a fine man with a good head on those strong old shoulders. Ah, he was a fine lad in his day.'

'He's given me some of his papers. He's been doing a history of the town.'

'That I know. And where his history stops, mine begins, and I'll fill in all the spaces for you.'

'I'm still not sure what you're talking about.'

'The Bad Summer. That's what I'm talking about. Like the summer of nineteen hundred and six, and the others. Like the one that started in sixty-one, when you were ten, and stopped sudden the night your grandfather and myself pulled the three of you from the rocks.'

She held up a hand to forestall my next question.

'No. Listen. You think Seumas is just an old man with an old man's night chill. He doesn't know the half of it. My history of Arden goes back to the start, when the land was low after the ice, when the people of the west came in

113

their curraghs and mixed their blood with the Sons of Life.

'It was then that they joined together to battle the hordes that flowed in from the south and the east and forced them to the shore between the Langcraig and the rock. It was there that they fought a terrible battle, but there were too few. When they drew themselves into the shadow of the rock, the shamans of the tribes made a ritual on midsummer night and brought to life the Cu Saeng, the dweller under the roots. The blood they spilled and the words they sang caused the rock to split and from the rock came the Cu Saeng and it brought madness to this place. But it fell on the hordes and massacred them all.

'But when they awakened from their madness, what was left of the people and their shamans realised that they might have been better to die in battle, because the Cu Saeng they had raised could not be sent back. There were many more deaths as the monster wreaked its havoc.'

As I listened to the old woman's voice as she told her tale, almost in a sing-song lilt, I couldn't help but be captivated. This was one legend I had never heard of. I hadn't even heard the phrase 'Bad Summer' until Jimmy Allison had mentioned it a few weeks back, and to tell the truth, I hadn't yet bothered to look through the stack of notebooks and papers he'd dumped on me. The old lady was spinning a good tale, the kind of thing you would expect from the old gypsies. However, I didn't believe a word of it.

So you can imagine how startled I was when she stopped her monologue and said: 'I know you don't believe a word of it. It couldn't be otherwise. But you will, in time, so do an old gypsy woman a favour and listen a while.'

I nodded and gulped the last of my tea to cover a twinge of embarrassment, like a little boy who's been caught using bad language by his mother. Kitty stood up, still staring at me, and went across to her old iron stove and started to make another pot of tea. When she'd poured two more cups, she brought them back to the table and put one down in front of me. I thanked her and she started talking as if she'd never stopped.

'They tried to send it back to where it belonged but they had no power left, so they used another ritual that served as a cage for the thing, hoping that when they were strong enough they could gather sufficient power to send it from the earth. They used a sacrifice and other words with force that made the Cu Saeng sleep long, and then they ringed it around on the rock with the walls to bind it.

'There were four walls that they made as barriers to form the cage. To build the first, they had to dig a channel from Cardross Hill where the clear spring rose from the foot of a rowan tree, because the rowan had the most power. They called it the Water of the Rowan, but you know it as Strowan's Well. The stream of silver came down the hill where they split it in two, one to the east and the other to the west, and flowing both into the Clutha – the Clyde firth.

'They built another wall, this time of the red sandstone from Langcraig that went parallel to the streams. And then another fence, a living one of hawthorn, which they planted one footspace one from the other to tangle together and bind each other.

'And the third wall was a ring of the bones of the dead hordes that had died in the great battle. They buried them in a line, with the heads removed from the bodies and all facing into the rock.'

Kitty looked at me with a half smile. 'That was that. They trapped that beast they'd brought from the far side with their spells and chants and their four walls. A wall of water, wall of stone, a wall of live wood and a wall of bone.

'And it worked. It worked so well that the sons of the sons of the men who wrought the spell let it lie, and they forgot, and the ravener passed out of their minds and into stories.

'You think I'm just weaving a story. Well, so did they, the ones who came after. For the Cu Saeng slept for five hundred years and more, and when it awoke it found itself trapped and it raged. And it sent out its mind like grasping hands to those who lived too close to it and caused them evil dreams and made them fall over the edge of madness. But though it fed, it could not get out, and when it was tired and had spent itself it went back to sleep again.

'But then, the walls were forgotten, and some of them crumbled because there were none who thought to tend them. And when the wall of stone was breached by the newcomers – the Roman soldiers – it rose again, stronger than the last time, and it was able to reach out further and further. Since that time, the sons of the MacConnor and the MacBeatha put a watcher on the shore, to ensure that the walls remain, at least one of them, to hold the thing until they come who can kill the Cu Saeng for ever in this earth and send it back.'

I looked up to see the old woman staring right into my eyes with such intensity I thought she was about to strike me. The piercing gaze was strong enough to be felt.

'I tell you now, Nicholas Ryan, that time is coming soon. You and they are the ones. You have to watch the walls, for the Cu Saeng is awake and it will send out its power to those who will break open its cage. It almost succeeded last time, and you beat it for a time. Yes. You and the others, although you don't know it now, defeated Cu Saeng and sent it back into the rock. But it stirs now, and a bad time is coming. A bad time.'

I was riveted. The old woman actually believed every word of what she was saying, just like Jimmy Allison had when he tried to tell me about the Bad Summers.

Kitty stared at me long and hard, then she reached over quickly and grabbed the teacup from my hand – a startlingly quick movement that took me by surprise. She swirled it around and turned and threw the dregs out of the open door and on to the path where years of her tread had compressed the earth into a hard-packed track. She turned back and looked into the bottom of the mug and then up at me with a sly smile.

'This the kind of thing we're supposed to be good at,' she said. 'Reading tea leaves. Ha, there's plenty more ways of seeing what's on the road ahead of us, but it's as good a way as any.'

She bent and frowned in concentration, murmuring to herself softly. The murmur went on in a sort of mantra for some time, a drone that was so low and monotonous it could have sent me to sleep, but then it started to get louder and I looked up at her to see that her eyes were half closed. She looked almost in a trance.

Then her eyes snapped open and she looked straight at me.

'A long life, Nicky Ryan of the MacConnors and the MacBeths. A long life to you, and that means that I can sleep. Born on the midsummer and conceived on half-night day. A joining and a rejoining. A life to be saved and a life to be owed, a child of one and a man child awakes, a storm and a battle. There's madness here, and slaughter and there's hate but there is love. Hold on to the love for it is for you three and for ever, and greater than you know.'

I didn't understand a word of that.

'You cannot write yet. But you will. You fear for your talent, but you have it. It will come after the bad days are past. The Cu Saeng reaches out to you and the others. It saps the strength, it snares the will, it sends fear. But you will win.

'Take care of the child. The man will grow. The woman will hurt . . . .'

Her voice trailed off and the fierce look which was drilling into the back of my eyes softened. She smiled again and her whole expression changed.

'The one and onlies?' she laughed. 'That was more true than you could have known. And I suppose you now know what a virginia is?'

'How the hell did you know that?' I asked, astonished. That last statement, straight out of a ten year old's memory, threw me right off balance.

'I told you before. It's not how I know, but what I know. And *that* you've got to learn. That was just to teach you that you should maybe believe an ancient lady down in a hut at the point.'

Then she laughed out loud at the expression on my face.

So an old woman had told me a tale. An interesting and scary old tale. And then she'd looked into the bottom of a teacup and she'd come up with some sort of riddling prophecy and then she'd plucked a memory out of my childhood and a thought right out of my head. I liked the legend, like something out of Slaine MacRoth, my favourite strip cartoon Celtic hero. I couldn't make head nor tail of the riddle, or whatever it was, but the last two threw me, as you can imagine. I suppose that's what they were meant to do. I'd gone down to the windy point to get some fresh air and clear out the cobwebs that were slowly filling my mind with self-doubt and I'd ended up just as off balance as before.

When old Kitty MacBeth had laughed at my expression, she motioned me across to her and put her arm on my shoulder, using me as an extra crutch, and half beckoned, half shoved me to the door.

'Come on, I'll show you something,' she said, still having a great old giggle to herself. She reached behind the door into a bag hanging on a bent nail and pulled out what I thought was a piece of stiff canvas, and braced herself on my shoulder again. We went along the path that led to the big standing stone, slowly, while Kitty half skipped at my side. She placed herself in front of the monolith, on the south wide where the salt-spray-laden wind had weathered the black face to a polished smoothness.

'The old folk knew a thing or two,' she said. 'Look here. It's all smooth with thousands of hard years facing that firth. But you look at every tree you see. The moss and lichen grown on the north side, and on this point the winds never come from the north, only the south and west.

'Come round here,' she said, gesturing me to follow as she did the crab walk round the other side of the basalt spine. 'Look at this.'

I looked. She was right. On the straight, slabbed north face of the stone, a thin sheen of lichen covered the flat surface.

'And look now,' she said, taking the piece of canvas in her hand and folding it around her fingers. It cracked as she wadded the material.

'Dogfish skin. It's as good as any sandpaper,' she said, reaching up to scrape gently at the slick green covering. She did that for a few minutes, then took the skin away and rubbed with a wetted finger.

On the surface, thin lines appeared, etched in the stone. It looked like some form of script, but what kind I couldn't tell.

The whole area, maybe the size of my hand, was completely covered in tightly drawn figures and letters which were etched in the stone and had been completely protected from the elements by the natural insulation.

'They told the whole story, but people forgot how to read it,' Kitty said. 'They told what they did and why they did it, and they wrote down the way to send Cu Saeng back, but there was not enough people to do that, not enough of the right people, so it must be killed.

'This part speaks in a riddle. It is a foretelling, and that's why I'm showing it to you, Nicky Ryan.'

'Why, what does it say?'

'If I tell you, will you believe me?' she asked.

'To tell you the truth, I don't know. It all sounds a bit weird to me.'

'Ah yes. That's the right word. It is your weird. And mine. But it will get through to you as time goes on, and I don't think we have too much of that. You can't avoid it, so I might as well tell you.'

She lifted her hand and pointed out some lines. They could have been Greek or runes for all I knew.

'Yet come three, alone yet one, earth-day born. Awakens one who sleeps and strays, two return to fight the wrath. Sacred flow and sacred grow and sacred stone to end the rule of Cu Saeng.'

'What does that mean?' I asked, not entirely convinced that the old woman could actually read those scratches on the rock, or even, if she could read it, that she could understand it.

'Well it could have many meanings, but I think that you three, your one and onlies, fit the first part.'

'How come?'

'Because there are three of you. That's easy enough. Alone yet one, only children, single children, but you were close enough then to be one, at least last time you did whatever you did on Ardhmor. And you're all earth-day born. You on midsummer, the girl on the autumn equinox and the boy in spring.

'The chances of that happening in a small place like this are surely millions to one. Especially when you consider that you all have the blood of the MacConnors and the MacBeths in you, though a touch more diluted than I'd like, but it's there.

'It has to be you, and the other two, and you have to watch the walls. The bad thing's coming, for I can feel it, and I cannot watch the walls.

'Look at me. Broke my leg like a silly old fool down on the rocks. Hobbling around like a shore crab. Set it myself, but it takes so long, and we don't have long.'

She nodded across the bay to where Ardhmor sat squat. 'I can't get over there, and something's happening that I can't see. You have to be my eyes and hands now. It's just like last time, when you were a boy. My mother was dying, and I was away from here. I came back on the night your grandfather was searching for you down at the rock. If I had not been away, maybe we could have ended it then. And now, with this old crippled leg, I might as well not be here.'

Kitty took one of my hands in hers and smiled again.

'Remember, a long life. You can believe that anyway, because I do. It means that you will beat this thing, although how you will do it, I cannot tell. But don't worry about not believing the rest. That's no problem to you or to me.'

I didn't know what to say to that.

'You will, Nicky,' she said. 'And when you do, you'll have some work to do.'

The night after I saw the old lady down at the point, I thought about what she'd said and what Jimmy Allison had told me, and wondered if maybe I shouldn't have a look at his handwritten history. Kitty had hit the mother lode a couple of times, especially when she went through that rigmarole of looking at the tea leaves in my drained cup. Now, I've never believed in that sort of thing. I'm a bit of an agnostic in more ways than one, but when she spoke of the one and onlies, and when she told me I couldn't write – not yet anyway – I felt uneasy.

The old legend I could take or leave. The west coast abounds with them. I suppose I would have been prepared to go along with the fact that every legend has a root in some truth, however paltry. Maybe something did happen on Ardhmor way back when the world was young, but I couldn't see the relevance of it today. True, recently one or two things had happened, like the lifeboat crew who disappeared and still hadn't turned up. There was my tangle with the undergrowth which, though it still gave me the shivers when I thought about it, I had dismissed as an extra-vivid imagination brought on by exhaustion and drink. There was the time when Colin and Barbara and I ended up in the rock, or under it, and Colin came out ruined. Nobody knew what the hell we'd been doing down there, least of all me. It was a blank.

Later that night I got up out of bed to close the curtains. The half full moon was beaming directly into my eyes and must have woken me up. Outside the window, a silver-blue haze outlined the trees and the rooftops. It was still hot, at the start of August, and the summer felt as if it was prepared to stay a good while longer.

I stretched and went downstairs for a drink of water, automatically missing the creak on the seventh stair, and into the kitchen where the moonbeams lanced through the lace curtain, dappling the water in the basin with amethyst. I turned on the tap and rinsed a glass which threw off shards of brilliant flashes as the cold water splashed down. The air was quiet and still. No owls hooted. There was not a sound in the world except for the quiet creak of the old rocking chair in the sitting room and the small drip-plink from the tap where it drained its last.

The sitting room was awash with the moonlight, which didn't strike me as odd, although it's not on the same side of the house as my bedroom or the kitchen. I padded through on my bare feet and my grandfather looked up from the rocking chair and smiled. His face was half in shadow and his old, big hands were curled around the smooth arm of the chair.

I stood there, paralysed. Just as I started through the doorway, I'd taken a drink of the cold water and now it stuck somewhere between my throat and my stomach and seemed to want to move two ways at once.

'Come in, come in,' the old man said. 'Come in and sit yourself down.'

He motioned me over to the armchair at the other side of the fireplace where the white coals had long fallen to dust since the last fire had been lit. I was rooted to the spot, which is a phrase I've always disliked, but it was nonetheless true. It was as if my whole body was clamped in a block of stone. My heart thudded wildly – I could hear it in my ears – and from way down in my stomach I could feel waves of panic layering up on top of each other, building up to one huge scream.

That's not what happened. My old grandfather's eyes caught the moonlight, black and blue under his brows, and he gestured again to the easy chair. Some force took my feet and lifted them one by one off the floor where they'd been nailed down and walked me across the room and sat me down. I didn't do it. It happened.

'Ah, Nicky boy, you've grown,' he said in that big gravelly voice that I had often remembered with that warm jolt of affection. It now seemed to come from a million miles away, dry and cold.

'And you've come back to stay with me, eh? That's good. Very good.'

He nodded, almost contentedly, and his eyes looked into the fireplace.

'But you've been a bad boy. A very bad boy. I've told you not to go down to the rock, and you went down there.'

He paused and seemed to consider.

'I told you not to have anything to do with that old witch, but you've been speaking to her, haven't you?'

I sat and stared. No sound would come out of my throat. I could hardly breathe.

'If you want to stay with me, you'll have to be a good boy.'

He raised his eyes from the fireplace and turned his head slowly round in my direction. I could hear his head turn on his neck, a dry sound like old hawsers taking up strain. And he grinned a huge grin. That wasn't my grandfather. Of course it wasn't my grandfather, for he'd been dead for years. But whatever this was, it wasn't even him. My old grandfather laughed, or he smiled, or he roared. But he never grinned.

I stared at the apparition. My eyes must have been opened so wide they were in danger of falling right out of my head.

The grin widened until it showed an impossible array of teeth that were long and thin and blue in the unearthly light.

'You be a good boy,' he hissed behind that row, 'and I'll let you stay with me.'

He started to giggle and the skin started to flake off his face. Hee-hee-hee. High pitched. Mad. And the more he laughed, the more the skin shrivelled up like leather on an old boot and split down the seams of his face and inside his head seemed to swell. The eyes got bigger and paler and the noise of old twisted ropes tearing and twisting got louder. The rocking chair creaked as it swung back and forth as the thing that had looked like my grandfather swelled and split and giggled.

123

Then the glass that I'd been holding in my right hand suddenly gave way in the pressure of my grip and a jagged edge went straight into my palm with such a force that blood just spouted out. That was enough to get my breath back and I let out a scream that must have been heard from the far side of the firth.

I leapt out of the chair in terror and instinctively hurled the base of the glass and what remained of the water, plus, no doubt, a fair quantity of the blood that was pouring out of the gash in my hand, right at the thing in the chair.

In slow motion I watched the glass tumble in the air, catching that light, and smash right into the writhing, giggling thing. It hit with a muffled thump, and then a crash as it struck through and into the turned risers at the back of the chair which tipped over with a thump. The thing just disappeared in front of my eyes as if it had never been there, leaving me in the middle of the floor cursing in words that I thought I'd forgotten, a stream of invective that reverberated back at me from the walls until I stopped, gasping for breath, and sank back down into the chair.

The light from the early morning sun awoke me through the space in the curtain that I'd meant to close the night before, and I suddenly jerked awake with the vision of that thing still in my head.

Everyone has experienced that moment of awakening when a dream disappears. I rolled over and out of bed, breathing deeply, still shuddering from the visual memory, and I crossed the room and opened the curtains fully to let as much daylight in as I could. As I did so, I felt a sharp stab of pain in my hand as it brushed against the curtain fabric. I looked down and there in the centre of the palm was a small, crescent-shaped cut that was just beginning to scab over.

Instantly I got a vision of the dream again but I shook it off. I've had falling dreams when I've ended up on the floor, or fire-engine dreams just when the alarm goes off. I couldn't remember cutting myself, but that didn't mean it

124

hadn't happened yesterday, maybe down at the point. I probably just hadn't noticed it. By the time I got dressed and slunged my face with cold water, the shaky feeling was receding. The day looked fine and fresh and I felt like frying up a good breakfast and then getting out into the fresh air and away from the house for a while. I'd fixed up with Barbara Foster to take her and Paddy across to Loch Lomondside for a picnic, so I thought after a stroll I'd go up to the shop to get whatever we'd need for a day out.

In the kitchen I had the pan sizzling with good Belfast ham and I threw in some mushrooms and set a couple of eggs on to poach. The kettle boiled quickly and I had a cup of tea while I was cooking and another one while I ate. I felt a whole lot better after that.

I took a third cup, which was quite strong and thick by the time I'd finished and cleaned up the kitchen leaving the plate to drain beside the sink, and carried it through to the sitting room.

There I promptly dropped it on my foot, which would have been badly scalded if the tea hadn't cooled down.

For the rocking chair lay on its back at the far side of the room.

And there was a broken glass and shards lying beside it.

The burn from the tea was painful enough to make me cry out, which I suppose helped release the breath that was getting ready to back up in my lungs, but the pain quickly receded. All sorts of explanations began to line themselves up in my head, but before I could think of any of them a face loomed into the window frame so suddenly that I jumped backwards in fright.

If I'd thought rationally, I suppose by this time I would have been getting a bit pissed off at the number of shocks my poor little thudding heart had been given in quick succession. But when the figure looming at the window lifted a black arm to cut off the reflection and peer into the room, I recognised Father Gerald O'Connor. He wasn't wearing his motorcycle gear, but the normal black suit and white collar. I motioned him around to the front door and he was standing there in the sunlight when I opened it.

'Sorry if I gave you a fright,' he said affably. 'You look as if you've seen a ghost. What were you doing in there? A war dance?'

'No, I spilled some tea on my foot.' We both looked down. There was a light red weal where the tea had splashed. It wouldn't come to anything.

'Ah, tea. I'd love cup,' said the young priest, eagerly, inviting himself in. 'I've been up since five o'clock this morning. I'm the duty man on the emergency service. I think I'll get a siren and a flashing light.'

'What was the emergency?'

'Oh, nothing serious. Mrs Black found her father at the foot of the stairs and thought he'd had a heart attack. She decided he needed extreme unction. What he needed was extreme black coffee and I suppose he'll have an extreme hangover later this morning. And when you think of the voice his daughter's got, you can expect he'll wish he had died before the week's out.

'What gets me is that she's not even a Catholic, but that's the third time she's called me out in the past year for the old man.'

I put the kettle on and the priest – he said I should call him Gerry – said he'd shoot his granny for a bacon sandwich, so I fired up the pan and put a couple of rashers in to sizzle.

'I just thought I'd drop by in the passing,' he said. 'I never got a chance to meet you up at Alan's house the other day. I'm sorry if I gave you a fright. Most people are glad to see us. We're on the good side, you know,' he winked conspiratorially.

'No, it wasn't you,' I said. 'It was something else entirely.'

'Why, what happened?'

'You wouldn't believe it.'

'Try me. I'm a good listener. It's all the hours we spend sitting in a little box.'

I'm not a religious person, but strangely it seemed a

126

relief to talk about it, even to a young priest who ran about on a racing Honda. I sat there and told him about what had happened last night, and how I'd woken up thinking it had been a nightmare, and then come back down and seen the rocking chair lying in the corner. Just before the kettle boiled I took him through and showed him.

'What do you think? Am I going crazy?'

'Not at all,' he said, smiling. 'You've been sleepwalking. I used to do it all the time when I was small. My mother was worrying but my old man said as long as I didn't pee the bed he didn't mind.'

'I've never walked in my sleep before, and I've been getting bad dreams almost every night.'

'You're probably tense. Are you worrying about anything?'

'Nothing that should make me feel like I've seen a ghost. I've not been feeling great, but what happened last night scared the hell out of me.'

'Well, that's pretty normal. But I wouldn't say you're crazy. I'd just put it to the back of my mind if I were you. Things always look different in the daytime.'

I made the tea and fixed up the bacon sandwiches. He started eating them with obvious appetite.

He took a gulp of tea to wash down a bite and said: 'The world's got a lot worse to throw at us than ghosts, you know.

'Look at that poor woman who killed her son and then took her own life. And there's that farmer, Mr Gillon; you were there, weren't you? If ghosts were all we had to worry about I'd be delighted.'

'That's another thing,' I said. 'Those two accidents, I mean. What could have caused them?'

'Accidents happen. No rhyme nor reason. And we've just got to try to help after they do.'

'Have you ever thought that these accidents might not have been accidents?'

'How do you mean?'

'I don't know. Not yet anyway. But I've got a funny

feeling. Ever since I've come back to Arden, things haven't gone right. Like those deaths. In a small place like this two freak accidents seem more than coincidence.'

'I could say something trite, like "The Lord giveth", but I won't,' Gerry said. 'These things happen. I can't explain them. Nobody can.'

'What if . . . ' I said, but I stopped.

'What if what?'

'Nothing. I'm just a bit shook up. Shaken up, I should say. I've spent too long in the States.'

'You're a bit too worldly wise for me to give parental advice,' he said, 'even though I am a priest. I know what I'm like after a nightmare. But at least we always wake up. I don't believe in ghosts and ghouls. The Holy Ghost maybe, but that's between me and him.'

'I can't say I'm much of a believer,' I confessed.

'Don't worry about that. I'm not an evangelist. Even priests have their own doubts.'

'So have journalists who aspire to be writers. Lots of them. Let's hope you're right.'

He finished his tea and we exchanged some chat as he was leaving.

'Will you be coming to the festival?' he asked at the gate.

'I suppose so. Everybody else will be there.'

'Yes, I'm looking forward to it. They're getting things ready up at the seminary, so I'll be kept busy with that for a day or so. Listen, why don't you come up and see the place? You'd like it. I'm still amazed, being a city boy, how self-sufficient the old timers have got it. Been doing it for hundreds of years, I'm told.'

I said I would come up sometime, and Gerry suggested Thursday – not having anything planned I agreed.

NINE

'Neat machine!' yelled Paddy as I stepped out of the jeep
after parking on the pebbled driveway at the doctor's big
solid house.

She'd come bounding out of the front door and through
the porchway to leap down the steps, landing with a
baseballer's slide in front of me. She was all blue eyes and
sparkly teeth and still a dead ringer for her mother.

'Where're we going Nick?' I could tell she was excited
at the prospect of getting out and away from the big house.
She bobbed up and down on the soles of her running
shoes, brimful of energy and packed with fun.

'Don't know yet,' I said, letting her take me by the arm
and pull me towards the house, feigning reluctance. 'Hey,
hey, at least let me keep my arm.'

'Are we going for a picnic?'

'Well, I thought we'd go for a drive across to Loch
Lomond. Maybe we can have a picnic there. I've brought
some stuff to eat.'

'Great. I'm starving.' The little girl's enthusiasm melted
away my night creeps like hoar frost under a hot sun. I had
only met Paddy that once, the time I'd accosted her in the
car park, and I had watched as she'd stuffed her face with
Mary Baker's finest. I'd taken to her, which is hardly a surprise, because she was so like her mother that she evoked a
whole string of pleasant childhood memories. But she was
also a good kid. Bright, intelligent, well mannered and
funny. She took to me as well. It was as if she'd known me
all her life. In a strange way, I felt really good about that,
though I couldn't explain why.

I'd thought about Barbara once or twice since we'd re-
met. No. That's a lie. I'd thought about her quite a lot. She

was terrific. I mean she was not just terrific looking. She had all the qualities her daughter had, and some that Paddy was surely going to inherit. Over our coffee and spiced buns we'd talked a lot about this and that and it didn't take long for the small talk to evaporate. Maybe we hadn't seen each other for twenty years and maybe we had been just kids then, but it really felt to me like she was an old friend – as if I knew what she was going to say, just before she said it. Her humour was quick and her brain was agile, and she had poise and confidence. On top of that, she really *was* terrific looking.

That estimation was reinforced when she came out through the porch and stood in the sun, the rays that lanced through the chestnut tree limping off the waves of golden hair.

'Hi Nick. It's a great day for a trip.'

'You betcha mom. We're going to Lock Lomond.'

'Lo*ch* Lomond, Paddy. You say it like you're clearing your throat.'

'I thought we'd take a run up there. I haven't been for years.'

'Sounds like a great idea. I need to get out in the fresh air. I've been stuck in with a cold or the flu or something.'

'Oh, you should have told me. I could have made it another day,' I said, secretly glad that she hadn't.

'No, I'm feeling fine. I just haven't been sleeping well at all. I've been waking up with the shivers in the middle of the night.'

For an instant I had the shivers, up and down my back.

'But I slept all right last night, so I think I must be over it. And I wouldn't give up a day like today for the world.'

'I've brought along some things to eat. Juice and crisps and some cakes,' I said. 'Plus some sausages and beans in case we want to make a fire.'

'Great,' Paddy said, jumping around excitedly. 'Can we make a camp fire Nicky? Can we mom?' she said, looking back and forth from me to Babs. Her mother smiled and ruffled her hair.

130

'We'll see. First I'll get the stuff I've packed,' she said, and went back into the house to reappear seconds later with a load of things wrapped in tin foil. It looked like enough to feed a platoon. Her father came out of the house with her. He'd aged a lot since I'd last seen him, but he still looked like an able old fellow. He took off his horn-rimmed glasses as he came down the stone steps and shook my hand.

'Well, hello there, Mr Ryan. Nick, isn't it? Haven't seen you in a long spell.' His accent was still Scottish, unlike Barbara's which, though not erased, was a mid-Atlantic hybrid. Paddy was strictly American.

'Nice to meet you again, doctor,' I said.

'Take care of those ladies for me,' he said. 'They're all that's between me and senility.' He laughed and I went along with it. He was probably right.

I opened the back door of the jeep and Paddy scampered in, bouncing up and down on the seat excitedly. Babs eased herself into the passenger seat and belted herself up while I started the engine, reversed and headed back down the driveway. The old doctor waved vigorously as we turned into the street.

We passed through the edge of Westbay and out along the Kilcreggan Road past the Langcraigs, a long ridge of buckled rocks that formed a low cliff parallel to the road. Out beyond that we took the Fruin Road that took us up by the old reservoir and past the Colquhoun battle monument and down the twisting leafy road in the valley between Cardross Hill and Black Hill towards Loch Lomond. It took less than half an hour to be on the main lochside road and heading up towards Luss and Inverbeg in some of the country's most breathtaking landscapes. The further we travelled from Arden, the better I felt. Barbara was lively and animated and frankly stunning. I put down my good humour to her presence. She was dressed in a cotton shirt and a pair of white tight jeans that made no attempt to hide her long-limbed shape. She had a light sweater as well, but it was at her back, with the arms tied

131

around her waist. Every time she moved her head her hair swung and bounced gently with it. Like her daughter, she smiled a lot and her piercing blue eyes sparkled.

The Lomondside Road twists and turns alongside the Bonnie Banks in a series of chicanes and hairpin bends, which is murderous for the driving tourist who has to keep his eye firmly on the road and therefore misses those stunning glimpses of the deep blue water and the sweeping slopes of Ben Lomond. Babs and Paddy were impressed with the views and kept up a running commentary for me while I concentrated on passing caravans trailed behind slow-moving cars. I stopped at Inverbeg where there's a nice little inn and an out-of-the-way art gallery that I made a mental note to have a browse through some time. I left the jeep in the car park and we took a farm road on foot behind the inn which led up Glen Douglas. We walked for no more than twenty minutes, which was enough to get us well out of earshot of the traffic on the road, and then followed a narrow path that took us down to the river. The walk was worth it for we found ourselves in a clearing at the bank of a crystal-clear stream that gushed down from a spectacular height into deep pot-holes in the rock. The sunlight slanted down deep into the water, giving the dell a fairytale quality. The only sound was the rush of water and the singing of linnets and chaffinches.

Barbara stood entranced while her daughter immediately slipped off her trainers and left them on a narrow strip of shingle while she tested the water with her bare foot.

'Ooh! It's freezing!' she cried out after wading in until the water was just above her ankles. She danced about, trying to get both feet out of the water at once, and failing comically.

'This is a lovely spot,' Babs said. 'I never even knew it existed.'

'I used to come here now and again during the summer holidays,' I said. 'There's some good trout in the water. We used to take a few and grill them over the fire.'

'Sounds lovely.'

'It was, but if we'd been caught poaching, the gillie would probably have shot us. They don't mind you walking up here, but fishing's a capital offence. We never did get caught.'

'The water looks so clean and cool,' she said, watching as Paddy minced back on to the shingles, shivering.

'She's right, it is freezing, but you get used to it.'

I pointed downstream to a huge, water-smoothed rock. 'Just beyond that there's a good pool that you can swim in. After the first shock you get your breath back and when you come out you feel great.'

'I think I'll try it,' Barbara said. 'I haven't swum in a stream for years.'

'Go ahead. I'll pass. It's too damn cold for me.'

'Cissy.'

'Too true. I'm no masochist.'

I did let her persuade me to take a dip later. It was absolutely freezing and I was blue with the cold. But I was right. After I got out of that pool and got dried off, my skin tingled and I felt wonderful.

Paddy insisted that I light a fire, so I got some sticks together and put some fair-sized rocks in a circle and got a blaze going. I cooked the beans in the can and put some small sausages on a sharpened stick. It was no gourmet meal, but there's something immensely appetising about anything cooked outdoors over an oak and pinewood fire. After we ate that, and watched as Paddy demolished most of the sandwiches her mother had brought, Barbara let her play about in the shallow pool and we sat by the crackling fire.

Barbara had been telling me about her life in America where she'd gone just before her eleventh birthday.

'I was absolutely devastated when my father told me we were going,' she said. 'I remember I cried all night and most of the next day, but nothing I said seemed to matter. He had kept it from me right until the last moment, probably because he knew how I would react. Suddenly I found myself on a plane and away. It was the most miserable time of my life. I must have cried every night for the first year,' she said.

Barbara was sitting with her back against the stump of an old oak tree. Her hands were clasped together around her knees, which she'd drawn right up almost to her chin. I was stretched out on the short grass, having a smoke. I'd cut down a lot since coming back, but one after a meal was still great.

'I remember being really upset when I went up to the house and found it empty. I thought you'd run out on me. There was nobody left.'

'My father never told me why he decided to leave, but it was quick. He'd been offered a consultancy in Vermont, but he'd had such offers before and disregarded them. His practice here was running well. I've got the feeling he just wanted me to grow up somewhere else. It's strange though, when he decided to move back, there was no question in my mind I'd come back too. And after all that time, it was a wonderful feeling to be coming home.'

'It was just after the accident, wasn't it?'

'What was?'

'When you went away.'

'Oh, you mean down at the point?'

'No, Ardhmor.'

'Ah, that was it. Yes. I think so. Not long after that.'

'Maybe your father thought you had bad company. But I felt as if I'd been deserted. Colin was in the hospital for months and you were gone to America. There was nobody left.'

Barbara leaned forward, away from the tree stump, trying to see what her daughter was doing further upstream.

'She's all right. I can see her from here. She's as happy as hell, but she must have anti-freeze in her feet.'

Barbara smiled. 'We used to spend a lot of time in the stream, I remember. The one and onlies. How did we ever come to call ourselves that?'

'Colin made it up. He thought we were unique.'

134

'Yes, I remember now. The one and onlies. It seemed to fit right, didn't it?'

'Like an exclusive club. We had some great times.'

'Yes, we did. My father didn't approve of you two.'

'I can't blame him. We were a bit wild,' I said. 'But you were just as bad as the two of us.'

'What the hell were we doing down at that place?' she asked.

'Where?'

'That rock. Ardhmor.'

'I haven't a clue. It's strange. I hadn't thought about it for years until I came back, and then a couple of people reminded me. Really, I just hadn't thought about it at all.'

'Neither did I. I just remembered it the day I met you down at the supermarket. I mean, I remembered what I'd been told about it, but I can't remember anything at all, subjectively.'

'Have you seen Colin?'

'God yes. I really had no idea. I was walking along the street with Paddy and this great thing lumbered out of a shop and started giggling at her and nodding. He tried to take her hand and I let out a yell. Hell, I didn't even know who it was.

'He jumped back as soon as I shouted at him and then he started to cry. I felt a bit silly afterwards, and a bit ashamed, but I really didn't know about him. He's so . . . different.'

'They call him Badger, you know.'

'Yes, I heard. I suppose it suits him with that funny hair, but it's a real shame. He was really so bright and adventurous. It's as if there's nothing there inside his head. Paddy and I have passed him by a few times down at the shops. She isn't bothered. He just stands and smiles, like a big shy kid, and she makes a point of saying hello. Children are instinctive about that sort of thing, but mothers are different. I know he doesn't mean any harm, but I can't identify Badger with Colin Blackwood.'

'Poor guy. He was pretty battered, so I'm told. What a

waste. I've seen him down in Holly's bar. They give him a lemonade shandy and he sits quietly and watches everything that goes on like a bewildered child. I don't know how much of it he understands. It's as if a switch has been clicked off inside his head.

'It could have been you, or me.'

Barbara shuddered: 'Oh, don't say that. I've always been terrified of brain damage. A friend of mine in the States was in a car smash and ended up in a coma. When she came out of it she was pretty near a vegetable. I was so screwed up I couldn't go to visit her, because it really wasn't her. I've got some sort of phobia, as if I'm scared it's infectious and I'll end up like that.

'Let's talk about something less morbid.'

'How about Paddy?' I ventured. 'I'm still amazed at how much she's taken after you. I swear that when I first saw her I thought I was in a time warp.'

'She's a good kid.'

'Yeah, I can see that. I wonder if she's as wild as you were.'

'I wasn't wild. Maybe just a bit wilful. I could climb trees as well as you.'

'Probably better. You were an honorary boy to us. That was the biggest accolade you could get.' I turned and looked her up and down with a mock leer. 'I suppose I'll have to withdraw that honour.'

Babs blushed. 'I've had twenty years to grow out of it, plus,' she said, nodding towards where Paddy was still splashing in the water, 'somebody to take over where I left off.'

'Just as long as she stays away from kids like me, she'll be all right.'

We both looked towards the stream where a flash of lights sparkled. Paddy was standing in the water up to her knees, and with one outstretched hand she was sweeping the surface of the water, sending up a coruscating curve of droplets.

'Look. Look at this. I can make a rainbow,' she cried in delight.

Barbara and I watched, laughing as the sunlight caught the shimmering droplets and laced them with colour. Paddy turned towards us with a wide smile on her face, and suddenly I was ten years old again and Barbara was . . .

. . . *standing in the water up to her knees, and with one hand outstretched she was sweeping the surface of the shallow stream, sending up a coruscating curve of droplets.*

'Look. I can make a rainbow.'

Colin and I were sitting on a rock that sat in the middle of Strowan's Water. He was whittling the point of a stick that he'd cut for an arrow. I had my head in my hands, feeling the sun on the back of my neck. We watched as Barbara squealed with delight, sending up rainbows into the air.

The stream gurgled softly through the glade, murmuring as it meandered through the shallow gully, down towards the bridge and on to the firth. It was one of those days that you could feel and smell and hear. The air was warm and still, sultry with pollen that settled on the surface of the little pools. Bees and insects buzzed in the trees and bushes and an occasional dragonfly would dart out like a fighter plane and buzz the calm surface, scooping up the mayflies as they hatched out. There was the smell of green that went with the dappling shadows on the water, and there was the delicious smell of pinewood smoke. A cuckoo called in the distance and wood pigeons threw their voices from the great branches hanging down from the beech and lime trees that lined the clearing.

Colin was using the sharp end of the slender stick to scrape off thin lines of moss that lined the back of the stone, and Barbara, with her slacks rolled up over her knees, was a tousle-headed pir-ouetting figure of an undine, delighting in the play of sun and water.

A fly buzzed up near my ear and I lazily swatted it.

'We could live here, you know,' Colin said. 'There's rabbits and fish and lots of things to eat.'

'Yeah, we could build a hut here. Maybe up in a tree. Nobody would ever know we were here.' The idea had enormous appeal. I picked up my bow and nocked an arrow on the string. 'I could be Robin Hood,' I said, and let an arrow fly into the air where it curved lazily and landed in a tree. It failed to come down again.

137

'I'd love to stay here,' Barbara said, 'but my father would never let me.'

'We'll just have to run away,' Colin said. 'My mum would kill me when I got back.'

'Don't be silly. If you run away you don't go back.'

'Well, I think we should build a gang hut where we can keep all our bows and arrows and stuff and come here anytime we like, even when it's raining.'

'Great, and we can bring things to sit on, and even a bed and pots and pans, and all that.'

'And nobody would ever know, if we hide it well enough.'

'It would be just our place. For just the three of us,' Barbara said.

We found an overhang later that afternoon and started piling up logs against it like a lean-to. The gales in the winter had dropped a couple of tall pines that had broken up, and there were any number of big branches that had snapped off the lime and beech trees. It didn't take long to build a shelter that could take the three of us fairly comfortably. We grunted with strain as we rolled up three fair-sized flat stones to sit on and Barbara and I collected clumps of fern and bracken to cover the gang hut with. It was rough and ready and pretty cramped – there was no way we'd get chairs inside, never mind a bed – but it was dry and well camouflaged against raiders. And it was our secret.

The lean-to in the overhang of the rock in the clearing at Strowan's Water was our place for the summer, our special hide-out, our headquarters and our galleon, whatever we wanted it to be in those long days, but there was something special about the day that we built it – that day when Barbara had stood in the water and swept up a rainbow, and Colin had caught the fish. It was a day when the insects murmured softly and the stream gabbled its way through the rocks and I felt the sun on the back of my neck and . . .

Somebody shook me gently by the shoulder.

I started out of my daydream and Barbara was saying something.

'You were miles away,' she said. 'I thought you'd fallen asleep.'

'Not so many miles, but a long way,' I said, shaking my head. 'I was thinking about the hideout.'

'So was I. That's one of the most amazing coincidences. It must be twenty years since I last thought about that.'

'It was just when Paddy . . . '

'Said she could make a rainbow,' Barbara finished for me. 'Yes, as soon as she said that I could see myself doing it down at the stream. The whole picture just came into my head, complete, like a film out of an archive.'

'Déjà vu, or something, they call it. No, more like a memory trigger. I was just thinking of that time, remembering how good I felt then. Those were the days.'

'But they didn't last,' she said, almost wistfully.

'No, nothing ever does. You went off to America and Colin was in hospital and even when he came out there wasn't anything left of the one and onlies. I stayed round at my grandfather's a lot after that, because I couldn't be bothered with anything else. I suppose I became a bit of a loner then.'

'Me too. It took me a long time to forgive my father for taking me away. I remember thinking then that you two were the best friends anybody could have.'

'I suppose all childhoods are like that. You think you're going to be friends for ever, but it hardly ever happens.'

'I'll tell you something, though,' Barbara said, sitting with her arms crossed over her knees again. 'Nothing was the same again. I mean I've had some interesting times growing up in America, but there was nothing to make it sparkle. I went to school, and then college, and then I sort of drifted into marriage, and it was as if I was just going through the motions.

'And then Paddy came along, and the sparkle came back. It was as if everything was in black and white and then went into full technicolour. She brought the magic back into my life, like nothing else could.'

'You're lucky,' I said, looking over to where the little girl was wading in the stream, her jeans rolled up over her knees, and her tanned, well-shaped legs cutting bow waves

139

in the water. 'She's a lovely girl.'

'I suppose you're going to say she takes after her mother,' Barbara said, and laughed softly.

'You can hardly deny maternity, can you? Yes she does take after her mother, and if she keeps on going she'll be every bit as beautiful as her mother is.'

'Oh Nick. I believe you just made a pass,' she said with a wry smile.

'Not at all. I just said the truth. I'll make a pass if and when I'm good and ready. Just don't get presumptuous.'

Barbara laughed out loud. 'Always ready with a put down, Nicky Ryan. You haven't changed a bit, have you?'

'Still the same crazy kid, I guess,' I replied, and leaned over and kissed her softly on the lips. She was taken aback for a fraction of a second, then kissed me back, gently but warmly, with her hand pressing on to my shoulder.

I drew back. 'That's the pass. I was good and ready. You weren't.'

'Crazy kid,' she said.

'Well, some things have changed. This crazy kid would never have kissed a tomboy.

'Good kisser,' I said, and reached up to ruffle her golden hair.

From across the stream Paddy gave a squeal of laughter.

'I saw mummy kissing,' she called out, then put her two fingers up to her mouth and gave out a wolf whistle that must have been heard up and down the length of Glen Douglas.

'Who the hell taught her to do that?' I said, impressed.

'You did,' Barbara said, almost proudly. 'By proxy.'

TEN

'Meet Professor Sannholm,' Jimmy Allison said, introducing me to a small, fair-haired man with owlish, round-framed spectacles. 'Arthur, meet Nick Ryan.'

We shook hands. The professor was wiry and had a strong, firm grip. His hands were rough and calloused, surprising working man's hands, on a lean body with an academic face.

'Arthur's been working on his dig,' Jimmy said. We were in the lounge of the Chandler on the evening after I'd taken Barbara and Paddy on their picnic. It was still warm and sultry. The lager was cool and welcome, and the professor was no slouch when it came to downing half a pint in one swallow.

'Thirsty work,' he said, 'but very rewarding. It's been a good summer. I'll be reluctant to get back to university, but what we've found on your rock should keep us going for a full term, thanks to Jimmy.'

'Arthur's found another wall,' Jimmy said.

'Not quite a wall. A ring. A concentric ring,' said the professor. 'Really quite amazing, really. It was Jim here who first led me to suspect the Roman fortification which we dug up some years back. Lovely work. A real solid wall.

'What puzzled us then, and still puzzles us now, is that they seem to have built it for nothing. There were no fortifications inside the wall, but there were some minor Roman artefacts outside. They must have just built it and packed up and left. In fact, their wall wasn't theirs at all. They just built up on top of an even earlier dyke. We think it's from a much earlier time than bronze age. It's got a typical paleolithic layer construction of old red sandstone. Quite fascinating actually.'

141

The professor was off and running on what was obviously his passion.

'And what's this other wall?' I asked.

'Well, it's hardly that, really. More an upraised ditch, as a matter of fact. It's concentric with the first wall, parallel to the dyke, but at least sixty yards away. If it's an earlier development, then it must indeed be old. I think we could be thinking in terms of about five to six thousand years ago. Much older than Stonehenge. In fact, if I'm correct, this will be one of the earliest fortifications on record.'

'I would have thought that the rock was fortification enough,' I said.

'Well, you would think so. But the dyke goes around the rock in a semi-circle. I'm assuming that it was a sort of stockade, maybe to keep cattle in and thieves out. Like a walled garden. We still haven't found anything on the rock itself. Maybe it was too exposed for actual habitation. Perhaps it was a last-ditch retreat in case the first defences were breached. We don't know yet, but the finding out is sure to be fascinating.'

Professor Sannholm – he soon insisted that I call him Arthur – took a second mouthful of his pint when he stopped for breath. His prominent Adam's apple bobbed up and down on his thin neck as he swallowed gustily, and when he put the glass down there was nothing left but a trail of foam slowly sliding to the bottom of the glass.

He smacked his lips. 'Lovely stuff, that.'

I ordered another two and a whisky and beer chaser for Jimmy. The barman was prompt and as soon as the drinks arrived Arthur lifted his to his lips and sunk another huge mouthful.

'Sweating like a horse, after a day's honest toil,' he said when he came up for air. 'Now, where was I?'

'Up to your armpits in mud, no doubt,' Jimmy said, winking at me over his glass.

'Ah, no, as a matter of fact, it's all pretty good clay, mixed in with shingle. Polished river-bottom stuff, you know. Probably that part of the peninsula was under water

142

just after the ice age. The land's been rising ever since, you know, since the ice retreated and all that weight was taken off.

'Anyway, the inside dyke is much smaller than the Roman wall. Just a series of small humps joined together and overgrown with moss and what have you. If you go past the hedgerow you'll see where we've been digging.

'I wasn't convinced that it was a wall until we did a survey of the whole line. It was too parallel. Too much of a coincidence. Possibly the first stockade was too small when the population expanded, and they had to build again much further out to give them more space.'

I suddenly thought of old Kitty MacBeth and her tale. Her story didn't allow for an expanding population at all.

'So after the survey, I organised a dig, just to see what was there. Over the last few weeks we've taken off the top soil, and we found the shingle, which made us pretty certain that it was indeed man-made. You don't get shingle so near the surface there. It's mostly clay under a thick humus, then a good sandwich of sand for a few feet, probably from when the peninsula was first formed, and then a layer of river stones before bedrock.

'The presence of shingle meant that it had been churned up a long time ago, but not as long as it had been since it was laid down initially. There wasn't anybody about here at that time, not unless they could have lived under two thousand feet of ice, that is.'

'Shingle doesn't sound like normal wall-building material,' Jimmy said.

'Yes, you're right of course,' Arthur said, brightly. He turned to me with a smile: 'If I could only persuade Jimmy to come and work with me I could get him a bursary, you know. He knows more about archaeology than my graduates, I'll swear.'

'Is there anything you don't know?' I asked Jimmy. 'You're a one-man book of knowledge.'

'I've just had more time than you to read the best books,' Jimmy said. 'Anyway, I wouldn't enjoy it if I was

143

paid for it. Hobbies are for fun.'

'What about your organ playing?'

'Oh, that's business. The church can afford it,' Jimmy said, chuckling. 'If I get a better offer I'll play the Apollo.'

'I'm sure you would, you old rogue.'

Arthur was winding up for his next lecture, gulping his lager.

'But today we found the definite proof. We'd dug down about six feet with nary a sign of anything but the conglomerate of shingle and clay, and then we hit the jackpot. It's tremendously exciting.'

'Well, tell us what you've brought up this time,' Jimmy ordered impatiently.

'Bones,' I said.

Arthur spluttered in mid-swallow, almost spraying the bar with lager. He turned to me, amazed. 'How the devil did you know what I was going to say?'

'Just a lucky guess,' I told him. Jimmy was looking at me with a strange expression. Arthur just stared.

'Well, you're perfectly right. That's just what we did find. And the remarkable thing about it is that it's unlike any other burial site I've ever worked on.'

'It's a burial site, then?' Jimmy asked.

'We're pretty certain it is, but as I say, it's like nothing else before. This one is an upright grave. The body was bound with reed ropes and buried standing up. It's in a remarkably good state of preservation. Almost every bone is intact and in its proper place, probably because of the dry cementing quality of the clay. In fact, there are still some remnants of clothing which will give us a fair idea, I'm sure, of what our friends were wearing all those years ago.'

Arthur stopped in his headlong rush and took his inevitable gulp of lager.

'But the strangest thing is that not only was our neolithic chappie buried standing up, but his head was not where it should have been. It was there, all right, but not attached to the neck.

'It was carefully placed on his feet, facing forwards. Don't ask me why, but it was obviously a decapitation before interment. Never seen anything like it before in my life. Wonderful.'

There was the inevitable pause. Arthur was wildly excited, and I could tell that Jimmy was interested.

I watched the two of them, and I felt a shiver. A cold wind played up and down my spine. It was a warm and sultry evening in our Indian summer, and for me alone it was suddenly overcast as a great dark cloud came creeping up the firth and settled right over me, casting a pall of gloom.

Jimmy and Arthur started talking, but I was miles away. Their voices seemed to recede into the background. Instead, I was hearing old Catriona O'MacConnor MacBeatha, old Kitty MacBeth, gripping my hand and telling me about the four walls.

'A wall of water, wall of stone, a wall of wood and a wall of bone.'

And when Arthur had been about to tell me what he'd found under the ground on his archaeological dig at Ardhmor, I had known, without any uncertainty, what it was.

Arthur had found and breached the fourth wall.

The MacConnors and the MacBeatha have always had a watcher on the shore, to ensure that at least one wall remains until they come back who can kill the Cu Saeng for ever in this earth and send it back.

The strong voice came back, clear and sharp, right into the centre of my head.

The tingling in my spine remained. I hadn't given too much thought to what the old woman had told me. It was a legend.

But I was beginning to get a little bit uneasy at the succession of coincidences. Things were a little too pat.

The world was beginning to get a little blurred at the edges. I wasn't sure at all what was happening. I wasn't sure at all that *anything* was happening.

But I sure as hell was beginning to get a bit edgy. I

didn't like that feeling of unease that was trickling its fingers up and down my vertebrae.

'Have another pint, Nick,' Arthur said, nudging me with his elbow and bringing me back to the here and now. I accepted and soon we were back in conversation, but my brain was still giving me muted alarm signals that I couldn't quite fathom out.

Suddenly, I had the feeling that I wished Arthur had gone and dug somebody else's cemetery. I didn't care too much for that thundercloud that was hovering just at the other side of my consciousness.

Long after Arthur had gone home to his flat in Glasgow's West End just off the university campus, and I'd strolled along the tree-lined street to Jimmy's house where I'd seen my old friend quietly ensconced in his living room, I had some time to think things over. Something was going on that I couldn't figure out, something that was making me uneasy. I couldn't write worth a damn. I couldn't even order my thoughts properly, which was not true to character. Yet when I'd taken Barbara and Paddy for a picnic on Loch Lomondside, only twelve miles away as the crow flies, the ideas kept bubbling up like a hot mineral spring. Out there in the fresh air and sunshine, I could feel the creativity I knew I had, welling up and overflowing. When we came back over the black hill and along the Kilcreggan Road to Arden, they all leached away like soil on a hillside under a steady drizzle. I didn't even notice it, taken up as I was with Barbara's conversation. It was only when I got back to my house and sat down to order up all those ideas that I found they'd disappeared again.

There were a few more things I thought about as I strolled along in the dim twilight. I was in a state of puzzlement, unsure, unsteady and certainly unready.

Certainly, I was unready for what happened next.

I walked round a corner into the main street, the continuation of Kilcreggan Road through Westbay, and came almost smack into Badger Blackwood. Even then I still had

146

to think and stop myself from calling him that to his face, although Colin wouldn't have the sense of self to mind.

Colin pulled himself up short just before he crashed into me and knocked me to the ground. He was breathing fast and heavy, obviously with exertion. An inch or two taller than me, but a bit heavier, Colin would have been a heartbreaker with the ladies, but for his childhood accident. Even the two lines of white that had grown in along the deep lacerations that had raked his scalp almost from brow to nape would not have seriously detracted from his face. He had a wide forehead and black eyebrows and deep dark eyes that would have set hearts a-flutter. But there was nothing in the eyes. They were all but empty; stupid, docile eyes. The boy had been a devil-may-care, quick-witted adventurer. The man that he had become was a baby.

At first he didn't recognise me. He just stood there, panting and trying to mumble some apology or whatever, not certain which way to go around me.

'Hello Colin,' I said, raising a hand up to his shoulder. His chest was heaving.

Recognition dawned, if dully. 'N-N-Nicky. It's them!' he wailed loudly, and jerked his hand behind him. I could see some figures coming along the street at a fast walk.

'Who?' I asked, trying to calm him down.. 'What's the matter?'

'Th-them. People,' he stammered.

'Hey you,' a voice came out of the gloom between the street lamps. I still couldn't make out the faces.

'Come here, you big daft bastard,' came the voice. Harsh and vicious, and full of drink.

Colin tried to push past me, but I stopped him.

'It's all right, Colin. Everything's OK.'

'You stupid big fucker. I'm going to kick the shit out of you,' yelled the voice, closer. Colin's chest started to heave again in a fit of panic. 'You hear me? I'm going to batter your thick brain in.'

I looked over Colin's shoulder and saw four people just

coming into the light. I could have guessed. Billy Ruine and his brother Tommy, along with two young layabouts from the Milligs. They were in their early twenties, a mean little bunch with the kind of low-life spite that seems to always be prevalent in small groups in small towns.

The four figures loomed closer.

'Well, well. Look who it is,' Billy Ruine said. 'Fuckin' local hero, eh?'

I stepped around Colin, who flattened himself up against the wall, trying to make himself disappear into it.

'What's the problem, Billy?' I asked, trying to sound calm and reasonable.

'No problem for me,' Billy said. He was a lean, mean little guy, maybe a couple of inches smaller than I, built like string and wire, with a narrow face and a wide mouth with a gap where he'd lost a tooth. The last time I'd seen him he was holding his nose and promising revenge after I'd straight-armed him. 'Big problem for you, and your thick-as-shit pal,' he said, and one of the other guys hovering behind him sniggered.

'I don't think we need any of this. Why don't you go and pick on somebody else?'

'Because that stupid bastard got right up my nose. And you get right up my nose. All right?'

I turned to Colin who was still backed against the wall, his face a picture of fright and bewilderment. 'Let's go home, Colin.'

I had just started to move when I felt a hand on my sleeve. I spun round quickly and dug my elbow under Billy Ruine's ribs and there was a fleeting satisfaction in the bellow of air that whooshed out. It was a lucky hit, but there was no point in hanging around to see if my luck would hold. The odds were against it.

The three others gathered around Billy who was still trying to suck air back in again, so Colin and I took advantage and ran down the alley. From behind us I could hear yelling voices. Almost at the end of the alley, and heading towards the turn that would take us down to Elm Street, I

148

heard that Billy had got his voice back.

'Get the bastards. I'll kill them. I'll fuckin' murder them,' he shrieked. Right in my ear I heard Colin whimper in terror.

Then from nowhere something hard came out of the night and hit me smack on the back of my head and everything went straight into slow motion.

There was a shock of pain and I started to pitch forward towards the wall just ahead of us. I remember a sudden instant wave of nausea as my knees gave way from under me. There was a sound of clanging in my ears and the other sounds, the thudding of our feet and the shrieks of the enraged Billy, faded away along with everything else – I took a long dive into darkness.

In the dark, faces loomed up at me coming out of the shadow and flickering in a grey light then fading out again. Processions of them. I saw:

Andy Gillon lying in the mud under the fallen tree on his farm.

His eyes were locked into mine, but they were white and wide and dead. The tree gave a great lurch off his body and everything that was inside him spilled out into the marsh, blue and green and red and purple, twisted and torn ropes that writhed like snakes and made a horrible slithering, sucking noise. They coiled and looped with a life of their own. Too much, too many. Gillon's eyes opened wider and wider; huge eyes with nothing in them, staring straight into mine and I couldn't turn away. The glistening slimy ropes slithered around him like slimy bonds and there was a smell like vomit. They piled up and around, binding his upstretched arms and coiling around his silently screaming mouth, and then they started to pull him into the mud. I could see his hands opening and closing like talons as they disappeared into the marsh and he was gone, leaving nothing but bubbles that oozed to the surface and burst sickeningly.

I turned and I saw Edward Henson – who I recognised although I'm not sure I had ever seen him before – walking

149

down the farm lane, with no hands at the ends of his shredded arms. He looked at me and his eyes were white, and black blood spurted from the rags he had instead of elbows and wrists. He walked towards the mound and the ground opened in front of him and a thing of bone and skin crawled out. It had no head. And all the time, I could hear the deep breathing from behind me, a rasp of dry leaves.

Grandfather said: 'You've been a bad boy Nicky. A bad boy.'

He towered over me and his eyes were white and the smell of his breath was foul. He raised his walking stick high and brought it down on the back of my head and made the world spin with my pain.

'Give me back the stick you made,' he roared and the wind took him and his voice and blew him into the darkness of Ardhmor.

Barbara screamed a long scream and I saw fire and a huge bird with a beak like a dagger, and then Colin and I were standing holding her hand on the bank of the stream when the big strange man in the fur cloak stuck the butt of his spear into the soft earth and disappeared.

'Come back,' Colin yelled. 'Come back.'

'. . . Come back to us, have you?' Kitty MacBeth said, and for a horrible moment I was still in the depth of a dream.

Light was in my eyes, causing needles of pain that orbited on the inside of my skull and set off bombs way at the back where the sickness bubbled. I tried to sit up and the nausea started to foam.

'No, just lie back and rest,' she said, and put a cool, surprisingly soft hand on my forehead. Her face was a blur.

'You're all right. You're in your own home,' she said. 'You've had a sore bang on your head.'

'What happened? How did I get . . . ?'

'Wait until you've had a drink,' Kitty said. 'I think you'll probably live. I put a compress on your head. The bleeding stopped a while ago, but you've been concussed,

I shouldn't wonder, and you've got a bruise the size of a cushie-doo egg.'

'Billy Ruine. He was after Colin,' I said, and braved the needles to sit up. I was in my own bed in my own room, which swayed just a little as I moved.

'Where's Colin? What the hell happened?' Recent memory was still in a fuzzy world.

She made me drink a large glass of cold water which made me feel slightly better than hellish, but not a lot.

'I sent him home last night after we put you to bed. He's all right, poor soul,' Kitty said.

'He says somebody threw a rock at you. Lucky you're not dead. Could have knocked your brains out, and then where would we be?'

'I remember Ruine and his mates chasing us, then something hit me. But how did I get here? And how did you get here?'

'From what he tells me, he picked you up and carried you. Somebody came out of one of the houses when they heard the racket and chased the others off. I met Colin just at the end of the street, still with you slung over his back. I had to stop him, for I feel he would have kept on going until morning.'

'And what were you doing out here at that time of night?'

'That must be one of those coincidences,' Kitty said. 'I was out looking for my cat. Maybe I shouldn't have, for the walk up from the point has taken it out of me. But look, I've thrown the crutch away and put on a smaller splint. I think the old leg is knitting together well. I'll soon be out and about like a spring lamb again.'

At the side of the bed were two walking sticks cut from branches, like the one I had made for my grandfather.

'Should you really be walking about yet?'

'Probably not as far as I did tonight, but the exercise is good for me, and I have to get myself in shape again. There's work to be done, and I need to be walking to do it.'

She looked at me with that wild, piercing stare. 'What was all the trouble about anyway?'

'Oh, Billy Ruine's been giving Colin a bad time for a while now. I just tried to get him away. Something hit me, and then I woke up.' I didn't mention the dreams.

'Well, you've been thrashing about and shouting at the top of your voice as if all the devils of hell were after you.'

'Maybe they were. Concussion's a bugger. My head feels as if it's been pulped.'

'You'll heal. You'd better. I need you,' the old woman said matter of factly. 'We all do.'

I phoned Barbara in the morning, just to let her know what happened, and probably looking for a bit of sympathy too, but there was no reply. I was hoping she might come down and minister to me while I bravely suffered. I had to make do with Kitty who hobbled all the way from the point about mid morning and shushed away my concern for her healing leg.

She forced me to drink something that tasted like liquid bramble jam with cinnamon which, despite being a witch's brew, was the nicest experience of the day so far. Whatever it did, it also brought back my appetite, and within the hour I was on my second plate of Scotch broth. Despite the sticks, Kitty worked quietly and efficiently with an economy of movement, although she favoured the damaged leg. She didn't say much either. I'd only met her once before, really, that day down at the point when she'd told me all those strange things, so I didn't know that much about her either.

When she saw I'd finished the soup, she took the plate away, and somehow made it downstairs, which I shouldn't have allowed. Then she came slowly back up again. There was a pause after six slow steps, then she must have eased herself over the seventh, because there was no creak. When she came into the room she looked at me and said: 'You wanted me to miss it. So I did.'

I had no reply to that. Kitty sat on the bed for a minute then she asked me if I'd thought about what she'd told me

152

down at her shack. I told her I'd thought some, but it was all a bit mixed up and fantastic so far.

'You'll be thinking more about it, then when you're ready, I want you down to my place, so I can tell you some more,' she said. 'I found my cat. It was on your front doorstep when I got back.'

'Must have followed you,' I said.

'I don't think so. Some of it was on the doorstep. Some on the grass and some on the pathway. It's been torn to pieces.'

I was about to say something. Some platitude or whatever you say to somebody who's just found their pet ripped to bits, but Kitty didn't let me.

'Before you say it's a coincidence, it's a message,' she said.

'From who? I mean whom?'

'Ah, you don't listen, do you? It was torn apart by some animal and left where we would see it. That's what happens you know. Anger and hate and violence is coming. You have to be protected.'

I sat forward quickly before I remembered about the pain involved in sudden movements. Whatever Kitty's brew had contained, it certainly helped dull the pain.

'I don't know what you're talking about. I remember what you told me the other day. About Ardhmor. But what's that got to do with your cat?'

'The cat's nothing. I don't keep familiars. It was just a stray that wandered in last year and stayed the winter. I looked after it and it kept me company, that's all. But now it's dead, and in your garden. And I'm in your house. It can't get out because of the walls, but it sends out its hate and infects.'

'Who does?'

'Cu Saeng. The sleeper. It made the dogs kill the cat to let me know it wants you. It wants revenge.'

'For what?'

'For what was done to it. For the binding. And for what you did.'

153

'What the hell did I do?'

'You stopped it.'

'When? And how?'

Kitty sat at the edge of the bed and stared at me.

'You've a lot to learn, you know. And little time to learn it in. Listen to me, and I'll tell you something.'

I leaned back against the pillow and Kitty told me about 1961. She told me how the summer had started warm and sultry and how Hugh Henson – father of the boy I'd dreamed about – had ended up under his plough with his hands cut off. And there was the dog fight down at the Milligs when the terriers had gone mad and ripped one of the men to death. And there were fights and accidents and a suicide. There was the herd of cows that had gone off the top of the cliff at Langcraig. There was a bad summer where everything seemed to go wrong.

'And then it stopped. You stopped it with the girl and the boy. It stopped on the night we took you from the jaws of that rock, and it has been gone ever since.'

'But I don't remember a thing about that.'

'Maybe you don't. But Cu Saeng does. That's what I've been trying to tell you.'

'Look, Kitty, I feel as if I'm caught up in one of these farces. I haven't a clue what's going on. I remember the legend you told me, but it's all Greek to me. This Cu Saeng. This spirit. What is it supposed to be, anyway?'

'Cu Saeng. The ravener. It is a hunger, a hate. That's what it is, and all your computers and radios and televisions won't change that. I told you how they raised it, and how they bound it with the walls.

'But I have to tell you now that the walls are wearing down. The Cu Saeng gets stronger and its force reaches out. It reaches for you. It will twist and turn everything against you. Watch.'

Kitty smiled, but it was no smile at all. 'Already you've taken a blow. And so have I. That is the start.'

'Those walls you were talking about,' I said. 'The water, stone and wood and bone . . .'

'Yes?'

'One of them's down.'

'What?' Almost a gasp. 'What do you mean?'

'I was speaking to the professor who's doing a dig there. You were right. They did find bones where you said they had been buried. And there was no head.'

Kitty's eyes blazed blue.

'Fools. Damned fools. And damned more than they know.' She put her head in her hands and rocked backwards and forwards. Then she stopped rocking and looked up. 'That's what's made it stronger. It reaches out.

'You had better get better, and soon,' she said. 'I think you are going to need all of your strength.'

Over and over, parts of what Kitty said came back to me, chipping away at my natural scepticism. The more I thought about it, the more I came to believe that something was definitely *wrong*.

Cu Saeng. The Ravener. The Sleeper.

I wasn't convinced. But I knew the old woman was convinced, and despite local rumour she seemed pretty steady on her feet, no matter how strange her tale.

But some *spirit*? Some age-old monster trapped by cavemen? I don't think I was quite ready for that yet. I've covered stories in South America where healers claim they have taken tumours out with their bare hands. I couldn't disprove it, so I can't say they don't. On Haiti I was shown a horrible something that a contact swore was a zombie. I couldn't say, one way or the other. I believe there could be a sasquatch or a yeti or whatever, and I don't laugh too loud at people who believe in the Bermuda Triangle although I don't subscribe myself.

But a monster spirit? Here in Arden? In the modern electronic eighties?

I would need more to go on before I put my money on it.

I thought about the dreams that were still scaring me out of sleep. I thought about Andy Gillon and what he said

155

to me as he spilled his life out in front of my eyes.

I recalled with a shudder that horrific thing that I had imagined, the one that looked at first like my grandfather.

And I thought of that night down on the rock when the wind was blowing the rain hard into my face and the bramble and dog-rose thorns had gripped and clung.

I seriously considered the possibility that good old Nick Ryan was quickly and quietly cracking up altogether.

Then I spent a couple of days reading through the wealth of Jimmy Allison's work on his history of Arden. That did me a whole lot of good.

On Thursday morning I woke up out of a dreamless sleep. Sometime in the night a whole lot of the information I had churned around in the past couple of days had settled itself into some sort of order.

I decided I wasn't cracking up. I wasn't exactly sure I knew what was happening. But I knew there was something awfully bad going on around here. And I knew that for some reason I was part of it.

ELEVEN

According to Jimmy Allison, Arden is older than all hell. That's probably how he would have put it, but that's not how he wrote. I was amazed at the depth of his research in geography and history, archaeology and palaeontology. He'd studied just about every major work ever written to find out what he could about the place of his birth. As he once explained to me, it had started with him a long while back when there was some dispute over whether the Priory – as it was then – was older than Westbay church, and Jimmy's research for the newspaper had settled the issues one way or another.

'It was the finding out of one fact that led to questions,' he would tell me.

'The more I knew, the more I realised how little I knew.'

So it had gone. The more Jimmy Allison discovered, the clearer became the pattern. Every now and again – and there was no clear regulation, no set timescale – Arden went through a period of disaster and destruction. Oh, the town stayed on, older than all hell, but there were times when it took long to recover. There were times when it almost never recovered.

Jimmy's history starts way back when the great lava plugs were cooling down. Ardhmor, Dumbuck, Dumbarton Rock, Dumbuie. Those vents of towering volcanoes that had spread their ash and dust and nutrient-rich rock all over the centre of Scotland. Just at that junction where the basalt welled up against the old red sandstone, a fault developed which lifted and twisted the hills into the highlands, while everything south was a shallow sea filled with sharks as big as a train and shelled monstrosities that have left their marks in the fossils of shale. Out of that sea poked the volcanoes that heaved and thrust up from the mantle of the earth and drained off the water and formed the basis for the level plain that would become the Clyde valley, the central lowlands of Scotland. Arden was right at that point where the plain butted up against the great folded ancient mountains that marched north. There were swamps, dragonflies as big as birds, centipedes that were six feet long and more. Later on there were reptiles and then mammals and then came the great ice sheets that covered everything and bore down the earth with such a weight that it sank. And when the ice melted the water came back, flooding the plain again; then the land started its slow rise with the weight gone, shuddering its way up from the depths around the dead volcanoes. And when the land came back, man came with it.

The man they found in the dugout canoe on the mudflats, so well preserved by the chemicals, had been one of the early explorers. Short, squat and strong.

Jimmy Allison's view is that these people, who hunted mastodon and elk, were of the same people as the Fir Bolg, the Irish tribes that lived throughout the west.

They were stone-age people, who made spears out of rowan and axeheads out of basalt. Their needles were bone and their hammers were antler. They killed the bear and the wolf and their descendants put up stone teeth to show that they had been here and had gone.

In more recent times, only four thousand years ago, there were more people from the west, from Ireland. The descendants of Bryan Boru, Conchobhar and Cu-Chulain, sailing in their big currachs up the Clyde and mixing their blood with the old people. They cut the ring stones and started the harvest festivals, burning their sacrifices in the wicker man at Samhain.

Then came the Romans and their legions up to the dear green place of Glasgow and beyond, building their wall that split the country north and south and sending raiding parties into the north to quell those who were not the

Picts, and the Scots, the blue barbarians. Some of those legions never came back again. The Ninth Legion has been a mystery since it left Old Kilpatrick, the most northerly outpost of the Pax Romana, and walked their hobnailed boots past Dumbuck Hill and into legend. They were never seen again.

St Columba came and St Kentigern, with their new way and their new god, and won over the chiefs of the western isles, the warriors of Argyll.

The Normans came next. They didn't conquer Scotland, but married it and wore it down that way until one Scot, Robert the Bruce, defied English rule and sent them home to think again. The Bruce and the Wallace won their wars, and the King of Scotland came back to the west to live by Arden. And when he came here he rotted away and died. He was not the only one.

The clans rose against the oppressors and the Colquhouns marched north into Glen Fruin just above Arden and were massacred. There was plague, and there was famine and there were killings.

Arden took it all and stayed put.

Every now and again, in all the records since written history began – pieced together fact by painful fact – was the evidence that Arden harboured some sort of curse that inflicted it with madness or war, or sickness or death.

Kitty MacBeth called it Cu Saeng, the ravener, the evil thing that lived among the roots, brought into this world by terrible spells in terrible times.

The monks called it the wrath of God. Jimmy Allison and the old people said it was a bad summer.

Whatever it was, an ancient scribe, writing on a goatskin, summed it up in his runic script, in a word that everybody would agree with. He called it a *bane*.

Father Gerry came roaring along the narrow street in his speed machine and did a wide sweep to the other side of the road to point the front wheel through the narrow space and right up to the front door. I was watching through the front window as he curved in, wrenching the throttle hard to bump the front wheel up on the pavement and dart, in a cloud of exhaust, between the stone pillars that held the gate with only an inch on either side of the handlebars. The sun gleamed on the shiny black dome of his crash helmet and reflected from the tinted visor that came down right over his face like a huge insect eye.

In the kitchen, he unstrapped the skid-lid as he called it and took several minutes to free himself from the expensive black leather jacket.

'Great jacket for the road,' he said, 'but too damned hot when you stop.'

The kettle hadn't long boiled and I poured him a cup of instant which he drank, leaning back in the pine chair with one boot crossed over the other on the top of the table.

'I heard you needed last rites,' he said after the first sip.

'That was days ago. I need the rites that come after the last ones.'

'Well, you look all right to me. Mr Bennett told me you'd been nearly killed.'

'By the time the story gets to the other side of town, I probably will have been.'

'What happened, then?'

'Some idiot threw half a brick at me. Nearly took my head off. At least that's what it felt like next day.'

'Jimmy Allison said you were feeling better. He's looking a bit unsteady on his feet with that bug he's had. Anyway, you look none the worse for it.'

'That's just my image,' I said, and he laughed.

'Listen, what are you doing today?'

I told him I'd planned to plough through some paper work. I was still reading Jimmy Allison's stuff, but I hadn't been out in the last few days and had been toying with the idea of a stroll down the shore or up Cardross Hill.

'I brought another helmet,' he said. 'Just in case you fancied coming up to the God spot.'

'God spot?'

'The big house. I've been planning this damned harvest

160

thing for weeks. It's about time I had a day off. Come up for lunch.'

He saw me hesitate. I didn't really feel like socialising, especially with a bunch of old priests, or eager young acolytes.

'Aw, come on,' he said, dark eyes flashing and mischievous. 'It'll get you out of all this. And I'll tell you what . . . we'll throw in some altar wine as well, blessed or unblessed.'

He nudged me on the shoulder and winked like an honest to God car salesman.

'Or are you still sworn off the drink after your last case of the heebie-jeebies?'

'OK, OK, I'll come on up, as long as I don't have to sit through a service or preaching or anything like that.'

'Come on, times are changing. Anyway, they don't let me preach. They think I'm the red under the bed trying to subvert the young ones.'

'You probably are.'

'That's right, and they know it. I'm the devil's advocate. A walking example of what a priest should never be.'

'Amen to that.'

'Here, and I thought you never prayed,' he said, raising his eyes skyward. 'There's more rejoicing for one sinner.'

'After the last couple of weeks I've had, I reckon I should start,' I said.

'Why? Are things still not going right for you?'

'You could say that. I don't think things are going right for anybody.'

'That sounds pretty deep,' he said, taking his boots off the table and swinging forward towards me. 'How do you figure that out?'

'I know you're going to think it's stupid, but I think something's going wrong around here.'

'Go on,' he urged, leaning forward even more, and staring intently at me.

'All right. Take the night when the lifeboat from the *Cassandra* went missing at Ardhmor. They haven't found a

161

sign of it ever since. Nothing, not a trace.'

'Accidents happen at sea. They'll find something sooner or later.'

'Oh, you think so? I don't. It's happened before, you know, years ago, and there was never any trace. An oar, or a hat, or a boot. Something that floats. Not *nothing*.'

'I'll concede that. All right, you have a disaster that takes place at night, in the middle of a storm, and a lifeboat goes down with all hands. Mysterious that they haven't found it, but not impossible. There was a storm, you know. So now what?'

'I'll tell you what. That fishing boat disappeared in exactly the same way, from the same stretch of water, back at the turn of the century. Calm sea and a bank of fog, and it's gone. Nobody knows where. Like it's just been spirited away. Again, not a sign.'

'So what you're saying is that we've got a Bermuda Triangle in the firth. A local disaster zone?'

'Wait until you hear more,' I said. 'We have the lifeboat, and the fishing boat years ago. Then we have Andy Gillon. I was there when he died. It was grotesque, horrible. But what's been preying on my mind ever since is what he said, just when he died. He told me the tree jumped. And I swear to God, when I looked at that stump, it must have. I just don't know how that tree could have fallen on him. It was yards away from where the roots were planted.'

'Wasn't there a fatal accident inquiry?'

'Formal verdict. Accidental death,' I said.

'And didn't you mention any of this?'

'I wasn't called to give evidence. I wasn't needed. But even if I had been called, I don't know if I would have said anything at the time. It was just too way out. And at the time, I thought I must have been mistaken. I'm sure Sergeant Morrison wondered, but when it came right down to it at the inquiry I don't think even he wanted to say anything. I can't blame him either. It's just when I look at it in the light of all those other things that I begin to see a pattern, and I don't like what I'm seeing.'

Gerry was about to interject, and I help up my hand to forestall him.

'After that came Edward Henson, who took off both his hands with an outboard motor. His mother shot him and then she shot herself. And before you say anything, I've got to tell you that his father lost both hands way back in 1961 in another weird accident. And that was the year there were a whole lot of crazy things happening in this town, although I didn't realise it at the time.'

'It seems to me you've strung together a lot of unfortunate coincidences and come up with some sort of reason for them. You must have seen a lot of disasters in your travels; a whole lot worse than this, I don't doubt. So allowing for the fact that these accidents have happened, and it's terrible that they have, why should there be any reason for it?'

'Some people believe this place is cursed,' I told him, watching his eyes for the merest hint of amusement.

'Cursed? Like in black magic? That sort of thing?'

'Yes, something like that.'

'And you believe it?'

'I didn't say that.'

'Well, what are you saying?'

'I'm saying that there's something weird going on here. There have been times when there have been chains of disasters in Arden. Whole bunches of them one after another.

'And they've been going on for a long time,' I said, and paused to spoon sugar in my cup.

'They call it a Bad Summer. The old folk do. The last one was in sixty-one. Before that it was 1906. There was another in the eighteen fifties, and yet another in 1720. And more, going back a hell of a long way.'

'How do you know all this?'

'I've spoken to a few people. And I've got a friend who's spent years studying this place.'

'Maybe it's just an unlucky town. But I imagine if you study any town's history you'll find terrible disasters, natural and otherwise.'

163

'Maybe you will. But in the old times, they believed there was some sort of creature, a demon or whatever, that woke up and haunted this place, and caused accidents and death.'

The look he shot me was one of total incredulity.

'Demons, eh? And you an agnostic! Do you really believe in all this?'

'Listen, Gerry, I don't know what to believe. I don't want to make a complete arse of myself, but I've got to tell you, I feel everything going wrong. I've got a horrible feeling of oppression, as if I'm at the centre of a cyclone, and just waiting for it to hit and blow me away. I know that sounds crazy. Really I do. But I've got a real bad feeling inside me that something terrible is going to happen.'

'Maybe it's you,' he said, softly. 'Maybe everything that's happened has unsettled you.'

'That's a nice way of saying I'm cracking up.'

'No, it's not. In your job you report on disaster. My job is to handle it when it happens, and try to prevent it happening. I think you may just be under a lot of strain. I've seen it happen. You need to give yourself a break, and just stop thinking about all this for a while. If you don't, then you will start to crack up. Believe me, it's hard enough, even for a priest, to hold on to his spiritual integrity with what the world can throw at us. We see the disasters all the time, at first hand, and every time we ask: how does He let it happen? But they happen all right. No curses, no demons. Just a crazy world and too many crazy people.'

'You're not crazy. Not even nearly crazy. But you could do with a break.' He pushed himself up from his seat. 'Come on, let's go for a wander and get some fresh air. Nature's best cure.'

Gerry spent ten minutes lacing and strapping himself back into his splendid leather jacket. He was dark and good looking and I could readily imagine the ladies of the parish, no matter to which denomination they leaned, seeking out the young priest for spiritual comfort. Or any comfort they thought might be available. He looked charming and roguish and clean cut and piratical all at the same time. The one thing he did not look like was a priest. I wondered why he had become one, and asked him straight out.

'Haven't a clue. I just woke up one morning when I was sixteen and knew that's what I was going to be. I hadn't thought about it before. I've thought about it since, though. Wouldn't be human if I didn't. My mother was delighted. Dad was furious for a while. I was supposed to take over the business. He's as rich as sin, you know. But they let me go ahead.'

'How about the vows?'

'Ah, you mean the *vow*. The big one?'

'I suppose I do.'

'Well, to be frank, it's like chronic haemorrhoids. A real pain in the ass. And all the time. Being a priest doesn't interfere with your hormone levels It just makes them more acute.'

I laughed, and he joined in ruefully. 'It doesn't help to have this film star's face, either,' he said, still grinning. 'The number of the blue-rinsed brigade who have told me it's a total waste, you wouldn't believe.'

'And you've never . . . ?'

'Broken my vows? Have you ever revealed a source? That's between me and Him upstairs,' he said, bobbing his head to indicate the direction of the third party. 'And He's not telling.'

When he was finally strapped in, he pulled on his gauntlets which completed the slightly menacing ensemble, and clapped me on the shoulder.

'I won't ask you to trust in the Lord,' he said, 'because that would be a waste of time. Just trust in yourself. Don't dwell on things. They give you headaches and constipation.

'Remember the final commandment.'

'And what's that?'

'Thou shalt not give a damn about things you can't do anything about.'

'Up yours too, padre,' I said, returning his cheery smile.

Before I knew it I was sitting on the back of the big Honda and roaring behind the Prince of Darkness past Mr Bennett's smallholding on the smooth tarmac that led to the seminary.

He handled that machine as if he had a death wish, but his control was superb. We slewed into the gravel fore-court of the big ivy-covered main building, kicking up half a ton of small stones. I'd left my breath and my stomach a quarter of a mile behind. Gerry took off his helmet and his face was flushed and alive. He might have made his vows of chastity and obedience, but he hadn't made any prom-ises about speed.

'I'll probably walk back,' I said, when I gathered enough saliva to make my voice work again.

'Rubbish. I was only doing seventy. That beast goes all the way up to a hundred and forty.'

'Not with me in the saddle. There's a law against suicide.'

'Trust me. If we come off, I'll hear your confession on the way up and give you absolution on the way down again.' He was loving this. My knees were being less than supportive.

'And who'll hear your confession? For murder.'

'God takes care of his own,' he said with a laugh. 'That's sacrilege, I suppose, but I hate waste, and it would be a waste of that lovely machine not to let her go now and again. The good Lord gave me good reflexes and told me to go forth and rev up. And if the monsignor heard me talking now I'd be on bread and water on my knees for a week.'

'Make it a month, you irreverent young scoundrel,' came a voice from the arched doorway, 'and clean your mouth out in the font on the way in.'

Standing in the dappled light against the worn red sand-stone was a tall, thin priest with a serious, forbidding face that was deeply creased on each side of a sharp, hooked nose. His hair was iron grey and cut short in what would have been a navy crew-cut if it had been taken any further. He had strong dark eyebrows and deep-set eyes that were hidden under the shadow of his brow, and his mouth, between those two furrows, seemed set in a line of grim and un-fun-loving determination.

He looked like how I would have imagined a latter-day Torquemada would have appeared. Self-righteous, virtuous, a man with God's message, and with God's personal permission to nail it home.

'Monsignor Cronin, meet Nick Ryan,' Gerry said brightly, totally ignoring the stern-sounding admonition of his religious superior. 'I've invited him up for a look around the place, seeing how I'm bored out of my brains running your daft harvest festival.'

The monsignor's eyebrows arched up, hauling away the great shadows under the crags and revealing a bright blue pair of eyes that fastened on me. I was prepared for the wrath of God to come and strike one or possibly both of us.

What I got was a deep rumbling laugh that was totally out of place in such a forbidding figure. It came storming up from somewhere deep, like a basso-profundo Santa Claus, shaking the whole frame of the man in the black cassock.

'Bored? Bored? I'll tell you young feller, you've got the best job in the place,' he boomed. 'There's priests here would fast for a month for the life of Riley you've got.'

I couldn't have been more wrong in my at-first-sight assessment of Monsignor Cronin, christened Michael, but known as A.J. for reasons fairly obvious to everyone but the students. He was a hugely humorous, witty man who, I was soon to discover, took great delight in almost everything he came across. He had a face that would scare an orphanage but a sunny nature that seemed incapable of taking offence or seeing anything but the best in people.

'Come away in, Nick. And you too, you rapscallion,' he roared in his great opera singer's voice.

The vigorous handshake all but jarred my shoulder from its sockets. The handshake and the voice were completely incongruous in the slender figure. Both belonged to someone ten stones heavier. Underneath that elongated robe, I assumed the monsignor must be all bone and steel.

I heard Gerry snigger as I almost stumbled under the friendly pat on the back and entered into the atrium. It was clean and smelled not of incense, as I'd fancied, but of flowers. There were stacks of them around a little votive statue to the virgin, beautiful chrysanthemums, fuchsia and freesia, arranged with loving care.

A.J. ordered Gerry to give me the grand tour and disappeared in a brisk swish of black, his long legs carrying him along the corridor at a swift pace.

'Terrific guy,' Gerry said. 'He scared the hell out of me the first time I saw him. I thought "God, what have I let myself in for?" '

'I thought he looked like Torquemada when he stepped out of the doorway,' I said.

'Oh, that's beautiful. He'll love that one.'

'Don't you dare,' I warned.

'Oh, don't worry about it. Old A.J. is aware that his face was never his fortune. He says it has outlived four bodies. His heart's his best feature. Big enough for all of us and more besides. He's a real hero.'

'How do you mean, a hero?'

'Just that. He's my hero. Everybody's hero. I mean, he's the boss here, and short of just about a papal decree, he can do what he likes here. But he treats everybody so well, from the youngest student up. He sees good in us all. He loves us collectively and individually. That's what I call a hero.'

Gerry paused for a moment, then laughed to himself. 'I suppose that's the kind of guy I want to be when I grow up. But A.J. declares that I never will.'

The guided tour was a delight. As a youngster, I had trespassed on the seminary's extensive grounds, stealing fruit from the orchards and trapping the occasional rabbit. To me it was just a big school-type building with a farm around it, but it really was a model of self-sufficiency. There were acres of potatoes in flower and almost ready for a main crop harvest, and lines of turnips mottled yellow and green in the light breeze. The orchard was smaller than I recalled as a boy, but still huge, and still filled with apple and pear trees that were getting heavy with fruit. There were plums turning that deep red of late summer and a vast greenhouse filled with an ancient twisted vine that was bearded with great black grapes. Not a weed dared poke through that hallowed soil in the walled orchard. Beyond the wall, fields of corn and barley gleamed gold in the sun in a bountiful harvest. In the distance, a big red combine harvester was cutting its swathe through the gold and shooting the ears on to a massive mound in the truck that ground alongside. There were men working in the fields, on tractors and on foot, young and old, sweating as the sun rose high towards noon.

We took a lane down to the mill at the Kilmalid Burn where a wheel turned slowly in a sparkling crescent of bright water. In the mill an old priest delighted in showing us the ancient wooden machinery of cogs and wheels that turned the giant millstones in an unceasing flow of fine flour. He pointed out the beech and oak, the ash and elm woods that were used to make the individual parts of the mill's elaborate workings. It was old and efficient and beautiful.

'Be sure to be at the harvest festival,' said the dust-covered priest. 'Father Lynn promises to be working overtime to make the best bread you ever tasted from all of this,' he said, gesturing to the bulging sacks with a white hand. His urging brought back the taste of that fresh bread in those long ago harvest festivals. Bread still warm from the ovens, delicious and soft where the butter melted through. I almost watered at the mouth.

At twelve o'clock a bell rang in the far away tower in the main building and in the fields, everybody stopped, dropped their tools and switched off engines and got down on their knees and faced the slender cross that topped the tower. Gerry, who had changed into a pair of cavalry twill smart trousers, did the same, regardless of the dust underfoot.

I shuffled about a bit from one foot to another, embarrassed with indecision and the feeling of being the odd man out, then compromised by sitting down on a hummock of grass. Gerry turned and flashed me a quick smile, then went back to the serious business of praying. After a few minutes, he got up and dusted his knees off, sending up little light clouds.

'Sorry about that,' he said. 'I forgot to tell you about the Angelus. It's a bit of a tradition here. Everything stops at twelve.'

'You do that every day?' I asked.

'Only on the premises. We don't get down on our knees if we're elsewhere, although we're supposed to say it to ourselves no matter where. But here on the farm, it's just part of the way of life.'

'What happens if it rains?'

'Well, we don't actually have to grovel in the mud. But some of the others do just that. It's their own way.'

We made our way down towards the seminary, and Gerry pointed out interesting parts of the farm. The Jersey cows with their huge promising udders; the big Aberdeen Angus beef bull that snorted and stamped in a paddock of its own. He explained that the farm itself was a mini-ecology of its own. No added chemicals, no preservatives. They made honey and jam, and flour and cheese and butter, and took care of their land as the priests and monks had done for centuries before them.

Lunch in the big, bright refectory was plain, but hearty. A good thick broth, followed by exquisite steak pie – and if you have never heard steak pie described thus, believe it – with new potatoes covered in butter, and fresh peas and carrots. Everything, I was assured, was completely home-grown and organic. There was a delicious red wine which the monsignor said was elderberry, but tasted like a full-bodied French vintage, and which he swore he'd made himself and bottled some years back. I had two glasses and that was enough, even though I wasn't driving. It had a kick like a jack-hammer.

During lunch, A.J. insisted I tell him all about my adventures, as he called them, and I regaled him with one or two tall tales from my roving days.

He laughed uproariously at all the funny bits and never seemed to notice how every time he did so a wave of silence swept through the ranks of young, clean-shaven faces at the long trestle tables down each side of the refectory. When the monsignor's great booming laugh bounced off the plain walls, the low, murmured conversations halted abruptly and a few of the more inquisitive turned to see what the hilarity was all about. I gathered that A.J. must be the light entertainment in amongst all that serious talking that seemed to be going on among the recruits.

The monsignor countered with a few tales of his own from equally far-flung places where he'd worked. He parried any light probes into his former profession with quick wit, telling me he'd joined the staff of the Great Brigadier, and expected a transfer any year now.

Later, he asked me to join him in the flower garden, which, it transpired, was one of his passions. He, I discovered, had grown the flowers for the array around the Virgin's statue, and had arranged them himself. When he told me that, I suddenly got a picture of a Samurai warrior, hard, and tough, and deadly if necessary, but with a love of beauty and a delicacy of thought and a gentleness of nature. He seemed a man who had come to terms.

As we strolled through the gardens, the tall priest pointed out his flowers that burgeoned in riots of colour. He knew all the names, and their Latin classification too, explaining the relationships between the varieties, their differences in colour and perfume; occasionally nipping off a bud or a leaf as we passed. Walking through the garden, I wondered what I was doing here. All right, I had accepted a casual invitation, then reluctantly allowed myself to be virtually hijacked by a suicidal, but likeable maniac, and found myself surrounded by a bunch of priests who I'd never met before. And now I was strolling in a flower garden with a tall, ex-commando who was explaining the joys

171

and rewards of horticulture. It may be strange, but I was enjoying myself. For a short afternoon I seemed to have found a hideaway from the anxiety and chill that had crept up on me. It was as if that cyclone had died down and dissipated, leaving me in a calm stretch of clear water. A.J.'s voice, deep and resonant, was telling me something which, in my momentary reverie, I missed.

'Pardon?' I begged.

'Our dark knight mentioned to me that he thought you might need some help?'

So that was the reason for the hijack.

'Dark knight?' I dodged gauchely.

'Father Gerry. Our caped crusader.' He wasn't fooled.

'He seems like a good guy,' I said.

'Oh, he is. One of the best. I worry about him, you know.'

'Why, in case he crashes that bike?'

'No, I trust in his reflexes and hope for the best. He's so gifted and dedicated. The motorbike is just his way – his lock on the land outside the cloister, his bridge to the other side. If he didn't have that I don't know what he would do.'

'Why do you worry about him, then?'

'Doing too much, working too hard. He never stops. I can't stop him. He just keeps pushing himself, and tries to carry everybody else. I gave him this harvest festival thing to organise, hoping it might make him drop one or two other things he'd got involved in, but no, he just added it to the rest. I fear he's going to burn himself out.' The monsignor paused to pluck a tiny white flower from a low cluster. He gave it to me and told me to smell it. It had a scent like wild honey.

'Alyssum,' he said. 'Delightful, isn't it?' It was.

'I expect he'll settle down, but until then I'll have to keep praying for him, otherwise he'll exhaust all his energies and his talents. I'd hate to lose such a gifted and dedicated man.'

The tall priest turned and beamed his blue eyes from

under the great crags of his eyebrows.

'I gather he's adopted you as one of his causes. I asked him to bring you up to lunch.'

'I think I know what you're talking about. I told Gerry something the other day which should perhaps be left unsaid.'

'Yes, he told me what you said, and he asked me what advice he should give you. On the question of curses and what-not.'

'He thought I was heading for a nervous breakdown.'

'Yes, I imagine he did. And does. I told him to bring you here for some peace and quiet.'

'That was really nice of you. I've enjoyed myself a lot,' I told him, genuinely.

'That must have come as a surprise,' he said, with uncanny accuracy.

'Well, I suppose you're right. I expected a lot of prayers and religious tedium.'

'That makes two of us. I expected that when I came here too,' he said, and laughed again.

When he stopped laughing, his face went all serious again. 'Tell me about this curse,' he said quietly.

'Why do you want to know?' I asked.

'Let's say I'm curious,' he said, and one side of his mouth turned up in a half smile.

'Do you believe in curses?' I countered.

'I believe in a lot of things. Like you, I've travelled, and I've done some things that man shouldn't do to man. All a long and misguided time ago, of course. But I believe in good and I believe in evil.'

'I'm not sure what I believe in.'

'I also believe in history. And we have a lot of it here. This place has been inhabited by religious orders since the time of St Kentigern – St Mungo to the Glaswegians. They kept records, you know.'

'Records of what?'

'Oh, the usual things. Births, deaths, marriages. Harvests. Battles. The usual comings and goings. Very efficient record-keepers, were the old monks. Had a mania for writing things down.'

'Go on,' I urged.

'We have them all here. In our library. It's a hobby of mine, since I've been here, to acquaint myself with everything that's gone before. And in reading through all those records, I've discovered that this place has had more than its fair share of turbulent times.

'I've got a roll of parchment skin that was written by a monk who was one of the few survivors of a famine in the seventh century here. He spoke of a plague of madness that afflicted the villagers, and said that the survivors had gathered here in the chapel to escape the curse. It is written in Latin mixed with Gaelic, so I dare say he was a local man. He said the ravener had awoken to steal the minds and souls of the people. At the time he wrote, there were sixty survivors in a village of seven hundred.'

'The bane,' I said.

'Yes. That's how he described it. A bane.'

'And do you take it seriously?'

'Let me say I don't close my mind to anything.'

'I'm surprised,' I told him.

'Oh, don't be surprised. I'm not superstitious, or a religious fanatic. Suffice it to say that I'm a man who has seen the effects of both sides and have chosen one. I believe in good, and I believe in evil, and there are many things that I cannot explain. And the trail of devastation that has centred on this little place is one of the things that I cannot explain.

'But if I believe in a good, and a God, then I must believe in the converse.'

'An evil force?'

'If you will. The archbishop would probably have me sent to Rome for decontamination, so I'd be obliged if this conversation was kept strictly off the record, for the moment, as you journalists like to put it.'

'I don't think anybody would believe it.'

'Quite.'

He paused again, gathering his thoughts.

'Father Gerry said you were concerned about some recent happenings.'

'Yes, I am.'

'Why?'

'It's a long story.'

'Well, if you're not in a hurry, sit down and tell me,' he said, taking my arm gently and leading me to a rustic bench that had been lovingly put together with natural branches of yew, and we sat down.

I told him everything. He just sat and nodded encouragingly as I started right at the beginning, the dreams, the deaths, the disappearances. My conversation with Kitty MacBeth and my study of Jimmy Allison's work. The dig and the discovery at Ardhmor. The legends, and the history. He soaked it all up like a computer assimilating data. At the end of it I asked: 'Do you think I'm cracking up?'

'No,' he said. 'I don't.'

The monsignor stood up when I had finished, and we started to wander around the flower beds again in the bright sunlight. The bees were toiling busily amongst the incandescent hues of the flowers in that little haven of serenity where I had spilled my soul about things that could not possibly be true in that place and on that day.

'Cu Saeng,' I said. 'Could such a thing be true?'

'Is there life beyond death?'

'I don't know,' I confessed.

'I do. Otherwise I would not be a priest. But I don't believe that we have the monopoly on such knowledge. Christianity is such a young religion. But my God is not young, and neither is man in this place.

'If good and evil existed from the start, then even primitives were entitled to believe and worship. It does not matter to me, nor, I suppose, to God, what they called Him, or any manifestation of Him. The same goes for the dark side, and when a minion of evil is in the world, it is difficult to get him out again.'

'You believe that?'

'Read your Bible laddie, with an open mind. I don't expect anybody to take in the Old Testament word for word. But the spirit of it must be true. The old legends have a basis in fact. Arthur found the secret of melting iron, and gave his people the sword that vanquished. Wotan climbed his tree to flee the wolves and hallucinated in thirst and became Odin. The legends couch what is true. Jesus Christ struggled with the Devil himself, and the Gazarene swine became lemmings.

'I ask you, what, under God's miracle that we call life, might *not* be true? Does the old battle still rage, or have good and evil so pervaded man that all is grey?'

'I don't know what I believe,' I admitted.

'Neither do I. But I am uneasy about what *not* to believe,' he said vehemently.

'I've heard the phrase "Bad Summer" before. Twice this year, from old people to whom I've given extreme unction, on their deathbeds. I too am aware of what has happened in this place of late, and it so resembles other times that I fear there is more than coincidence.

'That is why I am talking to you, alone, of this. Because I am afraid that there is something bad that I must fight, and I am considering how best to fight it.'

'You mean with prayer?'

'With whatever. I cannot say your Cu Saeng exists and that it is an evil entity. But I can say that there have been times when this place has suffered with an intensity and an agony that has recurred like a dormant disease, and there is something in my heart that tells me that the illness is coming back with a vengeance.'

'That just about sums it up for me.'

'There is another reason that I asked Father Gerry to bring you up here,' he said, staring intently at me.

'I dreamt about you two nights ago.'

'About me?'

'Yes.'

'But we have never met before.'

176

'That's true. But I don't ask for a reason. I just accept the gift.'

'What did you dream?'

'I dreamed that you were standing by the bed of a stream with no water. Not as you are now, but as a child. But I knew who you were, and I knew that you needed my help, you and the others. A boy and a girl. There was a wind that was blowing trees down and I had to get to you to give my blessing, but my feet were stuck in mud and I couldn't reach you before the darkness came down and swallowed you up.

'I awoke in fear that I had failed.'

I stared at him in surprise.

'What were the others like?' I asked, stupidly.

'A girl with golden hair, and a boy with dark eyes and a bow in his hand. But I knew you.

'When Father Gerry spoke to me of you, I had a certainty that you were the child I had failed to reach. There's a miracle for you. When I met you today, I realised the truth of it.

'That's why I insisted that he bring you here to see me, especially when he told me of your troubles, and asked how he could help you.'

We had reached the wooden doorway of the walled garden, and the monsignor opened it to let me through. The gravel crunched under our feet as we walked towards the arched doorway of the main building.

'Now I've been given another chance,' the priest said as we walked inside and into the shade where the little statue of the Virgin was enthroned in beauty. He beckoned me over to a little font set in the wall and dipped his hand in. I could hear the splash as he raised his dripping fingers to my head and marked a cross on my forehead.

'Bear this blessing and take strength in the name of the Father, the Son and the Holy Ghost,' he said with a strength of feeling and such conviction that even the agnostic in me felt the power. It was like being charged with force.

The water dripped down between my eyes, but I ignored it. It was a strange moment, one that I will never forget, ever. At that moment there was a bond between me
and that tough old, joyful, fearful, grizzled priest that was more than words could describe. He had given me something. I didn't quite know what, but it was something special, his backing, and the backing of Whoever was backing him.

'Thank you, Father,' I said.

'Call me A.J.,' he said, chuckling. 'They all do behind my back. But remember, not a word to a soul, or they'll drum me out of the Brownies.' He had shifted his position from being deadly serious to devil-may-care with one deft flick of his thumb over my forehead, and the spell was broken, as if the previous conversation about things beyond the reach of man had never taken place.

I walked home. Gerry had disappeared somewhere and had not come back to give me a hair-raising ride home, for which I was duly thankful. As I strolled past the pillars which marked the entrance to the long drive, I thought about what the monsignor had said to me. Really, it was hard to believe that he had actually said it. He had told me that I was not cracking up, not having a nervous breakdown. He, a man of God, who was in control of dozens of young men who wished to become priests, had actually put some credence in the curse, the bane.

I didn't know whether to be elated that I had a fellow traveller, someone who was as rational as anybody can be, but who was prepared to say he believed there *might* be something happening in this place that was way beyond reality. I didn't know whether to be happy, or to be truly shit scared.

My little, and altogether strange, talk with the priest, had left me a little bewildered, but a little stronger. Something bad was happening, something I couldn't identify, no matter what I'd been told. I still didn't really believe in the Cu Saeng, or demons or spirits. But like the priest, I had a strange certainty of foreboding badness seeping into Arden. Now I had an ally in that certainty. Whether this made things better, or a whole lot worse now that somebody else had put credence in it, I was unsure.

As I walked in the sunlight, the water bottle banged against my hip.

Monsignor Cronin had blessed me, then taken me to his study and given me the old, worn, canvas-covered bottle.

'Here take it. It's a memento of mine from the bad old days. It has seen me through a lot of dry spells. We get our font water from the spring at Strowan's Well. I've blessed you. Pass it on to the others if you can. I hope you won't need it, but it can't harm anybody.'

I took it, a bit nonplussed, and thanked him. I hadn't a clue what I was supposed to do with it then, but hindsight is a great clearer of mysteries.

TWELVE

The new Fruin road that would soon by-pass Arden was taking shape. Along much of the fifteen-mile length, rocks had been blasted and hardcore laid. It would become a two-lane dual carriageway to be used by the Ministry of Defence as their main transport route to the Trident base on the Kilcreggan peninsula.

On that sunny day, men were preparing to finish work on phase four, a two-mile stretch that skirted Cardross Hill to join up with five and three, completing the sections between Levenford and Kirkland.

It had been a long and hard day for Bert Milne, a big, grizzled digger driver who had been at the controls of his yellow monster since lunch-time when he'd sat with his mates round a brazier that they'd made out of a fifty-gallon drum, punctured with a pickaxe and loaded with wood chips and any debris left from the land clearance. They had made thick tea in their smoke-blackened cans that hung over the flames, bubbling and frothing over to sizzle in the red heat.

Bert Milne had sat down on a plank that was raised up on a couple of concrete kerb-stones and he had taken off his dirty cap and mopped the sweat of his brow.

He had waited for his tea to infuse – with a little piece of twig floating on the surface to draw all the particles of dust and ash – a trick that every labourer has known since tea was first brewed – and then he had guzzled his big box of sandwiches with a fervour known only to those who work in the open air. Cheese and pickle, corned beef and pickle, and a great treat – tuna and pickle. The subcontractors, earning huge wealth from the defence work, were paying handsomely. Bert's wife could afford tuna.

Bert sat with his mates, big and bulky in his chequered shirt, savouring the tea and the sandwiches, the sun and the heat from the fire. He belched loudly and satisfyingly and swapped jokes. He had another cup of stewed, sweet tea, lifting his can off the coals with a deftness born of experience and thickly calloused working-man's hands which defied the scorching. He enjoyed the tea, and two unfiltered cigarettes, and when he'd finished he and his workmates went back to the job. Some to lay pipes for drainage, some to manhandle the heavy kerbs into position, and Bert to his JCB.

He sauntered along the dusty road to the end of the built-up section, then out on to the hardened mud where all morning he had been clearing debris from the base of a rock face that had been blasted out.

The engine roared into life seconds after he had heaved himself into the tiny, dusty and oily cabin and the great shovel clanged down into position for the first thrust.

Bert liked his work, he could handle this big machine. It suited him. He was conscientious and drove the JCB forward and backwards, pirouetting like a forty-ton ballet-dancer, rumbling across the earth, and moving great mounds of earth. His hands juggled with the controls as the sunlight streamed through the plexiglass window that was smeared with dust. Bert worked and sweated all afternoon, feeling the throbbing of the great diesel engine underneath him. A slight case of haemorrhoids would start to give him gyp, no doubt, later on, a condition caused by sitting in his sweaty box all day long, but one which he bore with relatively cheerful stoicism.

Late in the afternoon, Bert's stomach started playing up. The muscles spasmed tightly, causing him to suddenly wince.

'Bloody pickles,' he muttered to himself in between trying to belch to ease the gripping pain. This action did not prevent him manoeuvring his big machine and lowering the jaw down for another foray into the mound of rubble.

The pain did not go away, and Bert started feeling

nauseous. He started to sweat, not in the way he had been perspiring all afternoon, but coldly, in copious amounts that oozed out all over his face and at the back of his neck and on his chest.

Then suddenly there was what felt like an enormous explosion deep inside the big man's ribcage, a huge pain that caused him to lurch forward over the controls. Bert was dead before his face hit against the screen as the hole that had suddenly appeared in the big artery leading from the top of his heart spilled everything into his chest cavity.

The JCB had a life of its own.

Unguided, with Bert's body sprawled over the levers, the machine lurched forward, its jaw raised high. Instead of digging into the base of the mound, the flat plates of the caterpillar tracks carried its immense weight right up the side of the slope without faltering. Then as it neared the top, it began to slew sideways. It seemed to pause on the crest, then with a rending screech of metal against stone it turned and started to tumble. The jaw slammed against the crumbling rock face and a welter of rock broke away, big jagged stones that battered against the cab. The machine just rolled over in a slow motion action and hit the near edge of the face, bring down an avalanche. Then it and the rocks that had dislodged crashed with a huge noise into the little stream below. When the dust cleared, the running men who were moving even before the digger had started to topple were sliding down the scree of the new avalanche slope, and were in the rubble that surrounded and half covered the JCB which lay on its side where the clear water had flowed. By the time they had prised off the loose rocks and hauled Bert Milne's body out of the wreckage, the water was brown with silt and had started backing up in a deepening pool. The yard-wide steel and concrete pipe that had carried the water from further up the gully that cut into the hillside was blocked with stones and shattered rock, mixed with mud and clay.

By evening, when the ambulance had come and gone, the backed-up water spilled over the low edge of the gully and found a new way out into a drainage ditch that had been cut and cleared along the length of the roadway to carry off the spill water from the wide carriageway. The ditch travelled more than half a mile, taking the extra load easily until it reached the Kilmalid Burn, the largest of the four streams that passed within the boundaries of Arden. The silted water soon cleared and the Kilmalid flowed, taking the water of both streams now instead of one, down its steeply etched valley past the grey concrete council houses and under the bridge on the Kilcreggan Road. It meandered more slowly now as the waters gurgled in a serpentine shape alongside the pigeon huts and shacks of the shore side of the Milligs, and out into the flat expanse of the mudflats, midway between the long rifle barrel of the sewage pipe and Ardhmor Rock. Then it drained into the firth and was dissipated in the salt water.

Below the backed-up pool, downstream from where the plugged pipe allowed the newly formed pool to grow, the clear waters of Strowan's Well ran more slowly, became a trickle that quickly drained away, leaving a punctuation of shallow pools that trapped some small trout. Through the good farmland the waters diminished and died away, and the silver fork of the stream that cut across the Ardhmor peninsula east and west became a patchy ditch of still water that started to evaporate as soon as the sun rose in the morning.

By nightfall on the following day the bed of the stream was just muddy and moist. Two days later it was dry.

Kitty MacBeth would have been the first to notice the disappearance of the water of Strowan's Well from her vigil watchpost on the point. But on the night that Bert Milne died in the cabin of his digger, the old woman took ill with what she thought was a summer cold, and went to her bed. Two days later, racked with a cough that seared her throat, and running a fever, she could hardly move.

That's how I found her in her neat little shack, shivering and coughing under the pile of blankets. There was no fire under the kettle and no air in the cramped space.

I knocked several times on the hardwood door that had obviously in a former life graced a more imposing homestead, but there was no reply at all. I assumed the old woman had gone beachcombing and was about to leave when I heard a weak, rasping cough. I stood on some of the logs that she had collected for firewood and had to rub the dust off the glass to peer inside. It took a few moments for my eyes to accustom themselves to the gloom, and at first I saw nothing, then I noticed the shape under the pile of grey blankets. I knocked on the window with a knuckle, but there was no further response, not even a cough.

The big door looked as if it was going to take a lot of shouldering to get it open, but it didn't. I turned the handle and it opened with hardly a creak. She hadn't locked it.

Inside, the air was foul, reeking of damp and sweat and more besides. I crossed over to where Kitty's pallet was tucked in against the wall and pulled a blanket back from her face.

Ghastly is the only way to tell you how she looked. In the couple of days since I'd seen her she had lost a deal of weight, and her blue eyes were sunken into sockets that seemed much too large to hold them. They had lost their sparkle, and only stared in a dull, confused way. Her hair was lank and sweaty, and her neck was like a chicken, scrawny and scraggy. A pulse beat in one of the blue veins that seemed to stand out against the pallor of her skin. I took hold of her right hand that was up close to her neck and she tried to grip mine, but there was no strength at all in the grasp. The movement ended almost as soon as it began. I could feel the heat from her body coming off her like a radiator.

'Kitty,' I said, bending low to speak.

Her eyes swivelled in their sockets, coming to rest, slowly, on mine. For a moment there was nothing, then a brief, tired moment of recognition before they glazed over again. She coughed, and the sound seemed to be coming from way down deep inside. 'Sick,' she murmured. 'Got sick.'

'Yes, I know you're sick. I've got to get a doctor,' I said quickly.

'Doctor. Yes. Please.' The words were just a dry whisper, but again I felt the pressure of her hand tighten on mine. I pulled away gently and tucked the blankets around her as tightly as possible. In the few moments that took, the old woman had drifted off to sleep.

The mile from Kitty's shack to my house was possibly the quickest I've run since I was a kid. By the time I got there I was panting like a dog, and I had to lean against the lintel to get my breath back before I could get my key into the lock. I barged in and ran through to the study where the phone was, and picked up the receiver to dial instead of using the phone book to find the local doctor's number. I just got straight on to emergency services and asked them to send an ambulance, then I ran all the way back down to Kitty's place, albeit at a much slower pace, promising myself that I must do something to get myself as fit as I should be.

The ambulance managed to get within a quarter of a mile of the shack, and quite quickly too, before the two men had to get out and foot the rest, carrying their stretcher between them. I had told the operator that an old woman was dying and needed a stretcher. For all I knew she was, but I didn't want to take any chances. Once inside the shack, the men were briskly efficient, checking pulse and heart rate almost at the same time as they lifted Kitty out of the bed and on to the stretcher.

'Dehydrated,' the older of the two said. 'She's pretty weak.'

'Any idea how long she's been like this?' asked the other. I shook my head.

'We'll get her on a drip as soon as we get to the van. Do you want to ride with us?'

'Yes, of course. Thanks.'

I helped spell the older man along the track and through the beechwood to where the ambulance was parked. Kitty didn't stir. As soon as we got there and put Kitty inside, one of the men ran round and started up immediately, while his partner hauled over some sort of intravenous array and affixed it to Kitty's arm. It looked yellow and thin, and the veins were sticking out clearly from the surface. I suppose that it made the job of getting the needle inserted a lot easier.

'What is that stuff?' I asked.

'Just a saline solution with some vitamins. I can't give her anything else until she's been examined, but the solution won't do any harm, no matter what.

'She's running a fair old temperature too, but if she's dehydrated, that stuff will help bring it down a bit.'

The journey to the little cottage hospital on the west of Westbay took ten minutes at the most, and within fifteen minutes Kitty was getting checked out by the youngish doctor. His work took less than half an hour, and when he came out he called me across from where I was sitting in the little waiting room. Through in his tiny office, he told me that Kitty had a temperature of a hundred and four, was thoroughly dehydrated as the ambulancemen had suspected, and had swollen lymph-nodes in various locations on her body.

'Too early to say at the moment, but possibly some sort of virus,' he said. 'We'll have to keep her here of course.'

I nodded.

'I'll need some personal details,' he said.

'I don't know how much I can help you there.'

'Oh? I thought she was your. . . .'

'Friend. No relation. I can tell you how old she is, and where she lives, and her name. Not much more than that.'

'Well, it'll do for a start. Do you know if she has any relatives in the area?'

'No, she has none that I know of. But if there's anything that's needed, I'll be available. You can put me down as next of kin for practical purposes.'

'I thought you said there was no relation,' he said, looking bemusedly over the top of his bifocals.

'Well there isn't really, but I suppose I'm all she's got.'

That seemed to satisfy the bureaucrat in him and he filled in a little form as I supplied him with what little information I had. Later he let me in to see the old woman. She was cleaner than before, but just as pallid against the while linen of the hospital sheets. I could see the orbs of her eyes move under the delicate thin eyelids. I sat down by the bed and was just looking at her when the eyes slowly opened.

She raised a hand that was pinned with the intravenous drip, so I leaned forward and held it still, hushing for her to relax in the way they do on television. She eased her head round slowly to face me.

'Wooden box. Under bed,' she whispered hoarsely. 'Take it. Use it.'

'Later. Talk later. Just rest now.'

'No. Now. Take it. Use it,' she said, with as much vehemence as she could muster. I could see that even that effort drained her.

'All right, Kitty. I will,' I assured her. Her eyes started to close, then they snapped open, gleaming brightly for an instant, beaming the full blue straight into mine.

'The walls,' she hissed. 'You take care of the walls!'

For the third time that day, I went down to the point. This time I walked, feeling depressed and oppressed. I knew inside myself that the old woman was seriously ill, and for some reason I found a weight of responsibility on my shoulders, although I was unsure *what* I should feel responsible for. I wandered, hands deep in the pockets of my bomber-jacket, in the shade of the huge beech trees, along the hard-packed path that skirted the shore. I stopped for a few minutes beside the big stone dragon's tooth where the old woman had shown me the inscription on the standing stone. The small part she had scraped away with the dog-fish skin was still lighter than the rest, but already the lichen was returning in a thin sheen of green. Already the script was invisible. Had it been real? Had it?

Kitty's shack door was open. I must have forgotten to

close it in my haste to get her to the ambulance. Inside, the little packed room was well aired. The stench of sweat and illness had blown out of the door and had been replaced with a fresher air brought in on the light sea breeze. To tell you the truth, I felt a bit ghoulish, but I had made a promise. I tend to keep them. Kitty had told me to find her box. I found it under the bed where she'd said it would be. It was small, made of polished hardwood that had been etched in a stunning labyrinth pattern all over its surface. There was a hole for a key, but the box was not locked. I lifted the lid a fraction, then lowered it again. I didn't feel like poring through the old woman's possessions inside her home. I decided to take it back to my place although, in fact, I would have preferred to leave it where it was until the old woman came out of hospital.

There was a big key hanging on the back of the door, which fitted the mortice lock. I turned it twice, hearing the clicks that would secure Kitty's home from any but the determined, and I gathered there would not be many of those in Arden. I hefted the solid little box under my arm, and was about to head back along the track to the stone and up to Westbay again when I heard a shout in the distance. Someone was calling my name.

'Hold on, Nick,' the voice came from the shore, carrying clearly from halfway along the curve, close to where the sand gave way to the marshes.

I raised a hand over my eyes to ward off the glare, and saw the figure striding towards me. I didn't recognise him and I remember thinking he must have bloody good eyesight if he could make me out at that distance. I watched as the man walked steadily across the sand, his feet kicking up little plumes of the fine grains. At about half the distance, I recognised the major, Donald MacDonald, the old soldier, and Gaelic singer, who was a friend of Jimmy Allison.

He waved when he was closer, and there was a smile on his broad face.

'Housebreaking or socialising?' he asked.

'A bit of both,' I said. 'The old woman took ill today. I got her up to the hospital.'

'Och, that's sad. She's a fine old one, that,' Donald said, 'despite what they say about her.'

'She asked me to come down and collect something for her.'

Donald nodded, accepting my explanation. He was wearing a peaked hunter's hat that was camouflaged just like his sleeveless jacket. Around his neck there was a pair of Zeiss binoculars that looked powerful and heavy.

'I often drop in to see the old lady when I'm here,' he said. 'Makes me a nice cup of tea and doesn't complain when I put a wee dram in it neither.'

He hefted the binoculars. They explained how he'd been able to recognise me from the far side of the bay.

'The birds, you know,' he said by way of explanation.

'Oh, I didn't know you were an ornithologist.'

'More just an observer. It's been a passion with me since I was a boy on the islands. And here is a wonderful place for the birds.'

He nodded back in the direction from which he'd come. 'Do you know we have an avocet there?'

Noting my expression, he went on: 'No, you wouldn't. And nobody else does, either, except for the old lady. She knows them all.'

The major reached into one of the dozen or so pockets that patched his jacket and pulled out a little silver flask. He offered me a taste and didn't mind when I declined. He sat himself down on a flat stone a few yards from the shack, where the grass of the point gave way to the stone dip that led down to the water's edge, and took a little swallow, smacking his lips with relish.

He gazed over the water of the bay out into the firth. The hulk of the *Cassandra* was a black curve in the silver blue, a great dead reminder of the storm in the spring. Between the shipwreck and Ardhmor, the water was calm, with hardly a ripple from the light sea breeze. Much further out there were two black buoys that marked the north sides of the shipping lanes for the decreasing number of boats that used the waterway up the firth to Glasgow.

Nearer in, about a mile offshore, a small dinghy was moored at anchor. I could just make out the yellow jacket of the angler, sitting hunched in the little boat, and if I strained hard I could see the rod he held over the side.

'That's the life,' Donald said. 'That and sailing and the wildlife. Give me them and a dram and some good singing company, and I'll never need anything else.'

I nodded in agreement. There were a few other things in life that I would have thrown in for good measure, like books and women and cool beer, but Donald was on the right track anyway.

'Oh, by the way,' he said, 'I'm planning to go up to the islands in a couple of weeks. Do you still want to come with me?'

'Yes, I'd love to. I could use the break. When are you planning to go?'

'Soon. Soon. They're just putting a new skin of paint on the old boat, so I'm planning to be away by the end of the month. Mind you, you'll have to work for your holiday. I need some young muscle.'

'Well, if you don't mind showing me the ropes. It's been a long time since I did any serious sailing.'

'Och, I'm only jocking,' he said. In his accent, it came out like 'choking'. 'I don't believe in all that heave-ho stuff. I've got a diesel engine in that beauty that would drive a bus to the islands. No, you come along for the company. Just as long as you can put up with my singing.'

'I think I'd rather be keel-hauled,' I told him, and he laughed so hard he almost choked on his sip of whisky. When his laughter subsided, and he wiped his eyes, Donald was about to say something else when out in the bay a movement caught his eye, and he raised an arm to point it out to me.

'Look, over there,' he said. 'The gannets. Just off the rock.'

Again I had to strain against the glare, looking out to

where his finger was pointing. At first I saw nothing, then a flash of white silver twinkled out over the water. A small flock of gannets was wheeling in the air over what must have been a shoal of sprats. They spun and turned, then, with their wings folded, they dropped like arrows, plunging into the blue waters, sending up tiny explosions of gleaming silver water.

'Ah, the lovely birds,' Donald said. He had his binoculars up to his eyes and was staring intently across the water, gently turning the focusing ring with his finger.

'Oh, look at that,' he muttered. 'Beautiful.'

To me they were just white dots in the distance. He was getting a close-up view. He stared rapturously for a few minutes, then realised the scene was practically lost on me because of the distance.

'Here, you have a look,' he said, unlooping the leather strap from around his neck, and handing the glasses over.

I put them up to my eyes, and the white dots swam into focus as great white birds. The binoculars were truly powerful. At that distance I could make out the yellow spears of their beaks and the black lines across their eyes as they wheeled in the air, catching the bright sun on their snow-white feathers. I would concentrate on one bird as it hung in the air, then it would turn, fold its wings and lance downwards.

With the glasses, I could easily follow the trajectory as the bird shot out its neck and speared the water like a missile, leaving nothing but a spray of spume. Perfectly designed bodies and beaks hunting through the shoal, the gannets were a beautiful sight.

'He won't be a happy man,' Donald said.

'Who?' I asked, still taking in the wheeling, plunging scene.

'The fisherman,' he said. 'He's in amongst them. They'll be scaring his catch away. He'll be cursing the birds.'

I handed Donald back the glasses and he swung them up to his eyes. Looking out, I could make out the birds – how small they were in the distance without the Zeiss's powerful magnification – now hunting close to the boat.

'Ha, I was right. He's trying to wave them away,' Donald snorted.

From out across the bay I could hear a faint noise. The furious angler was shouting at the birds that were wrecking his fishing. I saw some splashes close to the boat and turned to Donald, hoping for another shot of the glasses. The man's face could probably be picked out by the lenses. I wished I could see the expression on his face.

But even as I turned, the expression on Donald's face suddenly changed. His jaw dropped open and he let out a grunt of surprise.

'Good God would you . . .?' His voice trailed away. 'Dear God . . . it can't be . . . .'

'What's wrong?' I asked.

'The birds. The birds. They're . . . they're . . . .'

'They're what?' I asked. I hadn't a clue.'

'Look. Oh dear God. I don't believe it.'

I snatched the glasses out of his hands. In the split second before I raised them to my own eyes. I caught a glimpse of Donald. His face was white with shock. His mouth hung open in a slack circle and his eyes were wide and staring.

Again the white birds zoomed into view against the blue of the sky. I followed them down again and what I saw made my heart lurch so hard I almost dropped the glasses. Out there, nearly a mile from where we sat, the birds were spearing down out of the sky, but their target was not the shoal of sprats.

Their wings folded against their sides, they were lancing down with those great stabbing beaks and smashing into the fisherman in the boat.

As I watched, one bird plunged, its neck outstretched, and hit the man on the shoulder with a thump that I could feel across the distance. The beak drove straight through the coat and into the flesh and a gout of blood spattered the yellow of the coat and the white of the bird's feathers. The bird's wings beat for a second, and stopped, it's beak still jammed inside the man's body. Through the glasses I could see him waving his hand frantically as more birds lanced down. One of them hit the boat with a thump that I did hear rolling in across the smooth surface of the water. Another shot down and speared the man's stomach, and there was another great gout of blood.

An anguished scream, faint in the distance, but loud as all hell in my ears, came rending across on the wake of the other sound.

My eyes were jammed up against the glasses, mesmerised with the horror that was going on out there on the bay under the heat of the sun. Beside me I was dimly aware of Donald muttering curses and prayers, all in a jumble.

A white bird lanced across my field of vision, driving its beak into the bottom of the little wooden boat that was now rocking violently on the still water. Again came the muffled thump of the impact. The man in the boat was jerking about in agony, all red and yellow. I couldn't make out his face, which was turned away from me, but I could see his jaw working, stretching his mouth wide in what must have been a despairing scream. Just then his head turned towards me, splattered with blood, and as it did there was a flurry of white as another gannet plunged down. Its spear of a beak plunged straight across my line of sight, driving with phenomenal accuracy into the circular target that was the man's open mouth. The angler's head snapped back and more blood splattered. With a rising lurch of nausea, I saw the huge beak sticking straight out of the back of the man's neck.

I dropped the glasses from the eyes, the spell broken. Something inside my stomach gave way and my lunch promptly expelled itself, spattering on to the rock where I sat.

'Oh, fuck,' I said, helplessly.

Donald was still sitting, staring out across the bay. His eyes were still wide and he was shaking his head slowly, as if to deny the reality of what he had just seen.

In my throat, the bile was burning.

'They can't do that,' Donald said in a voice that was just a moan. 'Gannets don't do that.'

I couldn't think of anything to say. There were just no words, just pictures in my head, instant action replays of what we had just seen. My stomach lurched and heaved again, but there was nothing there.

Out in the bay, the action had stopped. Donald reached over and slowly took the glasses from my hands, prising them slowly out of my numb fingers, and raised them again, almost fearfully, to his eyes.

'It's stopped,' he said. 'They're all dead. And so is he. It's terrible. Just terrible.'

He stared through the glasses for a long time, then he said: 'It's sinking. The boat. It's going down.'

He handed me the glasses again. I didn't want to look, but I couldn't stop myself.

The dreadful scene swam into focus. Only minutes before it had been a wonderful picture of nature's beauty. The wheeling and diving of the beautiful white birds, so fitted for their way of life. Now there was a little boat, listing to one side, and in it was a red and white and yellow mess, tattered feathers and tattered clothing, the bodies of the birds and man bent and broken and torn. As I watched, the boat sank further in the water, tilting slowly until one gunwale was beneath the surface. Then it seemed to heave and in seconds it had disappeared, leaving a faint streak of pink in the bubbling water.

The bubbles soon stopped and the surface became calm again. There was nothing there, except for a few white and red feathers that floated on the surface, and soon scattered in the gentle breeze.

'Here. Take the glasses. There's nothing left,' I said, handing them back to Donald. He was still shaking his head numbly.

'How could that have happened?'

'I don't know,' I said. I was lying. There was no coincidence in this at all. Right at that moment I almost got a full-focus glimpse of the big picture. Almost, but not quite.

'We'd better go and tell them about this,' Donald said.

'I don't think they'll believe us,' I told him.

'But we have to, anyway. We have to.' Donald's face was chalk white. That terrible scene had robbed him of his appreciation of the wonders of nature. It had stolen his picture of the rightness of things, the beauty of the natural world.

It was only adding to my picture of one that was not natural at all.

Murdo Morrison, the sergeant up at the little police station, took our statements, slowly writing down everything we said in his neat, painstaking way, occasionally looking up, and glancing from Donald to me and back down at his sheet.

'And you say the birds attacked him?' he asked.

'That's right,' Donald said. The shock had begun to wear off a bit. 'Gannets.'

'Gannets actually flew down and, er, hit him? Stabbed him with their beaks?'

'That's what happened.'

'But seabirds don't do that.'

'Well, they do now,' Donald said, almost angrily. 'I've been watching the birds for forty years and they never did that before, not until today. But it happened.' Donald's voice had risen steadily during that statement.

'All right, don't get yourself all worked up. I didn't say I don't believe you,' Murdo said. He hadn't said it, but he certainly didn't believe it. I noticed when he was questioning me that he leaned in very close, as if to pick out every word. It was only later I realised he was trying to smell my breath. He probably caught a sniff of Donald's whisky, but there was nothing on me, and I knew, and it should have been apparent, despite the tale both of us were trying to tell him, that Donald was more sober than he'd ever been in his life.

Murdo took our statement, then said he'd be in touch. Donald asked him what he was going to do, and the policeman said he'd send out the inshore lifeboat to have a look round. He was as good as his word. Dave King took the boat out and quartered the calm bay for hours, and came up with nothing, not a sign. Murdo had quite wisely told him only that a boat had been in difficulties. He hadn't mentioned anything about gannets. Donald and I told the lifeboat cox exactly where the fishing boat had sunk, and the orange inflatable crisscrossed the area in ever widening circles until it had checked out the whole of the bay. There was nothing to be found.

Murdo called us back to the station that night and asked us to go through it with him again. We did. He asked us straight if we had been drinking, or smoking anything unusual. No, we told him, we hadn't. He looked as bewildered as a big, canny village policeman could manage. What we had told him took a lot of believing.

The next morning we were back in his office at his request. He wanted us to describe the boat, which we did in a limited fashion. You don't remember paint colours when a flock of birds are breaking all the laws of nature and spearing a man to death. We could tell him roughly what the boat was like, and what the man seemed to be wearing.

He wrote all this down again on the forms, nodding to himself as he did so.

When he had finished, he looked up and said: 'It's a strange tale to be coming to me with.'

'I know that Murdo. A terrible tale. But it's the truth,' Donald assured him.

'Aye, well maybe it is, and maybe it isn't. And before you say I'm calling you a liar just let me finish,' he said, and Donald sat back in his chair.

'I can't say you didn't see something out there, but I've got to tell you I'm not happy about sending this report to the fiscal. Not yet anyway, until there's something to show from the search. So I'll hold on to it for a day or two, just in case.'

'That's fine with me,' I said, wearily. 'I didn't think anybody would believe us.'

'Well, that's another matter. But in the meantime, we've got a search going on. It seems that one of Davy McGlynn's boats was hired out yesterday and the man hasn't brought it back. A Glasgow fellow down for a day's fishing. Davy tells me he was wearing a yellow oilskin.'

'That'll be the man,' Donald came in. 'A yellow coat with a hood.'

'Aye, that's what it seems like. We'll keep looking, but as a favour to me I'd like you to keep your story just between the three of us, just in case there's been a mistake.'

I agreed for the both of us and got Donald out of there before he started on the sergeant. The island man was a stolid, placid type, stocky and strong, but I could see he was still carrying the vision of what had happened out there on the bay, and he didn't like anybody telling him he'd made a mistake.

The search went on and Davy McGlynn's little dinghy didn't show up. There was not a trace of it, or the Glasgow man who had hired it for his fishing. Nobody was reported missing, and other events left the incident behind.

It was not until November that the currents threw the boat up on the rocks at Kilcreggan, some miles away. And on the same rocks, a bunch of children found the remains of the fisherman, and the remains of the birds, still tangled and nailed together in death as they had been on the day when Donald and I had watched the man die in agony and terror. By then, there was no point in telling Murdo we had told him so.

THIRTEEN

Kitty's box lay on the dresser beside my bed until the night after Murdo Morrison told us about the missing angler. In the afternoon I had visited her in hospital, but she was asleep the whole time, lying gaunt and frail, still with a drip connected to the vein in her hand, and a new one that they'd put in her nostril. Doctor Goodwin, the man I'd spoken to before, met me in the passing in the corridor outside, just as I was leaving. I stopped him briefly to ask about Kitty's condition.

He hummed and hawed a bit, taking off his glasses and putting them back on again. 'We're not quite sure yet,' he finally said. 'My first diagnosis was some sort of meningococcal infection, or inflammation, but the tests haven't shown anything so far. She's got a high temperature and a severe loss of body fluids, and of course, she's very weak. I'll need some more time before we know for sure.' He hurried away in a flapping of his white coat and disappeared beyond two fire doors that swished shut behind him. I went home and opened her little box.

Inside, it was plain red wood, and it contained an odd jumble of bits and pieces, objects of interest that she had no doubt picked up along her way.

There was a little book, bound in leather, with pages written in a neat, tight script, the early ones faded to light blue and even brown in some cases. The ones further on got bolder until, towards the end, they were sharply delineated in black. There were some small, water-smoothed stones, of varying colours, that had been beautifully etched with patterns of animals. I wondered if she had worked those stones herself. There was a piece of amber, which I recognised, for amber is one of my favourite stones. This one had been cut in a flat cabochon, and at first I thought there was a flaw on the major, flat plane. But I was wrong. Inside was a tiny fly, embedded in the clear stone, perfect and undamaged as it had been at the moment of its death millions of years before!

It was the name on the white envelope that caught my eye, as I curiously rummaged – still feeling graverobber's guilt – among the contents. My name, written again in that neat script. The words had rung in my subconscious even before I had actually looked at them, in the way that a phrase will stick in your mind as your eye flicks over a newspaper, caught in a flash of peripheral vision.

Nicholas Westford Ryan

I picked out the envelope and looked at it, blankly, for a moment or two. There was no other message, just my name.

In my drawer by the bedside, there was an old horn-handled penknife that my grandfather had given me as a youngster. The blade was still sharp from years of honing, and the slightly curved handle was smoothly worn from a lifetime's handling. It had a small, silver shield embedded in the horn, with the initials N.W. intertwined in flowing calligraphy. I'd had that knife on or about me since I was little, when my grandfather had overruled my mother's objections about little boys with knives, and had presented me with the knife I had envied.

The biggest of the three slim blades snicked open with a flick of a thumbnail and I eased it along the top fold, slicing the envelope open cleanly on the edge. Inside there was a number of pages of plain white paper, and I started to read.

Nick,

So much to say and so little time to say it. You are reading this, so therefore assume that I am gone on the long journey. Tonight, my bones ache and I'm cold. It will not be long. I have seen it coming, and other things.

The long night is beginning in this place, as it has before. I fear the morning will be long in coming. But if you are the one, then the dawn will come.

Watch the walls. Watch the walls, as I have watched them these fifty years and more. They are for you and the others, the rings to bind the Cu Sæng. Those fools that dig do not know what they do. Put back the stones, as I did. Plant the haw berries as I have. This is important. *Watch the walls.*

Now. You still see but your eyes have no vision. The vision will come. Read the book, it has my history. And that is your history. If only I had the time to teach you the writing on the stone. Then you would see.

In 1961, when I lifted you out from the rocks, you and the others had almost died. Look in the box and you will find the stone that you had in your hand. Remember! It is an old stone. It is your stone. Take it.

Take also the torc, that was my mother's, and her mother's back to the time of Cu-Chulain. The torc protects. Take it.

Remember. You watch the walls. You are the walls. And I will watch you from where I am.

Your friend.

Catriona O'MacConnor MacBeatha

I read the pages over again a couple of times. Kitty obviously thought she was dying. From the look of her, pale and still on that hospital bed, she was in no great shape.

But what did the letter mean? I knew what she was getting at. But what did she really want me to do? After watching those seagulls out there on the water, I was stunned and shaken and horrified enough to realise that my feeling of impending doom was rapidly racing towards proof. What I had seen had shaken my belief in the rightness of things, as it had with the tough little ex-major. The unnatural had happened, the unthinkable.

But what was I to do about it? I must confess that I was still floundering in a miasma, feet clogged in the mire.

I folded the letter neatly, and slotted it back into the envelope, which I put on the dresser. As I leaned across, something else caught my eye among the tangle in the box. Gold. I reached down and lifted it from the odds and ends. It was a thin, gold rod that had a ball at each end and had been curved until the two golden spheres almost met each other in a near-complete circle. A torc. A Celtic circlet. Beautiful in the simplicity of its design. I had seen one similar to this in the museum in Glasgow, but that one had been slightly dented and scratched from eons underground. This one was gleaming and glowing with a purity that spoke of real, unmixed gold, delicate and strong. It could have been made by a craftsman only yesterday. I had no reason to doubt that this was the torc that Kitty had told me to have, and I had less reason to doubt that it had been in her family for generations. How many I couldn't begin to count. And it had been passed on to me by that old lady who was lying sick and maybe dying in the cottage hospital. I laid it beside the letter and went back to the box.

I moved aside some of the polished stones, granite and feldspar, maybe a smooth garnet. There was an old, gold wedding ring that looked its age. Was it Kitty's? Had she been married?

The box tilted slightly, and something heavy and black slid from one corner to the other, clunking solidly as it connected with the wooden side. I picked it out, hefting its weight in my hand. It was a flat, black stone, almost the size of my hand, smooth as glass and wedge shaped. The thinner end of the wedge had been smoothed and worked to a sharp edge, just like a spear-head. Just as I thought that, I realised that was exactly what it was – an obsidian spear-head, worked by a stone-age craftsman from volcanic glass, shiny and perfect. A work of art, warming in the perfect fit of my hand.

I had seen one of these before, somewhere. Where? When? I could not remember, but there was something stirring at the back of my mind. I stared at the beautiful stone in my hand, and there was a soft click deep inside, as a door opened in my mind and light started to shine through.

FOURTEEN

Summer 1961.
*Sausages sizzled in the bottom of the old, battered frying pan,
sending up a delicious aroma that combined with the pine and oak
twigs that hardly smoked at all as they burnt in the little circle of
stone.*

'Sausages is the boys,' Colin said, sniffing the tang of crackling
fat. He was stirring the embers on the other side of the fire to make
a flat space for the equally battered little saucepan that was filled
with baked beans.

'I'm starving,' I said. 'I haven't eaten for hours.' That wasn't
true, but it sure felt like it.

'Real commandos can go for days without food, and still fight,'
Colin asserted. Today he was a commando. Today, we were on a
three-man mission of derring-do. Our gang hut was now our fox-
hole beside the stream. Sausages and beans were iron rations. My
bow was a rifle. Colin's spear of rowan was a bayonet. Barbara
was so far unarmed, because her father had confiscated her slingshot
after he'd lost a pane of glass in his greenhouse. That miss-hit had
almost put paid to our adventure in the woods at Strowan's Water.
Doctor Foster disapproved of his daughter hanging around with the
likes of us kids from down the hill, but we kept a diplomatic distance between ourselves and him, and the one and onlies were still
a threesome.

'They live off the land,' Colin said. 'You can send them anywhere and they can find their own food, rabbits and deer and everything.'

'And berries and mushrooms,' Barbara said. 'I can find berries
and mushrooms.'

'Berries don't go with sausages,' I chipped in.

'But mushrooms do,' Barbara said. 'I know where there's
plenty. I could live off the land.'

202

'They're probably poisonous toadstools,' I told her. Barbara was already starting off down the path.

'Some of them can kill you just by looking at them,' I said.

'Naw, you have to touch them first,' Colin refuted. 'And then you can make a cut where you've been touched and suck out all the poison.'

'What about the poison in your mouth?'

'That's easy. You just spit it out.'

'I don't fancy that much. If you touch one of them, you can suck your own poison out.'

'Some commando you are,' Colin snorted. 'They're supposed to defend each other to the death.'

'What if your tongue got poisoned when you sucked it out?'

'Then you'd go dumb, dummy,' Colin said, laughing at his pun. 'And then you wouldn't be able to ask a lot of silly questions.'

He got a slender stick and started rolling the pink sausages over, exposing the dark brown, sizzling undersides. Then with the same stick he stirred the beans. They were just starting to bubble.

'Look what I've got,' Barbara called from a little way down the track. 'There's hundreds.'

She came striding up, bright and smiling, her hair bobbing with her gait. She had an armful of big oatmeal-capped mushrooms.

'They're toadstools,' I said. 'They'll make you dumb.'

'Don't be daft, that's only after you suck the poison out,' Colin retorted.

'No, they're mushrooms,' Barbara said. 'They're just the same as the ones my mum gets. Isn't that right, Colin?' she added, looking to him for support.

Colin stood up, backing away from the fire, and he wiped the smoke out of his eyes. His face was streaked with the tears that had poured down his cheeks when we first lit the fire and the smoke had billowed into all our faces.

'Let me see,' he said. Barbara kneeled down and let her load spill from her hands on to the grass.

'They look all right to me,' Colin announced. 'My Aunt May picks mushrooms up here, and they're just the same as them. They're OK.'

To prove it, he picked up one of the big mushrooms and sniffed it, then bit a piece off, chewing quickly, like an expert tasting truffles. His tongue didn't go black at all and that settled it.

I used my penknife and sliced up the caps and we threw a lot of them into the fat with the sausages. They quickly went from white to grey, fat mushroom steaks that added their tantalising smell to the already mouthwatering mix.

We ate the lot, along with the beans and the sausages, scooping them out of the pans and on to the enamelled tin plates that formed part of our survival cache in the little hidden lean-to. Every mouthful was a delight. Afterwards, Barbara brewed up some tea in a dried-milk tin that we had punctured at the top to take a wire handle. We debated as to how much tea we should put in, because none of us were experts in that field, and there was brief argument over who forgot the milk, but the arguments faded as we sat in the shade of the huge beech tree and scalded our mouths on the tarry brew.

We decided to wait until it had cooled down. The plates were lying at the edge of the stream, lightly covered in the gravel which would help scour them clean of our outdoors dinner. Colin asked to borrow my knife and I warned him not to lose it and he promised to guard it with his life. He strode down to the stream edge and cut off a stem of saxifrage that swayed over the still water of a sunlit pool, and brought it back to where Barbara and I were gingerly taking sips of the smoke-blackened tin.

'Making a peashooter?' I asked. Colin cut the corrugated hollow stem into a little open-ended tube.

'Nope.'

'What then?' I asked.

'Wait and see, nosey,' he said, cutting the fragile tube with the sharp blade. Barbara and I watched curiously as he took a piece of bread from the slices I'd filched from the kitchen and nipped off a morsel between his finger and thumb. This he jammed into the base of the tube.

'Right, now watch this,' he said. Colin took the bag of tea and poured some out into his hand. I could see his tongue – still undamaged from the mushrooms – sticking out of the corner of his mouth as he concentrated on the delicate task of funnelling the tea into the open end of the tube. When he was done, he reached over to the fire, shielding his face from the heat of the flame, and stuck

the thing into the red base where the coals gleamed red. It immediately started to smoulder and he hissed to himself as the heat
started to sear his hand. He pulled back quickly.

'Right. Watch this,' he ordered, and sat back against the bole of
the tree and put the end of the saxifrage stem in his mouth. From
where I sat, only a foot or so away, I could smell the aniseed aroma
of the smouldering plant, and another, bitter-sweet smell which I
assumed was the tea. Colin sucked hard through the plug of bread,
and we watched in amazement when he blew out a thick cloud of
blue smoke.

'Great smoke,' he said, and then coughed a little.

'Where did you learn that?' I asked. 'I didn't know you
smoked.'

'Trade secret,' Colin said. 'Want to try it?'

Barbara screwed up her nose, then reached out and took the
smouldering stem from Colin. She sucked in hard, and then went
on to a paroxysm of coughing.

'Too much,' he said, and started beating her on the back. As far
I could see it wasn't helping the cough any. It took her a few
moments for the coughing fit to subside. Colin took back his
extraordinary cigar and said, 'Watch this.' He put it to his lips and
pursed them around it, and his cheeks caved in with the vacuum.
Then, to our astonishment, he blew out two blue plumes of smoke
from his nostrils. It reminded me of a picture in a book where a
dragon puffed out jets, and I started to giggle.

'Here, you try it,' he said, and handed it to me. I did. There was a
definite liquorice-aniseed taste from the smoke, and another that
was strange, and not at all unpleasant. As soon as the smoke filled
my mouth, I could feel saliva welling up, and when I blew out the
cloud, I had an immediate need to spit it. It landed on one of the
hot stones that ringed the fire and sizzled loudly and satisfyingly.

Barbara had another try, and this time she didn't cough, then we
all had shots each, passing it around like I would much later in sociable
company.

'Right. Take in some smoke. Not too much,' Colin said, dem-
onstrating. His voice was wheezy when his cheeks were full of
fumes. 'Then,' he said, smoke dribbling out as he did so, 'suck in.'
He took a big breath and it all disappeared inside him. When he

blew it out again, it was grey, not blue. I wondered how that happened. It took Barbara three tries, and me five, to get the hang of it. The smoke burned my throat, and I could feel my lungs starting to swell, but it was a nice sensation. The saliva ran, and we all spat intermittently into the fire and on to the hot stones, relishing the hiss as it evaporated.

I blew a smoke ring, and the other two fell about, helpless with laughter. I tried, but I couldn't repeat the action. We giggled together, sharing the tea-filled steam, and didn't notice at all that everything was getting hazy.

'Great shmoke,' Barbara said, and Colin nearly wet his jeans.

'Triffic,' I agreed, to another gale of laughter. Colin laughed so hard he fell over, and lay staring up into the trees, his belly shaking in spasms. I leaned back against the tree and wondered why everything went in and out of focus. Barbara, who had been sitting on a gnarled root, slowly slid off, landing with a gentle thud on the dry grass, and that set us all off again.

And a few moments later, the world started to sway and spin and I shot away from it in a blaze of colour that swirled and sparkled in front of my eyes and . . . .

I squatted at the edge of the stream, watching the sunlight catch the expanding rings from where the fish had risen to dipple the surface. Rings of gold, ever moving outwards. I was in a glade where the sun shone between the tops of huge trees. In front of me, the field was gone. Instead there were big-boled beeches and massive firs, wide and monstrous, marching up and over the hill and on for ever. I could see between their great trunks, but only for a little distance into that forest, for it was gloomy in there, dark and shadowed. The sun shone where I sat by the edge of the water, watching the slow movement of trout, big and fat, lazy in the pool.

I looked around me, curious, yet accepting that I was alone. This was a strange place, yet not strange. Familiar and unfamiliar. The big stone where Barbara had sat like the little mermaid was still there, but the stream was different. The trees were tall and mighty, bigger even than the gnarled beech that we'd been sitting under.

Somewhere downstream a bird called, a hooting cry that echoed among the trunks, and there was a reply from further away.

206

Behind me, something crashed through the trees, and I turned to look into the forest behind me, but there was nothing but shadow. I sat still for what seemed an age, and then a movement caught my eye, a flash of dark in peripheral vision. For some reason, I did not move, only sliding my eyes to where the movement was. Out of the trees, slowly and majestically, came a huge stag, the king of all stags, bigger even than the huge Clydesdale that towered over the hedges up at Kilmalid Farm. If I had stood up, my head would not have even reached its belly. I stayed rock still, and so did the deer, standing like a huge dark shadow as it surveyed the glade. Its nostrils flared like black tunnels as it sniffed the air, and its ears turned and twisted, quartering for danger. Satisfied, it slowly emerged from the gloom, one slow step at a time, grand and dignified, and as it came out into the light I almost gasped in wonder. For on its head it bore an impossible spread of antlers that I hadn't noticed in the background shade and tangle of branches. They were immense, a great two-handed sweep of pronged bones that were almost, to my eyes, as wide as a road. The far edge of one of them lightly scraped against the trunk of a fir tree, cutting a neat gash that started to drip resin. Out into the light, one silent step after another, the giant stag came towards the stream. And behind it followed another huge beast, though by comparison much smaller. Walking carefully behind the second beast was a slender fawn, tawny and speckled, picking up its dainty hooves with light, jerky motions of its impossibly spindly legs. The stag was magnificent, the fawn simply beautiful.

It followed its parents down to the waterside where the stag drew itself and its great antlers up high to scan the clearing, then, satisfied, bent down to drink, snuffling noisily at the clear water. The doe and the fawn followed suit, lapping thirstily. They drank copiously, then something seemed to startle the baby. With a smooth, clean jerk, it raised its head up from the water, its ear fanning like radar, and it looked round. Then one huge black eye, infinitely gentle, found mine, and stared. It was like looking into a pool. For long moments we watched each other, the fawn standing stock still, and me afraid to breathe, then it bent back to drink. Finally, the stag lifted its magnificent head and shook its thick mane, sending droplets of water scattering, then it walked across the bed of the stream, its hooves clattering on the hard rock. The doe and the fawn followed and the three animals moved into the forest and were lost in the shadow.

Only the glistening water that their hooves had splashed on the stones of the stream, now quickly evaporating in the sun, marked their passage. For a long time, my eyes were fixed on the spot where they had entered the shadow, hoping that they would come back, but they must have been far away. From somewhere in that general direction, far in the distance, a deep, bellowing roar, that kind of rumbling, numbing growl that you hear from lions in the zoo, came rolling through the trees, muffled by distance, but powerful and hard. There was a tearing screech and another bellow, this time a lowing, high and despairing. The lowing sound suddenly stopped, cut off. Then there was a silence that seemed to go on for ever, and then the birds in the trees started singing and twittering again. I turned back to the stream and looked into the water again, and in the water I saw a shape, dark and looming, wavering on the surface. It was a reflection, and when I looked up, there was a man standing there, staring at me with black eyes. Tall and broad, with a ragged, hairy animal's pelt that had a hole cut in it where his grizzled head popped through. A strip of different skin cinched the garment together at the waist, and there were other strips that formed boots with leggings. He carried some sort of satchel and in his hand was a long curved bow and a straight spear. The man's hair was long and straggly and tangled, just like his beard, and his arms were matted with a thick pelt.

Our eyes locked. I felt no fear. For some reason this was not a man to be afraid of. He looked at me, right into the back of my mind, reading all of me that there was to be read. Then he nodded big and broad, and as dignified as the stag that had glided out of the gloom.

With one hand, he took the spear from the clutter of bows and arrows and hefted it. The sun sent shards of light from the long, black head. He stared at me, without malice, but with an expression of infinite wisdom; then he swung his arm up high. I could see the muscles on his forearm bulge as he gripped the shaft tightly – then his whole arm flashed in a blur as he launched his spear towards me. And still I was unafraid. The wind from that spear tousled my hair in the passing, and I heard the hissing as it cut the air. There was a loud thud and I didn't turn around. I could hear the shaft of the spear thrumming as it vibrated with the impact. I kept looking at the man's eyes, and he kept looking at mine for a long time until the reflections of the sun on the water made them water and the world blurred in a riot of gold and green and then went right out of focus.

Everything slowly started to emerge from grey and I opened my eyes again. The sunlight was dancing up from the ripples the tiny fish were making, bright sunlight that came from the direction of the trees. But the trees were gone. The field, with its short, cropped grass and the buttercups and clover, was back, with its hoof-tracks and its cowpats. And I was back again.

Colin was sitting with his back against the big gnarled root of the beech tree. His sloppy-joe had risen up as he'd slid down against the bark, exposing a slice of his tanned belly. There was a dark blue patch on his jeans at the knee, a deeper shade than the rest of the weathered and well-washed denim. His feet were splayed out and one baseball boot, black and white and red and wearing thin at the sole, was slowly swaying from side to side. Colin's eyes were half shut, and I could see a glimmer in the dark where his iris was throwing back the light. There was a half smile on his face.

Barbara was lying down, spread out on the short grass next to him, her arms wide and her feet together. There were leaves in her hair and, though her eyes were closed, there was a radiant smile, an expression of joy that lit up her whole face. Her jeans, newer and better kept than Colin's, had muddy patches on the knees.

My head felt full of cotton wool, clouds that were very slowly dispersing. There was a buzzing in my ears, a deep tickly vibration that was more of a feeling than a noise, as if a bee had got into the back of my head and was busy spreading honey in there.

Colin muttered something, low and jumbled, the way children do when they talk in their sleep. I couldn't make it out, but as I turned to look at him, his eyes flicked wide open. His eyes were glazed at first, then seemed to find their focus. He shook his head, and put his hands up to his temples and screwed his eyes up tight, very much the way a man with a bad hangover does at the moment of awakening.

'Jeez-O,' he said softly. He took his hand down from his head and looked around him, looking a little shaken and a bit bewildered. 'Where are we?'

I was about to answer, still feeling as if the white clouds were drifting about inside me, as if my voice would come out all soft and cottony, if it came out at all, when Colin said: 'At the gang hut.'

He nodded, confirming it to himself; getting his bearings. 'The gang hut. Jeez-O. I must've fell asleep.'

'Me too,' I said, and my voice was all cottony, sticking at the back of my throat. My lungs felt stiff.

'Weird,' Colin said, this time with vehemence. 'What a dream! A knight in shining armour with a big gold sword. Like Lancelot. Or Galahad. A black knight. He was terrible.'

Colin stopped and looked around. Barbara had made a noise, and she was trying to raise her head up from the carpet of green. It slumped back sleepily at first, then she too seemed to shake her head to clear it. The radiant smile was still there.

'Ooooh. Beautiful,' she murmured with a sigh. 'She was beautiful.'

'Who was?' Colin said.

'The lady with the flowers.'

'What lady?'

'She came to me with flowers. Golden flowers, just like her hair. Didn't you see her?'

'Nope,' Colin and I said together.

'You must have,' Barbara said. 'She was there. Right there.' Barbara pointed at the bank of the stream. There was nothing there.

'You've been dreaming,' Colin said. 'We must have fell asleep.'

'Fallen asleep,' Barbara corrected him absently, her voice still soft and dreamy.

'Oh, she was so beautiful and kind. She put the flowers round my neck, like a daisy chain, and smiled at me.' Barbara's hand slipped up to her neck, feeling the skin.

'It was there,' she said, and her voice lost the dreamy quality. Now it had the tinge of ache of a lost dream.

'I dreamed I saw a knight with a sword. And he was riding around waving it and shouting at people. He was fighting everybody and chopping at them with the sword and they were screaming. He was terrible.'

'The hunter,' I said, and they both looked at me. 'A hunter. That's what he was. He came here, to me, out of the trees, over there.' I pointed.

'What trees?' Colin asked.

'There was trees. Big forest there,' I pointed across the stream. 'He came out and stood there and looked at me, and then he threw something at me.' I paused. That wasn't right. 'No. He threw something to me. A spear.'

I had been sitting down. In my mind's eye, the man in the furs and skins was still standing on the far bank. I heard the swish and felt the wind again as the long spear raked the air. I heard the thud and the thrumming vibration, and I knew where the spear had hit.

I scrambled on to my knees and crawled a few feet away from the others towards the bank. The turf was dry and hard.

'It landed right here,' I said, feeling the grass and earth with the palms of my hands.

'What did?' Barbara asked. The dreamy tone was gone from her voice. Colin was just staring at me as if I'd gone crazy.

'The spear. He threw it here. He wanted me to have it.'

'It was just a dream,' Colin said. 'I'm not smoking any of that stuff again. It gives you scary dreams.'

'Mine wasn't scary,' Barbara said, almost defiantly. 'And it must have been the mushrooms. They give you a belly-ache and you get dreams.'

'That's cheese,' Colin said. 'Cheese makes you dream.'

'And mushrooms too,' Barabara argued. 'I saw it in one of my dad's books, so there.'

All this was going on in the periphery. I was still on my knees, and there was something inside of me that knew, with clear certainty, that I had to rip up the turf right here where I was kneeling. I struggled with that long ruler-pocket in the leg of my working-man's cut-down jeans and worked my old penknife up the material until the horn handle poked out. I grabbed it and pulled out the big blade and started cutting a square of the turf.

'You'll break the blade, idiot features,' Colin said. He'd recovered from whatever was scary in his dream. I hadn't quite recovered from mine. Barbara's was real enough for her to watch me non-committally.

211

'Don't care. It was here. I saw it,' I said, sawing away rapidly, up and down, not caring if the old treasured blade was rasped down to a blunt nubbin. When the square was cut, I grasped the grass at the edge of one of the lines and started hauling, feeling my nails bend backwards under the strain.

'Oh, let me,' Colin said resignedly, as if he'd decided he wanted to humour me. The two of us tugged and then the turf came up with a rip, like wet cloth rending, and we fell backwards. The red square of earth underneath was just earth. Nothing more. I started to dig again with the blade of my knife, but Colin stopped me.

'That will break the blade. Here, use a stick,' he said, handing me the one he'd cut for an arrow. He'd whittled a sharp point on one end and I took it and started to hook the dirt out of the hole. In a few minutes I'd gone down about six inches, and there was nothing there. Colin and Barbara were watching me, and I felt a flush of embarrassment. The image in the dream had started to slip slowly away, and suddenly I started to feel as if I were making a fool of myself.

'Let me at it,' Colin said just as I was about to stop digging to spare myself further ridicule.

Colin's tanned arms jabbed up and down, hooking at the hole. Within minutes he was panting with the effort. Then the rasping of the stick in the dirt stopped and there was a little clicking sound and Colin's arms seemed to jar all the way up to the shoulders.

'Ow,' he yelled as the stick broke halfway up and he lurched forward, both hands plunging right into the dirt. Barbara and I scuttled across to the hole. The broken arrow had reached rocks, two big quartz stones that would become white when the rain washed off their coating of dirt. Between them, jammed upright, there was a thin, black, smooth stone, lodged in the narrow space between the two rounded boulders.

I reached past Colin and grasped the stone and tugged. It didn't budge and I had to work it back and forth about nine or ten times before it gave up its grip and came free.

'That's it!' I yelled. 'That's what he had!'

'What is it?' Barbara asked.

'Just a stupid lump of rock,' Colin said. 'Not worth all that hard work.'

'No. You're wrong,' I said coldly. It had been there. I walked to the stream, right to the edge where I'd been sitting, mesmerised by the sun in my dream, and knelt down with that flat stone in my hand. It was long and smooth, and rimed with caked-on dirt. I plunged both of my hands into the clear water and rubbed at the black stone's surface, watching the water go cloudy and brown as the earth washed off. It took only moments of rubbing the stone with my thumbs to clean it, for the dirt had no crevices to cling to. Then I lifted it from the water and turned triumphantly to Colin and Barbara, holding the stone in both my hands like a trophy.

The sun ricocheted off the polished surface, making it gleam bright and black.

'Hey man,' Colin whooped. 'It's a stone-axe. A real caveman's axe.'

'No, it's a spear. A point for a spear. And that's where he threw it in my dream.'

'I don't believe it,' said Colin.

'Me neither,' I said, and although I held the weight in my hands, marvelling at its smooth surface and beautiful simplicity, I didn't believe it.

'But it's ours,' I said.

FIFTEEN

There was a click in my head, and I was back again. But when I'd picked up that piece of smooth volcanic glass, it was as if I'd walked through that door into summer, taking the short route, a seven-league step right back to childhood.

I had flown back to *then*. I was *there*. Small and skinny, with Colin and Barbara, the original one and onlies. The image was so clear I could feel the grass under my feet, and smell the clover and hear the gurgling of that clear stream in the valley. Where had Kitty MacBeth found the stone? It was the same one, I was sure. Twenty years had passed, and there must have been many polished spearheads, lying under the dirt for people to dig up or turn up with their ploughs in this place that was steeped in human history since the dawn of time. There must have been others that were *like* it. But this stone from Kitty's box wasn't like it. Not merely similar, crafted in the same simple fashion.

Something in me knew that this was the same stone. The one that the huge man with the wise eyes and the raggedy skins had come in a dream to give. This was our stone. Our magic stone.

It was the one and only.

I sat and felt its smoothness, warm and hard where it picked up the heat of my hand and radiated it back to me. More than twenty years later, I was getting some sort of pre-cognition, a feeling of foreboding. Prescience is a terrific facility in hindsight. Everybody gets the occasional feeling of déjà vu: Jimmy Allison had a *feeling* that a Bad Summer was creeping up on Arden. The monsignor in the seminary, the old soldier turned crusader, had the feeling too. Kitty MacBeth went much further. She named the beast. The Cu Saeng. The ravener, the dweller under the roots, an old earth god that the people had brought into the world to fight their fights. Cu Saeng, trapped between the earth and what lay underneath it by chants and magics and powerful boundaries.

Yes, Kitty MacBeth knew a thing or two, and as I held that smooth black stone in my hand the juggernaut, the engine of death, was rolling towards Arden, and it hitched up into a higher gear, gaining speed all the way.

Kitty MacBeth, Catriona O'MacConnor MacBeatha, the last of the Sons of Conchobar and the Sons of Life, whose people had been in this place since *forever*, died in the cottage hospital. She never regained full consciousness since the time she'd told me to go and find her box. Doctor Bell, the resident who ran the two small wards, could do nothing for her at all, except pump in antibiotics and vitamins. Kitty just burned up with a fever that he couldn't identify despite the tests for bacteria and virus. There was no real reason, he told me, why she should have died, but she did, and that was that.

The nurse on the ward, a round and ruddy-faced smiling girl, told me that she'd been there at her desk, working on her notes under the swan-neck night-light, when the old woman had cried out in her delirium.

The girl had got up from her seat and gone to the bedside. Kitty was lying on her bed, heat radiating from her body and her head twisting spasmodically from side to side.

'She kept asking me who sang,' the nurse said. ' "Who sang?" all the time. I told her there was nobody singing and that she must have been dreaming. Then she grabbed at my wrist, really tight. So hard I had a bruise the next day.'

The nurse unconsciously rubbed her hand over her arm.

'But she kept on asking me. Then she opened her eyes and looked right at me, but I don't think she saw me at all. "Who sang is here," she said. And then her eyes just closed. She seemed to go back to sleep, but about an hour or so later I went back to check on her and she had slipped away. I'm sorry.'

I thanked the nurse and went out of the hospital into the bright sunlight. From the front steps, I could see past the houses on the other side of the street and across Westbay to the firth. I felt a sense of grievous loss that I couldn't explain. I jammed my hands into the pockets of my jeans and went down the steps, blinking hard to hold back the upwelling. Big boys don't cry. The little boy in me, the one who had been evoked when he held Kitty's black stone, felt he must.

The harvest festival came a week later, four days after Kitty MacBeth's quiet funeral in the little cemetery between the north side of the Milligs and the wood at the hill that led to Upper Arden. This was where the old parish church had stood until the fire of the Reformation. The walls were a jumble of rocks, but the churchyard remained inside the dry-stone walls. Kitty's grave went unmarked as yet, but I ordered a polished granite. It would be another four weeks or so before the stone was cut and put in place, so Kitty went into an unmarked grave for the moment, but it was a grave that she herself had owned, according to the parish clerk.

I had expected a quiet funeral. After all, Kitty had no family, and what friends did the old woman have here in Arden?

So I was gratified – and surprised – when I followed the hearse from the little undertaker's parlour and saw a line of cars following on behind. Jimmy Allison stood beside me at the graveyard, still a bit red-eyed and snuffling from the cold or flu that had sat on him for these past days. The major was there too, saying farewell to his fellow nature-lover. The monsignor came and, along with the Reverend McCluskie who ran the parish from the opposition, said a few quiet words over the grave. But what really surprised me was the number of the townswomen who came to the funeral. Women from Milligs and Westbay and even from Upper Arden. Wearing black hats and veils, young and old, they must have represented every household in the town. What had Kitty MacBeth been to them? The old witch-woman from the point, with her lotions and her potions, and her reading of the tea-leaves.

I don't know why the women came, but as I stood there and watched them crowd into the little cemetary I remembered what the old woman had told me about the time when I was born.

'I know you were conceived on the night of the equinox in forty nine. I know that because I knew your mother,' she had said, cradling her mug of hot tea and smiling mischievously at me. What, I wondered, had she done for my mother, that would give her that knowledge?

And what had she done, over the years, that these women would leave their kitchens and their washing and their shopping to come to her funeral?

Summer stuck with us, promising a typical festival of sunlight and song. All round the area, the farmers were harvesting their corn and barley in the yellow fields. Up at the seminary, the big red combine had been out all week with hardly a break, razing the stalks and leaving a stubbly beard that the field squads burned.

Now, at this time, unknown to anybody, the priests were reaping something that they had not sown in the wide fields that were bordered by their close-clipped hawthorn and privet hedgerows. They had planted in the spring on the red rich earth that they had turned over with their ploughs, and fed with the great heaps of manure that they swept out daily from the milking sheds. All organic, truly self-sufficient. A lesson in ecology. The priests were the masters of husbandry on the land that they had cared for since the time of Kentigern and Columba. Not for them the modern wonders of insecticides and chemical fertilisers. They did it their own way, the old way.

Good strong corn, they planted, not too tall that it

would bend and break in the rains that never came. Thick, heavy ears of corn that threshed easily and made the best wholemeal bread with its light frosting of flour on top. Good corn.

But not just good corn. Sometime in that summer, on one of the breezes that came and eddied around Arden, something drifted in and settled. Tiny almost infinitely microscopic spores came down in an invisible mist when the winds dropped. It landed on the grass and died; on the potato crops and just dissolved.

But on the corn at the seminary, the spores landed and found somewhere they could live and grow. And when they had grown, they spored, and those spores repeated the process. On the other farms, where the crops were sprayed with the polyglot protection from ICI, that killed the bugs and the threadworm and mildew and fungus, the spores were wiped out. But up at the seminary, the old way, the best way, held sway. The light fungus that grew from the spores was a thin dusting of yellow on the ears of corn, and nobody noticed it until the doctor, who had puzzled over Kitty MacBeth's death, finally put some of the fungus under his microscope. He had reasons for doing so, but the fact that there was reason meant it was too late to do very much about it.

The fungus was ergot, a strange, primitive parasite of wheat and corn, known all over the world for its effects on the human psyche, on the consciousness of man.

Why it grew in Arden, nobody knows, for certain.

But I now believe that this was yet another in the string of coincidences that were not coincidences.

Kitty MacBeth's last words, the nurse had said, were 'Who sang?' That's what they had sounded like, but that's not what she had said.

The old woman had warned right to the last: 'Cu Saeng. Cu Saeng is here.'

And if anything had brought the ergot and its madness to Arden, it was that stirring power.

The first to feel the effects was Father Byrne, a short,

swarthy priest, the one who had shown us with pride around his mill where the water from the well had turned the wheel that had made the heavy wooden machinery creak and groan and turn the big millstones rasping on each other to trickle out the stream of flour. The Kilmalid Burn, with its extra load of water from the dammed-up runnel at the new road, splashed over the top of the wheel and the flour poured out. The red-faced little priest hefted his sacks and the open cart came and took them away, some for distribution to some of the local bakeries, and some to the bakehouse that was tagged on to the seminary. Father Byrne toiled for two days with breaks only to eat and sleep, and say his breviary and kneel for the Angelus. The mill ground wheat for most of the local farms on a contract basis, and was in operation almost all the year round, but the seminary's own grain was milled in one operation, almost from the first cut of the combine harvester. In the two days he breathed in flour dust and his face was caked, ghostlike, by the time he swung the doors on the mill at night.

On the third night Father Byrne was not surprised at all to be speaking to his mother as he ran through his inventory in the little upstairs storeroom that also served as his office. He had buried her thirty years before, and his voice cracked with grief as he recited the Latin, despite his knowledge that his dear devout mother was almost certainly in the bosom of the Lord at that instant, and looking down joyously and kindly over her son. But there she was, dressed in her long black skirt and cotton blouse, the way she had been when she had bathed him as a little boy. Father Byrne was not surprised at all. He had a long conversation with his mother, and then she went away again, her skirt trailing on the dry boards, and Father Byrne went back to his ledger and wrote away for some time. In the morning, when he did not appear for early mass, or breakfast, and was not found in his room, there was some minor alarm, and someone was sent to the mill. They found him, still writing in his ledger, but none of the writing was legible, or could even be described as handwriting. Father Byrne had studiously covered every single page of the thick lined book with doodles and drawings and squiggly lines. They took him away from the book and he cried a little and called for his mummy, and they gave him a sedative and put him to bed in the infirmary.

Obviously, Father Byrne was overworked. The harvest had taken its toll on him, they said. He'd be as right as rain in a day or two.

SIXTEEN

Barbara called me on the morning of the harvest festival and I was enormously cheered up to hear the sound of her voice. Kitty's death had hung over me like a pall of heavy cloud and the last couple of nights had been less than good. I had woken up from those dreams again. Writing had gone right out of the window.

'Hi Barbara,' I said, trying to stifle a yawn, and still feeling muggy and shaky from lack of proper sleep. 'What time is it?'

'Oh, I hope I didn't wake you up. It's past ten o'clock.'

'No. Yes, well you did. But I should be up by now anyway,' I told her.

'I just thought you'd want to come to the festival with us today. It's been years since I've been to one and I thought Paddy would love it.'

'So would I. I was going to ask the two of you anyway,' I said. 'She'll stuff her face and be sick all over the place, but every kid has to go through it every summer anyway.'

'You better believe it,' Barbara said. I could hear the start of a laugh in her voice. What a nice way to be woken up from bad dreams.

'Right, I'll come up and collect you, if you like, and we can stroll down. About three?'

'Why not make it for lunch?'

'Sounds even better. I haven't tasted woman's cooking for months.'

'Well mine isn't that great, but I can rustle up a salad.'

'Cheat.'

'Suit yourself, greedy guts. Come up at one.'

I told her I'd be there. The day took on a slightly brighter aspect, and for once I managed to slip out from

221

under that cloud.

This was one harvest festival I was going to really enjoy.

On the way up to Upper Arden, I dropped in at Jimmy Allison's place and found him looking better than he had the other day in the cemetery. He was planning, he said, to drop in at the Chandler with Donald and old Duncan Bennett for a few light refreshments before the festivities.

'Just to get in the mood,' he said, with a smile. 'It's become a tradition, don't you know?'

'Yes, every night, I reckon,' I said.

'Well, when you get to our age, you take what fun you can get whenever you can. Anyway, it's good to be up and about again. That was a bugger of a bug.'

Jimmy paused for a bit, lost in thought, then he seemed to jerk back to the present. 'Anyway, did you read that stuff I put in the box?'

'I did.'

He looked at me, checking to see if I was bull-shitting him. 'I did, honest. From start to finish,' I said, and he nodded conceding that I might have. 'It's a remarkable history. Tell me, Jimmy. Have you ever heard of a Cu Saeng?'

'Cu Saeng? The Old Dog?'

'Yes, that's the one?'

'Of course. It's an old legend that one.'

'Where does it come from?'

'Who can say, but it's common to both the Irish and the Scots sagas, which shows they go back to the same origin sometime in the past.'

'Do you know what it is?' I asked.

'Sure. It's the spirit of madness. It lives under the ground, or the underworld, take your pick. Probably the god of darkness symbol. Anyway, it's supposed to drive anybody who sees it as mad as a hatter, or turn them into stone. Like the Gorgon, I imagine. Why do you ask?'

'I'll tell you in a minute. Go on,' I urged. 'What else do you know?'

'Well, it's supposed to be the spirit that haunts lonely

places, waiting for the unwary. Pops out from under the roots and scares the hell out of them.' He stopped to light his pipe, sucking in the flame that dipped down towards the bowl with every pull, and blowing out a plume of blue. 'Now tell me why you're asking.'

'Kitty MacBeth told me it was a Cu Saeng that caused the Bad Summers.'

Jimmy Allison's eyes flicked up from where they had zeroed in on the glowing bowl of his pipe, and fixed me with a hard stare. He stared so long and hard that the match he was holding burned right up to his fingers, and it was only the quick burn as the flame scorched his thumb that made him jerk away, dropping the blackened match on to the floor. He jammed his thumb into his mouth alongside the stem of his pipe and sucked on both.

'She told you what?' he asked, his face serious.

'She said that the Cu Saeng awoke to ravage the place,' I said, and I must confess I felt a little bit foolish, no matter how much I had thought about the situation over the past week or so, and what conclusions I had reluctantly arrived at.

'And how would that happen?' Jimmy asked.

'She said that sometime in the past, the people here had brought something to life – into the earth, she said – to help them stave off some sort of invasion. But once it had done the job they couldn't send it back again, so they trapped it in the rock and put up walls around it. It's all written on that stone down at Kitty's shack.'

'What rock?'

'Ardhmor.'

'And the walls? What were they?'

'Water and stone, and wood. That's the hawthorn hedge. She said she had to keep re-planting it whenever one of the hawthorns died or got broken. Oh, and there was another wall of bone where they buried the invaders with their heads cut off, just like . . . .'

'Just like the ones Arthur found,' Jimmy said, softly. There was a strange, half-puzzled, half-knowing look on his face.

'Well, what do you think of that?' I said.

'I don't know what to think. Seems a bit far-fetched to me, but I'll tell you, I can't gainsay it. I've seen too many far-fetched things in my time to say yea or nay. I know that the Bad Summer happens every once in a while, and some of them are worse than others. I've never heard of any explanation of them before, except to call it a curse or a bane. Like recurrent bad luck. Real bad luck.' He stopped off and took another pull on the pipe and watched the smoke billow, a frown of concentration pulling his eyebrows, grey and grizzled, down over his eyes.

'Could such a thing be true?' I asked.

'Who can say? It's a new one on me. I mean I've gone over all the old records, probably more than anybody has. But I've never heard or read of anybody saying why these things happen. Only that they do, and they pray to God that they don't ever happen again. What about you? What do you think?'

'Well, I've got to confess that I'm beginning to believe that it must be. Kitty shocked me with some of the things she knew about me. She knew she was dying and there was something else. She said that I had something to do with stopping it.'

'Stopping what?'

'The Bad Summer. She said that I almost stopped it before, and that this time I would have to finish the job. The only thing is that I haven't a clue after that. I wouldn't know where to begin.'

Jimmy looked very thoughtful as I left. He hadn't said one way or another what he thought of the things I'd told him except to say that it might not matter what had caused the bad times in the past.

'I think she was right about it coming again,' he said. 'And so soon. It's been only twenty years, near as dammit, since the last string of troubles, but I can feel it in my bones again. Who knows, maybe she was right. Maybe it would be better if she was. Anything that can be conjured up should be conjured right back again. That's a lot better

224

than waiting for the curse to strike again and not being able to do a damned thing about it.'

I told Jimmy I'd better get a move on to Barbara's place, and he told me to go on up, dropping the opinion, with a sly grin, that he thought she was a fine-looking woman and just my type. It was as close to a nudge-nudge, wink-wink as he'd ever get, but I got the message that he would give his blessing to any advances I might make on that front. He saw me to the garden gate, still pulling hard on the big briar pipe, and told me he'd see me in the beer tent later on in the afternoon. Just as I was leaving, he thanked me for reading his stuff and I thanked him for writing it.

'Do you think there's a book in it?' he asked. 'Can you use it?'

'Yes and no. There is a book in it. But it's your book. You've done all the work on it yourself and it reads right. There's no need for me to write *your* book, you lazy old bugger.'

'Less of your cheek, young toe-rag,' Jimmy said, all the time beaming with pride that his protégé, the one he'd encouraged all the time to get out there and write, had been the one to praise his own work.

'Anyway, I won't have the time. I don't have the gift.'

'Prove me wrong, then. I'll give all the stuff back to you, and you can send it off to a publisher. I'll bet a case of Strathisla they snap it up.' He said he'd think about it and I told him to do more than that. Just as I was leaving, he said it would make a better tale if there really was such a thing as Cu Saeng.

'I didn't think you'd believe it,' I said.

'Oh, I don't say that. You've sort of sprung it on me. I'll toss it around a bit and think it over. What I think doesn't really matter anyway,' he said. 'There's not a damn thing I could do about it.'

As it transpired, there wasn't. But there was something I was supposed to do about it, so I'd been told, except I didn't have the foggiest idea of what, or how, or where, or when. Or even why.

I had decided, even before my talk with Jimmy, that I would just wait, and watch and see what happened.

One thing was certain, if it turned out to be a whole load of hogwash, nobody was going to be more delighted than me. Then I could get out from under the raincloud and get on with my life, get on with my work and sleep well at nights.

Both Barbara and Paddy met me on the steps at their front door as I climbed down from the jeep, both of them sparkling with excitement. It showed more on Paddy, who had got to the jumping up and down stage.

'She's been driving me *crazy* since she woke up this morning,' Barbara said. 'It's as if she was high on something.'

'And you can't remember being just the same? Shame on you. The mother hen's got a convenient memory, hasn't she?'

'Oh, go on with you,' she said, giving me a light punch on the shoulder. 'I was never as bad as that.'

'Worse, if my memory's right. But don't worry about it. We were all like that.'

'Well, I must say, I've been looking forward to some light relief,' Barbara said. By this time we were at the top of the steps and Paddy was running around my ankles like a frisky pup. Barbara planted one on my proffered cheek and then I had to bend down for the same treatment from her daughter. When she gave me the required peck, I didn't let her spin away, but instead grabbed her by the waist and swung her up to sit on my hip. I grabbed her free hand and spun her around.

'Can I have the pleasure of this dance, miss?'

'Yessir!' she cried, right in my ear, her laughter almost deafening me.

'And you're next,' I called to Barbara, looking past her daughter's bouncing pony bob. Barbara did what would have been an elegant curtsey except for the fact that she was wearing a pair of slimline Levis and a halter top under which things were moving in that kind of way that takes your mind off dancing altogether. She caught my eye and I would have blushed but for the wink she flashed at me, and that overcast feeling went slip-slidin' away.

She shooed both of us into the kitchen where she'd made a big tossed salad with pepper and celery in a wooden bowl, along with boiled eggs in mayonnaise and a ham cut so thinly you could see through it. I ate more than I should have, but I suddenly found I had an appetite and Barbara didn't seem too displeased to see me demolishing it. In between stuffing her mouth with eggs and ham Paddy kept up the usual excited barrage of questions about what would happen at the festival. Her idea was the American dream. Would Mickey and Donald be there? Did they have majorettes? Would there be pop-corn and candy? I said there would be something like that, but different. Better, I said. Yes, there would be a band, and a parade and lots of things to do. Paddy still couldn't picture exactly what was going to happen at the festival. I think in her mind it was a cross between a rodeo and a fairground, but in any case she knew it was going to be *fun* and she was getting herself right into the mood for having plenty of it.

After lunch Barbara sent Paddy out to play in the garden while we sat in the living room watching from the mullioned window over the expanse of lawn that rolled away towards the vegetable garden and the big trees beyond. We were drinking coffee in the big comfortable room where the sunlight streamed in and lit up big oblong patches on the old parquet floor.

'She plays in our tree,' Barbara said, emphasising the *our* meaningfully. 'She told me only yesterday she'd found people's names carved on the bark, and wanted to know whose they were.'

'What did you say?'

'I told her that they were ours. Yours and mine and Colin's, and she said "Golly, they're *ancient*",' she said, laughing with exaggerated rue.

'They are ancient. From another age.

'Do you remember . . . .?' I said, just at the same time as

Barbara said the same thing. I broke off and she laughed and insisted that I go on first.

'All right,' I said. 'Do you remember the day we had the picnic? Down by the stream?'

Barbara frowned a little, obviously trying to picture it, failed and shook her head.

'It was the day the three of us found the . . . .'

'Mushrooms! Yes. I *do* remember. And we smoked some concoction that Colin made up. Yes I remember.'

'I had this dream about a man with a spear, and he stuck it into the ground.'

'Oh yes,' Barbara said. 'You were so convinced it was for real that you started to dig and Colin got really pissed off.'

'Yes he was a bit, but it *was* true, don't you remember? I dug and Colin helped and . . . .'

'And you found something. I can't remember what it was. A stone or something?'

'Yes, A stone spear-head, just like the one I saw in the dream.'

'That's it. I remember now. And the lady in the dream gave me gold flowers for round my neck. Oh, I remember I was so disappointed when I found they were gone. It was like gold, so beautiful.'

'Colin dreamed of a black knight with a sword,' I said.

'Did he?' Barbara asked in a small voice, she was still miles away in her memory. Years away, remembering the woman who had given her flowers in her dream on the bank of Strowan's Water.

'I found the stone.'

'What stone?'

'The one I dug up.'

'Really? The same one?'

'I think so.'

'Our treasure! Do you remember? That's what we called it. The buried treasure. You said it was a magic stone that gave us special power, didn't you?'

'No that was Colin's idea. He was always the imaginative one.'

228

'Poor soul,' she said with simple compassion. 'He was, wasn't he?'

I remembered something else just as Barbara said that, and I reached into the inside pocket of the light nylon jacket I had put on, a flimsy, almost wet-looking thing that was ideal for the hot weather because it could crumple up into a fist-sized bundle and fit into a pocket.

'Look at this,' I said, and pulled out the slender golden torc that Kitty MacBeth had unofficially bequeathed to me, along with the rest of the contents of her beautiful carved box.

'Ooh,' Barbara said, evoking yet another memory. 'It's beautiful.'

I reached out to give it to her and she took it. Our fingers brushed lightly, and I felt that delicious little sparkle, the *vibes* I would have called it in my teen years.

'Is it gold?'

'I don't know, but I'd bet any amount that it is.'

'Oh, it's the loveliest thing.'

'You like it?'

'Like it? It's exquisite,' she said, holding up the torc to the light so that the sun sparkled off the golden orbs that finished off the arcs.

'I'd like you to have it,' I said, surprising myself. I hadn't put the torc in my pocket for any reason that I could figure out, and I hadn't intended to come here and give it to Barbara, but all of a sudden, I just did it as if I'd been pushed from behind.

'No, I couldn't Nick,' Barbara said, shaking her head, with her eyes still fixed on the gilded glint. 'It's far too expensive.'

'Well, actually, it's probably never been valued. It was given to me by somebody who doesn't need it any more, so I don't think she'd mind if you had it. No, I don't think she'd mind at all.'

What was it Kitty had said? 'The one and onlies?' and she laughed. 'That was more true than you could have known.'

No, with a brief flash of certainty, I *knew* that Kitty MacBeth would not mind at all.

'I don't know what to say Nick. It's so gorgeous, I really shouldn't take it.'

Just then Paddy came into the room and leaned over her mother's knee. Her eyes had caught the flashing light from the torc.

She stared at it, with wide, unblinking eyes, as if the reflections had snagged her hypnotically.

'That's pretty,' she said, in a very soft voice. 'Is this a present from Nick? Can I see it?' She reached out a small hand and clasped the circlet and Barbara just let it go. I thought Paddy was going to put it on her head, but she just stared at it, entranced, almost hypnotised. Then, in one easy movement, she put it up to her neck, pulled apart the two golden balls and slipped it on. It sat there, gleaming bright.

'Can I have it, Nick?' The question was more like a command. Not like a little girl's appeal for a plaything. The torc sat perfectly on her neck.

'Paddy, that's not very nice,' Barbara said.

'Can I have it, Nick. It's for me, isn't it?' Paddy said, as if she hadn't heard her mother speak. The sunlight caught off the gold on her neck, beaming it back into my eyes, and for the briefest instant I saw rings of golden light, spiralling outwards on water. For a slender moment of time I heard the buzzing of summer insects and the clattering of hooves on rock. I smelt the pungent sap of pine.

Then my mind switched to the more recent past, and the words in Kitty MacBeth's letter. Take the torc. It protects.

And for some reason, it just seemed right that Paddy should have it. I don't know now, and didn't know then, what made me think that, but I just nodded my head.

'Yes. It is yours. If your mother says so.'

Barbara scolded me gently for falling for Paddy's plea, but she didn't object.

Later she said: 'It's strange. When Paddy put it around

her neck, I suddenly thought of golden flowers.'

The festival was just winding up to full swing when we got down to the field at Duncan Bennett's smallholding. The whole town was there, Upper Arden folk rubbing shoulders with the people of the Milligs, and the Westbay crowd rubbing shoulders with everybody.

Barbara had changed Paddy into a summer frock, which probably wasn't practical and caused a mother-and-daughter feud that died down as quickly as it flared, and the little girl bore the indignity with relatively good grace. I parked the jeep in the only free slot in the supermarket car park, and we strolled along the main street towards the sound of the brass band that was belting out an enthusiastic but tuneless marching jazz number. Barbara was stunning in a white cotton dress and sling-back sandals, and she'd put her hair up in a neat French roll that showed off the clean arch of her neck and did amazing things for my hormones. She cleaked her arm through mine and Paddy grabbed my hand, swinging it to and fro to match her bouncing step.

The marquee was blue and white, jammed in a corner against the hedge and in the opposing corner, furthest from the main road, the beer tent was a square box of green canvas that seemed to be bulging at the sides. I knew that in there it would be hot and smoky and jostling with bodies and swimming with beer. Ideal for the Arden men on festival day. I thought a beer would go down just fine on a warm afternoon. Along the edge of the hedgerow, there were stalls with cakes and sweets, home-made jams and buttered shortcake. There were little cuddly toys in profusion, baskets and pottery, all for sale at giveaway prices that would help swell the coffers of whichever charities the day had been dedicated to. When we arrived, the grass was already trampled flat under Arden's feet.

Paddy saw the slide and swings that some of the townsmen had put up under the trees the night before, hauled out from whichever hall they'd been gathering dust in for the past year. She slipped her hand out of mine and was off like a rabbit, with a quick wave of her hand and a flash of white tail.

'She was probably right about wearing her jeans,' I said.

'Don't you start.' Barbara said. 'I had a bad enough time with her.'

I held my hand up in surrender. We strolled around the periphery and Barbara ooh-ed and aah-ed at the handicrafts. She picked up a piece of local pottery that had been fashioned into a deep red stem vase with a narrow neck, and was turning it around in her hands when there was a loud report from the trees nearby. Barbara jerked and the delicate piece slipped from her fingers and thumped to the ground. It bounced, but it didn't break.

'It's all right. Just the clay pigeons getting warmed up,' I said. Barbara was relieved that the piece hadn't broken. She bought it on the spot.

The next stall offered a selection of arty candles in all shapes and sizes and some grotesque colours. The two men in the stall ran a little shop next to the Chandler that specialised in arts and crafts, picture framing and candle making and other such gaucheries.

'Mrs Hartford,' the tall, slender one gushed. He had a long face and a nose to match. One hand was cocked on his hip, and he sported a big silver belt buckle. 'How *nice* to see you.' His smile showed a row of milk bottles a yard wide.

'Isn't it, Brian?' he said, turning to his chubbier companion who was graced with a shock of silvery hair that was carefully coiffed, and had the faintest tinge of blue. He waddled from the back of the stall where he'd been arranging a set of thick candles with dark colours that ran into each other and reminded me of rotting toadstools.

'Oh, hell-*o* there,' Brian effused, wiping his hand on a natty little apron that only emphasised his paunch. '*Wonderful* day, don't you think?'

Barbara agreed that it was, and politely had a look around the wares. I'd met the two gentlemen in the Chandler one night, where they'd been described to me as 'raving berties,' a description that seemed redundantly obvious. They seemed civil enough to me, although I found their mincing just a little bit exaggerated. But having worked in TV studios, their effeminate mannerisms were less out of the ordinary to me than they must have been to some of the plain folk from Arden.

Barbara and I strolled into the marquee that was bustling with the woman of the WRI and the Round Table and what have you. The trestle tables were creaking under the weight of the home baking and garden produce, elderflower wines and sugared fruits. Contest was in full swing and, when Barbara met one or two matrons who insisted that she get a guided tour, there was nothing for it but a quick dodge through the flap. With almost one bound I was free of all that. I headed for the beer tent by way of the playground, where Paddy was in a crowd of squealing and laughing youngsters who zoomed down the slide or soared on the swings or jumped and climbed on the jungle-gym. There was big muddy mark on the back of her dress, I noted with some small satisfaction. Most of the other kids were in jeans.

In the beer tent it took my eyes a moment or two to adjust to the gloom and the fumes. It was sweating in the green half-light that filtered through the canvas, and there was that convivial hubbub of male voices, shouted orders and raucous laughter. This was man's country.

Jimmy Allison and the major with Duncan Bennett and a few of the older guys were sitting in a circle on upturned aluminium beer kegs. I beat my way through the fug and crowded bodies to join them and somebody poured me a lager that was so cold it froze my throat deliciously at the first swallow.

'You'll be wanting a half of whisky, I fancy,' Donald said, producing his trusty hip-flask from the pocket of his tweed jacket that must have been killing him with the heat.

'No, beer's fine for the moment,' I demurred, smacking my lips contentedly.

Jimmy didn't pass up the opportunity and Donald poured him a fair measure before charging his own glass. 'Slainte,' the highlander said, raising his whisky, and we all said cheers and good health. Jommy's hands were not so twisted and gnarled with the arthritis, I noticed, and I thought the summer warmth must be doing him good. I made a mental promise to bully him into seeing a specialist before the winter set in and made them useless. He was in a mellow mood, as indeed we all were. Some more mellow, I'll grant you, than the others who hadn't been drinking since the beer tent flaps opened at noon, but that's the way of it at the festival. Outside, the band screeched enthusiatically and nobody minded nor cared whether it was off-key or out of step.

Behind our group, World War Three, as they were affectionately known in the Chandler, Brigadier Watson and two of his forces friends who apparently joined him every summer for a yachting holiday were arguing in loud, plummy tones, adding their military wah-wah-wah to the conversation. They were drinking pints of dark beer and smoking cigars and having a jolly good time, their old war-horse faces getting redder and redder as they went.

Most of the farmers from the surrounding area were in the tent, with their greasy caps shoved back on their heads and sticks with worn, knobby handles tucked under their armpits. Along the side of the tent, in the shadow where the pegs held the canvas down to the grass in taut little arcs, their border collies waited with infinite patience, panting, sides heaving.

At one of the tables, a crowd of young lads were taking turns at arm wrestling, rocking the little trestle back and forth with their effort. Beer cans hissed open, and big John Hollinger, who had run the bar every year as far as I can remember, roared out with robust good humour to all and sundry, the sweat beading his brow and his customary bar cloth slung round his neck.

'Right, who's next?' he would bellow. 'No, not you Bert, you're third. Willie? Three pints, right. No, no

234

whisky. You bring your own,' and so it went on.

Somebody choked on his beer in mid laugh and somebody else slapped his back. Somebody stumbled and stood on one of the dog's feet and jumped back when it yelped with a high-pitched squeal of pain and surprise, and the owner cautioned him to watch the bloody dog. One of the arm wrestlers fell down when his elbow slipped in a slick of ale and the whole tent laughed. Everybody was getting juiced up for a real good time.

I stayed for another beer, sitting in that mixed company, just taking in the conversations that were going on all around. Donald challenged me to a clay pigeon shoot and one of the farmers laid a bet with another over the result of the quoits match. Another of the barrel-sitters professed that if his wife didn't win a prize in the home-baking section then it wasn't worth his while going home tonight. A crony said it would be nothing short of a miracle if he was sober enough to *get* home tonight, and again everybody laughed.

Outside I was garrotted by the sunlight, jerking back as I emerged from the gloom into the bright. The field was a riot of noise and colour. From outside, along the main street, I could hear the honking of horns that heralded the arrival of the parade, and as I walked toward the marquee, the big trailer did a wide swing to negotiate the gate and scraped through. On the back, the harvest queen was done up like a dish of fish, with a bright yellow cloak and a long dress to match. She had the corn-crown, woven by one of the townswomen from stalks and ears into a delicate, dainty headpiece, and behind her, slightly to the right, dressed in a jacket and a hat made of cornstalks, was the reaper-king, a tall, fair-haired lad, with his shiny, curved scythe. All the corn maidens were pretty as a picture in their colourful dresses, and the whole pageant was finished off with dollies and animals, roosters and intricate shapes made of straw. Everybody cheered as the leading trailer made a circuit of the field and then came to a stop in the centre. Following the leader came a horse-drawn flatloader pulled by two immense Clydesdales, great plodding beasts that were tricked up to a glossy shine, their burnished harnesses gleaming and jangling. Their heads bobbed up and down majestically with every step, showing off their pleated manes. The flatloader was piled high with the harvest gifts, stalks of corn and barley, tied together in the traditional hour-glass shape.

There were barrels of apples and early pears, mounds of potatoes that were so white they must have been dug up that morning. There was a forest of rhubarb from the smallholdings and pots of honey from Duncan Bennett's apiary and the other hives around Arden. There were round, soft cheeses and gallons of buttermilk, but most of all there was the bread. Big humped loaves with golden-brown cracked crusts, square loaves and crescents, cottage loaves salted with flour. You could smell them in the eddying breeze, warm and sweet and mouth watering. The produce float pulled up behind the pageant and everybody cheered again. In the front trailer, the harvest queen and her escort and their crowd of pretty little backers stepped down for their royal parade around the field, waving and smiling at the applauding crowd, who cheered enthusiastically.

By this time, I had found Barbara, and Paddy had come running with all the other kids as soon as the horns of the pageant had beckoned. We had a good position at the centre of the field where the queen would give out the bounty of the harvest. I'd been there once when the poor girl had been bowled back in the rush of eager children and had ended up with her backside stuck in a soft cottage cheese.

Paddy couldn't see what was going on, so I lifted her on my shoulders and held her steady with a grip on her ankle. Barbara watched with a smile of approval, and then gave my arm a brief hug that said thanks, and I got another of those little warm glows you get at such times.

Just when the queen and her retinue had arrived back at the middle of the field, there was another wave of horn-honking, and the deep growl of an engine, rough and powerful. The crowds parted and up the line came Father Gerry on his Honda, resplendent in his shiny hard-top and black gear. He zoomed past the cheering crowd and hit the ramp at the back of the pageant trailer at such a rate that, when he got up to the loader level, the bike actually leapt into the air, its front wheel spinning powerfully. He stopped dead centre, and the wheel thumped down on to the boards and with a flick of a thumb he killed the engine dead, and he jumped the bike back on its stand and whirled to face the crowd with one fluid motion. Great entrance, I thought, watching him standing there, black and magnificent, his arms raised high, willing the crowd to silence.

It obeyed him. A hush swept over the farmers and their wives and all the kids.

And in the silence, Paddy, from her vantage point somewhere above the top of my head pealed out: 'Look mummy, it's Darth Vader!'

Everybody heard it, even Gerry, who was unlacing his helmet, and a wave of laughter swept through the crowd. It made a mess of Gerry's entrance, but nobody cared. Beside me, Barbara was having a quiet fit of hysterics, and I could feel Paddy jostle up and down on my shoulders which were heaving with barely suppressed laughter.

Gerry got the lid off and beamed a big smile down at her.

'Don't I wish, young lady,' he told her, and everybody clapped. He was still smiling widely when he lifted his hands up again for silence.

'I'm not going to try that again, ladies and gentlemen, boys and girls. I don't want to risk my neck.'

Somebody at the back shouted: 'Oh, don't be a spoilsport, reverend,' and there was more laughter.

Gerry shook his head good-naturedly and the laughter fell away slowly.

'Ladies and gentlemen, boys and girls, everybody,' he called. 'Once again, it is our own harvest festival and we're all here to have a good time.'

He paused and looked around.

'But first, let's remember why we're here. To say thanks for the summer, and to say thanks for everything that's grown so well to let us have a festival today.

'So, boys and girls,' he said in his strong, clear voice, 'let's join hands and say thank you.'

Above me, I could hear Paddy clap her hands together, following Gerry's exaggerated gesture of encouragement. Beside me, I noticed a few other children doing the same.

'Dear God, we thank you for making things grow, for making all the nice things we like to eat. We thank you for making the sun shine on our harvest festival and for giving us this wonderful day. Amen.'

'Amen!' piped up shrill voices and adult tones all around.

'Now let's all have some *fun*!' Gerry yelled, and everybody cheered.

'Who is that?' Barbara asked.

'My friend, the hot-shot priest,' I told her. 'Father Gerry O'Connor.'

'He's delicious,' she said. 'What a waste.'

I felt a small twinge of jealousy, but I had to admit that the good-looking young priest did have more than the normal helping of good looks and charisma. I just said a thankful prayer that he actually *was* a priest, and a conscientious one at that.

'Sorry kid, he's spoken for,' I said, gesturing skywards with my eyes.

'Oh, don't be silly,' she said, and hugged my arm again, leaning in towards me so that I could feel the softness and warmth of her body. The little pang of jealousy evaporated in the heat of that moment.

Paddy asked to be let down off my shoulders and I caught her under the armpits and swung her, topsy turvy, over my head, spinning her so she landed on her feet.

'Can I go and play, now?' she asked, squinting up against the sun. Barbara told her to run along and be careful. As Paddy turned, her mother noticed the muddy patch on her skirt and was about to say something but Paddy slipped through the crowds like a fish and was gone.

'Oh, I forgot to tell you,' she said, still holding on to my arm, 'I've got an interview at the Western Infirmary on Monday.'

I told her I was delighted, and asked if she wanted me to drive her up to Glasgow.

'No, I've borrowed my father's car. He doesn't really use it any more. I've got used to the fact that the wheel's on the wrong side, and I'm just grateful that he's got an automatic. I'm afraid a stick shift would just be beyond me.'

'Best of luck, Babs,' I said. 'I hope you get the job.'

'Thanks, me too. I need to be working at something now that Paddy's going to school. I don't want to be cooped up in the house all day long.'

I said something phoney and masculine like they'd be crazy not to hire her, but she just smiled and took it as a compliment.

'I wonder if you could do me a favour, though,' she said. 'My father had arranged to go down to London to meet some friends this weekend, so . . . .'

'So you want me to babysit?'

'Well, yes. If you don't mind.'

'Not at all. It'll be a pleasure. I'll come up and pick her up and take her out somewhere, if you like.'

'That would be nice. Really. Thanks.'

'No problem. She's a great kid. More fun than most people I know, so I'll be having a good time,' I said sincerely. Paddy was one of those kids you just took to, although I suppose her strong resemblance to her mother was more than just an added bonus.

'I'll take her along Strowan's Well, and see if the gang hut is still there,' I said, on impulse.

'She'd love that. But don't you tell her about the things we used to do. I want her to grow up to be a lady.'

'Didn't seem to do you any harm,' I said appraisingly.

Back in the centre of the field, the harvest queen was

239

handing out goodies to the children who surrounded her in a yelling horde, helped by all her maids, some of whom were almost floored in the rush. Everybody got their little round loaf, and a piece of cake and some fruit. There was an abundance of fudge and drinks of fresh and sour milk, and every child's face and hands were sticky with something in a matter of minutes. Close to the beer tent, the barbecue was warming up nicely. The trench had been filled with coals and over the red heat there was a whole pig turning on a spit that was spun by a brawny young fellow with a painful-looking sunburn. Beside it slowly rolled what looked close to a full side of beef, and there were about two dozen capons going crisp red-brown and sizzling over a long hot trench that had been dug parallel to the main fire.

I left Barbara in mid-afternoon to have another vital pint of lager in the tent where I found everybody at that mellow stage of good fellowship and bonhomie. A pint was thrust into my hands and this one was a heaven-sent stream that slaked the back of my throat like a blessing. I took a huge mouthful and belched explosively and unstoppably to a round of raucous laughter.

'Terrific,' I said vehemently when I got my breath back. 'Bloody wonderful.'

'You'll be wanting a wee half of whisky now,' Donald said, and brought out his little hip-flask again. It was full to the brim, and I wondered if he had a magic flask, or a hidden bottle. I declined again and he shrugged and poured him and Jimmy another fine measure of heroic proportions. Another two candidates for the flatloader express, I thought. Every year, the horse-drawn buggy was the main form of transport home for everyone who found it difficult to walk. It could take twenty people, and normally made five or six trips. That's how much Arden liked its harvest day.

Donald MacDonald and I had a contest at the pigeon shoot where he outclassed me embarrassingly. We'd had a side bet on the outcome, but he refused to take the pound.

He'd scored ten out of ten, despite the fact that he'd drunk enough to floor me twice over. When we walked down through the trees back to the festival field, he was as solid as a rock.

We left the tent and came down the path where Father Gerry was surrounded by a group of sticky-faced kids who were jostling about him and hanging on to his sleeves. He'd changed out of the biker's gear into a light shirt and slacks. The monsignor was with him and everybody was laughing. The tall priest with the basset hound's face had a deep booming laugh that rumbled up within, giving out a resonance of good feeling.

'Hello Nick. And Donald too,' he said, shaking both our hands firmly. Gerry called out a hello over the heads of the children.

I made my excuses to both of them, for I'd seen Barbara out there in the crowd, beyond the beer tent, and waded through Gerry's congregation of children. I was passing the big square tent when something caught my eye in the narrow space between it and the bright canvas of an adjacent hoopla stall. There was a crowd of men fooling about in the shade there, drinking out of bottles. I was about to pass on by when a flash of white on black drew my attention, and I did a double-take. There was Badger, in amongst the crowd, which immediately struck me as being strange, and just as I looked I saw that he was being pushed about roughly by a circle of men.

I started up the narrow canvas alley, between the tents, ducking to avoid twanging the guy-ropes with my head.

When I got to the end of the passageway, I saw that Colin was drunk as a lord. He could hardly stand on his feet, and the circle of guys were shoving him about, from one to the other. The poor guy looked sick and drunk and terrified, and he didn't seem to know where he was.

'Look at him,' one of the men said raspingly. 'He's as drunk as a skunk.'

'Here, Badger,' another one said, and Colin was shoved across the circle. The man shoved at him and Colin staggered backwards and fell in a heap. Everybody laughed cruelly.

Colin tried to get up and one of them stuck out the toe of his boot and sent him sprawling into the leaves. I could hear him sobbing with fear and bewilderment, and then, just as he had got to a kneeling position, on all fours, he was suddenly sick, and a gout of vomit splashed out and spattered over one of the men's shoes.

'Fuck sake,' the young tough said, jumping back. 'He's been sick all over my boots.'

Somebody laughed and the man told him to shut the fuck up.

'Stupid bastard,' he grunted and swung one of his soiled boots forward and got Colin right under the ribs. He let out a whoosh of air that was mingled with a sharp yelp of pain and rolled sideways.

'You can have it back again, fucking idiot,' the man said. It was one of the toughs who'd ganged up on Colin before, that night I'd been floored with a half-brick. Billy Ruine, the mean little gang leader, was there too, smirking on the other side of the circle.

I couldn't hold back any longer.

'What do you think you're doing, you bastards?' I shouted out and came out from between the tents. All the heads turned.

'Oho, here comes the fuckin' hero,' Billy Ruine sneered.

'You get the hell out of here before you get it too,' he spat.

I was almost speechless with rage and disgust.

'You cretins. Look at you. Bloody animals. Picking on somebody who can't even defend himself.' They'd obviously got Colin tanked up on their cheap booze.

'Who the fuck do you think you're talking to, big mouth?' Billy Ruine said. 'What you want to do, take the whole lot of us on? Eh, that what you want?'

He stuck his chin out and made a come-on gesture with both of his hands. His team of hoods spread out beside

242

him, their faces flushed with drink, dark with violence. Behind him I could hear Colin snuffling his misery.

'Come on then, wise guy, let's be havin' you.'

I could feel my hands shaking with that burst of adrenalin you get with confrontation. There was no way I was going to come out of this well at all.

I braced my feet on the ground and prepared to hit out at the first one that moved. There was no way I could run away from this one, so I decided I might as well take a few bloody noses with me as they carted me off in the ambulance. This was looking very hairy indeed.

Billy Ruine took a step forward, with that sly, arrogant look on his face.

'Well, well now,' Donald said, loudly. 'This is a fine wee party we have going on here, do we not?'

I was never so glad to hear a human voice in my life. Billy Ruine turned and saw Donald standing off to the side.

'Now, is it a private party, I'm wondering,' Donald said in his mild, slow way, 'or is it that anybody can join in?'

'Fuck off, old timer,' Billy said, and one of his troops giggled. 'This is nothing to do with you.'

'Well, if you put one hand on him, then I'll have to make it something to do with me, now,' Donald said mildly. There was no hint of anger or menace in his voice.

Billy turned away from him. 'Ignore that old fool,' he said and ran towards me, swinging his boot up to catch me in the groin. I jumped back and Billy's foot missed me by an inch. I grabbed it and pulled and he went down, but he twisted and came back up again like a cat and swung a roundhouse that clipped me on the side of the ear and made my head ring.

That was the last hit he got in. An arm lashed out and caught him right smack on the chin. I turned, surprised, and saw that it was not Donald who had thrown the blow. Monsignor Cronin was standing off to the right. There was a bellow of pain and I saw Donald leap into the crowd. He spun and his foot came right up clear of the ground and connected with one of the group's head. He went down like a sack. Donald continued the movement and turned like a ballet dancer and his hands moved like pistons. Smack, smack right and left, and two of the young hoods doubled over. The monsignor swept past me like a black shadow and stepped over Billy Ruine who was lying still on the fallen leaves. He caught one of the guys and spun him around on his heels with a blow to the solar plexus, and grabbed another and head-butted him straight on the nose, like a bar-room brawler. But there was nothing of the streetfighter in the fluid grace with which the two men cut a swathe through the line-up. My ears were still ringing from that clip, but the pain had gone away. It was over in seconds. The two remaining young men turned and ran. The rest of them writhed and moaned on the ground under the trees.

Monsignor Cronin shot his cuffs out, and rubbed his hands together. He was breathing lightly, and his solemn face looked as placid as he could ever manage.

'Silly boys,' he said, shaking his head. He turned to me and raised his finger to his lips: 'Shhh. Not a word to a soul. Bad for the reputation, don't you think?' I was too surprised to do anything but nod.

Donald helped Colin to his feet and dusted him down. His nose was running and the tears had streaked his face. He looked very unsteady.

'Bloody animals,' Donald said. 'That's what they are. Come on, laddie, let's get you away from here.'

We helped Colin into the beer tent and sat him on the grass beside the barrels where he snuffled a bit before falling asleep, lying sprawled and ungainly beside the patient dogs.

'He'll be all right once he sleeps it off,' Jimmy Allison said after I'd told him what happened, or some of it.

'It's a damned shame, picking on that poor soul. You would think they had better things to do with their time.'

'Och, they're no better than pigs,' Donald said loudly and vehemently. 'Animals is what they are, and no

244

mistake. It does them good to get a taste of their own medicine. I'm thinking we were a bit soft on them.'

Donald was still in a fury over what Billy Ruine and his boys had done to Colin. I must say I was enraged as well, but I was still very grateful to Donald – and to the monsignor – for getting me out of that with nothing worse than a thick ear. Grateful and, frankly, amazed. Those two men, well past their prime, had made mincemeat of those young toughs with such ease that if I hadn't seen it I wouldn't have believed it. If it hadn't been for them I would probably be lying round there in a pool of blood, or worse. The cheap wine that band of thugs had been drinking from their bottles had obviously fired them up to a frenzy. They might not have stopped at a mere beating.

My nerves had calmed down by the time they started carving up the crisp brown meat of the barbecue. The sweating helpers hauled the beef and pork on to wooden planks set on sturdy workhorses and the carving knives were whipped up to ringing sharpness as Tommy Muir, the local butcher, and his son, both big and beefy men, set about carving everything up with a marvellous deftness into steaks and slabs of hot meat. The chickens were halved and quartered and everybody lined up for a share. The beer tent emptied, giving John Hollinger a break, and I saw him strolling off with a plate of beef and pork and potatoes that would have done a bear proud. He was a bear of a man anyway, so it made little difference. Barbara and Paddy joined Jimmy and Donald and a few others with myself who sat in the shade of a weeping ash, and we had our own banquet, washed down with some white wine and more beer. The guys kept the jokes clean in deference to the two ladies and we all set to.

As to be expected, from memories of childhood, everything was delicious, as freshly cooked food in the open air never fails to be. Paddy made a pig of herself and within minutes of settling down her face was covered in grease.

I was on my fourth can of beer of the day – and that was

245

just enough for me – washing down the gargantuan meal, when Duncan Bennett remembered he hadn't got his free harvest loaf. I couldn't have eaten another morsel, but Duncan wandered off to get his fair share, saying he hadn't missed his loaf in all the years and that, he said, was a whole lot of bread. Barbara told Paddy if she ate another thing she'd be sick, and that's just the way I felt too. Babs and I sat back against the tree, enjoying the lethargy of a big meal on a hot day. All round the field, under the trees and in the shade of the tents and stalls, families and couples and groups of friends were doing the same thing. It was the festival's equivalent of half time, Paddy fell asleep, and I almost dozed off too, while the murmur of conversation and laughter washed over me.

After dinner time, there were games for the children, egg and spoon races, and contests. The men threw weights over the bar and put their bets on quoits, and they drank more beer.

Later on, when it was beginning to get dark, they lit the huge bonfire with the straw man as a guy lashed to the centre pole. The last job of the harvest queen was to put her crown on the straw man's head, then they lit the fire and he was gone in minutes – his and her hour of glory gone in one glorious burst of flame. Everybody cheered for the umpteenth time that day and applauded. Father Gerry had got in a spectacular array of fireworks that lit up the night and we watched as Donald passed round his miraculous flask. Barbara took a sip and he beamed with pleasure when she declared it top class. He got up and sang one of his Gaelic songs with all the verses that sounded the same, and nobody minded. The monsignor, his fellow combatant of earlier, got up and sang a funny one that had the kids laughing.

Paddy fell asleep, and I took her and Barbara home. Jimmy and Donald and Duncan, and a whole squad of others, left for the flatloader.

SEVENTEEN

Barbara invited me in for a nightcap and Paddy insisted I come up and wish her goodnight, waking up briefly but dopily for as long as it took to get her bundled into her pyjamas, and then she smiled and her eyelids drooped and she was fast asleep in the way that only small children and drunks can do.

Down in the living room, Barbara see-sawed the cord on the blinds and shut out the dusk. She poured me a Drambuie and made herself a brandy with ice, and we sat down in the broad armchairs on each side of the hearth. The liqueur sparked on the tip of my tongue and blazed a hot trail down my throat.

We sat and sipped and spoke in soft voices about the fun of the festival and other things, the conversation just rolling along nice and easy. Barbara had liked all the old guys that I liked, and she did a quick take-off of Donald's interminable Gaelic, which was so like him I had to laugh. She got me another Drambuie, filling the tiny Edinburgh crystal glass, and shushing my half-hearted protest. It was going down a treat. She had another brandy, swirling the spirit around in a fine balloon glass, and dipping her head every now and again to catch the fumes.

It must have been way past midnight when Paddy started crying upstairs, breaking the mellow mood that we had fallen into. Apart from the hassle with Billy Ruine and his mob of nut-cases, I had had a ball, and when Paddy started up, yelling for her mother, I had a fleeting unchristian thought which I suppressed a little guiltily.

Barbara gave me an apologetic look and went upstairs. She came down a minute or two later with Paddy in her arms, red-eyed, but still half asleep. Barbara was patting

patting her gently on the back the way all mothers do, and Paddy's arms were tight around her neck.

'It's all right honey,' she said soothingly while her daughter snuffled into her neck.

'She's been dreaming again,' Barbara said to me. 'But it's all gone now, baby,' she said, in a different tone, to Paddy.

'She'll be all right in a minute or two. Must have had too much excitement.' Barbara sat down on the sofa, still patting her daughter between the shoulder-blades, and the girl's panicky sniffling began to fade down. In a few moments the night shakes seemed to have left her. Barbara looked at me over her shoulder. She was smiling a little.

In a few minutes, Paddy's breathing settled down and she was asleep on her mother's shoulder. Barbara took her back upstairs and when she came back she said: 'She's been waking up a lot these nights. And so have I.'

'Me too. Must be the heat,' I said, and stood up, putting my glass down on the stone mantelpiece.

'I suppose I'd better shoot off. You've got an early start in the morning. I'll come up for Paddy about ten, and we'll think of something to keep us both amused.'

'Thanks a million, Nick. It really is awfully good of you. If I get this job I'll have to get some sort of babysitting service full time.'

I shrugged and told her it was no trouble at all, and I meant it. Having a day with a ten year old isn't everybody's idea of having a good time, but hell, I still wasn't beyond the stage of hankering to go climb a tree or hook a trout out of the burn. It was just that there weren't too many people my age with the same hankering. There are some things which most people have outgrown, and some of these things I guess I'm stuck with. Anyway, I was looking forward to it.

Barbara came to the door with me, and I slipped my arms around her back and joined them together. She pulled herself close and her arms snaked around my neck and she brought my head down to hers and kissed me. It was not a friendly kiss. Not a sisterly gesture. Above us, the moon was bright and silver, with that shaved way that tells you it's only a day or so away from a full moon, and the light tingled the needles of the cypress trees that lined the wide lawn. I returned the kiss with interest and she pressed her body up against mine, lithe and taut and soft at the same time. We held the moment, and each other, for quite a while before we broke away gently. I held on to her shoulders and she looked down at my feet (at least I hoped it was my feet because I was sure that kiss had done some pretty evident things to my hormones) and I nuzzled the top of her head.

'Right, kid,' I said eventually. 'I'll see you in the morning.'

I took my hands off her shoulders, and she continued looking down, and I went down the stone steps towards the jeep.

I had just reached the driver's door and was fumbling in my pocket for the keys when she called my name, quite softly, from the shadow of the doorway. I had half turned to wave goodnight, and she came tripping a quick-step down the stair and pattered across the pebbles. The moonlight outlined her body and blued the edges of her hair like St Elmo's fire and she came right into my arms in a rush and kissed me. Hard.

Then she stopped and looked right up into my eyes.

'Don't go,' she said, like an order. Like a demand.

Stupidly, I said: 'Pardon?'

'Don't go tonight. Please Nicky, I don't want you to go. Stay with me, won't you?' She said it quickly, getting it all out in a rush as if she might not be able to say the words if she spoke them slowly.

I didn't say anything at all. I just looked into her eyes, seeing the green shift to blue, and sparkling with the little reflections of the nearly full moon. I turned her around with one arm across her shoulder and walked her back up the stairs. I shut the door behind me and clicked the mortice lock over. We walked straight up the stairs and into

249

her room and she closed the door and came right into my arms again.

The moonlight was a dim arc-lamp that shone a pillar of fluorescence through the pane.

Barbara and I made love on the eiderdown. The tomboy had become a stunning woman whose long legs entwined mine, and whose breasts gleamed slick with the heat of our bodies in the moonlight, and whose soft, rich voice moaned low and hungry in the night and whose tears ran cool on my cheek.

We held each other for a long time and her tears evaporated, and then we talked for an even longer time, before we slept. Both of us knew, without saying anything, that something had changed, clicked into place, and that we would have to do something about it.

Barbara fell asleep before me and just as she began to fade out she told me in a whisper that she thought she loved me. I felt a surge of happiness welling up inside me.

I slept for a couple of hours, I think, for it was still dark when I was whiplashed right out of sleep by another of those dreams. I was sitting up straight before I knew where I was, before I realised I had been dreaming. This was one clear as ice; no aftershock fade.

In my dream I saw a thing that swelled and pulsed, a thing that changed as I watched, from a black shadow that shifted in and out of walls and trees and smeared everything it touched with a dead darkness.

In my dream I watched as it changed shape and stalked through the town, spreading its black disease, ripping here with a claw, touching there, and burning with the pale white eyes that were so dead they sucked out life. And as I watched, stuck in the mud and unable to walk or talk, it changed and the wind took it high where it became a flapping sheet, pale against the dark, that fluttered in the wind and started to spiral down, and I saw a gaping beak open and screech with a great cry that sounded like mad laughter and saw that it wasn't a sheet at all. It was a huge white bird that dived and dived, and down there was

Barbara who was running frantically away from the winged horror and its great stabbing beak. I heard the wind of its wings and tried to call to her, to move to protect her, but no words would come out of my throat, and the wind became a roar and I saw that the great beak was going to . . . no . . . no . . . NO!

And I was awake, shattered into the world again, and gasping for breath that wouldn't come, and beside me Barbara was awake and had her arms around me and was asking me what was the matter.

'Nothing,' I said, 'just a dream,' and I could still see her running in the distance and that huge thing streaking down towards her with the screech of mania trailing in the wind.

'Some dream,' she said, and kissed me on the cheek, hugging tight, the way she had with her daughter. 'Come on, lie down.'

Numbly I did, and she soothed me in her arms, and gradually my heart slowed down a bit and my breathing regulated itself down from high gear to idle. After a bit, she started to kiss me again and I felt myself responding, and then there was a great urgency. I sheltered in her, driving away the picture that was freeze-framed in behind my eyes, holding on tight enough almost to crush her ribs into mine, and some time during it she grabbed my hair and shouted my name loud.

Afterwards, it was me who fell asleep first, under the soothing pressure of her fingers trailing my brow, and her whispered murmurings on the threshold of my hearing. As I drifted down, safe in her arms, I had a dim twinge of guilt that she should be sleeping to prepare for her interview, and then the curtain closed over the show and I did not dream again that night.

It was just going on nine, and the sun was high enough to make a big square of light on the wall, when Barbara gently shook me awake, ruffling my hair with her left hand. I opened my eyes groggily and she was lying beside me, propped up on one elbow and looking like a vision.

251

Everything came back to me and I smiled, a bit sheep-ishly.

'Morning,' I said.

She chucked me under the chin. 'Hiya.' She smiled, and added: 'Tiger.' I smirked, I'm sure, with embarrassment.

'Tigress,' I countered. 'What time is it?'

'Too late for any more of that,' she said.

'Pity.'

'Aw, come on. I haven't got the energy or the time,' she said with a laugh. Then she came off her elbow and leaned over me, trailing my chest lightly with her nipple, and sending ripples through my skin. She puckered up and kissed me a smack on the lips.

'Thank you. Thanks for staying,' she said.

'No ma'am. Thank you.'

She gave me another kiss then rolled over and out of bed. I watched her walk to where her robe lay on a chair. She picked it up and with a wide movement swung it on. For a brief and tantalising moment I could see her outline through the fine gauzy material. She caught my look and grinned.

'Voyeur,' she said. 'Come on, and bring your mind with you.'

'I'll leave that behind,' I said. 'I think it would just get in the way.'

She laughed brightly and ordered me out of bed and said she was going to check on Paddy and fix breakfast. For some reason, I didn't want her daughter to know I'd spent the night, so I got out of bed quickly and fumbled around for my scattered clothes. It took me a while to find my socks, but I located them under the dresser and pulled them on and followed her downstairs. Barbara was bustling in the kitchen and I sat down at the pine table. She'd put out some orange juice which I downed in one gulp and she started to make coffee. There was a plate of cereal on the table for Paddy.

I watched Barbara move about, and I had to say something but I wasn't sure what to say, or how to start. But she

252

got in first.

'You don't have to say anything.'

I looked up, and she must have read the surprise.

'It's all right Nick. It was terrific. It was wonderful. But that doesn't mean you have to . . . .'

'You said you thought you loved me,' I said, and she stopped in mid-flow. She looked at me for a while, twisting a coffee cup between her fingers.

'Right. I know I said it, I can't take it back. But you don't have to feel you've got anything holding you. I mean, I just let my mouth run away from me.'

'I hope not.'

'What I mean is. Oh, God,' she said. 'I don't really know what I mean.'

'Well, I hope you mean that what you said was what you mean.'

'It was. It is,' she paused and I didn't let her go on.

'Well, that's all right then. Because that's what I mean too,' I said, and took her in my arms. She raised hers up around my neck and clonked me good and proper with the coffee cup which was still in her hand. She jumped back with a look of surprised shock on her face. My head was ringing.

And then suddenly we were both falling about with laughter. Maybe the mood was broken, but it broke the right way, and we had to hold on to each for a bit just to stop ourselves landing on the floor. We were still grappling with each other and the gales of laughter when Paddy came wandering into the kitchen and asked us what was so funny.

'Nothing hon,' Barbara said, with difficulty.

'Your mum hit me on the head with a coffee mug,' I said sneakily. 'I don't think she likes me.'

'Well, I like you,' she said, primly, flashing her mother a look of disapproval. 'What're we going to do today? You're early too.'

'Yes, I thought we'd make a day of it, so I came as early as I could.'

253

'You're still wearing the same clothes,' she said. 'Didn't you get to bed last night?'

I looked at Barbara and she had to turn away to the sink to prevent Paddy seeing her next fit of the giggles.

'Something like that,' I said. From behind me I could hear Barbara snorting in a bid to stifle her laughter.

Barbara went upstairs to get changed and Paddy and I sat in the kitchen with our respective breakfasts. The radio was on in a corner playing early morning wallpaper stuff and then the local news and the weather. I wasn't really listening, I suppose, lost in my thoughts. Paddy munched her cereal diligently. The weatherman said something about storms heading in over the Atlantic, bringing rain to most parts later. I didn't quite catch it, but Paddy heard too.

'It's not going to rain, is it?' she said, pulling a disgusted face.

I looked out of the window. The sun was working over-time.

'Nah. Not today anyway. I don't think.'

'That would be really rotten,' Paddy said. 'Can we go on a picnic then?'

'OK, but I'll take you somewhere you haven't been yet.'

'Where's that?'

'I thought I'd show you some of the places me and your mum used to play when we were kids.'

'Really? I can't imagine my mom being a kid,' Paddy said. 'What was she like?'

'Well, she could climb better than anybody, and she was good with a slingshot and she could hit a rabbit with a rock.'

Paddy's eyes opened wide. 'My mom? My mom could hit a rabbit with a rock?'

Her face was such a picture of disbelief that I had to laugh out loud and that made her laugh too.

'You're kidding me, ain'tcha?' she said, falling into her American idiom. I realised then that I might have been just a bit iconoclastic and that Barbara might disapprove of her image being tampered with.

'Yeah, I'm just kidding. But she was a lot like you. Same colour of hair and same freckles. I reckon you'll be a lot like her.'

'Do you think so? Do you think I'll be like her? I mean, she's awful pretty and all.'

'Don't worry about it,' I said, on surer ground now. 'Even prettier probably.'

'Don't know if I want to be pretty,' Paddy said, thoughtfully. 'But hey, I'd sure like to hit a rabbit with a rock.'

When Barbara came downstairs I was still grinning and she asked both of us what was so funny. I turned around and there she was standing by the door and looking like something from the front cover of *Vogue*. She had put on a simple white suit and had shoes and handbag to match, and frankly she looked perfect.

I gave her a low wolf whistle that Paddy tried unsuccessfully to emulate, and Barbara shot me a look that conveyed pleasure and incredulity and disapproval all in one.

'Do you think I'll pass muster?'

'I'd say if they don't hire you they'll need their heads looked at.'

'Me too,' Paddy chipped in. 'You look lovely mummy.'

'Well, thank you for that,' Barbara said. 'I take that as a vote of confidence.'

I wished Barbara the best of luck and she smiled. Then she told both of us to take care of ourselves and not get up to any mischief, and made us both cross our hearts. We did.

Out front, Barbara pecked us both, me on the cheek and Paddy on the top of the head, thanked us for our good wishes and warned us sternly to behave. She swung the estate car out of the gate and was gone with two brief toots on the horn. If it was up to me I'd have hired her on the spot.

'Right, now what?' Paddy said.

'First, down to my place, young lady, so I can get changed. Then we'll decide.'

255

We went in the jeep and Paddy was jumping and excited, a condition that I was beginning to take as par for the course with her. I let her ride shotgun, but insisted she get strapped in, and as she leaned back to slot the belt into the mount she came close to me.

'Phooey. Boy, do you need a bath,' she said, wrinkling her nose.

'Less of your lip, young lady. I told you I didn't get much sleep last night.'

'What's lip?' she asked innocently.

'What you'll have a fat one of, kid, if you don't button it, and pronto.'

That brought on another fit of the giggles. I was beginning to enjoy myself already. Yesterday, apart from the scene with Billy Ruine and his bunch of nutters, had been good. The best day I'd had in ages. Last night was just incredible. Today promised to be fun, pure and simple.

Paddy loved my place. She sat in the big rocker and swung back and forth while I pottered about in the bathroom, trying to convince the shower that lukewarm was not going to solve the problem, but that was all I got, so I just used a lot of soap. I changed into a pair of faded Levis and a light shirt and had a quick shave before going down to attend to my guest. She didn't say no to a couple of bacon sandwiches and insisted, despite my disbelief, that her mother allowed her to have coffee. I split the difference and made up a cup of decaffeinated instant and she was none the wiser.

While we were eating and swapping tales – me about being a kid here, and she about being a kid over there – I flipped on the radio and heard the weatherman on the other channel promising a big change in the weather. As I'd driven down from the heights of Upper Arden, I'd noticed some cloud piling high over the firth, but there was hardly any breeze at all, so I thought we'd get a last day of it. Over the roar of the low gears on the steep hill, there had been a low rumble like distant thunder. I hoped the day would stay fine, otherwise Paddy and I would be relegated to playing I-spy and happy families, but it was still hot and bright.

I thought we might head along to Strowan's Water and take the forest path into the valley where our old gang used to be. I reckoned I could spin a few tall tales about the old days, what I remembered of them anyway, that still wouldn't spoil Paddy's image of her mother, and retain mine – both versions that is.

Paddy asked me where the bathroom was, and I gave her directions and she thumped up the stairs.

She was on the second flight more than halfway up to the top, when she stopped. I could hear the sudden cessation of her footsteps on the treads.

'Anything up kid?' I shouted up. There was no reply. I took the bottom flight two at a time and cocked a head over the banister. Paddy was standing at the sixth step, with her right foot poised for the seventh. She was standing stockstill, one hand on the banister and the other almost touching the wall. Then, quite deliberately, she lifted her foot higher, and put it on the eighth step up, missing out the previous one, the one that creaked like the crack of doom in the middle of the night.

How the hell did she know about that, I wondered.

'Are you all right?' I asked, and Paddy turned on the top landing and nodded. There was a strange look on her face, puzzled but not afraid.

'Yes, I'm OK,' she said. 'That step isn't right, though.'

'What do you mean?'

'It was going to creak at me. Step on a creak makes you weak.'

She went into the bathroom, leaving me with the puzzled expression.

EIGHTEEN

Paddy waited impatiently for me as I put on my treks and settled for my old denim jacket. I slipped my penknife into the pocket of my jeans, and on impulse I picked up the smooth old stone from the dresser and shoved it into my jacket pocket. It was hard and warm, a touchstone under my hand. At the door, I paused at the old umbrella rack that had stood there since before I was born, and I picked out the smooth, worn walking stick of my grandfather's. I plucked my ancient fishing hat from the top spike, a battered old affair with a peak that was threadbare and bent out of shape, with a couple of antique flies irretrievably embedded in the green cloth. This I spun in the air and plunked down on Paddy's head, flicking the peak up so I could see her eyes.

'Right. Now we're all set for the wilderness,' I said. 'Just watch out for the bear, kid.'

I opened the front door and was just stepping through, still looking down at Paddy's grin, when I bumped smack into Jimmy Allison whose fist was raised high, caught in mid-flight on the first knock.

'Jimmy,' I said. 'You nearly gave me a heart attack.'

His hand stayed in mid-air, big and gnarled, and swollen at the joints where the corkscrew of arthritis was digging inexorably. His eyes were bloodshot and wide. He stared at me for quite a while and I could hear his breath rasp heavily in his throat. There was something wrong with him.

'Jimmy, are you all right?' I asked.

'Where is it?'

'What?'

'Where is it? You've got it.'

'Where's what?' I asked.

'My book, you damned thief. You've stolen my book. And I want it back.' His voice was hoarse and he seemed really wound up, like the tension rope on an old frame saw. I just stood agape.

'Give me it back, you bastard. Thought you'd get away with it, did you? Thought you'd steal my book and have it published yourself? After all I've done for you, you little bastard.' He snarled, and I was standing close enough to feel a spray of spittle on my face. Paddy's hand, which had been holding mine, clenched tight.

'Wait a minute Jimmy. That's no language in front of the youngster,' I said, nodding down towards Paddy, who was staring up, her eyes flicking from me to him.

'Don't give me any of your excuses, you dirty thief. You've stolen what's mine, and I've come to get it back,' he said, spitting more flecks at me. Some of them had gathered at the corner of his mouth and were working themselves into a revolting lather.

Before I could reply, Jimmy blundered past me in the hallway. His big frame nearly filled the narrow space. For some reason, I noticed that his shirt had been buttoned wrongly, and that this was the first time I'd seen him outside his own house without a tie on. He hadn't shaved either, and the grey and white bristles on his cheeks gave him an unkempt, trampish look. The weird expression in his eyes was something else.

Jimmy lumbered into the living room and I followed him, pulling Paddy along with me. She stuck right at my heels, keeping me between herself and Jimmy. From the room I could hear things being moved about and when I looked through the doorway Jimmy was rummaging about, scattering books and papers on the floor.

'Right, Jimmy, enough's enough,' I said. 'It's bad enough you coming down here drunk and talking like that in front of a kid, but you've gone too far.' I walked towards him, leaving Paddy standing at the doorway, and took Jimmy by the elbow. He swung round and shoved me away and I skittered backwards in surprise and landed in the easy chair. Behind me, I heard the girl give a little cry of fear. I leapt up again quickly and faced him.

'OK, Jimmy. I'm not going to argue with you. Tell me what it is you want and you can have it. And I'll see you when you're sober enough to apologise.'

'Give me my book. You took it away. I want it back. Now. *Now*!' he shouted, his voice rising up the scale.

'Oh, your history? Is that it? Well, you can have it back. Just don't touch anything else.' He kept on rummaging, opening drawers and turning out the contents on to the floor. The place was a mess. I was torn between absolute fury at Jimmy's behaviour, and disgust at what I was witnessing. I had never, in all my life, seen the old man like this. I would have been hard pressed to even remember seeing him angry. I crossed over to the far side of the room to where I'd put the box with all his papers and jottings down in the corner beside the old dark dresser, and hefted it in my arms.

'Is this what you came for? The book? Well here it is.'

Jimmy turned and his red-rimmed eyes fastened on the box greedily. He whipped it quickly out of my hands and clasped it hard against his chest. There was still foam at the corners of his mouth, and he grinned, and then he let out a little laugh that was more chilling than any display of anger.

'Take it and go, Jimmy. Just go now,' I said. I was shaking a bit, from anger or dismay, and I'm sure it showed in my voice. I'm also sure he didn't notice.

He giggled again, a sly, triumphant little laugh that was chilling, and almost ran out of the room. Paddy shrank back into the hallway as he went past, as if she was afraid he'd turn on her, or maybe just knock her down and trample her. I was suddenly afraid of that too, but Jimmy didn't even notice her.

His mind was totally wrapped around the box and its contents, as tightly as the arms that clutched it to his chest, and he blundered up the hallway and out of the front door like a looter getting out before he hears the sirens. I took Paddy's hand and we went out into the pathway and watched as the old man hurried up the middle of the street, half walking, half running, his coat flapping behind him.

That was the last time I saw Jimmy Allison alive.

I loved that old man, and I believe I've told you already what he meant to me.

He scurried away and went home and some time later he was found there, lying at the bottom of his stairs, in a crumpled heap. His neck was broken, and nobody knew whether he had fallen or had thrown himself down the narrow flight. He was still wearing his coat and his shirt was done up wrongly, and I'm sorry now that I was angry and disgusted with him that last time.

Paddy asked me what was wrong with the old man, and I told her I didn't know.

'Isn't he a friend of yours?' she said. 'He was with us at the festival.'

'That's right, but I think he's not very well today. I'm sorry you were scared.'

'I'm not scared as long as you're there.'

'Well thank you ma'am, for that big vote of confidence,' I said, trying to raise the mood and shake off the bad taste that Jimmy's visit had left under my tongue.

I twirled the rough walking stick around like the fox in *Pinocchio* and made a deep bow.

'Care to walk out with me, ma'am?' I said, smiling as widely and as genuinely as I could. She caught on and took my extended hand.

'Why thank you sir, I'd love to,' she said, and laughed her momentary fear away. I flicked down the peak of the fishing cap and she said 'Hey, watch it, buster', and we went down the path and out through the gate. We went the opposite way from Jimmy Allison.

As we got to the corner of the street and took a left that would take us in a sweeping curve through Westbay and up on to the main street, there was a wail of a siren up ahead starting in the east of town and getting louder as it got level with us, then dopplering down in flat tones as it gained distance in the direction of Levenford.

'What's that? A cop car?' Paddy asked.

'Don't know, sunshine. Maybe an ambulance, or even a fire engine.'

'Pity we missed it. I ain't seen a fire engine here.'

'Haven't seen,' I corrected.

'Right. Haven't. Where's it going anyhow?'

'I don't know. Probably out of town. Sometimes the Kirkland

brigade gets called out to help out at Levenford and vice versa. Might not even be a fire engine anyway. It'll be long gone by the time we get up to the main street.'

When we got up to the middle of the town and past the shops, the place was fairly quiet, which was strange for a Monday morning. There was hardly anybody about, and I could see at a glance that a few of the shops hadn't even opened yet, which was even more strange. Mary Baker's was still closed, and there was nobody in Tom Muir's butcher's shop which normally had a queue at this time in the morning. The red-faced shopkeeper was standing behind his white marble counter and he tipped his white paper hat to us as we passed, before going back to sharpening one of his big knives on the long whet with the practised ease of long experience.

A woman passed us and we both said hello, but she didn't acknowledge, and Paddy and I looked at each other. There was a clatter, and we both turned and the woman was still walking slowly along, but she'd let go one of the handles of her shopping bag and a can of fruit or beans had rolled out on to the pavement and continued across to the kerb before toppling slowly into the street. Paddy let go of my hand and skipped back and picked the can up and caught up with the woman. When she got level, she handed it to her and the woman took it. Paddy came back to me and I watched as the woman looked at the can in her hand as if she didn't know how it had got there. She

262

was still looking at it when I turned with a shrug and continued along the road. We had got a few hundred yards along the main street when I turned back, and the woman was *still* there and still staring, as far as I could see from that distance, at the can Paddy had given her. Weird, I thought.

There was hardly anybody else about. It felt as if Paddy and I were walking through a ghost town.

Out towards the Milligs it still looked as if Arden was having a lie-in after the exertions of the harvest festival, but when we got to the bridge that went across Strowan's Water, just as I was going to turn left and take the path that would lead us up the valley, I saw a pall of smoke further ahead and caught, through the trees, the sapphire-blue sparkle of a flashing police light.

'What's that?' Paddy asked, pointing ahead.

'I don't know. Looks like a fire, or maybe an accident.'

Just as I said that my stomach did a slow, lazy flip, turned itself over as if the ground had just disappeared from beneath my feet, and suddenly I was shaken with a wave of certain dread. I remembered the rumbling, thundery noise I had heard as we motored down from Barbara's place – a deep, growl that seemed to shake the jeep. I had assumed it was thunder and I remember thinking that Barbara should take it easy if we did get a sudden rainstorm.

But it had come from the *east* of town. Suddenly I was sure of that. And the clouds that were far out over the firth were still far in the west. The thunder had come only five minutes or so after Barbara had left us. A cold, knife-hard fear probed at the back of my head and instantly I didn't want to walk a step further.

'Come on,' I said. 'We have to go quickly.' And we ran towards the flashing lights and that tower of smoke that was piling up high into the sky. Paddy kept up with me easily and we got along past the curve at Milligs and raced along the road to where I could see, in the distance, a couple of police cars and an ambulance blocking the road.

There was a fire engine there too.

Even from several hundred yards away, and despite the trees that hid most of the scene, I could hear that loud crashing roar that sounded like a giant blowtorch, and above the trees there was a sheet of flame that sent tongues of fire licking high. The smoke billowed upwards in a huge cloud.

My heart started thudding heavily in my chest and I wished I had felt fitter, but we covered the distance and got up to where the cars were parked just at this side of the Kilmalid Bridge, the old stone hump-back that spanned the stream that ran past the far edge of the Milligs and down to the mudflats. There were a lot of men, police and firemen running about, and not much else to see, unless you counted the thirty-foot wall of flame that seemed to spout up from the stream itself. The heat, from almost forty yards away, was intense, and I felt a searing gust on my face. I stopped to look, stunned by the white heat, and with my left arm I made sure Paddy was behind me.

The Kilmalid Bridge had gone. There was nothing left to span the stream, and there was a moraine of rocks and stone all round, scattered across the street and on the verge. The air was shimmering and, through eyes that were already watering, I could see the hulking shape of a lorry or tractor in the middle of the flames, angled down towards the stream. Even without the heat haze, it looked like a twisted mass that glowed white and red. And there wasn't that much of it.

One of the policemen turned round and saw us standing there, and waved his hands at us. Over the roaring of the fire, his words were lost, but there was no mistaking the gesture. He was a lot closer to the flames than we were – and it must have been *damned* hot where he was, and he wanted us to stay well clear. I took the hint.

I pushed Paddy ahead of me in the opposite direction from the inferno, crossing at the same time to the north side of the road, where there was some shelter in the trees. We got under the spread of an oak, well out of the heat, and sat down.

'What's happened, Nicky?'

'I'm not sure, Paddy. There's been an accident, but I think we'd better stay well away. It looks pretty hot out there.'

'It *is* pretty hot,' she said. 'It's like when mom opens up the oven.'

'Yes,' I said, and again that sick feeling of dread stole in.

For some reason, I had to get across to the other side of the demolished bridge and find out *who* was in that wreck.

We sat there until I got my breath back and Paddy stared at me from under the peak of my hat. She looked solemn and a bit scared. So was I. After a few minutes, I stood up and took her hand again, and instead of going along the road I headed into the trees and down the slope towards the burn, maybe sixty yards north of the road. The stream was fairly full, despite the dry spell, but we had no difficulty in crossing it, far from where the action was. When we were on the other side of the burn, we continued along a well-worn path until we were a good distance from that dreadful gusher of flame. Down on the main road – the Kilcreggan Road again – we followed the hedgerow until I could see another fire engine on this side of the bridge. I told Paddy to wait there and she sat down on a tussock of grass obediently and nodded when I told her not to move. Her eyes were wide and glassy. She knew that something had happened and she didn't know what, but I knew without being told that she had had that dreadful sinking feeling that, whatever it was, it had something to do with her.

I stepped out from the hedge and sprinted towards the bridge. There were two fire engines, obviously from Levenford, and two teams of men in their yellow helmets were wrestling with thick hoses, straining to aim their hard jets of water at the centre of the flames. Out of the corner of my eye, in a small stand of trees and saplings, I saw a car that was angled off the road, on its side. My heart did a dive and then it started thudding in my ears. It was

Barbara's Volvo estate, crumpled in on the passenger side. The front end had concertinaed and a wheel had sheared off. The windscreen was gone, and even as I turned to look directly at it, I saw the red mush that covered the white of the bent bonnet. I could feel my breakfast make a bid for release and swallowed hard against it. I turned back towards the fire and, as I did so, I saw something, maybe a rag, fluttering limply in the fork of a sapling, white and red among the green. It wasn't until later that I realised what it was.

There was another police car, parked well behind the fire engines, and a uniformed officer standing well behind that. The roar from the flames was enormous, and when I reached him I had to shout to be heard.

He tried to tell me to get back, but I shook my head. I pointed back to the wrecked Volvo and yelled in his ear.

'What happened to the driver?'

'Hospital. Ambulance has just gone,' he shouted into my ear.

'Alive?'

'Dunno. Couldn't tell. Looked pretty bad. Blood everywhere.' The left side of the policeman's face was red from the heat of the flames, giving him a two-toned look.

'Which hospital?' I asked, and again he shrugged.

'Western Infirmary, most likely.'

'What happened here?'

'Petrol tanker came off and hit the gas pipe.'

That explained the flames. From where we stood we had to shield our eyes against them, and I had to hand it to the firemen who were a lot closer in than we were, still huddled over their writhing snakes, jetting water into the heat.

'Must have gone up like a bomb,' the man said.

The main gas pipe spanned the burn a couple of yards downstream from the old bridge. It was an unofficial bridge that kids from Arden had used since time immemorial, balancing on the two-foot wide shiny black surface, teetering across its smooth length, with a jam-jar full of sticklebacks or minnows. Now there was nothing left of the pipe, a great hole where the bridge used to be, and just a white-hot tangle of wreckage that used to be the cab and the bowser of the petrol tanker.

I stood mesmerised by the giant blowtorch and I wished to God somebody would go and turn the gas off. The firemen were *never* going to be able to put out that fire, no matter how much water they threw on it. I left the policeman at his post and went back to where Paddy was still sitting quietly, and I didn't even look at the wreckage of Barbara's estate car in the grove. If I had, I'm sure I would have been sick. I didn't want Paddy to see me throwing up. I didn't know what I was going to tell her.

She looked up at me from under the peak, still holding on to my walking stick like a little shepherdess, with inquiry in her eyes. I sat down and put my arm around her narrow shoulders, and two big tears sprang up and rolled down her cheeks.

'Is it my mommy?' she asked. 'Is she dead?'

I pushed myself back and looked down at her, wondering how the hell she'd read my mind.

'What makes you ask that?' I asked, backing out of the question.

Paddy didn't say anything. She just pointed past me, through a gap in the hedge that looked on to a curve in the road. At the other side of the curve, I could see clearly the battered and bent shell of the Volvo. I had made Paddy sit here alone in the one place that gave her a window on to the wreckage.

I fumbled for words, casting about blindly, and came up with nothing. All I had was the truth.

'It's your mum's car,' I said. It sounded like a confession. 'I don't know what happened, but they've taken her to hospital.'

'Is she dead?'

'I think she's hurt. I don't know how bad. But we're going to find out right now.'

Tears were rolling in a steady chain down her cheeks

and I felt her give a little sob. But that was all. I gave her what I thought was a reassuring hug and I felt I could have done with one myself.

'Come on, let's go and find out. We'd better go quickly, 'cause your mum'll need us right now.'

I helped Paddy to her feet and took her hand again and she just came with me, her face blank, but the tears still rolling. I wished I hadn't sat her on that tussock. I could have spun her a line, maybe, delayed the moment, but I hadn't and there was nothing I could do about it. We crossed back through the trees and over the stream to the far side, and by the time we got past the roaring of the fire geyser I just picked her up and carried her. The fast walk back to my place seemed to take for ever. Paddy just put her head into the curve of my neck and soaked me with those big tears and I felt sick for her.

Back at the house I tried to phone the ambulance service and the police, but there was nothing but static on the line. I didn't know right then, but discovered soon after, that the explosion that had wrecked the bridge had also burned away the telephone cable and the main power line that serviced half of the town, in one neat blast. All the time I was trying to get a line, Paddy kept looking at me with hope and fear and misery fighting for pole position in her eyes. I didn't have the guts to look away.

Finally I gave up and decided that we just had to go. Getting out to where we could find out what had happened to her was better than sitting here fretting. In a couple of minutes I had Paddy strapped in the jeep and we were heading towards Kirkland to double across the moor road, taking the long way round. I was in a panic the whole time. Paddy said very little.

NINETEEN

Barbara gave two toots on her horn as she swung the big estate out of the driveway and down the hill to the town. She was still smiling with pleasure at what Nick had said and at the compliment from her daughter.

It *was* a vote of confidence but, then again, they were probably both biased. Having said that, she had taken care to ensure that she was looking good and she was *feeling* good. It had been an interesting night and today she was going to give them her best shot.

'They *will* need their heads looked at if they didn't hire me,' she thought as she spun the wheel at the main road and headed east past the shops. In her head she thought through all the questions she might be asked and she hoped she wouldn't be overcome by nerves when she finally got right down to it. It had been a long time since she'd worked, but her qualifications were still good and she wasn't the nervous type.

Out through Westbay, past the allotments, round the slight curve at Milligs the big Volvo cruised smoothly. The streets were quiet, and there was hardly any traffic on the road. She'd passed by the shops, there was hardly anybody to be seen, but that didn't register.

Barbara hoped that Paddy wouldn't tire Nick out, but she was sure her endless chatter and boundless enthusiasm just might. She was glad they'd taken to each other. Since that first day they'd met in the car park, and she'd suddenly been overcome with anger and fear when she saw the stranger talking to her daughter, she'd been thinking about him a lot.

He was different, naturally, from the boy she'd known, but there was something about him that was still the same.

Yes, she had invited him home last night, then invited him upstairs and she had no regrets. She knew there was a feeling between them, and if she talked straight to herself she would have said it was too early to have that sort of feeling. Maybe she wasn't ready to talk straight to herself just yet. She had Paddy and she had the rather remote elderly man she called father, but there was something *missing* from her life and it wasn't just a man.

There had been something missing from her life for a *long* time.

And recently, she had begun to think that that blank space, that nagging empty spot, would be empty no longer. Barbara had not pondered the compulsion that had sent her back to her home town again after almost a lifetime away. She had just done it, without questioning the drive. There were some things in her life that just demanded to *be*.

Out across the low bridge over Strowan's Water, and the power steering took the sharp turn as easy as thinking, then rolling swiftly along the solid mettle, Barbara thought she was *glad* she had come back.

Ahead the road took a lazy left and a matching right. The trees whipped past on either side, heliographing sunlight through on the firth side, darker on the north. After the second bend, the Kilmalid Bridge hove into sight. There was a sign before it giving the usual exaggerated picture of a hump-back bridge, which in this case wasn't too exaggerated. You couldn't see oncoming traffic from either side. Barbara slowed slightly, but the Volvo had enough momentum to whip over the hump and down the other side with a slight judder from the rear shockers and an exhilarating stomach wrench like a roller-coaster drop.

Barbara was still thinking her thoughts when something flashed over the trees ahead and to the right, catching her eye.

The big white bird wheeled in the air, stalled and spun on a wingtip, then it back-beat twice before folding its wings and dropping from the blue sky. It dived straight for the car.

270

Barbara had seen the flash of white and her eyes flicked back down to the road again. She didn't see the big bird swoop until it was only yards from her windscreen, and by then it was just a blur of white flashing in front of her eyes.

Instinctively, her hand left the steering wheel and came up to protect her eyes and her head jerked back against the tough headrest.

The gannet hit with a crashing thump that instantly snowed out the windscreen and covered her with bulleting glass. In slow motion she saw the great yellow spear of the beak slide right through, followed by the head and two brilliant blue eyes. Blood spurted all over her white suit and she screamed. The eyes stared at her and the blood gouted, squirting from a jagged hole in the bird's neck and out through its beak that was opened in a wide, silent seabird shriek. Suddenly, the whole window started to cave in, and that looming head seemed to lunge towards her. Barbara's other hand came off the wheel and she instinctively jammed her foot hard down on the brake. The car started to fishtail on the road, swiping the hedges on either side. Barbara was still in the world of slow motion, as if unaware that she was in a car, and that the car was hurtling along the Kilcreggan Road. Her eyes were transfixed by that gaping yellow and red maw and those piercing blue eyes that were now changing to white. The beak opened wider, impossibly wide, as if it was going to rip the head apart in beak-hinges, and a gout of blood flew out on to her face. And then the dead eyes turned pure white, and from the gaping stretch of that awesome mouth she heard a sound that was like a croak, but it was more like a low, vicious laugh.

The Volvo hurtled forward, despite the screeching of her brakes that left twin black snakes of burnt rubber on the road. Even then, Barbara might have walked away from this, but for the petrol tanker that was rumbling around the corner ahead.

Jim Semple was taking the bends at a fast clip. Not too fast on a narrow road like this, but enough to give the

271

satisfaction of handling his machine. Up high in the cab he could see pretty well ahead over the hedgerows except for the places where there was a stand of trees, but he never drove beyond his limit. He'd been driving heavy goods, low loaders, artics and tankers for a quarter of a century and had never had a bad one yet, touch wood. Anyway, this high off the road, if he did hit somebody, even head on, the chances were that he'd be way above any trouble.

He whistled as he drove his first load of the day. He'd pump out at the BP station in Kirkland, then across to the little station at Luss where he'd shed the rest of it, and have a nice ploughman's lunch at the bar of the hotel and then back to the terminal at Old Kilpatrick.

Jim got round a tight bend, just skimming the hedge, and then powered up the gears on the straight, feeling the big engine pulling ahead, fairly *shoving* the load. At the end of the straight there was a left bend and Jim dropped down again at the right moment, keeping the revs just right on the dot, and giving the air brakes just a touch, just a hiss. Then he put the foot down and hauled on the wheel and was round this one, then same again for the right, smooth and powerful, the brakes sneezing hard to take the weight, then just as he was getting into the far straight the Volvo shot right out of nowhere coming fish-tailing straight at him.

Jim's eyes flew wide at the same time as he jerked on the wheel and hit the brakes. The Volvo was careering from side to side. Its front window was frosted right over, and there was something like a sheet, all white and red, cluttering across it.

He yanked hard on the wheel, pulling the tanker right into the hedge, and he could feel the big tyres digging hard into the soft soil on the verge and the rat-a-tat of small branches clicking off the nearside mirror and scraping along the bowser. The car shot past on his right and he flicked a glance down. There was a face at the window and then it was past. Jim hauled back again at the wheel, whipping the tail round, hoping it was moving fast enough in the swing to miss the car. He felt, rather than heard, the jarring bump as the Volvo's front headlamp and bumper clipped the rear wheel.

In the estate, Barbara's world whirled dizzily. There was a *crump* and a sickening jar, and then she was upside down. The seat belt socked her right across the chest, and everything started to lurch around, as if her eyeballs were loose in their sockets and she was being shaken like a rat in a dog's jaws. Then there was a huge, devastating thump as the dashboard and steering wheel came up and smashed her. Inside her chest she felt something break and there was a huge, sickening pain in her head and everything spun away to nothing.

Jim Semple saw the Volvo in his rear-view mirror. He didn't see the car hit, but as soon as he felt it, he shot a look at the glass and saw the estate car spin crazily, like a ballet dancer, on one headlamp, and then it tumbled out of sight.

All this had happened in about the space of one second and Jim was still hauling on the big wheel and still standing on the brakes to try to get his speed down. The nearside wheel, still in the soft earth at the side, hit a rock and the wheel jerked hard to the left, and Jim felt himself losing control. That sick feeling of losing it swept through him.

The big tanker ploughed down twenty feet of hedge and tore a gout out of the grass as the momentum carried it forward. Ahead, the hump-back bridge loomed into view and Jim wrestled the wheel around. He felt the cab swerve back on to the right line and almost had time to breathe a sigh of relief. But that last wrench out of the verge had been enough to set the back of the tanker just off line and the big wheels dug up the grass as the whole load began to shift. The rear clipped a small ash tree and broke it off at waist height and then it just started to slide, jack-knifing round, demolishing the fence. It started to roll just a bit and then the cab spun round on its pivot, bit off the main tanker, bounced and its wheels left the ground as the lorry rolled, like a dying caterpillar. Jim Semple was thrown against the roof of the cab and back down on the floor as the tanker flipped over and down the gully, crashing through the saplings just at the edge of the bridge. There was an immense crashing sound as the cab hit the big black pipe, and then it was all over for Jim Semple. The pipe just broke in two, and the two-foot-wide high-pressure stream of gas caught fire with a huge *ker-whump* that melted the glass and roasted Jim Semple to a cinder in the space of three seconds. Five seconds after that, the whole tanker caught fire and the bowser, nestled under the bridge, roared into a fireball. The immense upward pressure of the explosion under the bridge lifted the whole arch in one and scattered the rocks and stones all over the road.

By the time the fire engines arrived, the cab of the tanker had completely melted, and there was hardly anything left of the ruptured tank. There was nothing left of Jim Semple.

It was another ten minutes after that before anybody noticed the wrecked Volvo in amongst the trees. Two ambulancemen clambered through the undergrowth and found Barbara Foster lying in a pool of blood underneath the crushed steering wheel. It wasn't until they got her into the ambulance that they found a heartbeat, weak and fluttery, but a beat none the less.

It took them less than half an hour to get her to the Western Infirmary, and by that time her heart had stopped beating three times. A team of doctors worked on her for four hours, cutting, stitching, injecting, draining. She had shattered her left thigh. There was a bad fracture on her skull, and severe swelling of the frontal lobe of her brain. She had been given twelve pints of blood, and had four splinters of bone removed from her lung. Added to the multiple lacerations, contusions and abrasions, Barbara was in a bad shape. But she was alive.

She was also in a coma.

TWENTY

When we got to Kirkland, I stopped at the first pay phone and the operator gave me the number for the ambulance service. While I was thumbing coins into the slot, I glanced out of the kiosk at Paddy who was still sitting in the jeep. Her face was white and set, a picture of misery.

I finally got through to the depot and fretted while a telephonist put me on to the operations room, and then I had to wait for a few minutes, worried in case my money would run out, before somebody came on to tell me that Barbara had been taken to the Western. The guy was good enough to give me the number there: I wrote it down on the back of my hand, thanked him and hung up. Paddy didn't say anything when I went back to the jeep to rummage in the glove compartment where I normally slung my loose change. She just looked at me with the question in her eyes.

'Just hang on for a few more minutes, Sunshine,' I said and ruffled her hair. Normally she smiled at me when I did that, but not this time. I found enough coins for another call and got straight on to the hospital where I had to get through to admissions, and then on to a ward where a sister transferred me to intensive care.

'Mrs Hartford is in surgery at the moment,' the flat, matter-of-fact voice told me. 'It's too early to say yet.'

I got in a few questions that got short replies. You know the kind of words they use in hospitals. *Critical.* Poor. Intensive care. That sort of thing. But at least she's alive.

I hauled myself into the driver's seat, and Paddy just looked at me with those big blue eyes that were doing all the talking for her. I reached down and plunged the release catch on the belt that held her against the back of the seat and it pinged up and slid into the reel above her head. Then I pulled her across to me and put my arms around her. I could feel her tremble, all stiff and jangly, against my ribs.

'She's alive,' I whispered. 'They've taken her to hospital and the doctors are looking after her right now, so don't worry. We'll go straight there and see how she's doing. OK?'

Down somewhere around my chest, I felt Paddy nodding her head, and then she gave a big shudder and all that fear and grief that had been written all over her face since she'd seen her mother's car crumpled and battered in the stand of trees, it all came out of her in a released torrent. She sat there with her face buried in my chest and her shoulders heaved, and she bawled her little heart out. I held on tightly to her until she was over the worst of it, and then I loosened my grip. I fished a paper hankie out of the door pocket and tilted up her chin. The tears were flowing freely and I wiped both eyes. She sniffed and her breath was catchy from crying.

'Will we go now?' I asked. She nodded. I pulled down the seat belt again and clipped it home. Then we drove out of Kirkland.

The Western Infirmary is a big tower of concrete and glass built on to the old university hospital that is now mostly used as offices and storage. I stuck the jeep in the underground park and took Paddy up to the reception where we followed the blue lines on the vinyl floor tiles to the elevators and up to the seventh level. The floor was hushed. Nurses moved economically and quietly, padding about in cloth slippers. Most of them were gowned and masked. Some of them had blood on the green gowns and I hoped Paddy wouldn't notice.

The SRN at the desk told us to wait a while and I sat Paddy down on one of the moulded plastic seats while I leaned against the wall. I would have shot somebody for a cigarette. The nurse came back and motioned me across to the desk. Barbara was still in the operating theatre, she told

276

me. She was in very bad shape. The doctors thought she had a chance, but that was all. It was too early to say.

I went back and translated this into something a bit more hopeful for Paddy and she nodded. A little smile flickered across her face. We had a choice to wait here or wander. I thought I should get the girl out of the hushed atmosphere of the hospital, because there was nothing for us to do but think about chances and odds and what the emergency team were doing with Paddy's mother. Paddy came willingly enough. I took her to the art gallery at Kelvingrove which was only a half a mile away, and we strolled through the grounds for a while, watching all the normal people saunter about. In the art gallery I had a coffee in the cafeteria and Paddy surprised me by eating a danish pastry with her Coke. Then we wandered around the exhibits, and the fascinating collection of dinosaurs and fossils took her mind off the immediate problem for a while. I spun it out for as long as I could, so we toured the animal exhibits, then round through the archaeology department where I dredged up all my knowledge to answer the questions that she started to throw my way. Halfway round the stone-age exhibit, I saw a selection of arrowheads and spear points. One of them was very similar to the one that I'd found in Kitty's box. I pointed it out to Paddy and said I had one of them, without realising that in my pocket my hand was clasping around the thing. When I discovered this coincidence, I laughed and pulled it out of my pocket: Paddy did a quick double-take, thinking at first that I'd opened the display case and stolen the piece. Mine was almost exactly like the one behind the glass.

That was not the only coincidence. In the next display, there was a collection of Celtic jewellery, and in pride of place was a gold torc, pinned to black velvet. I pointed it out to Paddy, and her hand flew to her neck. I looked down, and there, peeping out from the V of her collar, were the two gold spheres of the one I'd given her. The one Paddy was wearing was finer and more simple than the museum's piece. Absent-mindedly, she rubbed her gold necklet as if it was a charm.

We walked back to the hospital and followed the lines and took the elevator up again to the hush zone where we found we still had some waiting to do. Paddy was a bit brighter than she had been, but I wasn't feeling great at all. There were a few things flitting around in my head that were demanding urgent attention, like how to contact Barbara's father. Paddy knew he was in London, but she didn't know where he was staying or with whom. I didn't know what to do about that at all. I wondered what to do about the girl, and decided that there was nothing for it but she should stay with me.

It was getting well into the afternoon when Paddy turned to me – I had just gone outside for ten minutes for a cigarette and she'd sat patiently for me to return – and said: 'It's going to be all right.'

I thought maybe somebody had come out that swing door, the one that keeps the secrets of scalpels and clamps safely away from the uninitiated, and had spoken to her.

But Paddy said no-one had come through.

'I just know. That's all,' she said. 'She's not going to die.'

'Of course she isn't,' I said, with as much sincerity and optimism as I could muster, which was probably very little. Paddy didn't know about the bone splinters in the collapsed lung, and all the other broken bits of her mother's body.

'The doctors are just fixing her up. They just take their time to get it right,' I said.

'Yes, But she's not going to die. I just know it.'

I looked down at her, and she looked up at me and there was that bright smile on her face, as if she *did* know it. There was a look of complete surety there that took me by surprise. I hoped it wasn't shock talking.

Just then the swing doors with their fogged-over portholes banged open and a tall man, still wearing a green gown and a cap, came towards us. I stood up and Paddy grabbed my hand.

'Mr Hartford?'

'No, my name's Ryan. I'm a friend of the family. This is Mrs Hartford's daughter.'

'Ah,' he paused and seemed to consider this.

'Mrs Hartford's father is out of town at the moment. I'm looking after Paddy here.'

'Right. Well, I might as well let the young lady know that her mother is as well as can be expected under the circumstances.'

He looked down at Paddy and beamed reassuringly.

'She's in intensive care now, and in a few minutes you can go in and see her.' The doctor bent down and took Paddy's other hand. 'Now, she'll be all wrapped up in bandages and there are some tubes to help her breathing and to give her the right sort of medicine, but you've not to worry about that, all right?'

Paddy nodded and smiled up at him. He told her to go and sit down for a moment and she did as she was told without question. The doctor took my arm and edged me away from her. When we'd got to the other side of the room, he started telling me what had been going on in there for all those hours. Basically, the surgeons had done all they could to repair the damage. They'd set the broken femur and bound up the ribcage after getting in to get the splinters of bone out. I got a blow by blow account, like a bill from a garage mechanic. The bottom line was that Barbara was in a coma, which was not surprising, the doctor said, because of the skull fracture and the swelling on the brain.

'We think we've repaired all the damage quite well. She'll have a few scars, but the ribs will be fine and her leg break wasn't as bad as we thought at first. Her heart's beating normally and we've got the lung inflated. But that's as much as I can do at the moment. We've got a specialist coming over from the Southern General later. In fact we may have to transfer her there, because they're the experts on head injuries. That's the worrying thing. She may come out of it in a day or two, or it may take longer. We just

279

don't know at the moment.'

I called Paddy over. He took us along a corridor and into the intensive care unit. Barbara was close to the door in a high hospital cot that was surrounded by high-tech machinery, and she was festooned with wires and tubes.

Lying in the cot, she was swathed in bandages and deathly still. She could have been dead, except for the very slight rise and fall of her chest. There were tubes in her arm and one up her nose, and under her eyes was puffed and bruised. It just didn't look like Barbara.

Paddy stared at her mother for a long time, and then a nurse came round and asked us to let her in to check some of the machinery. I took the hint and pulled gently on the little girl's hand, and she came along. Even as we were going through the doorway, her eyes never left her mother's face.

In the jeep, I concentrated on the city traffic until we got on to the expressway that headed west. Paddy was pretty quiet, but when we got closer to Levenford she turned to me.

'She will be all right Nick. I just know it.'

'I think so too Paddy. She's just been through a lot.'

'She's sleeping and I know she's hurt awful bad. But she'll get better I can feel it.'

'That's good, Paddy, you go on feeling that way and it'll be just as you say.' I thought she was being a mite optimistic. I sure as hell wasn't.

'But you don't understand Nick,' she said, in her piping voice. 'It *will* be. I don't know how I know but I know my mom's going to sleep for a long time and then she'll wake up. She's *safe*.'

There was something in her tone that made me realise that she was truly certain that Barbara was going to pull out of this, and that made me feel a bit brighter myself. There's nothing so good for the spirits as an optimistic kid who holds your hand and says 'There, there.'

I drove on a bit and stole a glance at the girl. She was leaning back on her seat and fingering the two spheres on the torc, and she had a smile on her face. Suddenly, I don't know why, I just accepted what she said as the truth. I realised that Barbara *was* going to pull through this. She was safe. And she would come back to both of us.

The storm clouds were thick and towering in the west as we crossed over the span of the Erskine Bridge; dark and heavy, they came piling together down the firth. When we left Glasgow, the air still had that clear, high-pressure sharpness that had kept the summer going long and hot, but as we zipped across the bridge the dividing line between summer and autumn was written in the sky. We hit the first rain in almost two months when we passed Levenford and out along the Loch Lomondside Road to take the detour route back home. Just at the turn-off where the dual carriageway was nipped into a single road, there was a blue-yellow flicker of lightning over the hills on the left and big heavy raindrops started to spat on the windscreen. In seconds the first drops became a downpour that spun silver pennies on the road ahead. The surface went from slick as the dust soaked up the rain, then to wet, and then it became a stream in the space of about half a mile.

When we turned to come over the Black Hill Road, the rain got steadily worse and I switched on the big halogen beams as visibility closed down, and I slowed even further to cope. The big radials sent up spume in clouds on either side and the rain never changed beat on the roof. Over the crest of the hill and down towards Kirkland we could see the expanse of the firth in the distance, a slate-grey blanket that reflected back the flares of fork lightning through the gauzy curtain of rain. By this time the road was awash and even at lower speed there were a couple of times I felt the steering slide that little bit, telling me I was aquaplaning on the bends. I came down a gear and slowed further. The wipers were toiling and even the inside of the screen was beginning to mist up.

On the long straight of the Kilcreggan Road back to Arden, the clouds above were like a barn roof and the air seemed even thicker. The lightning was coming down in arc-lamp sizzles and the thunder was like heavy artillery, rolling in on the rain and bouncing off the Langcraig face as we splashed past. Paddy nearly jumped out of her seat when an almost horizontal bolt of white light snaked out right in front of the jeep and sizzled the air in a jagged line. There was an instantaneous crack of sound that almost shook us right off the road, an *immense* wallop as if the atmosphere had imploded, and the bolt slammed into a stunted oak in a small field. The tree just came apart in an instant of blue and yellow and for seconds afterwards I had a purple after-image running right across my vision.

We passed Langcraig and I confess I speeded up a bit because I was getting nervous of those lightning strokes. The rain beat down relentlessly and already it was beginning to spill down the runnels of the stone faces that had been dry for the whole hot spell, and it came washing down across the road, bringing silt and debris. As we passed the big fan-shaped face, there was a white and brown column of water peeling off and dropping nearly fifty feet on to the scree below, and I could hear the rush of it over the drumming of the rain. Just as we were coming level with the instant waterfall, there was another cataclysmic peal of thunder that rocked the jeep on its chassis, and the crackling bolt of lightning seemed to snake right down the waterflow, sparkling it with blue St Elmo's fire, and seeming to wash with the flow in a sizzling blue carpet right across the road. Even with the window closed I could smell the nose-tingling odour of burnt air. I don't know what caused that lightning on the water, and I've never heard of it before, but there was nothing I could do about it anyway, because I was doing about forty-five and it was too damn close. We skittered straight into that flickering stream and there was the weirdest feeling of tension all over. I could feel the hairs on my neck and the back of my hands begin to crawl about and there was a ringing in my ears. For an instant the windscreen wipers just stopped in mid swipe and the screen was immediately flooded. The engine cut right out and if I hadn't put my foot on the clutch there and then we would have slewed round and into a ditch or a fence post. But suddenly we were through, the engine coughed back into life again, the wipers began their frenetic beat and the lights came on. My skin stopped crawling. From behind us came an immense booming sound, but I couldn't see what was happening in the rearview. I just supposed it was another bolt of lightning, but it sounded like an avalanche, and the road seemed to vibrate under the wheels. I couldn't have cared less at that moment.

Five minutes later I was bundling Paddy, under the shelter of my jacket, up the garden path, and I got completely soaked while I fumbled with my key. Finally we barged inside and shut the door on that incredible downpour. Outside, there was still thunder and lightning, but inside it was dry and safe.

I put the kettle on and made both of us a cup of coffee. Paddy talked about the lightning. She was more animated than she'd been since this morning, and I suppose the superb display had taken her mind off her mother. But later she told me again that Barbara was going to be all right. She couldn't explain how she knew, but she was completely assured of it anyway. As along as she felt that way – and it was reassuring even to me – I was not prepared to make any dents in her optimism.

I put on the central heating and lit up the coal fire in the living room which soon made the place a bit cheerier. Paddy and I graduated from happy families to draughts and then we played a game of chess with my grandfather's old wooden set that was worn smooth and warm with years of use. Her game was simple but she was good for her age and she had the killer instinct. It kept our minds off things. Not entirely, but for whole minutes at a time. Outside, the rain beat steadily down and there was a steady gusher from the gable gutter that was spilling over. I remembered the slates that had come off in the big storm on the night that I'd arrived. I'd always meant to get somebody up there to fix them and now I was hoping that the roof wouldn't leak.

Later on I scrambled some eggs and put them on toast for both of us, and we watched the lightning arc and fork outside the window. After that, I ran a bath for her and sent her upstairs and let her splash around until her fingers wrinkled. I threw in one of my old chambray shirts that came down almost to her calves, and she came downstairs to get her hair dried in front of the fire looking like a hillbilly.

When she'd gone upstairs later, I sat and tried to watch television, but the lightning was playing havoc with the reception, so I gave it up and read a bit of a paperback for a while. Without Paddy there, my attention kept slipping from the pages and back to the morning. I kept seeing that battered Volvo in the trees, and the sight of Barbara, lying mummified and tube-fed in the intensive care room, came springing back to me. Eventually I gave up and climbed up the stairs. I looked in on Paddy and she was sound asleep. In my own bed I listened to the hammering of the rain on the slates and took a long time lying there in the dark to get to sleep.

TWENTY-ONE

The shadow knocked on Tom Muir's door and went in. Eadie Muir, the butcher's well-rounded wife, was fast asleep, a beached whale that caused the other side of the bed to sink alarmingly. Tom Muir was no lightweight either. He was a big-boned man with a bristling moustache that was connected to mutton-chop sideburns, and he combed his hair from his left ear in a couple of tightly-stretched lines across the dome of his head. He was a ruddy-faced man, partly from his taste for whisky and partly because he spent a lot of time in his big walk-in freezer. Tom Muir was a jovial fellow who always had the time of day to pass with the customers of his shop.

That night, Tom was far from jovial. He'd woken early to get the shop ready early on the morning after the festival and he'd had a splitting headache. Not unusual, for Tom had been hungover many a time, but the morning's pounder made his eyes water. He'd gone down and got the joints from the freezer, cut off steaks on the saw and laid out the enamel plates just so, the way his father and grandfather had done for years.

It had been a quiet day. Hardly anybody came in, and those that did were quiet and distant, but Tom had thought business might be slack after the late night celebrations, and there were bound to be people with worse hangovers than he had. *He* hadn't needed the flatloader express with the rest of the drunks. He had walked home with his wife, and his sons, Andy and Bill, had come in sometime in the morning looking much the worse for wear. The shop had been quiet, but that dull ache at the back of his head was enough to make him more than a little grateful. Mrs Hardy had come in and spent ten minutes deciding what she wanted, which was strange because she always took six mutton pies on a Monday, but she'd looked around and seemed as if she'd forgotten why she'd come. Eventually Tom had bundled the pies into a package and put them in her bag, and she'd wandered off without so much as a thank you or good day but, even stranger, she'd forgotten to pay, and when Tom called to her at the door she just kept on as if she hadn't heard. No matter, he'd remember next time and she was a regular anyway, so a day or two would make no difference.

It had been a strange day, sure enough, but the headache did start to subside a bit from the jackhammer of the morning to pillow-thuds in the afternoon. By evening, it was almost gone, but Tom's eyes had started to go funny. Nothing bad, just flashes on the edge of his vision, as if something was moving in at the corners, but every time he turned his head there was nothing there. He'd told Eadie about it and she'd said maybe he should get his eyes tested and gone back to demolishing the prime sirloin steak that was oozing just a little too much blood on to her plate.

At night, Tom lay in the dark, trying to get to sleep, but he kept seeing those flickering movements out of the corner of his eye. He started to worry in case he was getting a brain tumour. He'd seen a programme on television about somebody who had one of them and it affected his sight. He kept seeing things.

Then Eadie started to snore and that made it even worse. She lay on her back and her mouth flapped wide open and her jowls, sleek and rounded, seemed to flabber with every breath. The snores were long and loud and, no matter how much Tom dug his elbow into her yielding girth, it never let up. Eadie just wouldn't wake and she wouldn't stop that disgusting noise at all. And those little coloured figures that had been staying just out of sight were jumping up in front of him every now and again, too quick to *really* catch, too fast to see clearly, but they were coming right out into the open. Eadie snored on, and Tom got angrier with her and more infuriated with those things

286

in his eyes or in his brain.

Tom's headache flared up high and hard in a wave that started way down his spine and shattered itself in bright sparks inside his skull, and Eadie's snore became a roar that was shaking him to pieces. The things in his eyes were flickering in and out and Tom knelt up in the bed, throwing the blanket off. He was holding each temple in his hands, pressing hard to kill off the noise and the flashes and the powerful pulses of pain. Eadie snorted and Tom whirled in the dark. He grabbed the rest of the blanket and flung it right off the bed, exposing Eadie's bulk like a lighter mound beside him. He grabbed her by the shoulders and shouted to her to shut up, but she never paid any attention to him. She just ignored him and carried on snoring. So Tom got her fat neck in his hands and squeezed and squeezed until the snoring stopped, and the pain in his head started to ooze away.

Gratified, he turned and switched on the light, and the little dancing figures were banished. Eadie lay beside him with her arms splayed out at right angles to her body. Big, pink, meaty arms. Her tongue was blue and swollen as it poked through her full lips. Her eyes had rolled up in their sockets so that all he could see were the whites. Eadie's nightdress had opened up and a large, soft breast had spilled out and seemed as though it was trying to drip down the side of her ribcage. The lightweight, voluminous gown had rucked right up to her hips and Eadie's heavy pink thighs splayed apart below the bulging curve of her belly. Tom thought she looked like a pig, with little feet at the end of plump rounded legs. There was an acrid smell of urine and a damp stain on the mattress where she'd wet the bed during the operation.

'Cow,' Tom said and got up out of bed. He went out to get a fresh blanket for he sure as hell wasn't going to sleep on a puddle of piss, but out at the top of the stairs he got lost and came back into the room again. What had he got up for?

It was time to go to work.

287

Tom dressed, looked out a fresh apron, put on his hat and went downstairs to the shop and five minutes later he came back and went to work.

It took him no more than half an hour to flense the carcass and take out the heart and liver and kidneys. The rest he just dumped. When that was done, he cut off the head and put it to one side, then, with efficiency born of years of experience, he took off the limbs. The torso he carried downstairs and he came back for the rest which he slung over his shoulder. The bedroom was covered in blood and the bed itself was a red mass, but the meat didn't bleed much at all once it had been cut into sections. Down in the shop, Tom ran the carcass over the saw, cutting the spine down the middle, and he used the handsaw to split the ribs, and he had two halves to work on. There wasn't much waste. He laid out the ribsteaks and small chops. He rolled meat and tied it into joints. He slung the spare fat into the rendering pot, and with what was left he filled the mincer and flicked the switch. Good red minced meat came squirming out through the perforations.

The enamel platters in the window were dressed nicely. Appetisingly.

And once Tom had finished, he stood there and waited for the customers to come in. He hoped it would be a busier day, because yesterday had been slack. Strange, wasn't it?

But there was always another day.

George and Brian weren't doing too well. They'd been bickering all day like two bad-tempered hens that were cooped up too close together. Brian had gone into a mood early on, and George clucked and fluttered around, nagging incessantly.

In the workshop at the back of their handicrafts store, Brian had been having problems all day. He'd planned to fire up the kiln and make a set of his vases while George worked out some candle designs. Normally they worked well together, helping and complimenting each other in mutual admiration. But today, things had been wrong. Brian was all fingers and thumbs at the wheel, and it had cost him two lots of clay that had slipped off on to the floor as he'd tried to get them into shape. That had never happened to him before, for he'd always been deft in clay. What was worse, George had laughed that high-pitched giggly way that got on Brian's nerves.

George had called him butterfingers and after laughing at the ruined clay he had flounced off.

Brian finally managed to get the clay centred and made his first piece, a plain grey vase that would end up earth-coloured when fired. It had taken him much longer than usual, but he blamed that on George and the fact that he wasn't feeling good. Probably had too much to drink at the festival, he reasoned. The other pots shaped themselves under his fingers and by the time he'd made his first two dozen the kiln was warming nicely. Brian was about to load it when George came back in and looked at his handiwork and simply *burst* into laughter again.

'What's that, then? A new design?' he snickered. 'Pottery Martians perhaps?' he said, chortling at his infinite wit.

Brian looked at his trays. The vases looked all right.

'What's wrong with them?'

'What's wrong? Are you joking? Look at them!'

Brian did. He shook his head.

'Nothing wrong with that lot,' he said.

'Have you gone *mad*?' George screeched. 'I mean to say, you're not seriously considering firing them, are you?'

Brian nodded.

'Of course, what else?'

'What in heaven's name are they supposed to be?'

'Vases, of course.'

'*Vases*?' George went into peals of laughter.

'They're just blobs of clay,' he said.

'Look George. I don't come and disturb you when you're working, so I'd appreciate it if you just buggered off and let me get on with it.'

'Buggered off?' George pouted. 'That's really nice.' He waddled out of the room. Brian looked over his vases.

'Blobs of clay, indeed,' he muttered. The vases were probably the best he'd ever made.

He shook his head in annoyance, carefully lifted his works of art on to their trays and slid them into the warming kiln. He closed the door and the crude, almost shapeless lumps of clay started to dry out in the heat.

In the afternoon, George almost went into hysterics when Brian brought them forth.

The tall man looked at his vases. They were beautiful.

He looked at George. He'd never noticed it before, in all the years he'd known him, but George was particularly fat and ugly. What did he know about art anyway?

It was late in the evening, an evening during which George nagged and harried, and Brian became more and more morose. George had made a meal and then he'd taken offence when Brian couldn't finish it. Whatever it was, Brian hadn't been hungry and there was a bad taste at the back of his throat, a sort of burning sensation as if he was developing a cold or something.

George had sat opposite him, chomping loudly. Brian could see his tongue coming out almost every time he chewed and it seemed that George's face, already pudgy, was getting plumper with every mouthful.

He was beginning to look disgusting. Brian tried to remember what he'd ever seen in him, and failed.

George kept popping in and out of the workroom, waddling like an angry duck firing off his barbed jibes. Eventually, he came in and plumped himself down in front of Brian and put his pudgy hands on to the table. Brian thought they looked like little sausages stuck together in bunches.

'I don't see why I have to do all the work around here, while all you do is mope around and make these monstrosities,' George said, gesturing at the tray of vases.

'It's about time you got your hairy arse off that seat and made yourself useful,' he rasped, leaning right across the heavy table. A speck of spittle landed on Brian's cheek.

290

George's face seemed to have swollen like a balloon and had taken on a bluish tinge. His lips seemed fuller and there was a dribble of saliva at one corner that was beginning to foam with the action of speaking. The lips looked as if they were about to burst and behind them Brian could see in great detail tiny little cavities in George's teeth that he had never noticed before. Brian was fascinated with that mouth and scarcely heard the words that were coming at him. His mind seemed to focus on those blubbering lips and the stains on the teeth and that foam that was being whipped up. It looked as if the mouth was getting bigger and getting ready to swallow him up.

'And don't just sit there staring, you great hairy oaf!' George shouted, his voice tailing off in a high register.

The volume seemed to jerk Brian back and the words came at him as if a speaker that had been turned down low had been swung right up to full volume.

'. . . great hairy oaf . . .' was what came blaring out at him, and something inside Brian just cracked.

The high pressure that had been building up all day suddenly gave way in a devastating flood of rage that shook Brian to his feet. In one movement he picked up one of his vases and swung it round at that bloated face that was hovering in the air in front of him. The vase smacked right into the swollen mouth and split it like a pumpkin. Blood just seemed to splatter into the air.

George gave one yelp as the hard mound of clay hit, and he dropped. On the way down, his head hit the table and he crumpled in a heap on the floor.

'Hairy-arsed oaf, am I?' Brian bellowed. His heart throbbed mightily. 'That what you think then? Hairy arsed? You little fat bastard. I'll show you.'

Brian lunged round to the other side of the table to where George was lying on his side, one arm flung across his face. His mouth was just a red mush.

He never felt Brian haul him up and he never heard the smash of china clay as Brian cleared the table with a sweep of his hand. In fact he didn't regain consciousness for several minutes and when he did it took him a while to remember where he was. From his point of view, the world was looking strange. His face was pressed down against a hard surface, and there was an enormous pain around his mouth, and a thick metallic taste of blood. There was another huge pain in his temple that pulsed like living fire and made him dizzy and weak. He tried to move his arms and legs and couldn't figure out why he couldn't. Then it dawned on him that he was tied to the table, spreadeagled across the rough wooden surface. He couldn't puzzle out why.

Brian had hauled George right on to the table and spreadeagled him on his face. He'd grabbed a roll of the cotton twine that they used for wicks for the thick, ugly candles that filled their window space, and used it to tie George's wrists and ankles to the corners, twisting the hands and feet down with great force to tie the twine to the thick table legs. All the time he was muttering and mumbling.

George tried to speak but his mouth wouldn't work properly. He was sure he'd lost teeth and there was a horrible grating sound that felt as if his jaw had been smashed. All he could manage was a burbling wail. Brian went away and George tried to pull his hands free, but the thin cord cut into his wrists so painfully that he had to give up.

Brian came back and hovered over him. The prostrate man tried to beg him to let him up, but all that he could manage was a sob. Tears were running down each side of his nose and dripping off the end.

Then there was a tug at his neck that whipped his head back off the table top and he felt his shirt rip right down his back. When the cloth gave, George's head came smack down on the table again and his nose smacked into the wood, sending another excruciating pain through him, and almost causing him to pass out again. He was hardly even aware when Brian ripped off his shirt and trousers and tugged at his boxer shorts until the elastic at the waist snapped and they sprung off in one movement.

Brian looked down at the fat body displayed before him and felt a twist of revulsion. George's soft form now seemed maggoty and shapeless. Every time he moved, a ripple seemed to spread out as the rolls of fat wobbled. Little golden hairs glistened all over the sleek-looking skin.

Brian grabbed a hank of silvery hair and jerked the man's head back and showed him what he held in the other hand. George stopped blubbering. He started to whimper in an ululating whine that quickly hit the high notes. Brian was holding the heavy metal pot they used for melting the wax for their multi-coloured candles. George, despite the numbness in his nose, could smell the boiling wax, and suddenly he was very, very frightened. His breath started coming in gulps and his stomach lurched alarmingly so that he broke wind at either end.

Brian swung George's head back on to the table and moved out of his line of vision. George's whine was now a muted shriek and he strained frantically at the twine that held wrists and ankles, despite the cutting pain.

Then the first splash of the boiling wax hit and the whine went up so high it went right off the register. It was as if somebody was holding a blowtorch right up against George's back, and he could feel, in that first instant, his skin blistering up in the searing heat. The pain was a solid force that hit him so hard his body arched up from the table. It stayed there for about a million years, pure intense fire, and then George's scream, that had become just a hissing of air, was cut off and he fainted.

The tall man didn't seem to notice.

With great care and thoroughness, he poured the still-bubbling wax down George's back and on to the buttocks and down each leg. He was careful along the arms, making sure every inch of skin was covered in a quickly congealing coat. Underneath the stream of wax, the fat body writhed and shivered spasmodically. Finally when all the wax was done, Brian took the thick metal urn away and put it back on the electric stove and turned off the power. He was always meticulous.

Brian waited until the wax had set and then went back to look over his handiwork. George was beginning to stir, and there was a low moan coming out of the smashed mouth along with a thick rope of saliva. The tall man patted the wax. It was set, but still warm and malleable. He went to the sink and poured out some cold water into a bowl and brought it back and splashed it all over the wax coating. Underneath it all, George's body arched again.

Then when he was satisfied that the blue-green mass was hardened sufficiently, Brian came round to the head of the table and tapped George between the shoulder-blades smartly with the heel of his hand, and poked a finger under the leading edge of the wax, sliding it along, left to right, to raise it. When there was enough space, Brian braced his feet and pulled hard. There was a ripping sound as the sheet of wax came up in one segment, like an elastoplast coming off slowly.

With it came George's skin and the small man, who was half-conscious during this phase of the operation, started to screech again. Brian pretended not to notice the writhing underneath him. He just kept pulling and the blistered skin peeled off like toffee, red and raw, in strips and patches. Brian hauled steadily and was faintly amused to see the wax split at George's buttocks, and then continue to strip off the hair and everything else down the back of the thighs and calves. The strips on the arms weren't so easy, but Brian wasn't too concerned.

George's screech had become a low moan again. The fire on his back was an immense blanket of pure pain. He was dimly aware of what had happened, but even despite the agony he did not realise the extent of the damage that had been inflicted on him. There was hardly one piece of skin left on his back or his legs. What was left was a red and yellow cratered surface of scalded skin scraps and boiled fatty tissue. Every nerve was screaming out and sent bolts of agony into his brain.

But Brian wasn't quite finished. He looked at the body before him for a long time, watching the twisting of the flayed muscles and listening to the slobbery moan. He realised that he had been right about George. He *was* disgusting.

And to think he'd . . . *they'd* . . . .

He went back into the store room and came back again with one of their prime products. It was almost two foot long and as thick as an arm, and a knobbled, gnarled concoction of different coloured wax from midnight blue to garish red. One of their best sellers. He hefted it in his hand and grinned.

Despite the huge tide of pain that kept rolling over him, George was suddenly acutely aware of the other thing that intruded, forcing and tearing. He felt the thuds of the mallet, and a vast rending sensation that convinced him he was being ripped apart.

Brian hammered and hammered, and blood started leaking out of George's mouth in a steady trickle. His eyes bulged wildly in his sockets and looked as if they would just spring out on their own. The pain didn't last long. Brian used the mallet with all his force and with great satisfaction, and all the time he was humming a tune.

'All the nice girls . . .' he sang in a low, deep voice.

On the table, George's body arched up for the last time as the agony reached a crescendo and shot bolts through every nerve in his body. Blood welled from his wrists and ankles and the..., with a snap, three of the bonds that were holding him gave way and, like a suddenly released spring, George's body catapulted off the table, crashing into a chair on the way down. His left leg, which was still securely tied, snapped as he fell, but George didn't notice. He was dead.

The shadow came and knocked on Mary Baker's door in the early hours of the morning and slipped inside.

It had been a strange day for the jolly woman who ran her bakery and teashop with the same delicate expertise that her mother had taught her as a girl. Mary was proud of her confections. People even came from Kirkland and

Levenford for her sponges and spiced buns. They ordered potato scones by the dozen and, in season, Mary's strawberry tarts were second to none.

Monday was just a haze, lost in the distance. At night, Mary couldn't even remember what she'd done in the shop. Normally, she'd spend hours behind the counter chatting and picking up the gossip. She had two nieces who came in to help, but although Mary was always up half the night and early in the morning, mixing and baking, she just couldn't resist the gossip. She knew everybody and just about everything about them. Everyone had something to tell Mary Baker about everybody else.

Not that Mary herself was a gossip. She would never bad mouth anybody. No, she meant none of her neighbours and customers any harm, and would never say a bad word about them. But she just liked to *know*. That was the real currency she worked for.

Strangely, she could not remember anything she'd been told today. Normally, she would sit and piece together the bits and pieces that formed her own personal view of Arden. Who had bought what. Why so and so hadn't been at church on Sunday. Whose wife was making dangerous eyes at whose husband. Mary knew it all. But as she sat in bed at night, she couldn't recall a word, which was not surprising because Mary hadn't been down to the shop all day, the first day off in years. At the festival, Mary had been one of the judges in the home-baking contest – her pride of place every year – and had delighted in sampling the wares. Some were not bad, others were disgusting, but she smiled at the amateur bakers one and all. What she liked best was the bread from the seminary, fresh and yielding and melting in the mouth. It was, she considered, on a par with her own wares. And she had three large pieces to herself.

And on the Monday she'd sat in bed all day staring at the wall, her mind far away or deep down inside her, but not aware in *this* world.

Well after midnight, Mary had clambered out of bed

and gone down to her shop. She'd heard a noise and won-dered if she'd forgotten to lock up. That had happened one night years before and a crowd of youngsters from the Milligs had noticed, and within minutes almost every kid in town was having a little private picnic. Mary pulled her big dressing gown around her and crept downstairs into the darkened shop. It was quiet, except for a slight, hollow-sounding drip from the tap in the back room.

She moved into the shadows and turned the tap off with a deft twist. Then she heard another noise from the shop and bustled through. The shadows in the corners seemed to move, and there was a line of light down the edge of the door. It *was* open.

Mary went outside and looked up and down the length of the street. There was no-one about. But maybe some-one had come *in*.

Her heart was thudding in her breast as she went back inside, into the shadowy shop. There was no-one there, not behind the counter, or hiding in the shadow of the big push-button till. She looked behind the rack of bread boards and then went through to the bakehouse that extended to the rear. It smelt of flour and spices, a deli-cious aroma that Mary had been born to. There were lots of shadows here and, despite the thudding of her heart, Mary searched around. There was no-one there. She breathed a sigh of relief and then her breath caught.

What if someone had *been* in the shop and stolen her cakes?

That thought propelled her through to the shop and behind the counter where there were still trays filled with spicy buns and tarts, covered in cling-film to keep them fresh.

In one of the trays, the wrapping was peeled back as if someone had tried to open up and get at the cakes.

The thought appalled Mary. Her cakes.

She lifted the tray out and sat down on the stool that she sat on while getting her daily charge of gossip. How dare they try to steal her cakes, she thought. Absent-mindedly, she lifted up the tart to her mouth. It tasted a bit stale, but she never noticed. She nibbled. It was an apple tart with a hint of cinnamon. She ate it and wiped the crumbs from her mouth.

'They won't steal that one,' she thought. 'They can't.'

And with that thought in her mind, she reached down and picked up another tart. They couldn't steal that one. Nor the next. Nor the one after that.

In the darkness of the shop, Mary finished the tray and reached for another. She set it down and went to the big fridge and hauled out a carton of cream which she opened with a deft twist and took a large drink of the cold smooth liquid. She smacked her lips and sat down again. Rhubarb pies. She ate steadily.

Sometime later, long before the grizzly dawn and while the rain still beat down hard on the roofs and streets of Arden, Mary was still munching and still slurping cream. She was on to her fifth carton and she was unaware of the pain in her grotesquely distended stomach. She kept on going, making sure nobody would steal *her* cakes.

Her breathing stopped when she had demolished an astounding array of delicacies. Her heart and lungs, labouring under the pressure from within, were on the verge of collapse in any case, but Mary slowly choked to death on a large raisin-filled piece of spiced bun that was generously iced. It got stuck in her throat but Mary didn't notice that. Even as consciousness faded, she was still trying to cram the last piece of bun into her mouth, and she was tring to chew it as she slumped back on to the stool against the wall. It was some time before she was found.

In the police station, Murdo Morrison sat with his feet on the desk while his assistant, John Weir, who was more or less the town's beat policeman, typed reports on the big Imperial that he pecked at with two fingers. Murdo had taken a turn in the blue and white Panda car round the streets which had been cleared by the pounding rain. Everything was quiet. In fact, everything had been quiet all day, which was welcome for Murdo, but not all that unusual in Arden. The day after the festival was always subdued, as if everybody had got their excitement out in one big burst and had to recover for a day or so while the batteries charged up again.

Down the corridor, in the three little cells, two of the more unruly drinkers who had been brawling on the streets at dawn were still cooling their heels. John Weir was writing up their reports, but there was every possibility that Murdo would crumple them in the bucket later and kick the prisoners' arses out with another warning. They'd have learned their lesson anyway.

The constable clacked away on the typewriter and Murdo started to doze off.

Murdo woke with a start when one of his feet slipped down from the desk and thudded to the wooden floor. At first he didn't realise where he was and shook his head to clear the blurred vision, but there were still wavery lines in front of his eyes. He yawned and stretched and shook his head again. John Weir kept on typing. Down in the cells, one of the prisoners was humming a tune. There was a slight ringing in Murdo's ears.

He got up from his chair and moved to the door that separated the office from the corridor that led down to the cell room.

In front of him, the wooden door seemed to waver and buckle, and Murdo stepped back, confused. He rubbed his eyes and looked again. The door still seemed to be warping outwards, but slowly. Murdo grabbed the handle and yanked the door open. There was nothing behind it, nothing that could have made the door bulge. He stepped into the narrow passageway and looked up and down. There was something wrong with the walls. They seemed to be slowly pulsing in and out, as if they were breathing.

The humming still continued along in the cell and the buzzing in Murdo's ears got worse, fuzzing down the noise. The walls bulged in towards each other and then subsided.

Murdo went down the narrow way, wondering what the hell was happening. He felt strange and dizzy, and the bulging walls made him feel claustrophobic. He stopped at the line-up of three cells and looked inside. Sam Caldwell was lying on the bunk, sound asleep and snoring softly. He moved on to the next and Alec McGrath looked up when he approached.

'Hey Murdo, am I going to be here all bloody night?'

Murdo stared into the cell. The shiny round bars on the cell door were expanding and contracting on their own, as if they were pulsing with life. He stared at them bemusedly for a while, wondering why they were doing that, when McGrath shouted out again.

'How about it, Murdo? I've been here all day. I'm dying for a drink.'

Murdo looked from the wavering bars and stared at McGrath. There was something wrong with the man's face. It was moving about too, as if the skin was crawling about all over, changing it. McGrath said something else, but Murdo watched fascinated as the man changed his shape and became a hunched thing that sat on the cot, a twisted, gnarled creature that screamed at him. Murdo stared in disgust. How the hell did that get in here?

He reached down into the pocket of his tunic and pulled out the bunch of keys, and correctly selected the big mortice from the collection and slipped it, clattering, into the lock. The thing on the bed, screeching and slobbering, stared up at him as Murdo, who hadn't said a word, loomed into the cell.

The big policeman grabbed the creature and started to shake it, and it kept screeching and slobbering. He slipped his strong hands round its neck and squeezed and lifted at the same time until the thing stopped moving.

In the other cell, Sam Caldwell who had been startled awake by the noise stared, his eyes popping out, as he saw Murdo Morrison squeeze the life out of Alex McGrath. He whimpered in fear, slowly sank to the ground and very, very quietly crawled under the cot.

Murdo went back to the office. The walls had stopped bulging and the buzzing had subsided in his ears.

'Everything OK, sarge?' John Weir asked, looking up from his massive report.

'Yeah,' Murdo said. 'All quiet.'

TWENTY-TWO

The butcher, the baker, the candlestick maker. Like something from a children's rhyme, I suppose, but they weren't the only ones. What I've said about them is as true as I can make out, although I wasn't there, and despite the fact that those who *were* there, or actually did those things, are stumbling around the blank and hazy quagmires in their memories.

The rest of Arden was in a state of stupor, hungover in the aftermath of the festival and the shock of the storm and the mind-expanding grip of the strange mix of the bread. Catatonia set in and many people just sat, or stood, or sprawled out, their eyes glazed and their minds far away. Others did things they would never have done before and there were those who went through their daily rituals in a trance-like state. A few seemed to be unaffected. That was the way it was.

Sometime around dawn, the storm broke, the thunder rolled away over the hills and the lightning became a distant battleground that gradually stopped its far flashing and died down. The slow sun peeked through watery clouds on to a waterlogged scene of dripping rivulets and muddy pools, rain-trampled grass and sodden earth.

I had awoken in the middle of the night in the usual fashion, with my heart thudding between my ears and my mouth dry and croaking out fright. Somewhere in my sleep I had been replaying the scene from today when I had left Paddy under the tree and walked towards the wrecked car and the white inferno of the ruptured gas pipe. I was walking in slow motion and my feet were padding on cotton wool, and I could feel the blast of that giant blowtorch on my face, singeing my hair and eyelids. I passed

302

the wrecked car and saw the blood flow down from the smashed windscreen and become a river that covered the crumpled bonnet and gurgled steadily on to the weeds below. Just out of direct vision, something white and red was flapping in the branches of a tree, and when I passed it I got a wave of pure coldness, a searing frost that soaked up the sizzling heat of the gas geyser, but it was a coldness that was so bitter that it was not a relief. I felt it pierce right through my body in a repulsive wave and I turned and looked into the white eyes of the big bird that swung to and fro, like a bloody, tattered pendulum. The eyes rolled down, piercing me with blue, and then they turned again to maggoty white that had no iris and no pupil, just a sickly white surface that was malevolent and riveting.

I tried to walk away, but my feet were tangled in the soft mush that sucked and tugged, and my eyes were fixed on those blank orbs. The head turned towards me so that both the eyes had me dead centre, and the big stabbing beak opened wide, impossibly wide, as if the head would split in two. And then there was a gurgling noise and from that gaping gullet came a gobbet of black stuff that jetted straight at me and caught me full in the face. It splatted into my eyes and nose and mouth and it burned. The smell was sickeningly putrid and the taste of it on my tongue caused my throat to contract violently, trying to eject it. My eyes stung right through to my brain and I went blind, and I fought and struggled to get away from it, but the black stuff spread all over my face and stuck to my hands, binding and choking, and I wrenched myself as hard as I could towards the light and suddenly I awoke, with that foul taste still in my mouth, panting for air and sanity. I sat bolt upright on the bed and immediately the sweat that lathered me started to evaporate, sending cool shivers up and down my spine. I heaved a huge sigh of relief when I realised it was a dream, and then the picture of that big bird, dangling in a tree, came zooming back into my mind again, and with a sickening lurch I realised what I had seen out of the corner of my eye down in the trees at the

Kilcreggan Road. It had not been an accident. What had happened to Barbara was as deliberate as the unbelievable scene Donald and I had witnessed down on the bay.

A scream from the other room jolted me right out of bed and the mental image disappeared like a bubble bursting. Paddy's scream was high and piercing and jarring in its intensity. I leapt out of the room and across the landing and barged right into the room where I'd tucked her up in the old double bed. She was kneeling up on it, tangled in my old chambray shirt, and her eyes were wide and unfocused. Her hands were up in front of her eyes and she was warding off some unseen presence, screeching at the top of her voice. She fought like a cat, shoving me away with surprising force, but I wrapped her in my arms as tightly as I could and yelled her name and suddenly she awoke with a start. I could feel her heart beating against my chest, fast and drum-like, like a terrified bird.

'There, there,' I said. It was all I could think of. I patted her back as reassuringly as I could, feeling her narrow shoulders shudder under my palm.

'It's just a dream. You're all right now, sweetheart.'

Paddy's breath hiccupped and caught in her throat, and then she let out a long wail of despair and relief and fear rolled into one. I kept up the steady patting between her shoulder-blades. The wail dissolved into honest to God sobs that were much better, more normal, and then they started to subside.

Finally she was silent and she was sniffing against my chest. I rubbed her back a couple of times, feeling the shivering die down, and then loosened my grip. She looked up at me and her eyes were pink with the force of her tears. Poor kid, she wasn't having the best time of her life.

'Are you all right now?' I asked. Of course she wasn't all right, but what else do you say?

Paddy nodded and sniffed.

'It was the bird,' she said, her voice still catchy. 'The bird did it. It broke the window and tried to get my mummy.'

'But it didn't get her, did it?'

She shook her head.

'I don't know. It was bad, and mummy was scared and now she's hurt awful bad.'

'I know honey, but she's safe now. She's away from it and it's dead now.' I think it was at this point that I stopped believing in coincidences and finally gave in to the fact that there was a shadow, a *bane*, a Cu Saeng. Finally and unequivocally.

Paddy shook her head.

'No. It's not dead. It's still here and it wants me.'

'What does, honey?'

'The bad one. The thing that gets inside the birds. It wants to kill me.'

'Nothing's going to get you,' I said. 'Not while I'm around.'

She looked up at me, and I swear I saw a thirty year old, or even a sixty or eighty year old, looking out from that short mop of fair hair. It was the kind of look that Barbara would have shot at me, or the kind of measuring stare that I would have been dealt by old Kitty MacBeth.

'You have to stop it,' she said.

'I know,' I said. 'I'm going to try.'

'We have to kill it, because it wants us. You and me, and the other one.'

Where had I heard that before?

The sun had managed to beat a path through the clouds by the time Paddy and I got in the jeep and splashed through the puddles and up to the main street. I'd tried the telephone again, hoping to get the latest on Barbara, but it was still dead. The town was still quiet, even though it was mid-morning and there was still dampness in the air. The sun was pushing through, but there was definitely a feeling that summer had finally called it a day and moved over to let autumn in.

I nosed the jeep into the main street and past the shops. I considered going into Mary Baker's for some bread and a

305

couple of cakes for Paddy, but I decided to wait till later. That spared me from being the first to find her. I had to head west to get to the turn that would take me to Upper Arden, and just as I slowed near the harbour a car ahead flashed its lights a couple of times. I peered through the windscreen and saw Alan Scott waving at me from his car. I stopped the jeep, pulling the nearside wheel on to the kerb to let any passing traffic through, and I got out and crossed the road. Alan wound down his window. His pretty wife Janet was in the passenger seat and his kids were together in the back.

'I wouldn't go that way if I were you,' Alan said, jerking his thumb back, indicating the road he'd come along. 'The road's blocked.'

'What happened?'

'Some rocks came off the Langcraig last night. Must have been the storm, but nothing's going to get past that today. It's a pure bugger. I'm supposed to be in Levenford this morning. I'm having a look at Harry Wilkinson's place. It looks like I can get a deal on it.' He looked at his watch. 'I should have been there now. I've got a surveyor going along too, and Janet and the kids are going shopping.'

'Well why not take the other . . . .' I trailed off. The other road was blocked, of course. It's strange how things like that don't really register for a while.

'A pure bugger,' said Alan.

'That was some bad smash yesterday,' he went on, and then lowered his voice. 'I'm told there was nothing left of that tanker driver. Bloody hell. What a way to go.'

I agreed.

'I don't think you'll get over that landslip, even in that thing,' he said, nodding at the jeep. 'There's a pile of rock ten feet high.'

'You're right. It is a . . .' I paused and looked at Janet. '. . . A shame. I've got to get to Glasgow today. That's Barbara Foster's girl. Her mother was in the smash yesterday. She's up in the Western.'

Janet gave a sharp intake of breath. 'Oh, the poor soul. And just arrived from America too.'

'Barbara Foster. Was she at school with us?' Alan asked, and I nodded. 'I thought it was her. Is she all right?'

'Pretty bad, but she'll probably make it. We're just about to go up and visit.'

'Well, I've got to get to Levenford today. If I can persuade old Wilkinson to sell up, then I've got myself out of a hole. I'll have to take that old farm road up by McFall's and get across the old Kilmalid Bridge.'

I knew the road. It paralleled the other road up to the seminary and took a loop round past a succession of smallholdings and came round again to join another good farm road just at the east of town. There was a network of narrow lanes that intersected each other all round Arden, some of them only single-track with passing places, but they were all connected and there were a dozen different short and long cuts that either took you over the moor out on to the Blackhill Road, or back down to the Kilcreggan Road on either side of town. Great roads for summer-day leisurely driving, or for bramble-picking, but not for those in a hurry.

Alan started winding his window up.

'I reckon you'll have to take the old road too,' he said. 'After last night's rain, I envy you that four-wheel drive. If I knock my sump off in one of those pot holes, it's going to really spoil my day.' He finished winding the window back up and waved. The kids all waved too and Alan pulled away back into town.

Neither Paddy nor I had a key to Barbara's house, and her father hadn't shown up. She wasn't the kind of woman to leave a key under the mat, but eventually I managed to find a window with a catch that was just a bit loose, and I wiggled the frame until it sprung, and slid the sash up. Paddy was impressed. I lifted her up and through the space – a minute later she opened the front door.

'That's a neat trick,' she said. 'Were you ever a burglar?'

'I've been a lot of things,' I said, conspiratorially.

She insisted on having a shower and came downstairs dressed in a clean pair of faded jeans and a bright jumper. She had obviously adopted the torc. It still glistened round her neck, matching her hair. While she was upstairs, I made a pot of coffee and poured myself a cup. I had considered helping her choose something to wear, but my experience of children was understandably limited, and although she was temporarily in my care I reckoned she knew more about ten-year-old style than I did.

Paddy begged me to let her have a coffee although Barbara's stuff was straight and strong and came out of the pot like treacle. It went down like a bitter-sweet burst of fire that put some of the go back inside me. What the hell, I thought, and poured her a cup, but I put a lot of sugar and milk in it just to be on the safe side. I didn't want her to be up all night. Not after last night.

I had a second cup and decided we should wait until the afternoon before taking the farm roads to get out of town and up to Glasgow. Paddy agreed. She was naturally concerned about her mother, but not *concerned*. I thought a couple of hours would make no difference and visiting in hospital is always better done after lunch. Barbara's phone was out too, as was every one in Arden, along with a lot of the gas and electricity supply and the two main routes out of town.

On the radio, the accident, even though it was a day past, was still prominent, even on the national channels. The local station gave it big licks, and my hand hovered near the knob, getting ready to turn it off if the announcer started saying things that I thought Paddy shouldn't hear. Fortunately, they said that Mrs Barbara Hartford's condition, while serious, remained stable, and Paddy smiled when she heard that. Police, the announcer said, were still investigating the cause of the accident, and the funeral of the dead driver was to take place the next day. Then the item went on to talk about the gas pipe and how Gas Board workers were trying to reconnect the supply, while other teams were busy on the other services that had been hit. It was estimated that the work on the bridge repair would take some longer, unspecified time, at an unestimated cost. Then the item finished by talking about the landslip at the other end of the town. Effectively, Arden was cut off from the rest of the world, unless you count the radio and television stations, and those winding farm roads.

If I'd thought about it, it couldn't have been neater. It just didn't strike me then.

It didn't strike me until two in the afternoon, after Paddy and I had had a bite of lunch. We'd sat around and talked for a bit and listened to every bulletin on the radio. I'd picked up a paperback out of the selection on the living-room shelves and Paddy had read one of her own books, occasionally looking up to ask me a question or to state an opinion. Barbara had some ham in the fridge that I sliced along with a hunk of cheddar and made a ploughman's lunch with coleslaw and lettuce. I made Paddy drink milk with this and got no argument.

I pulled out of the driveway with Paddy strapped beside me and went down the hill. I still had that biting taste in my mouth from the cheese, a delicious aftertaste, and I was full enough to feel set up for the afternoon. Paddy was eager to get up to Glasgow to see her mother, although she was still confident that everything would be all right. We got down to the main road and took a left to get to the field where the harvest festival had been held only two days before, to take the road up past Mr Bennett's cottage and through past the farm. Like before, I had almost reached it when lights flashed in an oncoming car which slowed down to a stop. I matched it on the other side. It was Alan Scott. I got out of the jeep again and crossed the road. Alan rolled the window down and even as I crossed the street I could see his face was white.

'What's up Alan? Are the other roads out too?'

'I don't know what's happening,' Alan said. He looked dazed. I looked from him to his wife. She seemed downright scared. She was holding on to her bag so hard her knuckles were white. In the back of the car, the kids were sitting very quietly.

'We can't get out,' Janet said in a brittle voice.

Alan held his hand up to stop her, looking quickly at Janet and then flicking a glance over his shoulder to the kids. He patted his wife on the shoulder and then got out of the car, motioning me to join him. When we got out of earshot, he leaned in close to me, holding my arm at the elbow. There was a slight tremor in his grasp.

'She's right. We can't get out.'

'Out of where?'

'Here. I kept getting lost.'

'Alan, you can't get lost here.'

'Listen Nick. There's something funny going on around here. I've been going around in circles since I left you. I'm telling you, we just can't get out of this place.'

'I don't understand,' I said.

'Look. I've tried every road I know. They all just come back to the one place. It's like a maze.'

'Alan, I don't know what you're talking about.'

'Listen, will you? I went up by McFall's farm and along the road that goes along by Cardross Hill.'

'Right, the old Carman Road.'

'That's the one.'

'It takes you out at the Lea Brae.'

'Yes. It always did. But it doesn't now.'

'How do you mean, it doesn't now?'

It just doesn't. It doesn't go anywhere. Except back to McFall's farm. You know that stand of trees? The one at the other side of the old Kilmalid Bridge?'

I nodded.

'I've been past that a dozen times. That narrow bit where the road nips in, and there's tracks on the verge where cars have missed the curve. That's where it happens. I keep going through there, and when I get out past the trees I'm back at the farm again. I can't explain it, but it's scaring the shit out of me.'

I tried to visualise the road. It's not easy to picture every bend in a winding farm lane, no matter how familiar. Obviously Alan had taken the wrong turning.

'Well, have you tried the Black Hill Road?' I asked. It would have been my second choice. Taking a left bend about five hundred yards past the farm and looping round in the direction of Kirkland before joining the wider road that crossed the heights of the Black Hill moor.

'Of course I tried that. And the same thing happened. I got to the crossroads that's going to take you to the reservoir or up to the radio mast. But then I just found myself back at the junction at MacDonald's croft.'

Alan's voice was getting higher and louder. I put a hand on his shoulder and tried to calm him down. His face crumpled.

'Listen, Nicky. I'm dead scared. There's something really weird going on around here. I'm either going crazy, or something's happened that's screwed up everywhere.'

He leant in closer and dropped his voice.

'And there's other weird things going on up there. Not just the roads.'

'Like what?'

'Look at the side of the car.' I looked. It was stove right in across both doors.

'What happened?'

'A cow. It came right out of nowhere and hit me. I mean it attacked the car. A cow, for Christsake. And up by McNulty's croft there's a family out having a picnic in the marsh. I mean they're just sitting about in the mud, covered in it. I must have passed them a dozen times and all they do is wave. It's crazy.'

Alan's voice was rising again and I motioned him to calm down. He looked at his wife, who was still sitting rigid in the car, and went quiet.

'I don't know what to do,' he said, and his face crumpled again, as if he was going to burst into tears.

'Well, I can't explain it. I'll have a look myself for I've got to get up to the hospital.'

Alan grabbed me by the sleeve. 'No. Don't do it.

There's something wrong. I mean something *badly* wrong.'

'There's got to be an explanation,' I said.

'Well I hope to God there is. I've done a hundred and fifty miles since this morning and I've got nowhere. It's scared the hell out of me. It got so I was terrified in case I ran out of petrol. I tell you Nicky, I don't want to be stuck up there on those roads. No way.'

'Listen, why don't you go home with Janet and the kids. There's no point in getting them all worked up. Maybe we could both go together later on.'

'Would you do that, Nick?'

'Of course. We'll check it out together. There's bound to be something to explain it.'

'OK Nick, and thanks. I feel terrible, but it's true. I've been driving around up there for hours, and I just can't get anywhere.'

I assured him that I'd call up for him later. Frankly I didn't believe him. It had probably been some time since Alan had driven up those winding roads. He must have taken a wrong turn. Alan went back to his car, and I hopped into the jeep. I did know for certain that the main roads out of town were blocked, but all the other tracks and farmways couldn't be. I started up the engine. I had a half tank of petrol that would have taken me halfway to London if I'd wanted. Just before I pulled away from the kerb, I reached forward and turned the little winder that put the mileometer back to a line of zeros.

An hour and a half and almost fifty miles later my mouth was dry, and Paddy had gone quiet.

Alan Scott had been right. There was something gone badly wrong. The more I drove, the more I could feel it. The roads took us nowhere, except back again. We drove at a fair clip through that stand of trees that leaned their branches in a green umbrella right over the narrow road, and when we came out into the light again we were back at the copse that is just a hundred yards or so past McFall's farm. There was nothing to explain it, but we were going into one set of trees and coming out another, but almost

312

two miles back the way we had come, and heading the way we had been going in the first place.

We tried the Blackhill Road and went left at the cross-roads and drove a hundred yards with the dry-stone dyke high on either side, and suddenly we were past the walls and moving right by the croft . . . a mile and a half from where we'd been.

It was as if somebody had taken time and space and twisted them around and cut everything up and stuck it back together again in a never-ending loop.

But it was scary as all hell. And that wasn't the only scary thing.

We were doing about forty along a straight stretch just under Carman Hill when a big dog came running along the road towards us, loping like a wolf in big strides that bobbed its shoulders up and down as it raced down the straight. It was right in the middle of the road and going full out. When it got closer, I could see its tongue lolling out the side of its mouth, whipped back by the air. I batted the horn a couple of times, but the dog kept on coming. I slowed down to about twenty-five, but the big dog, it looked like a labrador-shepherd cross, kept on loping down the straight. There was nowhere for me to go, and at the last minute I could see that the dog wasn't going to shift. I jammed my foot down on the brake pedal and Paddy jerked forward in her seat, but it was too late. The dog simply sprang at the front end, with its jaws wide open and its lips drawn back over a fearsome set of teeth in a vicious snarl. There was a loud thump as it hit, and even as the big roo bars caught it smack on. I saw it snap at the metal. There was a crack as the teeth connected and then the animal was spun right up and over the top of the jeep, hitting the road just where it merged into the wet grass.

'Jeesus,' I gasped. I glanced at Paddy. She was squirming around in the seat, tangled in the belt, to look behind the car. I looked in the mirror, and saw the dog trying to struggle to its feet and turn back. Just before I got to the corner, I looked again, and it was staggering along the road. Following us. It looked as if it wanted another go.

We didn't see the family who Alan said were having a picnic in the marsh, but we passed an old guy who leaned against a dyke with his trousers at his knees and held his equipment in his hand. The first time we passed I didn't notice, until we were right up close to him, what he was doing and waved to him. He shot his buttocks forward, displaying as much of himself as he could and waved himself back at us.

I did a double-take and then flicked a glance at Paddy. She had a half-amazed, half-amused smile on her face.

On the second time round that particular circuit, before I realised that we really weren't going anywhere, we came across the old man again. This time he had come off the wall and was standing closer to the road and, again, he had all working parts ready for a vigorous display. Fortunately I saw him with plenty of time to spare before Paddy did, and I told her to reach into the back seat to get my cigarettes. She squirmed out of the belt and we were past him before she turned back to face forward again. But as she did so, she caught a glimpse of him out of the rear.

'There's that funny old man waving his *thing* again,' she said brightly. 'Haven't we come this way before?'

I felt my face go red again.

We tried a couple of other, more narrow, roads but they all led back to the starting point again. I was prepared to give it a couple more tries, still reluctant to believe the evidence of experience, but on one of those little-used tracks we came past a gnarled beech tree that was wind-blown and stunted, its branches sweeping eastward, under the relentless pressure of the wind on the hillside. I had to slow down and slip the gears to take the narrow bend, and that tree moved. I caught it out of the corner of my eye, and I saw the branches *move*, twisting down impossibly towards the jeep. I yelled in fright and Paddy let out a scream. The thick grey twigs at the end of the branches thudded against the roof like twisted fingers and spanged off the windscreen.

'Did you see that?' Paddy said. 'It moved.'

'Probably the wind, kiddo,' I said. I didn't risk any more because my heart was beating so hard, I could hardly talk. I didn't even look at her, but I knew she had seen it. Suddenly I got a flashback of Andy Gillon lying there in the mud at his farm, under that massive tree trunk, and the look in his eyes when he told me '*The tree jumped.*' Now I believed him.

I gave up and went back to Arden.

And as I drove, I realised that the town was cut off, totally, from the rest of the world.

How it was done, I don't know. Whatever had awoken under Ardhmor Rock – I was now convinced that something had awoken, and by this time, in my mind, I was calling it the Cu Saeng – seemed to have some elemental power.

Cu Saeng. There it was. At last out in the open, in my mind at least, if not quite in fact.

And what was Cu Saeng?

I know what Kitty MacBeth said: the ravener, the dweller under the roots. Something out of old Celtic, or pre-Celtic mythology.

The folk tales are a bit hazy on what this thing really is. It appears rarely in the myths and the great Celtic sagas, and I reckon it's got much diluted down through the years. The latter-day version is that it's some kind of goblin, or hob-goblin, or an vil sprite that lives in the lonely places, the isolated rocks and moors. The stories go that just to cast your eye on it kills you by driving you mad. And in the old days, any traveller lost in the hills and bogs was deemed to have been a victim of Cu Saeng. Whether there was supposed to be just one entity, or a whole host, I've never discovered. I don't know whether it was Cu Saeng, the individual, or a whole species of cu saengs. I don't even know whether the bane that had come to life again under that black rock was even the same kind of creature – or un-creature – as the folk tales told of.

What I was certain of was that *something* had stirred and

stretched and yawned a gaping mouth that slavered at the corners and realised it was hungry.

And *angry*.

I also knew that somehow I was to be a central character in what was to happen next, because of something that had happened as a child, or something that had been ordained long before the time of the Romans. That knowledge made my stomach churn and my knees go weak and my heart pound achingly against my ribs.

It was me against something that could cause landslides and cause tankers to explode, and twist the world around inside my head so that I didn't know left from right. It could make birds kill men and dogs attack a car with intent to kill, and it could make trees twist and turn and *grab*.

What else could it do?

TWENTY-THREE

At Alan Scott's house I found him sitting at the kitchen
table, staring at the wall in what could have been blank
bewilderment. The large glass of whisky shook in both
hands, as if it had a life of its own. Janet had been pasty-
faced with worry when she'd opened the door and silently
motioned me to come in. Now she sat on a chair in the
corner of the kitchen, wringing her hands. The children
were nowhere in sight.

Alan looked up as I sat down beside him, and seemed to
spend a few moments struggling to recognise me. Something flashed across his eyes, and he seemed to start, as if
coming out of a daydream.

'Tell me then. Was I right?'

I nodded slowly.

'I told you. It's crazy. It can't happen.'

'I can't figure it out either.'

'It's that road. That's what's done it,' he spat out in a
voice that seemed close to hysteria. 'The bastards have
buried us good and proper. That's what they've been up to
all this time. They just want rid of us, that's what it is. I
knew this would happen.' All his words tumbled out in
that strained, cracking voice. Alan brought his hands up
again and took an enormous gulp of whisky and clattered
the glass down on the table again. I saw Janet wince in
alarm, out of the corner of my eye.

'Maybe it's got nothing to do with the road,' I ventured.

'Must be,' Alan said quickly. 'That's why they've built
it. So everybody would go past Arden and we'd all starve.
But they're not content with that. Oh no. Not them. They
want to seal us in. They've fixed it so we can't get out and
tell everybody what's going on.'

He lifted the glass and took a swallow that would have made a man's eyes water and slammed it back down again. Some droplets spilled over the edge and dotted the table. I don't know how many he'd had since he'd started, but I was willing to bet it was a fair amount. It didn't seem to be doing him any good, but he didn't seem drunk. He sounded scared, and angry, and maybe close to the edge, but his words, rising on the wave of hysteria, didn't sound like whisky talk.

He lurched to his feet suddenly, in a jerk that toppled the chair. He didn't bother picking it up.

'Right, I'll show the bastards. They can't shut me in.'

'Hold on a minute, Alan,' I said, and put a hand on his arm.

He shook it off roughly.

'Leave me alone. I'm getting out of here. I'll find a way they haven't thought of fixing. And when I do, I'm going to let them know all about it.'

'But there is no other way. I've tried them all. The same thing happened to me. And it's got nothing to do with the road. It's something in Arden.'

'Don't give me that crap,' Alan said. He turned and looked straight at me, and I could see the shift in his eyes, as they narrowed with suspicion. 'I know what it is. You're one of *them*.'

'One of what?'

'You know what I'm talking about, Ryan. You're with the Ministry, aren't you? That's why you've come back. All that guff about writing books was just so much shit, am I right? You're just a spy. Come back to spy on your own kind, haven't you?'

With a swift movement, he reached across the short distance and grabbed me by the shirt, twisting it hard so that his fist was right up against my windpipe. I could smell the sweetness of alcohol on his breath. His eyes were red rimmed, like a bull terrier's.

In the corner, I heard Janet gasp out a little sob.

'That's not true, Alan. I've got nothing to do with it.'

I brought both hands up and grasped his wrist, pushing hard to break his grip. His eyes weren't his only resemblance to a terrier. His arm felt like iron.

'I'll show you,' he spat, right in my face. 'You can't come here and fuck up people's lives like this. You're just jealous that I've made it up here. I've come up from down there, where you are, and you just want to take it all away.'

'Please, Alan. Stop it,' Janet urged in a small, whimpering voice.

Alan whirled, tugging me right around and almost snapping my windpipe.

'You shut your mouth. I'm getting this sorted out, woman. This is man's business, so you just keep your nose out of it.'

Janet winced as if she'd been struck.

'Alan, listen to me. It's nobody's fault. There's something going wrong around here. I'm trying to find out. I'm trying to help.'

All that took a great effort, for Alan's fist was still jammed hard up under my chin. His grip never slackened.

'You shut up too. I'm going to fix you.'

With that, he whirled me round again in a tight orbit, and let me go. I pinwheeled backwards and the back of my head connected with the wall with a dull thud that made the room spin crazily for a second or two. There were tiny pin-points of light, like distant fireflies, dancing in front of my eyes.

When they cleared, moments later, Alan was standing above me, staring down from eyes that looked as though they'd seen the end of the world. In that instant, he just looked mad. He turned and picked up one of the chairs and raised it above his head. He brought it down with immense force, aiming it right at my head. Fortunately his backswing gave me plenty of time to jerk myself out of the way. The chair hit the floor with a splintering crash and one leg broke off. The force of the impact spun the thing right out of his hand and it skittered across the floor to smack hard against one of the neat fitted units.

Janet screamed.

Alan whirled and looked as if he was about to pounce on her, and I scrambled to my feet, with the sick feeling that I was going to have to fight him and take a real beating for my trouble. But then, he seemed to forget all about her. In the blink of an eye, it was as if something else had caught his attention. He stopped, stood dead still, as if listening to a voice inside his head. Then he turned and barged out of the kitchen, knocking his shoulder off the doorpost. He didn't seem to notice.

As he shambled down the hallway, I heard him mutter: 'I'll show them. I'll find a way. They can't stop me.'

Janet called to him. 'Please, Alan, don't go. Stay with us.'

Alan barged into the door and scrabbled for the handle. He pulled it open and lurched out. In the space of a few moments, he seemed to have lost his co-ordination. He was jerking along like a puppet with loose strings. I went quickly to the front door and watched him heave himself into the car. The keys must have still been in the big limo, for the engine started up immediately. There was a screech of tyres as the car leapt forward, cutting right across a neat display of flowering azaleas, demolishing the shrubbery and leaving a scored tyre track on the short lawn. As the car swerved towards the gateway, the driver's door, which hadn't been shut, flew open and smacked with a noise like a gunshot into the stone pillar of the gateway, and thumped back on the car.

Behind me, Janet was sobbing loudly. In the living room, the children were almost hysterical. They had picked up Janet's anguish the way kids do, and were crying inconsolably. I heard one of them call out: 'Daddy, don't go and leave us. Daddy, come back.'

Nobody saw Alan Scott again. Not alive. It was to be many days before his car was found, nose down in a gully, with its grille crumpled against a rock in the middle of a small rivulet, and Alan bashed and broken inside it. By then the blowflies had had ample time to get to work on his body and the maggots had multiplied in their thousands. There was not that much left of him inside his jacket. But then it was just one more to add to the list.

There wasn't much I could say to Janet and we soon left. As I drove the jeep away, I could see her and the three kids, pale faces up at the window of the living room, scared stiff.

Paddy had gone quiet and I had a dull headache, the kind you get when the tension builds up and starts to thud at the back of the head like a muffled gong. I stopped at the chemist's shop for some Hedex but it was closed, which was unusual. The streets were still quiet, and I noticed there were a few shops which still had their shutters up. I couldn't recall if it was a half-day or not, but I did remember that Holly's bar stocked up a selection of hangover cures like Askit powders, so I parked the jeep in the alley beside the bar and told Paddy to wait for me. I wanted rid of that headache so I could think about what to do next.

Holly's was open, but there were none of the regulars inside, which was not unusual at that time of day. It was between opening hours, the official ones that is, but big John Hollinger's swing doors always swung open, and his licensing hours were generally worked on an arbitrary basis that suited everybody and didn't offend Murdo Morrison.

I pushed through into the bar and had to wait to allow my eyes to adjust to the dim light. There was nobody about, but I could hear the sound of movement from down in the cellar. I called out and I heard a crash and a mumbling from beyond the cellar hatch. I called John's name again, but there was no reply. Then, from upstairs came another sound, and there were footsteps on the stairs that led to Holly's living quarters that took up two storeys above the bar. The soft footsteps came closer and I waited until the adjoining door opened. It was Helen, John's wife, still in her dressing gown. She peered round the door, and then started when she saw me standing at the bar.

'Oh, hello Nicky,' she said and smiled. Her black hair was piled high in the way she'd worn it ever since I could remember, but a couple of wisps had fallen down over her forehead, giving her a slightly unkempt look.

'Didn't get you up, did I?' I asked.

'No. I was having a long lie. I've been as tired as hell.'

'Oh, I'm sorry to disturb you. I thought Holly would be about.'

'He is. He's down there,' she said, pointing at the floor. 'And as far as I'm concerned he can stay there.'

Helen was a statuesque lady, amply proportioned and always ready to smile. There was always a running battle of banter between Holly and her that was always jovial. I had never ever heard her criticise the big landlord before.

'What's up?' I asked.

'He's drinking the place dry, the big fool.'

'Holly? Drinking? He never drinks during the day.'

'Tell him that. He's been at it since yesterday. He went down last night to change casks and he's been there ever since. Drunk as a fucking lord. He's been into everything, and he's been smashing the place up something terrible. I've just let him get on with it.'

I had never heard Helen swear before, and I'd never seen John Hollinger drunk. The big man took a drink all right, but always at night, and it never seemed to affect him except to make his one-liners sharper and his banter more witty.

'I just came in for some Askit powders,' I said, to change the subject. I didn't really have the energy to get involved in a domestic dispute. 'I've got a bit of a headache and nothing for it in the house. The chemist's shop's shut too.'

Helen looked at her wrist where her watch would normally have been, looked puzzled and then asked me for the time.

'It's nearly half past four,' I told her.

'That's strange. I thought it was still morning. He must

322

have come up and opened the place.'

She leaned forward over the bar and her dressing gown wedged open a little bit, exposing an expanse of smooth skin split by a large cleavage.

'If you ask me, he's flipped,' she said knowingly. 'He was rattling about there all night, and the language! I've never heard some of those words.'

'He'll feel bad about it when he sobers up. He's going to have a helluva head if he's had as much as you say.'

'I hope it kills him. I hope his head's . . .' she paused. 'Headache? That's what you came in for isn't it?'

I nodded. There was still a bit of a thud between my ears, but it was lessening off. I didn't want to leave Paddy in the jeep too long.

Helen rummaged about the gantry and lifted aside boxes of crisps and peanuts, shaking her head.

'You can never find these damned things when you need them most,' she said, then she turned away from the tumbled pile of cartons.

'I've got some upstairs. A whole box of them. Come on and I'll give you what you need.'

'That's good of you,' I said and followed her through the connecting door.

In the flat above, Helen rummaged around in the bedroom, while I stood and looked out of the window into the main street where a handful of people were wandering around aimlessly, dazed-looking.

I stood and watched, baffled, until Helen's voice jerked my attention.

'Come and give me a hand, would you, Nicky?'

I dragged my eyes away from the strangely unsettling scene and walked across the room and through the short hallway to the bedroom. Without thinking I strolled into the room where a king-sized unmade bed dominated the space. There was a noise behind me as the door snicked shut and I turned, and then I nearly fell on my backside.

Helen had shucked off the wraparound nightgown. It lay pooled and ruffled around her ankles. And the rest of her was totally, massively naked.

'What . . . ?' I tried to ask something but the words locked in my throat.

Helen reached up both arms in a gesture of invitation, and maybe supplication. The movement caused her massive breasts to sway, jiggling the large, dark nipples in little circular movements.

I must have stood there for ten seconds, just staring, glued to the floor.

'Come on, Nicky,' she said. A slow, lazy smile spread her lips apart. But there was nothing funny about her eyes. They looked hungry.

'It's just the two of us,' she said, almost wheedling. 'We can have some fun, can't we? He's been no damn good, lying down there drunk all night.'

She swayed towards me, stepping out of the crumpled gown, Junoesque and rounded. Her belly met her thighs in a thick, black tangle that contrasted with her pale, smooth skin. In any other circumstances I'm sure I would have found it inviting. In fact inside me I could feel guilty little hot stirrings.

But the truth of it was I was suddenly dead scared. I was rigid with fright.

Because this wasn't Helen. The face and form were undoul.edly hers. But the expression she wore was not. It was something else. The sleek smile that beamed at me was a grimace that was shudderingly awful. And the light in the dark eyes didn't even look human.

Suddenly I thought of Paddy, down there in the car, alone in that street of strange, dazed folk, and as suddenly I realised that's where I should be.

'I've got to go,' I said, turning from her, trying not to look. She was standing in front of the closed door.

I tried to avoid looking at her and moved to brush past her, when she suddenly lunged at me, clamping her arms around my neck. Her great breasts were pressed pneumatically against my ribs and her lips sought mine, frantically.

I could hear her moaning in my ear as I twisted and turned my head away from her mouth, and I could feel the hot breath on my cheek.

'No, Helen. Please. I have to go now,' I said, feeling panic well up inside me. Paddy was down there. Alone. I had left her. And some instinct inside me knew that this little performance was something aimed at keeping me in here, while Paddy was out there.

Helen thrust herself against me, hard and strong, clasping herself to me in a smothering embrace. Her moans had become a sort of frantic slobbering. Her hips swivelled and punted against my thigh, pushing hard in a series of pulses. Even through my jeans I could feel the heat and wet. I forced myself away, shoving hard against her shoulder, and she clung on, no lightweight, with an animal ferocity.

My hand went down, almost of its own volition into my jacket pocket and curled around the stone spear-head. Instantly I felt a surge of something shiver through me, cold and bright, and in the same moment I felt Helen stiffen against me. Her grip faltered, and I brought the stone up under her encircling arms, up between her massive breasts and held it against her face.

I don't know why I did it. It was some sort of instinctive imperative, an act carried out without thought.

Helen let out a great gasp of air, as if she'd been holding her breath and had been punched, hard, in the gut. It was as if she'd been strung up with a powerful tension that had suddenly been released.

Her black eyes rolled up to white and her arms just fell away from me. She stood there, rigid, for all of three seconds, and then fell backwards, as if she'd been poleaxed, to land on the floor with a thump that seemed to shake the whole house.

She lay still. For a moment I was torn between checking up on her and racing from the room. My heart was pounding in my chest from the fright I'd got when I looked into Helen's eyes and saw something else. I shook my head, ignoring the deep, drilling pulse that spasmed inside my skull, and went for the door.

I stumbled downstairs, not giving a damn that I didn't

get the headache powders, taking the steps two at a time and swinging myself round on the banister in my haste.

Outside, I stood blinking in the sunlight, catching my breath. For all I knew, Helen was lying dead upstairs while Holly was lying dead drunk down in the cellar. Uncharitably, I couldn't have cared less.

TWENTY-FOUR

I walked out of Holly's bar and into the sunlight that weakly slipped through the grey clouds overhead, and all around me was bedlam. There was noise everywhere and there was movement all around, blurred as my eyes struggled to focus, and then everything sprang in clarity and I almost fell back inside the bar again.

The main street was like a rodeo. Somebody had let the horses out at the riding school up on the hill and they were galloping through town, clattering right along the road, like a scene from a bad western. There was a woman against a wall on the far side of the street cowering against the stone while the horses raced by, neighing and squealing and arching their necks. As one big roan passed, it kicked out its hooves viciously and almost took the woman's head off. One of the shoes clattered against the wall and sent up sparks. Further down the street, a teenager came round the corner into the street and saw a bunch of horses streaming towards him and took off. Instead of ducking back the way he had come, he ran away from them. He got about ten yards and the leading horse, a big grey mare, stamped him down. I could hear the sickening thud even from that distance. There was a brief yell that was cut off quickly and I didn't even want to look. There must have been more than a dozen horses, all milling around at breakneck speed. The sound of their passing was like thunder. I braced myself on the sides of the door and then flung myself out, gauging the distance between me and the alley and the nearest horse. I made it with plenty to spare and got round the corner and got the fright of my life.

A big black horse was rearing up on its hind legs and

bringing its front hooves smashing down on the jeep's bonnet. By the time I got round the corner, it must have been at it for a while, because the smooth new bonnet was just a dented moon-crater surface, and half of the front window was starred in cracks. But that wasn't all. There was a dog on the roof, scrabbling at the paintwork and howling dementedly, and there were two other dogs, one a big doberman type that jumped up and smashed against the passenger window where I could see Paddy cringing back, terror slashed right across her face. There was another dog, a small, squat one that was spitting and snarling at the front tyre. It looked like one of those pit bulls that some of the men down at the shacks on Milligs shore-side used to breed.

I took a deep breath and sprinted down that alley towards the jeep and took a dive past the haunches of the horse that was pounding the car into the road. Just at the door, I slipped and almost skittered along the cobbles right under the car on my ass.

On the roof the dog whirled and took a snap at me when I scrambled to my feet and jerked frantically at the door-handle. I backhanded it with a satisfying swipe that made its teeth click together and I hauled the door open. The look on Paddy's face was worth any risk. The door was what saved me from getting my back broken, for I was just about to pull myself on to the driving seat when that horse lashed out at me and got me a sickener right on my shoulder. I'd been too busy watching the dog line up for another spring, and watching at my heels in case the other two came round for a bit, that I'd been unable to watch the front.

The blow almost knocked me to the ground again, but I had one hand on the steering wheel and the top of the door-window took most of the force, denting the rim right out of shape. If it hadn't been for that, I would have been writing this one-handed, or, most likely, not writing it at all. The pain was a huge hot dagger in my shoulder that was so intense the grip of the dog's teeth on my thigh almost went unnoticed. I took a hard swipe at it and I felt the big canines drag past the denim of my jeans. It hadn't broken the skin, but I was going to have a really decorative set of black and blues for a long time. The dog took a tumble backwards and the horse reared for another shot at me. It was whinneying and foam was flicking out of its mouth, splatting the windscreen. I leapt into the cab and slammed the door shut as hard as I could.

My hands were shaking, and my right arm was almost paralysed from that horse-kick, but I managed to get the key into the ignition and get it started. All the time I was yelling at Paddy that everything was all right and she was safe now. Looking back, I must have just added to her fear.

The engine roared and I slammed it into first, gunned the accelerator and shot the clutch. The jeep jumped forward with a squeal of the four-wheel drive and I hit that big black fucker such a slam I must have broken both its legs and caved in its ribs. I heard the crunch as the bars hit, and despite its weight the horse was thrown backwards on its hind legs and thudded against the wall. I don't suppose the animal nuts will give me points, but I swear I let out a whoop of manic glee and I wished that mad horse in a hot hell. On the passenger side, the big black and tan dog slammed its nose at the glass a couple of times, leaving smears of blood and saliva, but I shot out of that alley like a cork from a bottle and heaved right to get away from the rest of the rodeo madhouse.

There was a blur on the left as the other dog flew up near the front of the jeep in a tumbling arc, its face just a wilderness of blood and mush. The jeep took a lurch to the side and there was a juddering that pulled the steering so hard I had to lean on it, near-broken shoulder and all, to keep it on a straight line.

It wasn't until I managed to get to the relative safety of the cut-off road to Mr Bennett's smallholding that I unsnapped Paddy's harness and eased myself painfully and gingerly from the jeep. I went round the other side and helped Paddy out, and again felt her little frame shiver against me, and I was flooded with a white-hot tidal wave of guilt at leaving her in the car and going upstairs with Helen Hollinger, no matter who was pulling those strings. But Paddy didn't cry, and she didn't look accusingly at me. She just held on tight.

Then I looked down at the nearside front tyre and found why the steering had gone. It was ripped to shreds, and the jagged, gaping hole in the rubber was matted with blood and hair and bits of bone. That little bastard had gripped on tight until its head was crushed.

By the time my nerves were wound up tight enough to play tunes on, and Paddy was in a state of shock. I stood her by the fence at the side of the road and pulled the jeep in on to the grassy verge. It was still wet from the rain, and the jeep lurched along with a mechanical limp. I opened the tailgate and rummaged around that little compartment where they kept the jack and bits and pieces for emergency repairs and hauled out what I thought I'd need. The jack was there, one of those hand-cranked things that lifted the thing on to its inside wheels, but when I went back to the box again I couldn't find the wheel brace, and without that I wasn't going to move that chewed tyre. If I couldn't get that, we weren't going anywhere, and I for one did not relish hanging around in nightmare country more than a minute longer. We weren't far from Duncan Bennett's cottage so I grabbed Paddy's hand and made to go along the road. She came away from the fence like a zombie and tagged along.

The old man wasn't in when I rapped on the door. His storm doors were wide open and when I tried the inside one it opened easily, which meant he was around somewhere. I checked in his garage which was more of an open-ended lean-to built against the gable wall. The place was littered with tools, and there were a couple of wheel braces and a few big shifting spanners, so I knew that I'd at least get something to take the wheel-nuts off and loosen the big spare from the back. I shouted a couple of times and wandered round to the neat little back garden. The

330

late crop of potatoes was still in bloom, but the early stuff like lettuce was long gone. I was about to turn back when I saw the smoke from the far end of the field, in against the trees where the old man kept his rows of beehives. I went into the garage again and Paddy was standing silhouetted in the entry way and I called her through. Watching Mr Bennett collecting honey might take her mind off the last ghastly episode for a couple of minutes, and the old man would at least be able to watch her while I fixed the jeep.

She came through and we climbed over the rickety stile and through the long wet grass in the direction of the smoke plume. It swished and caught at our ankles and the bottom of my jeans was soaked in seconds, but neither of us cared. The closer we got to the tree-shaded corner of the field, the more we heard the buzzing of the bees. Right in at the big oak that spread heavy branches several metres over the far fence, we could see a grey haze of insects and we moved towards them. As we did so, I was telling Paddy all about the bees and how hard they worked and what delightful creatures they really were. Then I stopped sharply and Paddy looked up at me. The smoke canister was lying on its own, about ten yards from the end hive, smoking away lustily into the air. The old man was nowhere to be seen. I scanned right along the neat row of white boxes and the buzzing of the bees was a drone in that cloud right at the corner.

Then my eyes caught a splash of red on the ground at the far hive and I stepped closer. I walked about fifteen yards and stopped right in my tracks, and I must have tightened my grip on Paddy's hand because she gave a little yelp.

The red splash was Duncan Bennett's shirt.

The old man was lying spreadeagled face up on the patch of short grass that surrounded the hives.

At first I thought he must have taken a heart attack and I started forward, but already my subconscious was telling me that there was something wrong. Something wrong with his face. I got a bit closer and halted again. Paddy started to say something and I hushed her to silence. There were bees crawling all over the old man, but that wasn't what was wrong. His whole face was purple-blue, and swollen up like a grotesque hallowe'en mask. The swelling was all lumpy and so severe that his neck had expanded to the width of his head, and those little wire-framed specs he always wore were embedded into the skin so tightly that they were hardly visible. I stood there, horrified for a minute, until it dawned on me what had happened.

By that time it was almost too late. The buzzing was much closer now, a fierce humming, like electrical wires arcing. Paddy noticed it first.

'Nicky,' she called. 'Look over there. What's that?'

There was more than a hint of panic rising in her voice.

I looked up and almost fell backwards. The dark corner of the field, right under the shade of that oak tree, was a mass of bees, an immense swarm that must have contained every bee in all the hives. There were mounds of insects that hung in brown clumps from the trunk and branches, bearing some of the thinner twigs down with their weight. And all around them was a thick fast-moving cloud of flying honey bees. I must have stared at them for ten seconds, and as I did so, more and more of the bees came off the tree and joined the cloud, darkening it, making it buzz more angrily.

'Paddy, walk away,' I hissed. I couldn't remember if loud noises antagonised bees, but I sure wasn't in the mood to experiment. Waving my hand behind me, I motioned her away, and gingerly tiptoed backwards, away from that giant swarm, and away from the poor old man who was surely dead (please God, I hope he is, I remember thinking), and with every step I took, more and more of the cluster launched themselves off the bark and the branches until the air was thick with them. The noise was so loud it vibrated in my head. When I got to the furthest hive, I turned. Paddy hadn't got far and she was standing, staring at the bees.

'Come on, let's go,' I said, and started walking across

the field. She came. But the noise, if anything, got louder rather than softer, and when we were halfway across I stopped to take a look back and my heart, which should have been used to it by now (but wasn't), took another leap into my throat. For the cloud suddenly billowed out in a dark explosion from the shade into the light and came rolling, buzzing across the grass towards us. In my mind a picture of Duncan Bennett, that gentle old man, flashed in a horrific vision, and I pictured clearly what had happened to him.

That gave me enough of a jolt of adrenalin to scoop Paddy right off the ground and, without breaking my stride, go into a sprint for the stile.

There was none of the dreamscape stuff about my flight. My feet did not become tangled in the grass and I did not slip back in the mud. I was not, as was normal, rooted to the spot, which was perhaps a pity because if I had I would have known it was just one of the usual nightmares. This was for real.

Paddy was a feather in my arms and my strides were ten feet long, and if there had been a clock on me I swear I would have broken any Olympic record for that hundred metres or so. And when I got to the fence I was in too much of a hurry to gingerly climb. I went over that like a champion hurdler, me, and Paddy as the baton, and landed clean as a whistle on the flagstones on the far side with nary a slip or a stumble. I scooted up that path and through the garage and round the front where I barged straight into Mr Bennett's house and slammed the door with a deft flick of my free hand.

Then I let my breath out in one huge whoop, dumped Paddy on to the floor, and straightened up. Then the adrenalin reaction hit me like a kick from that horse and I spun round so that when I was sick she wouldn't be splattered. I was, quickly and heavily. It all missed her.

I staggered through the to the kitchen, wiping my mouth with the back of my hand and gasping for air. When I finally got my breath back, I called out to the hallway.

'C'mon kid.' My voice sounded like an old man's.

Paddy came through the door backwards.

'They're at the door. I can hear them,' she said.

I could hear them too, even over the pounding in my ears.

'Yeah. But it's all right. They can't get in.'

I wasn't entirely sure of that and wondered what the hell I would do about it if they *did* all get in, but I was reasonably sure that no more than a few would manage to find a way inside the house through whatever cracks there were, and I could handle that. I've been stung before.

The bees continued to batter themselves to death on the door, and later, a good while later, when we ventured out, there was a mound of them on the door-sill. But they never did manage to find a way inside.

Paddy and I sat in the kitchen and listened to the low buzzing and the steady patter of kamikaze insects and my breath slowed down to a steady pant. What with Helen Hollinger and then that crazy horse and now my all-time world-record achievement, I'd been having an energetic day.

There was nothing for it but to light the gas under the stove and make a pot of tea. I turned on the tap to fill the kettle, but nothing came out. then there was a deep gurgling sound, and a thick brown sludge burst from the tap and spat into the sink. The water pipes must have ruptured.

Having thought of a cup of tea, I now realised how *badly* I really wanted one. The British cure for all ills, hot and strong. I almost swore in frustration, and then I discovered that Mr Bennett's big iron kettle was filled to the brim, and I sat down thankfully to wait for it to boil.

It really was the cure-all. Or at least it made me feel better, and it helped dispel that personal video that was re-running recent events in full colour inside my head.

I made Paddy's tea sweet and she drank two cups. Sitting across the table from her, I couldn't help but feel she'd had the raw end of any deal. Her mother in hospital and then the drive around the country to get to her. And she'd been attacked by a mad horse and a pack of dogs.

And the bees. I thanked every God I knew for the fact that I was able to get us out of that field ahead of the cloud. If I'd stumbled once, or if I'd twisted my ankle or broken something whilst leaping that fence, we would both still be out there, probably dead, but having taken a long time, oh, much too long, to get there. The thought made me shudder.

'Paddy?'

She looked up.

'How's it going, kid?' I tried an encouraging smile.

'How's it going for you?' she asked back quickly.

'Good and bad.'

'Is that good, or is that bad?'

'Well, we're still in one piece, aren't we?'

She nodded. 'S'pose so.'

She looked straight into my eyes.

'What's happening? Why has everything gone all horrible?'

'I don't know, sunshine, but I'm going to try to get you away from it.'

She kept looking at me, and fingering the torc around her neck. Maybe there was something about that beautifully simple necklet of gold. I was about to think more on that when Paddy's voice cut right across my thoughts.

'I don't think we can get away. I think it wants us. It wants to kill us.'

'Aw, come on,' I said, reaching over to ruffle her hair, 'you don't really believe that, do you?'

She saw right through me, but although I saw that in her eyes, she didn't say so.

'I do Nicky. I *know* it.'

'What makes you think that?'

'I don't know. I just *do*. I can feel it. It's weird, like there's something that hates us, waiting in the dark to jump out and swallow us up. I just know it, the way I know my mummy's going to be all right.'

'This thing, whatever it is, what does it look like?'

335

'I don't know. I dream about it, down in the dark. It's got white eyes and it keeps calling my name. But it's in the dark and I can't see it properly, but it changes and it's horrible.'

'We see lots of horrible things in dreams. And lots of nice things too.'

'But this thing. I've seen it *before*, but I don't know when.'

'How can you have seen it before? I mean, you've just come to Arden, haven't you?'

'I don't know. But I have seen it before. A long time ago. And the old lady was there, the one who gave me the flowers.'

'What flowers were these, kiddo?' How could she know about the flowers her mother was given way back then?

'The golden flowers. The lady comes in the other dreams and puts the golden flowers round my neck, and she smiles, and I know the flowers are *good*, just like that thing with the white eyes is *bad*.'

'When the old lady gives you the flowers,' I said, 'where are you?'

'Down at the stream. I'm with other people, but I can't see them.'

'And you're sure it's an old lady? Not a young one with golden hair? And pretty?'

'She's got gold hair all right, but she's not young. She's *old*. But she's smiling at me and her eyes are all twinkly, and I know she wants to help me.'

I sat back, amazed. Paddy was having a recurring dream that was twenty years older than herself, a dream her mother had had long ago when we'd taken the mushrooms and smoked the saxifrage mixture. How the hell could that be possible?

What the hell, I thought, after the last couple of days, when my whole world had turned itself inside out, what was a little touch of ESP compared to roads that took you back to where you'd started and seabirds that went for people, and trees that grabbed at four-wheel drives?

A couple of days more of this and I would take levitation as par for the course.

Paddy interrupted my train of thought again.

'What'll we do now?'

'I don't know, love. I'm trying to think about it. I think we should stay put here for a while, until they go away,' I said, jerking my head at the pattering of bees against the door. The flow seemed to be slackening off, and outside the clouds were gathering again. I felt bad about leaving old Mr Bennett out there beside the beehives, but he was dead and there was nothing I could do about it. He wouldn't have minded us using his little cottage as a haven from whatever was being thrown at us.

'Maybe we should stay here tonight,' I ventured, and Paddy quickly nodded in agreement.

'I don't want to go out there again. Not until they're gone.'

'Me neither,' I agreed heartily. I just hoped that they would eventually give up and go.

We did stay the night. The sound of the bees outside died away when the rain started. I lit a coal fire and Paddy sat on my knee, leaning against my chest while I smoked and looked into the embers, and then she fell asleep after darkness fell and I carried her up to bed. I pulled the blanket over both of us and wrapped an arm around her shoulder, listening to her soft, child's breathing in the night, and fell asleep soon after.

I don't remember dreaming.

Paddy woke up before me and shook me until I came swimming up out of it. I was stiff, and my shoulder was giving out messages I would have rather ignored. I'd been lying on one arm and it went into pins and needles and I had to rub it vigorously with the other, which jolted pain up and down my back. I had felt heaps better on other mornings, but it could have been worse. I could have been lying out there with a face like a peeled plum, and worse, the little girl I was supposed to be minding for a friend – a very special friend – could have been lying there with me.

'Nicky,' Paddy said right into my ear. I shook my head groggily.

'Yeah Paddy, what is it?'

'Do you want me to make breakfast?' she asked brightly. It was a new day, and I suppose, through the drizzle outside, the sun was making a go of it.

'Coffee first, if you can find any,' I grunted.

'Sure,' she said, bounding off the bed. I felt a bit tacky, and my jeans had rucked and folded behind my knees, digging into the skin. There was a sour taste in my mouth.

Paddy came back into the room.

'I don't know how to light the stove,' she said. 'I've never seen one like that before.'

I ended up making the coffee. At first I forgot about the water and spent a few moments looking blankly at the thick, glutinous mess that glopped from the tap. I got the stove lit and stoked up the fire, remembering how to push out the damper to get the back boiler heated, and put some porridge oats on to boil in a big aluminium pan.

The coffee was a lifesaver and I had my first cigarette of the day. Paddy frowned, but said nothing. Then came the porridge, hot and thick and drowned in milk. Paddy said she'd never tasted it before and was a bit put off by the thick, turbid mess I'd concocted, but after the first spoonful she ate ravenously and then proceeded to scrape the pot and the ladle clean.

Both of us felt a whole lot better after a hot bellyful, and we sat together at the table deciding what to do next.

I decided I should go out and check on the bees, but before I did I searched around until I found a piece of muslin in a drying cupboard, a large square piece of transparent cloth that Mrs Bennett probably had used for jam-making, and in an old wardrobe in the tiny upstairs bedroom I found a large blue hat with a wide brim. There was a little posy of silk flowers tucked on the outside band – probably the old woman's best hat for weddings and Easter service.

The hat didn't fit and I didn't care. I plonked it on my

head and spread the muslin right over it, gathering the corners together and tucking them down the collar of my shirt. I went downstairs and got a delighted, healthy laugh from Paddy, and that made me smile for the first time in days. I got some dishcloths and wrapped them like scarves round my neck and used two tea-towels around my hands for protection.

Then I cautioned Paddy to wait inside the house, with all the doors shut, even the room doors, and went out the front door, gingerly opening it a crack first, and peering through the line of light. Everything was fogged by the muslin, but the only sound was the pattering of rain.

I opened the door and slipped out, closing it quickly behind me, and carefully went along the path, ready at any moment to dash back inside again.

But there was nothing there. The bees had gone. And if they had flown back to where the hives were down in the corner of the field, I was content to leave them there. Under no circumstances, I was sure, could I repeat yesterday's feat of athletics.

The wheel brace in Duncan Bennett's lean-to fitted the nuts on the nearside wheel, and after much effort they came loose. Paddy watched from the window as I worked, leaning with her elbows on the sill and her head in her cupped hands. I knew she was watching out for the bees. I had made her stay indoors just in case they came back. I felt sure if that dark cloud had buzzed me I would have made it back to the cottage on my own, but I didn't want to risk having to find Paddy and get her to safety. As it happened, there were no bees and as I worked I even had the confidence to strip off the protective muslin and the silly hat.

The wheel came off and I dumped it at the side of the road. The tyre was a ruin. That little dog had gripped it so tightly that there was a bite-sized chunk out of the rubber, and the rest had been chewed by the rims as I drove away on the flapping flat. I unscrewed the spare that hung on the back and heaved it into position and almost racked my

339

back getting it on to the bolts, but the job didn't take too long, though I was beginning to sweat a bit when I spun the jack lever and the four by four settled back down on its wheel, swaying a bit on the springs. The jack went right into the back along with the brace, next to my waterproof coat and my walking stick and that old worn, canvas-covered bottle that Father Cronin had given me.

Paddy waved back when I gestured to her and came out of the house, gingerly at first, looking warily for signs of attack, and she carefully closed the door.

I opened the passenger door for her and helped her into the high seat and fixed her belt. I went round the jeep making sure the windows were tight, for I didn't fancy driving with a swarm of bees down my neck, and something made me check all the doors to make sure they were locked from the outside too. Maybe my survival instinct was taking over, or maybe it was just paranoia, but by then I didn't really care to analyse myself.

We went along the main street, past Ronnie Scott's garage – or Alan's garage now – and out to the far end of town to the blown-up bridge. I had half hoped that the four-wheel drive could have got us across the stream, but there was no way the jeep could take the steep banks. Even in low gear and all wheels turning, the jeep started to slew round dangerously and dig itself into the mud. I back-tracked a bit and went down by the shacks at shore-side where there was an old ford, but after the rains the stream was in full spate and that way was blocked. I reversed away from the roiling brown water and went back up the track and turned right at the pigeon huts and wire-fenced dog-runs. Then I had to step hard on the brakes. There were people on the path, four of them standing right across it, and a few more lounging against the grey-weathered wood of the nearest hut.

When I braked, the car slithered forward and the four men jumped out of the way, and as I passed I recognised Billy Ruine and the rest of his pals who had been giving Badger a bad time at the festival. He recognised me in the same instant, as the jeep lurched past them.

Over the whine of the engine, I heard him yell something, and then a beer bottle came from nowhere and landed smack on the roof just above my head and skittered off without breaking, bounced once on the bonnet and was gone. I twisted round in my seat and saw Ruine dive off the track and pick something up. I thought it was a stick or a club and I swung round to watch where I was going.

'Bloody idiots,' I thought to myself, pushing the stick up into third, and ramming down on the pedal. I flicked a glance at the rear-view and saw Ruine standing in the middle of the rutted track, pointing the thing at me, and in the same instant that the realisation flitted into my mind there was one almighty roar and a thumping clatter on the back of the jeep that fogged the rear window to a white blanket.

Paddy let out a little squeal and my hand jerked the wheel so hard I almost went off the path and into a scrubby hedge. That was a stroke of luck, because the second barrel hit the side panel instead of the back window which would have caved right in and showered us with flying glass and Hy-max goose shot.

I swung the jeep on to the straight with one hand and shoved Paddy's head between her knees with the other and took off up that track like a ferret up a roan pipe with the clutch whining in protest. At the main road I swung left hard, feeling the rear wheels fishtailing on the slick tarmac, but there was no traffic about, and when I was headed back into town I started to calm down.

'It's all right, Paddy,' I said, 'you can come up now.'

She lifted her head warily and squirmed round to look at the back window.

'What happened?'

'Somebody threw something,' I told her.

'That was a gun,' she said. 'I heard it.'

'All right. It was a gun. Somebody shot at the car, but they're gone now.'

By this time my heart had settled down to a mere racing thud that I could feel in my ears, and I slowed the jeep a bit as we rolled through Milligs.

'Why did they shoot at us?' Paddy asked.

'Drunk, or crazy, or maybe both. There's a lot of crazy things happening.'

'They want to kill us.'

'No, they're just drunk. They'll shoot at anything. Anyway, we're all right, aren't we?'

'I guess so,' Paddy said, dubiously.

I was just beginning to settle back down when I caught a movement in the wing mirror and glanced down. A car had come belting out of a side road and swung along behind us. There was a cloud of blue smoke belching out from under the chassis, and I saw the car sway from side to side on the road. I stared into the mirror. It was an old Cortina, dark blue with grey patches of glass filler.

'Shit,' I said, and it should have been under my breath, but wasn't. Paddy must have seen me looking in the mirror, for she leaned forward to see in the nearside one too.

'It's them. They're coming after us.'

I dropped a gear and boosted the pedal and the jeep lurched ahead, accelerating fast. That old Cortina was packed with people, and there was something sticking out from the side window and this time I was sure it *wasn't* a stick. The jeep hammered along the road and the old car followed us in its cloud of blue exhaust and somebody leaned bodily out of the window. I started swerving the jeep from side to side on the road, and there was a flash in my eyes and a patter like heavy hail on the back again, followed by another roar.

Then there was another shot that smacked across us again and I shoved Paddy's head down again, hard, although at that distance the shotguns weren't able to do much damage. I had to keep well ahead of them though, because if Ruine and his mad team got closer they could blow a hole right through the jeep. I preferred to avoid that scenario.

The team in the Cortina let off a couple more shots that didn't do much more than chip the paint and I decided to

342

get out of their sights. When we got closer to the field where the festival had been held, I jerked the wheel right and dropped to second gear at the same time and slewed up the side road that would take us back past Duncan Bennett's place. I was going far too fast and my attention was diverted when I looked in the rear-view again and saw that beat-up old saloon skitter in behind us. One of the wheels caught the verge and the jeep jumped about a yard into the air and I went nose-first into a hedge. The engine roared, coughed and stopped. All sorts of swear words were tripping in a non-stop litany as I fumbled with the key and slammed into reverse. The wheels turned on the soft earth and I came back about a foot, and then the engine died again. I didn't have time for another try, for right behind me the Cortina came shooting up the road and there was a screech of brakes as it slithered to a halt.

I punched down on Paddy's belt release and it sprang out of the socket and pinged up behind her ear, and in the same motion I grabbed her by the arm and hauled her across to my seat and I flung the door open and rolled out with her on to the ground on the lee side of the car.

Paddy landed on top of me and I got a brief shock of pain as my hip hit something hard when I rolled into the hedge. It was full of thorns and sharp, rigid twigs, but there was enough space between the gnarled boles of the hedgerow bushes for me to shove her right through to the other side and for me to scramble after her, all the time expecting to have my ass shot to mincemeat, but I must have been quicker than I realised for no shot came. Out on the other side there was a wide garden, then a row of cottages ahead, and I got to my feet, spurred by the slithery fear in my spine, and took off at full pelt, not bothering to heft Paddy in my arms. Instead I grabbed her collar like a policeman making an arrest and literally ran her right across the flower beds to the small fence at the far side. I could have choked her to death but I never even thought about that, and I don't think her feet even touched the ground.

There was a whole string of curses and plenty of shouting from the other side of the hedge, and then a loud crashing noise as my pursuers realised where I'd gone and started to follow me. I reached the fence and lifted Paddy over and vaulted it, slipping as I went over and landing with a bump in somebody's cabbage patch. It didn't hurt. Paddy grabbed at my hand to help me to my feet and I got a glimpse of her face, white and shocked. By this time I saw two figures clambering through the hedge and although I couldn't see whether they had guns I didn't wait to find out. Paddy and I went through the row of gardens behind the line of cottages like marines on an assault course. Every time I came to a wall or a wicker fence I just boosted her over like a ruck-sack, trusting to her reflexes to land properly. Bruises were infinitely preferable to what Ruine's crazy gangsters were offering, but I have to say that Paddy was running like a cat and landed like one every time, on her feet and moving fast.

At the second to last garden we faced a six-foot-high lattice. I grabbed Paddy and hoisted her on to the top and shoved her over, but in doing so I had lost momentum, and when I tried to climb over my feet slipped and scrabbled on the thin wooden fence. I took a dozen steps backwards then took a run at it and jumped, crashing one foot almost right through the partition, but I gripped the top and just swung my legs. As I did so, there was another huge bang from behind and the fence started to disintegrate underneath me. The shot blasted a hole two feet wide just where my back had been only a second before, and the thump rattled the whole latticework so hard it threw me off the fence and into the other garden. Fortunately Paddy hadn't waited around for me and was into the next flower bed by the time I got to my feet, or I would have found her in a pool of blood where I fell. I caught up with her and instead of going straight across the dyke at the end house I grabbed her arm and swung her round the gable end of the cottage and round to the front of the houses, doubling back the way we had come, but out of sight of our pursuers.

I reckoned that they would run straight on, and if I got back to the jeep before they realised their mistake we could be miles away before they got back to their car.

What I didn't realise, for I hadn't spent too much time looking over my shoulder, was that not all of Ruine's gang had chased us through the hedge.

I was almost doubled over from breathlessness and had an appalling stitch in my side by the time we got back to the first cottage, and angled across a wide lawn that would take us back to the hedge, although further along the road where there was a wooden gate that allowed on to the verge. We got to that and I hung on the heavy peeling green bars for a few seconds, whooping air into my lungs and pressing my hand into my side to try to dull the gripping pain. The gate swung open when I pushed it and I grabbed Paddy's arm and pulled her behind me on to the road and turned back to where the jeep was still nosed into the hedge. Paddy stopped suddenly and I looked at her. She was rigid and staring past me. I followed her look and froze on the spot.

That was when I discovered that only two men had crashed through the hedge after us.

Billy Ruine was standing only five yards away with a big grin all over his weaselly face and a twelve bore over-and-under in the crook of his arm. Paddy let out a little whimper and I gripped her hand tight.

'Well, well. Clark fucking Kent came back to us, did he? And nobody to back him up this time,' Ruine said, and there was a strange look of hate and glee in his eyes that I swear wasn't human.

I took a step backwards, thinking of making a dash back through the fence, but Ruine swung the gun up and aimed it right at my belly which lurched uncontrollably in anticipation.

'Don't even think about it. I've got you now, right where I want you.' He grinned again and looked around at his cronies. Ruine was the only one with a gun, but the others had sticks and somebody else had an angle-iron fence bar. They all sniggered like drunks.

'Kill him, Billy,' somebody said. 'Take his fucking head off.'

'I want the girl,' said a big beefy boy with a sparse, gingery beard. 'Let's have the girl.'

When I heard that, my stomach did even bigger somersaults, and I didn't know what I was going to do. Instinctively I pulled Paddy behind me and Ruine kept the gun steady right on my belly.

'Two for the price of one, eh?' he said quietly. 'This'll go right through you and blow her to bits.'

'Do it, Billy. Give it to 'em,' one of the men said, but I couldn't take my eyes off the two black holes of the gun barrel.

Just at that moment, the gate crashed open and two men burst out and Billy Ruine's gun swung right off me. One of the men had a gun and was whirling round when there was an almighty roar from Ruine's shotgun and an instantaneous ripping sound right behind my ear. I whirled and saw a mist of red billowing out behind the man who was standing only a few feet away from me.

It seemed to take me an age, although it must have been less than a second, to figure out what was wrong with the man. Then it dawned on me as he stood swaying for a moment. He had no head. The full blast of both barrels had exploded it into a rain of red fragments that painted the side of the tight-packed hedgerow.

For that second we were all frozen. Billy Ruine stared at the toppling headless man and for an instant the madness in his eyes was changed to disbelief. There was a crump as the falling body hit the grass and everybody stared, wide-eyed, as its legs jittered, as if they were trying to run.

I started out of immobility first and my mind had gone into hyperdrive. I grabbed Paddy again and took off along the road to Mr Bennett's cottage before anybody had a chance to move.

From behind I heard somebody shout: 'It's Tommy! You've killed Tommy!' And then there was a whole lot of screaming and yelling and I was dragging Paddy along like a rag doll, in a blind panic to get to the safety of Duncan's dry-stone wall before anybody had the sense to pick up the second shotgun. All the way along those brief yards I was kicking myself for not thinking of it first.

Billy Ruine had taken off his brother's head with both barrels.

Paddy and I had made it to the corner of the wall when the gun went off again, maybe about sixty yards behind, but Billy Ruine wasn't as accurate at that range with me as he had been at point blank with his brother. The shot rapped off the wall and ricocheted into the back of my leg, smacking into the wet canvas of my jeans like a paddle. My right foot shot away from me with the force of it and I went down in a heap, almost dragging Paddy down with me. My calf muscles were shrieking out in pain, but even through that I yelled to the girl.

'Run, Paddy. Get into the trees and keep going.'

She stopped for an instant and looked at me, her face all open and pale, then she was off up Mr Bennett's path and through the open lean-to, and gone from sight. I hauled myself up on to my feet and limped around the wall. My leg was hurting like hell and the muscle had gone numb and there was no way I was going to make any speed until it settled down, but I hoped to get into Duncan's cottage and bar the door to hold them off for a while, at least until Paddy got clear. I was sure that Duncan had an old four ten somewhere, which, while not as powerful as a twelve bore, would be just as effective at close range. It was a chance anyway of getting out of this.

I almost made it to the door when Billy Ruine's voice from the gate made me spin round.

'You fucking bastard. You made me kill Tommy. You made me shoot my own fuckin' brother,' he said in a screechy voice.

That was when miracle number two happened.

Billy Ruine slowly lifted the shotgun and pointed it at my head and started laughing hysterically, but not enough to make the black hole of the gun barrel waver at all. I had nowhere to run.

At that moment there was a buzzing roar and a black streak caught the corner of my eye and Billy Ruine turned again just in time to see the motorbike that was almost upon him. In that same instant he fired and the whole window of dead Duncan Bennett's cottage caved in with a loud crash.

Just then Father Gerry swung his golden sword over his head and hit Ruine a massive blow on the shoulder that felled him where he stood.

The priest was like a black knight on a black charger, his visor shining in the daylight, and in his hand what I had thought was a sword was the big crucifix that stood on top of the tabernacle in the seminary chapel.

The priest was wielding it by the short end, and as he waved it about his head the gold and precious stone inlays caught the weak sunlight, making it look just like a sword, an exquisite Excalibur.

Over the roar of the engine, I could hear Gerry roaring out a chant, although I couldn't make out the words. He charged down that road and into the bunch of men who still stood across it, close to where Tommy Ruine's body was still twitching, and the black priest's arm came up high in the air and the golden cross came down in a great sweeping arc and crashed into the beefy bearded man's head. Even at that distance I could see the blood fly and the man who had wanted Paddy dropped like a stone. Gerry went right through the group, still waving his sword, and turned at the road and came back again. This time the other three men scattered, and started running towards where I was. Gerry came right on, and although I should have taken advantage of the second miracle, I couldn't move. The golden cross went up again and came sweeping down on the slowest man, caving in his skull. The faces of the other two were twisted in fear as the black priest chased them up the road.

Suddenly I could move again. Gerry was shouting

something about the soldiers of the Lord and I left him to fight the good fight. I went through the lean-to and into the garden behind. The pain in my leg was still burning, but there was no blood, and the numbness was wearing off. I got to the fence and clambered over and went straight across the field and into the trees, avoiding the corner of the field where the horror of the swarming bees might still be waiting in ambush. I hoped Paddy had avoided that area. I hadn't thought to tell her, although something inside me was pretty certain she was too smart to have gone near the hives, no matter how scared she was.

TWENTY-FIVE

While I was staring down the tunnel at the end of Billy Ruine's shotgun, Paddy was running across the field behind Duncan's cottage. I needn't have worried about the bees, for when she was halfway across the meadow, leaping over the clumps of knapweed and thistle, she suddenly realised she was heading directly towards the hives and veered sharply to the left before she got within fifty feet of the white boxes where Duncan's bloated body still lay. In seconds she was in the shelter of the trees and stumbling down the far side of the little gully and up the slippery slope of the far side. By the time Father Gerry had sung his holy war chant and caved in the head of the running man, she had come through the trees on the far side of the gully and into the pasture at the south side of McFall's farm, still running fast and panting for breath.

She got near to the gate at the corner of the field when the hedge erupted with an almighty crash and McFall's black Angus bull tore itself out of the brambles with a furious bellow. Paddy screamed in fright, slipped and fell heavily. The bull swivelled and hooked at the hedge with its stubby horns then turned around to face her. There was a long rope of saliva oozing from its mouth. It stood there, sides heaving and breath juddering asthmatically, and Paddy stared at the black bulk, frozen in fright. Then the bull moved one foot forward and Paddy launched herself to her feet and ran for the hedge. Behind her, the bull bellowed again and charged. She could hear the thudding of its hooves on the turf and could almost feel its breath on the back of her neck, and panic rose up inside her like the scream she felt was trying to burst out.

She knew that the gate was too far away and that the

bull was going to get her. The huge head was going to crash into the small of her back and the horns were going to gouge and gouge until there was nothing left.

That's exactly what would have happened for sure. But with twenty yards left between Paddy and the gate, twenty impossible yards, a minor miracle brought another shape that came rushing in from the left. Paddy only caught a flicker of movement in the corner of her eye, because her entire being was focused on the five thick bars that spanned the entrance to the field. There was a screech and a thud and a bellowing roar. Paddy's foot caught in a tangle of reeds and she tumbled headlong to the ground, knocking her breath out in a gush that left her gasping for air. But the horns didn't slam into her back; nor did they crush and pulp her into the ground.

Paddy rolled over, wild eyed and sobbing with panicky fear. The bull had turned and was now attacking a man who had a big stick in both hands and was slamming it with all his strength at its nose. There was another thud and another bellow, not deep, but high and furious. Paddy couldn't take her eyes away from the battle. The bull kept jinking on its hind legs, trying to avoid the club that slammed into its nose, while at the same time determined to gore the man who battered at it furiously. The man raised the heavy stick like a baseball player and his whole body torqued with the force of the swing and the club took the bull on the side of the mouth with a sharp crack. This time the bull didn't hesitate. It just charged straight at the man and he made a dive to the right and the animal crashed halfway through the hedge. It bellowed again and shook its massive head from side to side, trying to unlock its horns from the tangled branches. The man scrambled to his feet, almost falling flat again as he slipped on the wet grass, and sprinted towards where Paddy still lay, frozen, on the ground. He didn't stop when he reached her, but merely bent and grabbed the front of her jacket with one hand and kept on running. Paddy was jerked off the ground like a rag doll. At the gate, the man just bundled her over the bars and on to the lane at the other side and clambered over. Paddy felt her arm being gripped roughly and she was propelled along the lane at such a speed that she almost tripped. She was forced to take great leaps just to keep up with the big man. But as soon as she heard the first crash as the bull battered into the gate, cracking the bars and almost taking the whole thing right off the posts, the fright lent her all the speed she needed.

Badger Blackwood hustled Paddy along that lane as fast as his big frame could carry him. Behind them, the bull was rampaging at the gate and, if it kept it up, it was only a matter of time before it would break out into the lane.

They got to the metal gate that led into McFall's farmyard and Badger hauled the little girl across it and they made for the shelter of the brick and wood pen at the back of the byre. He gave another heave to get her across the stout fence and Paddy flopped to the ground on the other side, spent and gasping for breath. The big man crouched down beside her, sides heaving from exertion, and his arms grabbed her close to him. She could feel the racing beat of his heart through the thick plaid of his workshirt, and she looked up to see his face contorted, as if in pain. The two white streaks of hair that lined through the black were almost standing on end, and his whole forehead glistened in a sheet of perspiration. His grip on her was almost painful, but Paddy didn't mind. It was worth it to feel safe.

In the distance, they could hear the bellowing and crashing as the bull pulped the gate. It seemed to go on a long time, and eventually the thudding of the big man's heart slowed down from its express rhythm and his breathing seemed easier.

Badger opened his eyes and looked down at the little bundle that was crushed in his arms. The girl stared up at him and gave him a small smile. He grinned back in return and loosened his grip to wipe the sweat from his brow with one hand.

'Barbara?' he asked in a hoarse whisper.

'No, I'm Paddy.'

'Paddy? Not Barbara?'

'No, she's my mum.'

The big man seemed to weigh this up for a few seconds. His expression went from puzzlement to delight in six or seven stages, as if his mind was wading through mud, moving slowly and carefully every step of the way. 'Not Barbara. You're Paddy,' he finally agreed.

'That's right. What's your name?'

'Badger Blackwood.'

'Badger? That's a funny name.'

The man's eyes went vacant for a second and his brow creased in concentration, then for another moment the dark eyes focused again and seemed to gleam with sharp brightness. He shook his head, as if clearing it, then shook it again from side to side in a certain negative. No. Not Badger. Colin. I'm Colin. That's who I am.'

'You saved me from the bull,' she said. 'That was very brave.'

'Colin Blackwood,' he said again, as if he hadn't heard what she'd said, and the light in his eyes flickered, became dull with doubt, then brightened again. 'And you're not Barbara. You're Paddy, who looks like Barbara,' he said and nodded, as if he had solved a major problem, and come to a great decision. He grinned widely like an enthusiastic child. 'That bull nearly got us both, eh? But we beat him, didn't we?'

His arm hugged Paddy closer, confirming their shared victory. The girl nodded.

'I thought it was going to kill me. I was dead scared.'

'You too?' Me, I was scared. I'm always scared.'

He nodded to himself again.

'I've been scared all day, since my mum hit me. She called me names and used bad words and hit me with a pot, and I ran away. There's something wrong with her and I don't know what it is.'

Again he paused, as if considering an immense problem.

'There's something wrong with *today*,' he finally said when he'd puzzled it out. 'Everything's wrong. Every-

353

body's different today. It's *bad*.'

As the big man slowly put words to his thoughts, Paddy's mind formed a picture of how *bad* things were, and suddenly the picture of Nick sprawled against the dry-stone dyke of Duncan Bennett's garden sprung into the front of her mind. She started and struggled against the big arm that held her close.

'What's wrong Ba . . . Paddy?' Colin said, a look of worry flitting across his face.

Paddy squirmed and pushed at his arm.

'It's Nicky,' she said. 'We've got to help him. They've got guns.'

'Who is it?'

'I don't know. Men. They were chasing us and they've got Nicky. They want to kill him and me.'

'Nicky?' Colin asked.

'Nicky Ryan. He's my mum's friend.'

'Mine too. Nicky's my friend too, Paddy. He helps me when I'm in trouble. He's *good*.'

'We've got to find him. Will you help me?'

Colin nodded and got to his feet. Behind them, they could still hear the bellowing and crashing as the bull kept up its attack on the gate. Colin took Paddy's hand and they stepped away from the corner of the pen where they'd been sitting, and moved towards the maze of alleys that served as a corral for the livestock on the farm. He opened a stile gate and let Paddy through first and let it click shut behind them, and both of them walked quickly across the churned up mud and straw towards the brick wall at the far side that ran parallel to the farm lane. From there they could quickly get to the Bennett cottage.

They were halfway across the muddy square when there was a movement at the right that caught their attention and brought them slipping to a halt.

Old Boot, the big boar that ruled the paddock behind McFall's byre, had been standing stock still when the man and the girl came through the swing gate and started cross-ing the yard. His great bulk, a sandy pink, merged with the rough pine pickets and bricks of the fence, and he stopped chewing as soon as he saw movement. As the two squelched in the mud to the centre of the yard, his little red eyes swivelled to follow the movement. A trail of red saliva dripped from the corner of his mouth. The big animal waited until the man and girl were furthest from the nearest fence, and then he suddenly whirled round and ran towards them, his snout wrinkled back and his mouth wide open to let out a harsh screech like a stone-saw.

This is where I came back into the picture. I had roughly followed Paddy's trail through the trees and up the side of the gully, but I'd come out further up along the lane. Behind me a big bull was bellowing and madly butting at the five-barred gate that was cracked and splintered but still holding. I jogged along the track to the farm, because I was sure those bars weren't going to hold much longer, and I didn't want to be stuck in the lane with that thing at my back.

Up at the farm I could see no sign of Paddy, and there was no-one else around either. I didn't know that she and Badger were huddled on the inside of the pen, and if I had it would have made things a whole lot easier.

I came round by the side of the byre and leaned over the wall of the sty where the big boar was standing near the barrier, a great mound of meat and muscle, scoffing away in that awkward breathless way that pigs have. I could see the powerful jaws working away and hear the snuffling chomp as they closed on its feed. The big animal turned its head a little and suddenly my stomach did a heaving lurch.

For in Old Boot's jaws was the shin and foot and black shoe of a child.

I was mesmerised with the shock of it and I couldn't draw my eyes away. Then the boar shook its head, flapping its big ears against its cheeks, and there was a crunching sound as the bone in the leg was crushed. The little shoe dangled at the corner of its mouth and then fell off into the mud that was scarlet with blood. That was just enough to break the horror spell and I turned and threw up what little else was left in my stomach, leaving me with heaving sides and a burning sensation in my throat and nose. I sank down to my haunches and then to all fours where I retched again, a dry racking spasm that brought forth nothing but a weak cough. My eyes watered so hard I thought they were going to pop right out of their sockets.

For a minute I was paralysed and I remember moaning a little to myself, feeling so ghastly that I just wanted to sit down for a while and cry until all of this went away. A child, for God's sake. That's what it was eating! And all of a sudden my heart and my stomach did a double tango when the thought flashed through my mind that the child was Paddy. Then I realised she hadn't been wearing black shoes and I almost cried with relief.

I eased myself on to a sitting position and turned away from the slick of bile I'd left on the ground, still shuddering in the aftermath of dry heaves, and waited a moment to get my breath back, wishing I would suddenly wake up from this prolonged nightmare and find myself and the rest of the world sane and safe and normal.

That was when all hell broke loose on the other side of the barricade. There was a high screech like metal being scraped off stone and a simultaneous scream and instantly I was on my feet again. Paddy was halfway across the muddy corral with a big man by her side and that immense boar was racing towards them away from the wall behind which I'd cowered and been sick. For an instant Paddy's face was stretched and white and the next the big man had grabbed her by the waist and was off and running for the far side of the yard with that huge pig in hot pursuit.

Ordinarily I would have run a mile in the opposite direction, but I didn't. I jumped that fence in one go and ran as hard as I could at an angle towards where man, girl and pig were certain to meet. The boar made a lunge and caught the heel of Badger's shoe and I heard the jaws snap together and the big fellow went down. Paddy was flung about three yards forward into the mud but she was run-

356

ning when she landed and started towards the fence. Old
Boot had a grip of that shoe and was shaking his massive
head from side to side, and big though Badger was, he was
being tossed about like a rat in an angry dog's jaws. Then
the pig let go and dived in for Badger's belly and he rolled
in the mud to avoid its tusks.

I arrived just then and without thinking I sunk my boot
as hard as I could right into the big rough scrotum that
pushed out just under its wiry tail. If the screech when it
attacked was loud, the one it let out when I kicked its balls
would have woken the dead. Instead of snapping its jaws
shut on Badger's belly, it missed its footing and seemed to
nose-dive right into the mud. Badger rolled to the side and
scrambled almost upright, then the pig whirled round and
had another go at him and he slipped on to his backside,
frantically kicking both feet at the boar's snout. I ran in
and booted it again, this time in the ribs under the flank,
and I nearly broke my toe. The animal lurched and came
round to face me. Its jaws were wide open and it was
screaming in fury and pain and the little beady eyes looked
as if they would drill me to the spot. It came at me with
the mouth snapping and if those razor tusks had connected
they would have taken my leg off at the knee. I jumped to
the side and it swung as it went past to have another snap
at me, catching the flap of my jeans and whipping me right
off my feet.

The long flat-curved tooth that had snagged my denim
sliced through the material with one tug of Old Boot's
head and I scrabbled away on my backside, slipping in the
mire. The boar lunged for me with its mouth agape and
those yellow curves jutting out each side of its mouth,
getting ready to slice and crunch me to shreds. Then the
pig stopped in mid lunge, with its fore feet scrabbling in
the sludge. I kept scrambling backwards out of bite reach
and saw the amazing sight of Badger heaving so hard on
the pig's tail that the hind hooves were right out of the
mud and bucking at the air. The weight of the beast must
have been enormous, for even though Badger strained like

357

a tug-o-war champion his feet slid forward allowing Old Boot to get a purchase on the ground again. Its screech of pure anger was eerily high, like nails scraping down a blackboard. Still Badger hauled, and when Boot found he couldn't go forward he spun around to bite at the big man. The movement swung Badger almost off his feet and the ensuing chase would have been funny if it had been slapstick. Badger held on grimly and the big sandy bulk spun and the jaws snapped until both pig and man were covered in shit and mud.

I had got to my feet by the time Badger's grip slackened and he was thrown again, sliding against the brick barricade, and he went down with a wet thump. The boar screeched shrilly and heaved itself forward and my feet were stuck in the mud when I tried to move in to help.

The big broad snout went in and I heard Badger let out a whoof as the breath went out of him and in my mind's eye I saw his blood splattered all over the wall. There was a loud roaring in my ears and a spray of red and a shock from a few yards away that almost knocked me off my feet and back into the mire. Old Boot's back was a gaping red hole just at that hump where the neck joined the shoulders, and a mass of blood and gristle and fat splattered on to the wall close to the ground.

The animal gave a lurch to the side and swung its head round low and I could see a raggedy flap that used to be an ear and a big bloody mass that should have been a cheek. The little eye swivelled in this mess and caught hold of me.

Then there was another loud roar and the right flank of the thing just seemed to blow out in a red explosion. Old Boot's hindquarters slipped from under him and he crashed to the ground. His jaws were working but the scream was gone, and the ungainly front hooves scrabbled for a moment and were still.

I was still three frames back and stared bemusedly at the heaving red bulk in the mud, unsure of what had happened.

And then a voice from the other side of the wall called

out: 'By God man, you'll be all the better for a good wash. And I can think of better ways to get bacon for breakfast too.'

Donald MacDonald leaned against the wall with what can only be described as a grim smile on his face, and a gun that looked as if it would put a hole through an elephant.

The four of us stood frozen for a long moment. Badger had hauled himself to his feet with hardly a scratch to show for his battle. His leather belt had been sliced clean through in Boot's last lunge, but the tusks had missed his belly. My jeans were tattered from the knee down, and both of us were black with mud. Paddy's face peered at us through the slats in the fence.

'Well, don't just stand there,' the major called out. 'Unless you really like playing around in that stuff.'

I waded through the sludge and clambered over the wall and Paddy ran round from the fence right into my arms, almost knocking the wind out of me for the tenth time that day. Badger followed me over the wall and bumped into both of us, knocking us against the major, and suddenly we were all holding on to each other and talking all at once in the aftermath of the adrenalin burst. I could feel my left knee shaking uncontrollably, and Paddy was crying and Badger was hugging her and slapping me on the back and through the mud I could see his face was split with a wide white grin.

Donald broke the spell when he jerked back and told us to be careful where we were putting all the mud and that sent me off into a fit of hysterics that got a lot of the tension out of me before I started to cry.

'It's a fine sorry mess you've got yourself into now, Nicky,'
Donald said, slipping the catch on his big rifle, and leaning it against the wall.

'Me and the whole world, by the looks of it,' I said.

'What the hell in God's name has come over the place?' Donald asked with an exasperated expression. 'It's like Dante's inferno down there.' He nodded in the direction

359

of Arden. 'And up here it's just as bad.'

'What's happening in town?'

'Och, you wouldn't believe it. Everybody is running about like chickens with no heads. You couldn't get any sense out of anybody. And them three old buggers, World War Three your friend Jimmy calls them. They've barricaded themselves up in that big house and they're shooting shot at anybody who goes near. I tell you, this place has just gone mad. Mad.'

'That's some gun,' I said, indicating the rifle.

'Aye, it's an Armalite. Just a wee souvenir from my active days. There's a lot of trouble down here in the town, and the horses and dogs are running around wild too. I thought I should take this out for a breather, just in case.'

Donald looked over the wall to where the old boar lay, now still, in a mass of blood.

'Just as well I did too.'

'How did you know we were here?'

'I didn't. I was just coming across the field, for I wanted to avoid the town, to get up on to the high road, the new one, and get to Kirkland that way. Somebody's got to go there and tell them what's happening here, for there's nobody in Arden knows which way is up today.

'Even down at the police station, Murdo Morrison and his constable have disappeared and there's a dead man in his cell and another who screamed for mercy as soon as I looked at him. Scared out of his wits, the poor fellow, and he was saying something about the sergeant killing the other one. The way things have been going on around here, I'm not sure I don't believe him at all.'

'Things are going crazy all right, and they've been going that way for a long time,' I said. 'I'm not sure what we're going to do about it, apart from trying to stay alive.'

'It's bad,' Paddy piped up. 'It wants to kill us all.'

'What does?' Donald asked.

'I don't know what it is, but it's bad.'

'We have to kill it,' said a deeper voice that was strong and hard.

Donald and I both looked round at Badger, who was still holding on to Paddy's hand. For a moment I caught a look in his eyes that was different from the Badger who drank his half-pint shandy in Holly's bar and gazed around him with his dim-witted dull expression.

'It tried to kill us before and now it's trying again. We have to kill it now,' Badger said.

'What do we have to kill?' Donald said quietly.

I looked at Badger, and his eyes dimmed again, as if the fire that had flared had been snuffed out again.

'I don't know,' he said slowly, shaking his head from side to side and frowning hard as if trying to recall something that had slipped from his mind.

'Something bad. I can't remember.'

Donald clapped him on the shoulder. 'Well, if it comes back to you, let us know, and we'll see what we can do.'

He looked the three of us up and down.

'I think the best thing is to get out and up to the new road and take it from there. I don't think it's a good idea to get into Arden at the moment, and I think we should stick together, especially since I've got this,' he said, hefting his gun from where it stood against the wall.

'But before that, I think you three should get yourselves cleaned up a bit. You're a sorry sight.'

Neither myself nor Badger nor Paddy wanted to hang about the farm any more, so we went back through the trees towards Duncan Bennett's cottage, skirting beyond the hives just in case. Donald strode ahead, with his peaked camouflage hat perched on the back of his head and his gun pointing forward. I told him about Billy Ruine and his gunslingers and I reckoned the major was in the right mood to shoot first and ask questions later. Instead of angling across the field straight to the house, he made us head for the road and he crossed the fence first and looked up and down each way before deciding the coast was clear and beckoning us forward.

The four of us walked in a line along the tarmac and had got halfway to the cottage when Paddy jumped beside me and let out a startled gasp, gripping my hand suddenly tight. I turned and Badger and Donald must have caught my look, and they all stopped and stared.

Father Gerry sat astride his black bike that had driven into a tangle of saplings which bordered the road. His front wheel had lodged between two of the stouter trunks and kept the machine upright. His hand was still raised high, and in it gleamed the upside-down crucifix that he had been using as a sword. The ornate carved end had caught in a fork, and that's what kept the priest's arm raised high. That was obviously all that kept it up. For the back of Gerry's black leather jacket was torn to shreds and there was a hole the size of a dinner plate and a hands-breadth deep between his shoulders. His head lolled to the side, just above the gaping wound, and the weak sunlight reflected off the shiny black helmet in the bits that weren't spattered with blood. He was dead.

'Oh, Christ,' I said softly, between my teeth. 'They've killed him.'

I owed the dead priest my life, and there was no way I could repay him, except maybe by finding a way to put an end to this bane that had swept the town into a nightmare. Why he had been careening down the road like a crusader on a holy war, I had no idea except that possibly the dead man had been affected by the madness that had turned Arden into an insane obscenity. Or maybe he was fighting the madness, trying to combat the forces of evil, using the crucifix as his own weapon and talisman against the evil all around. Whatever the reason, his sudden and startling appearance had given me the time I needed to get away from the cottage. If he had not come roaring down on his black charger, it would have been me who had the bloody dinner-plate hole.

'Come on,' Donald said, at last. 'There's nothing can be done for the poor bugger now.'

He set off down the road, and I made to follow, pulling Paddy behind me. We walked about ten yards, and I turned around to look again at the priest. Badger was still standing there, gaping.

'Let's go, Badger,' I called.

Paddy pulled my hand. 'It's Colin. He doesn't like Badger,' she whispered scoldingly. She was right, and I felt a twinge of shame.

'Colin, come on,' I said, a bit louder, but still low, just in case Ruine and any of his mob were anywhere nearby. The big fellow stayed where he was, shaking his head slowly from side to side. I had to turn back and take his arm.

'I saw him,' Colin said. 'It was him. The black knight. I saw him before too.'

There was that flash of brightness in his eyes that had sparked in him before.

'I didn't know it was you here. I was over at the trees,' he pointed behind the cottage in the direction Paddy had taken when she ran from the guns. 'I saw him come on his bike, but I thought it was a horse. He was holding his sword, and killing people, like before. I got scared and I ran away. I thought he would kill me.

'But it is him. It is the knight from . . . . from before.'

'From before what?' I asked him.

The brightness was beginning to fade from his eyes, and Colin stood there, shaken, bewildered, just a big, mild, frightened boy.

'I don't remember now. I don't remember when I *was*,' he moaned.

'When you were what?' I asked, still pulling him away from the scene by the crook of the elbow.

'When I was *before*,' Colin wailed.

Suddenly, with a clarity of vision I had not experienced in days, it came to me that Colin's far-off daydream had been some sort of prescience.

Who would have believed, then, that a priest would be screeching along a country road in black leathers, on a powerful motorbike, and wielding a gold crucifix like an avenging angel?

Hell, who would believe it today?

No matter what, that long-gone hazy summer day was linked by some sort of time-twist to what was happening now.

And the one and onlies were almost together again.

TWENTY-SIX

We got down to Duncan's cottage without incident, and Donald lit a fire, piling on the logs until there was a good blaze going, and we stripped off the muddy clothes and put them over the horse in front of the glow to dry them off. The water in the tap was still like sewage, but there was enough in the big kettle for us to have a cup of tea and to share the remainder for washing. It wasn't great, but it got some of the grime off. When our clothes had dried, the mud had caked and we just rubbed it until it fell off in flakes, and then rubbed some more until eventually, while not squeaky clean, we weren't covered in grime.

The four of us sat down round the table drinking hot tea. Donald and I did most of the talking, while Paddy listened, cocking her head between us like an umpire. Colin sat to the side with his face still creased with concentration and conster-nation. I didn't know what kind of battle was going on in his head just then, and I was too busy to find out. Anyway, I knew he would do what he was told. Paddy had told me, while we were washing, about the bull, and I had seen Colin in action with Old Boot. He may have been deficient in some areas, but he was big and strong, and no matter how scared he was of people, he obviously lacked nothing in guts. Despite the fact that I knew I would have to take care of him most of the time, I was glad he was with us.

The major and I went to have a look at the jeep. It was stuck nose-first deep into the ditch that ran alongside the hedge, and there was no way we could have got it out of there without a tractor. The nearside tyre, the one I'd replaced only an hour or so before, was flat, probably burst when we hit the hedge.

'We'll have to walk,' Donald said.

'I don't think driving's a good idea anyway,' I told him, and explained what had happened when we had tried to drive out the back way.

He looked at me sceptically, then shrugged.

'Sounds like some sort of illusion. But I've seen enough in the last day or so to tell me anything's possible. The world's joined the Book of Revelation as far as I can see. From where I stand, it looks just like they say the apocalypse should be. But maybe this illusion thing won't work if we go on foot.'

'Maybe not, but I wouldn't bet on it. And we'd better go careful. It's not just people we have to watch out for. The whole place seems to be against us.'

'What's doing it, I'd like to know.'

'You wouldn't believe it if I told you.'

'Try me. I'm an old soldier.'

So I went ahead and told him, standing in the lee of the nose-down jeep. I told him all about Kitty MacBeth and her tales of Cu Saeng and of the old curse that had caused the bad times in Arden since the iron age. I told him about Jimmy Allison's history, and its periods of disaster, and about the same histories as told to me by Monsignor Cronin from the vellum chronicles of the monks. I mentioned Andy Gillon under the fallen tree, and Edward Henson's mangled hands. I didn't have to tell him about the gannets that attacked the fisherman, but I told him about the bird I saw hanging beside the crumpled bonnet of Barbara's crashed Volvo. Donald nodded when I told him about the horses and the dogs in town. The piece about the roads out of town that led nowhere he had heard before, but I told it all again. And I told him about the night of the big storm when the *Cassandra* had rolled over and the lifeboat had struck for Ardhmor and there was nothing seen of it since.

Even as I told it, it was a sorry catalogue. I had gone past the stage of believing that Arden was just suffering from a summer of bad luck, but frankly, getting all that off

366

my chest was like drawing in fresh air.

Donald was a good listener. He didn't interrupt for most of my story. At the end of it, I asked him what he thought.

'I wouldn't be writing this up in any of your newspapers Nick,' he said. 'But it's got the beat of me. I've been too many places to be believing in ghosts and goblins and whatnot, but this time I just don't know what to think. That day down at the shore I saw nature turned inside out, and I know that just doesn't happen. And if it does, then there's something abroad here that is bad, I can tell you.' He stopped and considered, then came back. 'Tell me. If it is this Cu-thing, or whatever, what on earth are you planning to do about it?'

I shook my head. 'Haven't a clue, Donald. Maybe your idea to get out of here and let the rest of the world know is the best. If the Cu Saeng does exist, and I've got to believe that it does, for there's no other rational explanation for what's been going on here, I don't know how to send it back to wherever it came from.

'Old Kitty MacBeth was going to tell me more about it. She says there is a way. Some old prophecy in the stone down at the point. But she never got around to it. I wouldn't even know where to begin without her.'

'Well, we won't be going far in that thing,' Donald said, hitting the jeep with the flat of his hand. The sound was too loud and made me jump.

'Well, if we've got to walk, I'll get my stick,' I said. I opened the door and reached in for the old hawthorn. Beside it lay the water can in its canvas holder. I grabbed that as well and Donald and I walked back to the cottage.

Colin and Paddy were watching from the window of the cottage when we came back from the jeep. I had warned both of them to stay inside just in case Ruine and what was left of his mob returned, or the bees decided to swarm again. Both of them looked at me expectantly when we went into the front room.

'We're going to go now,' I told them, 'and when we do

we've got to be very careful.'

Paddy nodded and Colin just stared attentively.

'We'll keep in the fields, close to the hedges, and if you see anybody don't shout out. Paddy, you stay right by me all the time and Colin, you stick with the major here. Just be very quiet and I'm sure we'll be fine.'

The girl gave me one of her best smiles and came away from the window ledge where she'd been sitting, fingering the torc around her neck. We all went out of the cottage, me with my stick and the water bottle bumping off my hip, the major with his gun and Colin with that frown of concentration on his face. He hadn't said a word. It looked as if there was some minor battle going on in the maze inside his head.

We went left at the dyke and along to where Billy Ruine had taken off his brother's head. The rest of Tommy Ruine was still lying where he fell, but there was no sign of the others. Despite Father Gerry's seemingly deadly swipes with the crucifix sword, it seemed likely that some of them, maybe even all of them, had lived to fight another day. I made Paddy look the other way when we passed the corpse and went through the gate in cautious single file with Donald bringing up the rear. I remember wishing that I had a rifle or a shotgun in my hands instead of the old hawthorn walking stick but even having something, some weight there, was better than nothing.

Behind the row of cottages where Paddy and I had used the garden fences as hurdles, we angled away from the front lawns towards the heavy iron fence that bordered the slope leading down to the belt of trees that lined Strowan's Well.

There was an odd silence from the row of houses, as if they had suddenly been evacuated by disaster. There were no faces at the windows, no smoke from the chimneys perched on the slated roofs, no washing on the clothes-lines. Not even a dog barked. It was eerie, for despite the quiet, I could feel eyes watching me from dark shadows. There was tension all around, in the earth and in the air, as if the world was wound up on a tight spring. I could feel the little muscles in my back flutter like piano keys, and there was a high-pitched singing sound that was just below the threshold of my hearing, like the sound of small bats at night. I kept waiting for the ground in front to burst asunder and swallow me up.

We got to the fence without incident.

The slope down to the trees was muddy and pitted where the cattle had churned the dirt and clay into a red ochre slush that soon covered our shoes and the bottoms of our jeans. There were no cows in the field, and I was glad of that. Even with Donald's gun, I didn't fancy our chances against a herd of cows while we were crossing the mud slope. Not if they were anything like the horses and dogs in Arden, or McFall's bull, or worse, the boar that the major had blown to bits. A picture of that child's boot flashed through my mind when we were halfway down the hill and I had to bite down hard on the temptation to just pick Paddy up and bolt for the trees.

Rain was dripping heavily from the high beeches, pattering down on the red russet carpet of leaf litter and beech mast that was soggy enough not to crackle underfoot. There was no wind between the trunks and not a bird sang, as we headed further down the slope towards the stream.

There was another reason for the silence, we discovered when we followed the single track between the immense grey pillars of beech and got down to Strowan's Well. I had been in these woods a number of times since my return to Arden, and hundreds of times when I was a youngster. They had always been filled with the steady murmur, like far-off voices, of the running water. On a day like this, after heavy rain, we should have heard the gurgling rumble of the stream in spate.

But when we got to the bank, there was nothing. No steady clear flow, just a muddy trickle of runoff water from the valley sides that seeped between the exposed boulders and filled the deeper pools with cloudy water.

Colin stopped abruptly, almost causing Donald to walk into his back. He stared at the gully and its trickle of water and his brow creased itself into corrugated lines.

'Come on, lad. Let's keep moving,' Donald said. Colin acted as if he hadn't heard. He was concentrating hard.

'What's up, Colin?' I asked. 'Are you all right?'

'It's – it's *wrong*,' he said in a faraway voice.

'What's that?' Donald asked. He was impatient to keep moving.

'I don't know,' Colin said. He shook his head, like a sleepy man shaking off slumber. 'I can't remember. There's something wrong, but I don't know.'

'There's a whole lot of things that's wrong,' Donald said lightly. 'And if we don't get out of here, they could get a whole lot worse, laddie. Come on. Let's get across the stream.'

I went down the steep bank and stepped on to one of the boulders, twisting to ensure that Paddy was on sure footing
behind me. She kept a tight grip of my hand.

I was halfway across the stones, which were scattered around where the stream used to be, punctuating the slick muddy water. I don't know why we bothered using the stones, because our shoes were caked and the water was only six inches deep at the most, but I suppose old habits die hard. I'd always crossed the stream this way.

Colin came behind Paddy, following on the moss-covered rocks, and then angled to the side when his momentum threatened to carry him forward on to the stone where Paddy was standing. He ended up with a foot on each stone with his legs stretched so wide he was almost split in half, and the mud on his boots slipped and he started to lose his balance, cartwheeling his arms backwards like a jerky windmill.

Paddy and I reached out instinctively for him and our hands caught Colin's simultaneously, pulling him back upright. As soon as our hands joined in that little triangle, I got such a jolt through my body I was almost physically sick. It was as if I was suddenly inside out and two places at once. It hit me with such a force, it swept through my entire being like a cold black wind that shook me and froze me to the roots. The lurch passed through and out the other side and left me feeling as if I'd been invaded, raped and ravaged. Suddenly I knew there were things inside my head that I *knew*. They had always been there and in that wrenching second or so doors had been unlocked inside my head to let a watery light shine on dark memories that had been hidden in the deepest cellars.

I pivoted on the stone, still holding their hands, and got a look at Colin's face.

It was white with fear and shock and revulsion, and I could see the muscles on his cheeks bunch out, and for a second I thought his eyes were going to roll so far back in their sockets that the pupils would appear again from the bottom. There was a strangled moan that gurgled from his throat, as if he was choking back on a scream and his hair was standing right on end, and I could tell he was going through that outside-in feeling that I had experienced, only his was worse. Much worse. It looked as if it was tearing him apart.

I swung on Paddy and she was standing on a stone, with our hands grasping hers and her eyes were closed, but there was a picture of such serenity on her face that she could have been sleeping. Then suddenly her eyes snapped open and for an instant I could see Barbara there. Not the young Barbara who was the living image of her daughter standing there on the stones between her childhood friends, but the Barbara who I'd just begun to know again. The one I was beginning to fall in love with.

The moment passed and Paddy was herself again, but something had happened which made her more than that. She just seemed more *aware*, but I can't now, and couldn't then, tell you what made me see that in her.

But I can tell you that in that instant of gut-wrenching jolt something had happened to Colin. When our three pairs of hands had joined over the trickle of muddy water that was all that was left of Strowan's Well, Colin Blackwood awoke, and his awakening had all the trauma of a bad birth.

His face was drained of blood and his eyes had come back down again from where they'd been and he threw back his head and let out such a scream of pain that it just about made *my* hair stand on end and caused Paddy to slip off the stone.

Colin jerked his hand free and I grabbed Paddy to me, and we watched while his jaw worked with the force of the scream. His fists went up and pressed against his temples as if he was trying to squeeze the hurt right out of his head. The hoarse yell echoed away through the trees and Colin bent forward, both feet now in the water, slowly crouching until his head was almost on the slick surface, like a giant foetus. Then, all of a sudden, his voice stopped dead, as if his windpipe had suddenly been cut. I knew it wasn't, because the silence was followed by a huge swoop of breath, and slowly Colin's frame unwound until he was standing upright. He raised his head and looked at Paddy, then at me, and that frown of bewildered concentration was gone. The blank look that Colin had shown to the world for twenty years had vanished.

And for the first time since that long-ago age when Colin and Barbara and myself were the one and onlies, I saw the real Colin Blackwood. His eyes were clear and bright. Whatever doors had been slammed and padlocked inside his brain for two decades had been thrown open with such a force the pain almost killed him right there on those stepping stones.

I was to find out that there were more doors for him to open, one at a time.

But right there, I could see that something weird and wonderful and *right* had overtaken the village dullard. His eyes told their own story.

Donald broke the spell.

'What the devil's going on?' he said, still keeping his voice down. He looked to right and left, upstream and down, to see if the ruction had been heard.

'I thought I said we have to be quiet? What's wrong with that boy at all?'

I motioned him to be quiet and he looked at me uncomprehendingly. I stepped forward into the trickle and took Colin by the hand and pulled him to the far bank, hauling Paddy along with the other. On the way over, Donald bent and picked up my old grandfather's walking stick and brought it to me.

We didn't stop until we were at a flat part where the rain couldn't get through the dense foliage of a spreading beech and the three of us sat down in the dry leaves. Donald followed us and hunkered down, watching the three of us shrewdly. He knew that something had happened, but he didn't know what. I didn't know exactly either.

'All right, Colin. You tell us,' I said. His head was bent as he stared at the ground, and I could see the two white lines reaching back from his forehead right to his crown. He sat like that for a moment or so, then raised his head and stared at me. His eyes were black and fiery, as if they were letting out all the energy that had been stored all those years in his lacklustre, vacant gaze.

'It's happened again,' he said, quietly, but succinctly.

'You'll have to tell us,' Donald said. 'What's happened?'

'Don't you know, Nicky? Don't you remember?'

'Remember what?'

'The time before. Before I was like . . . different?'

Inside, behind my eyes, a picture was trying, but failing, to get through. I had the sure feeling that, if I could only catch the tail of it, I could capture something elusive that I should have known, but it slipped out of reach.

'I'm not sure, Colin. You'll have to explain.'

'Something happened. Then. Long ago. Something bad, and we were there. It is coming back to me, but I can't remember yet. It's too soon.'

Colin frowned again, but this time it was not like before, when he seemed to be fighting his way through fog. He was peering into awakened memories for an answer.

'It's the stream,' he said, suddenly, too loudly. Donald started and immediately looked around him with his soldier's caution.

'That's what was wrong. There's no water in the stream. Like before! Don't you remember?'

Suddenly the mist parted in my brain and I saw Strowan's Well again.

Summer 1961.
Colin crashed after me through the rhododendrons that covered the west side of the gully and almost knocked me into the stream. Barbara was standing on the far side looking past us into the bushes.

'*Hurry,*' *she hissed.* '*Come quickly.*'

Behind us we could hear the crackling of the branches as the others bullied their way through. Colin grabbed my hand and pulled me across the dry bed.

'*Stream's dried up,*' *he said, conversationally, as if we were just on one of our usual jaunts. Behind us came a harsh shout and I didn't give a damn whether the stream had dried up or gone to hell.*

The rhododendrons parted when we were halfway up the far slope and Fraser Beaton came out into the clear.

'*They're here,*' *he bellowed at the top of his voice.* '*Come on you lot. We've got them.*'

My heart was hammering against my ribs and at the top of the gully Barbara was panting. She'd ripped her slacks and cut her knee. A small bead of bright blood welled up and left a lighter trail against her skin.

'*Start running down that way,*' *Colin said quickly, pointing downstream.* '*Come on. Follow me.*'

He was up and running and we trailed behind, scooting along the path, darting between the grey trunks, while behind us we could hear the yells of the bigger boys who were chasing us and the cracking of the undergrowth as they gained the stream. The little valley through which Strowan's Well ran took a dog-leg to the left and when we got round that bend, running alongside the three-

string wire fence that kept the sheep out of the trees, Colin darted suddenly and leapt behind a dogwood bush. I was going so fast I almost ran past him, but he stuck out his hand and grabbed me.

'This way. They won't know where we've gone,' he hissed. He scaled the fence and I boosted Barbara over, quickly following behind and almost falling flat on my face as my small frame fought for equilibrium on the sagging top wire. In the sheep pasture Colin started doubling back upstream again, running at a crouch so that he couldn't be seen from the valley floor. We cut across that field at a sprint and got back into the trees, well up from where we'd started down the valley. Behind us the crackling of branches and the hoarse cries of our pursuers started to fade in the distance.

We stopped under the branches, straining our ears like deer, ready to bolt at the first sign of danger. The sounds diminished downstream.

'They fell for it,' Colin said, like the Texas Ranger used to say when he'd outwitted the Indians. He grinned, and I returned it, though I was still panting for breath and my heart was still doing boop-de-boop under my khaki shirt.

'Why are they doing it?' Barbara asked. There was a big smudge of dirt across her face, and on a normal day in the valley it would have made her the butt of our jokes. Today it didn't look funny.

'I don't know any more,' Colin said.

'Nor me. There's something funny going on here,' I said, and Colin nodded.

'You bet. They're crazy. I mean they've always been weird, but they're off their heads now.'

'I thought Beaton was going to kill you with that stick.'

'And he would've done if you hadn't knocked him down, pardner,' Colin said, sticking out his hand for me to shake.

'But why?' Barbara asked, plaintively. 'We never did them any harm.'

'I don't know why. But there's something weird happening. That guy down in the Milligs that got torn up by the dogs. That's weird.'

'It's horrible,' Barbara said.

'But there's more. I don't know what. But people seem different. Scared.'

375

'I'm scared,' I volunteered. 'If they had caught us, they'd beat the living daylights out of us.'

'Well, they've gone now.'

'But what if they come back?'

'Oh, they're too stupid. They'll be across the road by now,' Colin said with a smug look. He stopped and seemed to mull the situation over.

'Remember those cows yesterday? They broke down the fence and started charging along the road. They really messed up Alan's dad's van. I've never seen anything like that before.'

'And that Mr Henson, too,' Barbara said.

'Those two kids that were drowned down at the bay, and all. And the fire at the church. I'm telling you, there's something funny going on around here.'

'Who's laughing,' I said, and Colin actually did laugh.

'What should we do now?' Barbara asked, and Colin nodded ahead.

'Upstream. I want to get as far away from those nutters as I can. And I don't fancy going into town again today. There's a weird feeling.'

'I've felt it too. My dad said I had to stay inside all day. If he finds out I'm not there, he'll go crazy,' Barbara said.

'So will my mum.'

'And mine.'

'They're all scared,' Colin said. 'I wonder why?'

None of us knew. We all started out together, following the line of trees upstream.

'Did you see the burn?' Colin asked suddenly, after about fifty yards.

'Yes, you nearly knocked me right into it.'

'Well you wouldn't have made much of a splash, anyway. There's no water.'

'I didn't even notice,' Barbara said.

'Always going about with her eyes closed and her nose in the air,' Colin said, and winked at me. Barbara made a face.

'Probably dried up,' I said. 'It hasn't rained for ages.'

'But it's never been like that before.'

'It's never been as hot before.' It really was hot. The summer

376

had been lazily dragging on in a sweltering heat wave. Inside my shirt I could feel the sweat trickling down to the waistband of my jeans, and inside my black and red baseball boots, my feet felt hot and slick.

We kept on walking in single file, along the sheep rut at the edge of the trees, me taking up the rear, occasionally grabbing at a piece of rye grass and pulling it, squeaking, out of its green sleeve to chew on the cool succulent end.

Beyond the line of trees, the valley gave onto an undulating semi-moorland pasture that was dotted here and there with tall stands and clumps of ferns. We pushed our way through a green patch and down the slope towards the bottom of the valley.

Colin had been right. The stream was dry. There were a few warm and sluggish patches of water that looked stagnant and let off clouds of caddis flies and clegs when we passed, and just under the surface there were long trailing brown-green slicks of feather algae. Colin reached down and scooped up a handful of slimy candy-floss and made to throw it at Barbara. She squealed and then we all laughed. Colin threw it into a greasy pool with a splat.

'It must be blocked up there,' he said, pointing further up. 'Want to have a look?'

No matter how much I was going to have my backside smacked when I got home, the prospect of heading downstream and into Fraser Beaton and the rest of the bigger boys, with their sticks and stones and that funny look in their eyes, was not something I wanted to consider just then.

'Why not?' I said, and we both looked at Barbara. She shrugged and we headed upstream, carefully avoiding the slimy patches of water.

It was half a mile further up that we found the block, a natural dam in the narrow valley where the burn cut through what I was later to discover was the layered strata of debris left in the last ice age. Heaps of shale had been brought down along with a huge mound of lighter, harder rock by the trunk of an old blasted oak that had finally lost the battle with gravity as its roots were undermined by the wind and rain of past winters.

'Wow, would you look at that,' Colin said, excitedly, punctuating his explanation with a long whistle. He ran ahead and scrambled up the mound of stone and shingle to stand on the lip of the blockade.

'Hey, look at this!' he yelled, and I remember wishing he wouldn't yell so loud, just in case the others had worked out our doubleback ploy, but Colin had obviously forgotten that in the new excitement. He was jumping up and down on the dam, and beckoning us up with a frantic hand. Barbara and I clambered up and stood shoulder to shoulder with him.

'Jeez-oh,' I gasped, for it really was a sight to be gasped at in ten-year-old wonderment. Strowan's Well had backed up as far as the eye could see, forming a narrow lake that curved round the meandering valley. The water looked cool and clear, deep and inviting. Because of the long, hot summer, there hadn't been enough of a flow to push down the natural waterbreak, but even as we stood there on the wall, I could feel the rumbling underfoot that told me it was only a matter of time.

'Hey, I know,' Colin said. 'Let's bust it.'

'It's worth a try,' I said. 'And anyway, I don't like seeing the stream with no water. All the fish will die if they're not dead already.'

'How are you going to do it?' Barbara asked.

'If we can move this, the water will do the rest. You'll see,' he said, tapping the heavy trunk that stuck out from the dam wall.

'It looks too heavy.'

'We'll just have to work at it.'

Colin scrambled on to the trunk and jumped up and down on it while Barbara and I levered away with a branch, and there was a lurch that almost flicked Colin off balance and on to the rocks below.

What we did just added to the relentless pressure of the water on the up-side of the dam. It would have taken a week, or maybe even a fortnight, for the water to break through if the warm weather had held. We just moved things forward a bit, and as it turned out, this was the turning point in our young lives. Nothing was every going to be the same again, not for another twenty-odd years.

The lurch was accompanied by a huge, grinding rumble, and Colin yelled and leapt off the log, down the scree and over to where we were standing, holding on to the log that was jammed in the dyke, and now quivered violently in our hands.

'She's going to go,' Colin screeched joyfully. 'She's going to blow.'

Just as he said that, a thin jet of water shot out from near the base of the dam, like a high-pressure hose. Then there was another, then another, until the fine spray made a dazzling display of rainbows in the afternoon sun.

There was another great rumble and the whole dam wall seemed to shift, bowing out towards us.

'Get out of here,' I yelled, grabbing Barbara's hand and shoving Colin up the valley slope. If we hadn't moved then, it would have been the end of the story. We made about thirty feet going up that steep side like mountain hares, while behind us a thundering roar ripped up and down the valley.

All three of us turned round, holding on to clumps of the coarse grass to prevent us slipping back down, and watched as the dam wall split wide open with a thunder that almost shook us back down the slope, and a great curve of white water exploded out, snatching up the oak tree like a matchstick and hurling it on the crest of its wave as it lurched down the valley. It was the most magnificent sight I had ever seen.

From our shaky perch, high on the steep, crumbling side of the valley, we had a perfect view of the immense bow-wave that burst out and bore down the narrow defile, lashing against the shale curves and sending its spume in white clouds high above the froth. The roar as the backed-up weight was suddenly released literally made the earth throb, and it was multiplied by the crashing of rocks that were picked up by the force and smashed against the banks. The big oak trunk disappeared round the first bend, tumbling and corkscrewing high on the bow-wave.

'Kee-rist!' Colin murmured between his teeth. 'Did you ever see anything like that in your whole life?'

I shook my head, but couldn't take my eyes off the violence just below our feet.

'We did it,' he said, again in muted wonderment. 'We flamin' well did it. We bust the flippin' dam!'

From downstream, the roar of the wave-front came crashing back to us as the avalanche ripped into the alders and hazel that grew on the stream bank, and we could see the tops of the slender trees whip back and forth in a frenzy over the top of the slope that hid the next bend of the valley from our view.

Right below us, there was nothing left of the dam. When it went it went completely, shoved out and then demolished by the inexorable weight of the water. Where the first blast of stone and water had hit, on the right side of the valley and carrying on to the first dog-leg, the short turf that grew on the shale had been ripped up and scoured away.

'Hey, look at those trees go!' Colin yelled. He was first to come out of the frozen shock at the immensity of what we'd done.

'I bet it knocks them right out of their roots.'

'What if anybody's down there?' Barbara asked in a small voice.

'I hope they are down there,' Colin came back quickly. 'I hope those crazy dumbos figured it out and started following us. And I hope they get smacked right in the kisser by that lot. I hope it drowns the lot of them 'cause they're crazy bastards!'

Colin's voice had got higher and higher until he was shouting hard enough to burst his lungs, and my left ear which was closest to him, but his shout was smothered by the vast noise from the flood below. Barbara flashed him a quick look of disapproval for his language, but I'm sure she agreed, as I did, on the sentiment.

'Well, that's what they are,' Colin said. 'They would have killed us if they got half a chance. I hope they got what they deserve.'

I didn't say it aloud, but I hoped so too, in that strange, exciting, frozen moment.

It couldn't have taken more than ten spectacular minutes or so for the water to subside, and slacken down to something near normal.

By that time, Strowan's Well was flowing again, forking at the neck of Ardhmor peninsula and into the firth. What happened next was instantaneous and ferocious.

Barbara noticed it first. A great black cloud was boiling upwards, seeming to originate from the rock itself, as if something wild and terrible was overheating the air down there. In seconds the cloud roiled high and dark above us, flickering inside with caged electricity that sparked and flared and shot down to the ground with crashes of vast thunder.

We raced down the valley as if our lives depended on it, with forks of lightning stabbing the ground, causing it to shake and shudder. It felt as though something blind and angry was stabbing for us in the dark. Just as we got to the trees, the hailstones started, marble-sized, then pebbles of ice that smacked down on our heads like hammer-shots.

Colin, Barbara and I skitted through the trees, scared witless and stunned by the hail, until we got to the narrow cleft that formed the entrance to our lean-to garage. We tumbled inside and sat in the gloom, shivering with cold and fright, waiting for the storm to die.

TWENTY-SEVEN

Donald listened in silence as I briefly told him the twenty-year-old story that had been stored, wrapped up and unopened, until now. I told him of the chase, and then the wonder of wrecking the dam, and then how the whole world seemed suddenly to turn its hand against us.

'That was just the start,' I said.

'What happened next?' Donald asked.

'We stayed a while and then we followed the stream again. We were *made* to follow the stream.'

I was about to go on when out of the blue I got an echo of what Kitty MacBeth had told me down at the point. It seemed like a million years ago – A wall of water, wall of stone, a wall of wood and a wall of bone.

I suddenly got to my feet. 'That's it!' I told them. 'It's the stream. This is Strowan's Water and it's gone dry like before. The stream is one of the walls. We have to get the water flowing again. The old woman told me. The stream keeps it in Ardhmor.'

Donald looked at me as if perhaps I'd gone a bit crazy, but he didn't say anything. He just leant against the barrel of his gun that had its stock stuck in the dry leaves and raised his eyebrows, waiting for me to go on.

'I know it's hard to understand, but it is important. The last time Ardhmor had a Bad Summer was when the stream was blocked, and they did the first dig down at the rock. At least two of the walls were gone, the walls that were made to stop it, the Cu Saeng, from getting out. That's what Kitty meant and she was right. The last time we bust the dam and the water kept it in.'

'And then what did you do?'

'I don't know. We got hurt. Me and Colin and Barbara.

It'll come back to me.'

'We have to get the water back,' Colin said from behind me, in a clear voice. 'If we don't, we can't do anything.'

Paddy was holding his hand and staring up into his face. Colin was looking hard at me and already his face was different. It was as if, all of a sudden, he'd gone from childhood to manhood missing out all the bits in between. His eyes were bright and his brow creased in a frown. I still wasn't certain what had happened to him and I didn't have time to find out. In any case, there was no doubt in my mind that he was right.

'Will you help us, Donald?' I asked the major.

'Help you what?'

'Somewhere up there,' I said, jerking my thumb in the direction of the hills upstream, 'the burn's blocked somehow. We have to get the water to flow again down to Ardhmor.'

'Do you really believe that's going to help?'

'I do. It will help. At least I think it will.'

Donald sat and mulled it over for a minute, then he smiled, a little bit grimly.

'I suppose it can't do any harm,' he said. 'The whole place has become a Hammer horror film overnight. I still think the best idea is to get ourselves the hell out of here and keep on walking. I've been in some scary places in my time, but I have to tell you, laddie, this is beginning to give me the shivers. The hand of God is on this place and I don't really want to be a part of it, you know.'

He hauled himself to his feet using the gun barrel for thrust. Short and stocky, he looked like the grizzled old veteran I knew him to be.

'Right, let's be having you. We'll find out what's blocking your stream and we'll see what we can do about it. But I've got to say that if it makes a blind bit of difference, I'll eat my rifle.'

He slung the deadly gun over his shoulder and stepped out along the path. Colin looked at me and gave me a wide smile that for a moment cleared all the other, more troubled expressions from his face, and we followed the major.

It took us not much more than half an hour to get past the place where we'd found the natural dam, but there was no blockage there and the stream was still just a runoff trickle where the rain water seeped down the valley sides. A quarter of a mile beyond that we found what we were looking for when we reached the Ministry of Defence by-pass road. On the rubble slope that they'd built up to carry the four lanes a concrete pipe jutted out into the cleft where the stream should have been. When we scaled the slope and crossed the deserted road where the navvies and builders had left their tools in the portacabins when they clocked off, we discovered what had happened. The big digger, bent and buckled, had been hauled up by a winch and lay on its broken tracks on the rubble at the side of the new road. Down below there was a mound of rocks hard up against where the north end of the pipe should have been, the inlet to take the flow of Strowan's Well. Beyond that pile, a familiar back-up of water formed a narrow, twisting lake.

'It's another dam,' Colin said. 'I *knew* it.'

'How are we going to clear it?' I asked, and Donald pointed along the road to where another digger sat on its tracks.

'The way they intend to,' he said.

We gathered round as Donald hauled himself up into the grimy cab. The big jointed arm was closed, like a mantis-claw, with the big-toothed shovel pointed down against the packed earth.

'You ever driven one of these?' Donald asked.

'No. Have you?'

'I've driven most things,' he said. 'I think I can handle this.'

We stood back and watched through the rimy glass as he fiddled with the controls inside and suddenly the monster roared into clattering life in a thick cloud of blue smoke. I pulled Colin and Paddy back to the far side of the road and Donald wheeled the digger round and trundled it over to the lip. The arm that wielded the big bucket swung the wrong way, jerked and swung back again, opening and flexing as Donald tried to get the hang of it. Then it opened and lifted before sinking down like a feeding dinosaur. We heard the thud and crunch and then the bucket came up again with a huge scoop of stone and dirt. The digger swung round and the jaw opened and dumped a ton of rubble on the middle of the road. Donald wasn't going for points for neatness.

The major took less than half an hour to scoop up enough landfill to clear a way to the pipe, then the jaws started to come up dripping water. They sank down a couple of times and Donald lifted it high and let it drop hard down into the cavity he'd made, sending out thumping vibrations under our feet. Whatever he was doing he did it right, for the vibrations must have dislodged the stones that had jammed inside the pipe and that the big shovel couldn't get at. Colin ran to the other side of the road and peered down at the pipe. There was a rumble under the road and then a wad of mud and rock flew out of the pipe like cannon-shot. It wasn't quite as magnificent as the first time, when we were kids, but Strowan's Well was back, flowing again. Colin let out a yell and Paddy jumped up and down in excitement as the yard-wide brown bore of water arced out of the pipe mouth and battered its way down the dry gully. Behind us, the roaring of the engine stopped and Donald climbed out on to the tracks.

'Success?' he bawled, his voice barely audible over the tumult down below. I turned and raised a thumb, and he grinned again.

We must have stood there for five minutes, watching the water rush out of the pipe. Nobody came. The road was deserted.

'That's that, then,' Donald said. 'You've got your water back, and I hope it does what you said it would, although I have my doubts. I think now that we're here, we should just follow this road along to Kirkland. It's a fair hike, but we should be there in an hour or so.'

'No!' Colin said loudly. Donald and I turned round to face him.

'We have to go back.'

'What nonsense is this, laddie?' Donald demanded to know. 'We've just come from down there. It's a mad-house.'

'But we have to go back down there. We have to do it right this time.' Colin's face was a picture of fear and doubt, but the overlying expression was resigned determination.

'There's murder and mayhem down there, son. You'll be risking your life.'

'But it's not finished yet. We have to finish it now.'

Donald turned to me in exasperation. 'Can you not talk some sense into him?'

'I would if I could, but he's right. We have to go back.'

'Well that's just plain stupidity,' he said, harshly. 'Can't you see that?'

'I can see how it looks, but if we don't go down and face it, it will never go away. This is our only chance.'

Donald threw his hands into the air. I knew that if he thought he could order us to about turn and march along the road to Kirkland, he would have done so.

'You've got more guts than sense, the pair of you,' he said through his teeth. 'But what about the wee girl?'

'I'm going too,' Paddy piped up and my heart sank a little.

'Now that's just not on, at all,' Donald said. His voice was getting close to a shout. 'That's just plain stupid and criminal. You can't take a child back to that,' he said, pointing down the slope to where Arden showed its rooftops between the bays.

'You don't understand, Donald. It has to be now. Will you help us?'

'You are serious, I take it?'

I just nodded, watching his face. He was furious. He turned his back and folded his arms, legs planted wide on either side and the black gun aslant his shoulder-blades.

'Will you help us again?' I asked.

He breathed out heavily and didn't move for a minute or so, then he slowly turned and stared at me.

'I don't have much option, do I? I still think you're wrong, but I can see you're determined. Somebody has to look after the wee one.'

'Thanks,' I said. Donald looked at me accusingly, then looked away.

'Don't thank me. Just hope to God that when you get down there we can all stay out of trouble. I hope you know what you're doing, because I don't.'

'Me neither. It just has to be done. I'll just have to play it by ear, because I can't remember what I'm supposed to do, but I have to go down there and face what's been causing all this mayhem for all these years. It's as simple as that. If there was any other way I'd be right along that road beside you, but I can only go on what I believe.'

Donald stood for a while, chewing that over, then he lifted his eyes up from the new road surface that was scarred from the digger tracks.

'All right. I'm coming with you. I can see you believe what you say, and I can see that there's something gone badly wrong with Arden. I don't know what to believe, but you, and him,' he said, nodding towards Colin, 'seem to be the only ones with half a clue, even if it is just a wee bit too much for me to comprehend. I just hope you can do whatever it is that brings some normality back to this place, for it's gone to hell and beyond.'

I was about to reply to that when Paddy shouted to us, her high voice piercing the dull roar of the torrent below.

'Look, Nicky. Over there.' She was pointing to the south. Both Donald and I had to turn to look and we followed her gaze out on to the firth beyond Arden where the black hump of Ardhmor Rock sat in ambush beside the dull pewter of the distant water.

There was a swirl of mist, thick and grey, rolling out from the tall trees at the base of the rock, while above it

387

the already grey sky was beginning to darken into a thunderhead that was tinged with green.

'Ever had that feeling of déjà vu?' I asked Donald.

'All the time,' he replied.

'That's what happened the last time.'

'It's like a volcano. I've never seen the likes of it before.'

'I have, and it's not good. We have to get out of here and fast.'

'You mean that's what happened the other time you were telling me about?'

'That was just the start of it.' Above Ardhmor, the cloud rolled thick and oily, with that perceivable flicker of static electricity inside the dark, piling up to the sky.

'So what now?'

'We get ourselves out of here right now.' I beckoned to Colin and Paddy and they came over to where we were.

'Remember last time, Colin?' He nodded, his eyes fixed on the rising cloud and the spreading mist that was reaching out towards Arden, over the flat farmyard at the peninsula.

'I think it's going to happen again. We have to get right down to the trees again, and you know where we're going then, don't you?'

'Yes,' he said, firmly. His face was white.

'Right, let's get to it.' I took Paddy by the hand and set down the slope to the sheep track on the hill at the edge of the narrow valley. We ran as hard as we could. Donald brought up the rear, his boots thudding the track behind me, while Colin barged through the stands of fern clearing a path for us all. We were within a quarter of a mile of the trees when the wind struck, suddenly picking up to a roar that almost swept Paddy off her feet and buffeted us about on the exposed rim.

The big cloud blotted out the entire sky and the wind shrieked in a howling gale that lashed us with pieces of fern and pine needles that it plucked up in its frenzy. Behind me Donald banged me hard on the shoulder and had to shout to make himself heard. He pointed into the valley where Strowan's Well was in wild spate.

'Down there. There's more shelter.'

'Wait until the lightning,' I thought, but still I reached to grab Colin's arm and tug him down the slope.

The lightning was worse than before as the anger that moved inside that thunderhead sent bolts of fury down into the narrow ravine, sending cascades of shale down into the turbulent stream. The blue light flickered in a massive stroboscopic display that crashed and seared the air all around us. We didn't stop, not for the thunder nor the lightning, not the rain nor the hail. We made it, almost exhausted, to the trees, but the fury of the storm didn't abate. Instead the wind rose to an even greater fury that rattled the tall firs against each other and brought great branches crashing down on us as we dodged between the trunks.

I jostled Paddy along like a small sack of potatoes as the crashing and pounding went on all around us. The great trees groaned with the stress, and ahead of us there was a tearing crash as one of the giants gave way to the wind and came toppling down. Even as I ran, dodging the twigs and branches that came tumbling from the heights, I felt a fury rising inside me that this Cu Saeng, this so-called ravener, this darkness that had invaded and pervaded Arden, should have so much power to destroy.

Having said that I was scared out of my mind, underneath that surface fury. And I was running blind. The doors in my memory had still not opened wide enough to tell me what I should do next. It was like having a name on the tip of your tongue, stuck there, refusing to budge. I *knew* I had the knowledge. I knew it had not been knocked out of me in the concussion of the rock fall. But it just wouldn't come out into the open.

There wasn't much left of the gang hut when we got to the big rock. The years had rotted the branches and made them fall down into the little cave, but there was still enough of a depression there for us all to squeeze inside and shelter from the wind. Donald spent ten minutes gathering thick boughs which he expertly fitted up as a roof and a door, to give us adequate protection. In the semi-darkness, I lit a crumbled cigarette and inhaled gratefully.

'What now?' Donald asked.

'Ardhmor,' I said, blowing out a plume of smoke.

He nodded with resignation. 'I believe you now. I didn't before, you know, but I've never seen anything like that before. I can't gainsay you now, for you've been right so far. But I'll tell you one thing, if there's something down there that can cause all this, I don't give tuppence for your chances.'

I was forced to smile at this. 'Me neither, but I have to give it a try.'

'What are you going to do?'

'I don't know yet. I'm trying to remember.'

'Scared?' he whispered in my ear.

'Shitting myself,' I whispered back so that Paddy couldn't hear. 'But we'll beat this bastard. I'm going to send him back to where he belongs.'

'And you'll still not be writing this in your newspapers either,' Donald said.

'But I'll watch you eating your rifle. That's a certainty,' I said, and he gave a soft chuckle in the dark.

It was late into the afternoon when we moved out of the bivouac and followed the stream down to the main road. Overhead the wind howled and lashed at the trees and the lightning flickered and cracked in searing stabs that split the dark sky. By this time the flow of the stream had settled down to a more normal speed. Donald was for going up on to the road and across to the Milligs shore-side, but while I had a lot of trust in his rifle and his ability to use it, I didn't want to be caught by surprise by Billy Ruine or any of his team. We went through the old tunnel under the bridge, down into a long dark and damp stone tube that didn't offer much in the way of light at the end of it.

Colin's breathing started to catch when we entered the dark and he paused.

'What's up?'

'There was something there.'

'Where?'

'Here. The time before. Something bad.'

I couldn't remember that bit. 'What was it?'

'I can't remember. It tried to get us.'

A memory tried to force its way through. Dark shapes twisted in the tunnel, and an eerie scratching noise filled my ears, echoing off the moss-covered cobbles of the cavern. But I wasn't hearing anything. It was all in my mind.

I waded to take up the lead, still holding Paddy's arm, but keeping her behind me.

And up through the darkness in my head came the memory of the time Colin and Barbara and I waded through the little nightmare that the thing sprung on us. Ghosts of the past swirled out of the damp and turned their eyes towards me.

I was out in the lead with my spear in my hand that I'd picked up in the gang hut. Colin was behind Barbara with his little hawthorn bow and his Robin Hood quiver of arrows as we stepped out of the half light and into the dark under the road.

Summer 1961.

There should have been a semi-circle of grey at the far end, on the other side of the road, but the tunnel was pitch black.

'We should go over the road,' Colin said behind me, and his voice reverberated off the walls and down into the distance. They seemed to go on a long time, getting fainter and fainter. The water that gurgled past our legs made slopping noises ahead and I stopped to peer in front. I could see nothing.

Then the hairs on the back of my neck started prickling up as a soft vibration came up the tunnel towards us.

'What was that?' I asked. 'That . . . that . . . that . . . that' the tunnel said back, and then the noise returned, louder.

'I heard it,' Barbara said. 'There's something there.'

The soft noise became a low moan that got stronger and stronger, rising in pitch to a wail, like a hurt animal or a bereaved woman, then a high ululating scream that crackled in our ears before breaking off into a dead silence.

'I think we should go back,' Colin said, with the flatness of dread in his voice. I could feel the backs of my knees shivering as the nerves twitched and jumped. I took two steps back from the dark, almost knocking Barbara down, and turned to face the mouth of the tunnel where we'd come in. Suddenly I froze and my heart leapt right up into my neck and my mouth went dry a. a bone. It was pitch black there too. I heard Colin and Barbara gasp at the same time, and suddenly I wanted to feel the two of them right next to me. I took a step forward until I could feel them both.

'Oh, Jesus,' Colin said in an agonised whisper. 'We're stuck.'

'What'll be . . . ?'

I didn't even get a chance to finish. Behind me, in the black depths, came a gurgling roar, as if something with a huge mouth had opened it and vented its hunger. A wind like the smell of a slaughterhouse dump came blasting up the tunnel, thick enough to make me want to gag. Barbara screamed. I was too scared to.

'Oh, Jeeees,' Colin moaned again. 'I want outa here.'

The roar broke off in a snap that sounded like two great jaws shutting, and there was a slobbering sound, like some monster sniffing the air through flapping nostrils, and then, oh worst of all, came the sucking, splashing sound that something big and mean and horrible would make as it came up that tunnel towards us.

I whirled into the darkness holding my caveman's spear right out in front of me. My knuckles on the stout rowan staff must have been sticking up stark and white and something made me take a step forward. My heart was pounding in my temples and I took another step. At the end of my spear I had lashed the smooth stone I had found in the valley, the way I had seen it in the museum, the way I had seen it in my dream. Even in the dark, I could feel the gleam of it, sharp and hard on the end of the stave.

The mind-numbing roar came again, filling the whole tunnel with the rancid blast again, and then I realised we weren't in darkness any more. Up ahead there was a dim glimmer of greenish yellow light that slowly resolved itself into two huge, wide-spaced orbs, the size of footballs.

That was it. That was the monster. It was coming to get us and eat us and there was no way back. I thought of my mother and my father, and my old grandad and his walking stick, and a million other things in that brief second when I knew that this was it all over and washed up for me, a little boy in wet jeans in the middle of a stream in the middle of the worst nightmare, and something inside me just snapped.

I remember letting out a scream that seemed to come up from my baseball boots and out the top of my head and the whole world seemed to flip for a minute; before I even knew what I was doing, I started running down towards those green headlamp eyes and that mouth that must have been between them, getting ready to open and snap, grinding and rending. I spattered down through the stream holding my spear ahead of me like a bayonet, while behind me I was dimly aware of Barbara screeching in fear and Colin shouting at me to come back, and I aimed my spear right into the blackness between the eyes. Everything went slowly, as if I was running through treacle or a time-warp and every atom of my being waited for the snap and crunch and the oblivion that I was certain would come, when suddenly my feet came out of the morass and I hit the light at the end of the tunnel. Right out into the daylight on the Milligs side of the main road.

There was nothing to see, except the brown waters of the stream.

Behind me, Barbara screamed my name and I turned to look into the inky dark mouth of the tunnel. There was a lighter shadow that seemed to be miles back from the stone rim, moving slowly towards the pitch-black curtain from under which the stream flowed into the day. The movement got closer, then, as if in slow motion, as if she was pushing her way through a yielding solid, Barbara bust through and Colin was right on her heels, both hands grabbing hold of her shirt, as if pulling her back into the dark.

'. . . come back!' he was yelling, panic in his voice, hauling at her savagely. The sound of his voice was suddenly switched on as soon as he emerged from that black. Barbara jerked back in the light and fell on her backside into the water, with her eyes wide in amazement.

She just sat there and stared, as the brown water slicked around the seat of her slacks, with eyes like blue saucers.

393

Then she just burst into tears and launched herself to her feet and threw herself at me.

'Oh, Nicky,' she yelled right in my ear, while I staggered back and almost ended up sitting in the stream myself under the impact. 'I thought you were . . . Oh I thought. . . .'

'Hey. I'm all right. There was nothing there.'

'Look,' I said, gesturing around. 'There's no monster.' I looked into the tunnel and that stark blackness was still there. No light entered and nothing came out, except for the muddy water.

'Hey,' I said. That dark gave me the shivers, and I still had a re-run of the thing with the big eyes and the slobbering unseen mouth running around inside my skull. 'Let's get away from here. That place gives me the creeps.'

'Me too. Let's beat it,' Colin agreed.

'Where will we go?' Babs asked, and Colin said anywhere but back up that tunnel.

'We can head down the stream and cut behind the huts and along to the farm,' Barbara said.

'Not Henson's farm,' Colin said quickly. 'Not after what happened to old man Henson.'

'What was that?' Barbara asked.

'I told you. He got his hands cut off. That's just one of the weird things I was telling you about. I'm not going near that farm.'

Colin started to suggest something else when I heard a noise behind us and whirled quickly. I thought the thing in the tunnel was coming out, but I was wrong. I looked up to the worn stone parapet of the bridge and stared at the line of faces that gazed back at me.

Charlie Ballantine, Fraser Beaton and a dozen other big lads were lined up, leaning over the wall.

Big Charlie, who was maybe three years older than us, started laughing, and a couple of others, really old guys, maybe about sixteen or seventeen, from the far end of Milligs, joined in. There was something mad and harsh about the way they laughed.

We were standing in the middle of the stream, huddled in a tight little group, staring up in fright.

One of the big guys picked up a rock, and heaved it right at us. It whizzed past Barbara's head and crashed into the tangle of brambles on the bank.

Another guy prised one of the stones, a big lump of rock, off the wall and used both hands, like a footballer taking a shy, to hurl it down. Fortunately the stone was too heavy and he wasn't strong enough to get the distance. It landed about three yards in front of us and hit the water with a big splash that drenched the three of us. We cowered back.

'What's wrong with them?' Colin muttered. 'They all look as if they've gone looney.'

He was right. Up above us the cackling laughter continued. Then one of the big guys shouted down: 'What the fuck are you standing in the water for? Come on up here and take what's coming to you.'

'What for?' Colin shouted back.

'Just get up here you wee bastards. Come on. I'm not going to wait all day.'

'I'm not going up there,' Colin said softly. 'We'd really better make a run for it.'

I heard Barbara whisper 'Yes.'

'Are you coming up, or are we going to have to come down?' yelled the big guy.

'Aw stick it in your ear, pig-face,' Colin yelled back, and the big guy's eyes widened so far I could see white top and bottom. Suddenly I wished Colin had never said that.

'You're going to be sorry you ever opened your squeaky little mouth. I'm telling you. You better get your arse up here pronto or I'm going to cave·your fucking head in.'

As he said it, he lifted up a gnarled stick that was about three inches thick.

'Do it, Scobie,' one of the other guys shouted gleefully. 'Go and spatter the cunt's brains out.'

Colin hit me on the shoulder. 'Let's go Nicky. Run like shit.' The three of us turned tail and ran, as he said, like shit, splashing desperately through the shallows. Behind us came the hoarse cries and Indian whoops of pursuit.

TWENTY-EIGHT

All that came back to me in that dream-like déjà-vu feeling as we waded deeper into the tunnel.

Three yards under the arch, and the light just went out at the far end, as if somebody had closed a door over the arch on the south side. Suddenly it was pitch dark again, for as soon as we were all under the tunnel's damp wall the light from the entrance faded. The little stone tunnel could have been a million miles long. I held my stick in front of me and tapped my way along, trying not to slip on the smooth, water-worn cobbles, and keeping a tight grip of Paddy.

'You might hear funny noises,' I told her softly. 'But don't worry.'

'I won't worry, Nicky. Not with you all here,' she said, sweet and clear, and her voice echoed away down that vast black distance. I knew now that Cu Saeng had the power to make us see things that didn't exist. Hell, the tunnel was forty yards long at the most, and there should have been enough light to read by in there, but whatever we were heading down to face had the power to change all that. I tapped along in the dark, with half a mind trying to remember what we'd done before, and the other half trying to prevent myself. I was scared, not with the panicky fear I'd had as a kid. It was more like the panicky dread you get as an adult. To tell the truth, there's not a lot to choose from.

Up ahead, there was a noise, like a low moan. I gripped Paddy tight and over my shoulder I told Colin not to worry.

'It's just trying to scare us,' he said. 'I know. I remember.'

'Just stay cool and we'll get to the other side.'

I was beginning to wish we'd taken the high road, shot-guns or not. It was stupid to come this way and get our-selves all worked up again.

The low moan subsided into a rumbling gurgle, then faded to silence. Even the sound of the water was muted. Then there was another noise that was more of a slithering sensation that sent the hairs on my neck to attention again. I could tell myself that it was only imagination and I'd done this before, but it wasn't much consolation. The slith-ering grew louder, but I kept on going until something soft and sticky was drawn right across my mouth. It tugged slightly and gave. A cobweb, I realised, almost giggling with relief. Then another one, and another one, until I was blindly clawing my stick through a sticky, tuggy mass that seemed to fill the entire tunnel.

The slithering got louder, as if something was sliding along the cobbled stones. I held my stick out in readiness and something jarred against it, knocking it slightly to the left, then to the right. Something that *moved*.

Instinctively I jerked my hand back and there was an added weight on the stick. I hit it down on to the water, hearing the muffled splash, as if through several layers of gauze, and brought it up. I thought the weight was gone, and then something cold and scaly touched my hand.

Something had crawled up the stick and on to my hand. Something cold and scaly.

The wave of repugnance that swept through my entire being like an electric shock made me almost lose balance. I jerked my hand up spasmodically and snapped it down again, and whatever it was, whatever cold scaly creature that hadn't been dislodged from my first attempt, flipped off and into the water. I took two steps forward and felt something crunch under my shoe. It gave, then crunched with a palpable pop. I didn't even want to think about it.

I took another step, still tapping with my stick, when Paddy let out a shriek of pure horror.

'Get it *off* me! Oh get it off me!' she screamed in such a high voice the words were almost unintelligible. I pulled her close to me and let go of her wrist. She was writhing there in the dark and I grabbed her round the shoulder, feeling her body shake convulsively as she beat her arms around. There was something on her neck, and I swear to God it felt like what a big spider would feel like if it was built like a peeler crab, hard but yielding, cold and clammy, and all legs going. Without thinking I just grabbed at the wriggling thing and gave it such a squeeze that it popped right there in my hand. I felt some stuff spurt all over my hand. Then something landed on my shoulder, and a smaller something that felt just about the same plopped, scrabbling, on to my head. Behind me I could hear the sharp intakes of breath as loathesome things descended on Colin and the major, and Paddy let out that unearthly screech again.

That was it for me. There was no point in delaying this any longer. Cu Saeng might be interfering with our minds, and it *might* all be just in our imaginations, but I sure as hell didn't want to suffer it a moment longer. Something that was a much bigger brother to the thing I had pulped in my hand put some legs or feelers or whatever around my legs and I kicked out savagely. There was a squeaky grunt as I connected hard, and it all felt to bloody real all of a sudden.

'Come on!' I bawled at the top of my voice. 'Run for it. Colin, Donald. Get the hell out of here.' I just held Paddy's arm tightly and lashed out savagely with the old walking stick at the cobwebs that were in my way, and whatever disgusting things that sat in them. I blasted my way out of that tunnel like a runaway express. It seemed to take a long age as I powered my way through the cloying darkness and shot out like a grape seed into the open air, tugging the girl into the light.

I skittered to a halt and Paddy stopped yelling. I pulled her down beside me, keeping an arm about her shoulder to steady her. There was something on her head, something that looked like that thing I'd pictured back in the darkness, that seemed, in the instant I looked directly at it, to change shape and substance and melt into the air. My hand was still covered with a greenish-yellow glop that also

398

evaporated in the light.

Imagination maybe, but it seemed all too real to me. Paddy put both her arms round my waist and sobbed into my hip.

There was a scuttering noise behind us, and I watched as Colin and the major made that slow-motion run through molasses in that dark place where time seemed to be stretched out, before they popped through the black warp and into real time.

If Donald had been a disbeliever before, he sure had got the faith in that forty yards of tunnel. He was an old soldier and no doubt he'd seen and done many things, as had old Jimmy Allison and the monsignor at the seminary, but his face told me that he'd sure as hell never gone through anything that came close to that forty-yard, million-mile stretch. Colin's face was pure white, but he'd become a believer, become whatever he should have been all along, when the three of us had joined hands on the dry bed of the stream.

'Dear Jesus Christ Almighty,' Donald said with true fervour. 'What on earth was . . . ?' He paused. 'No don't tell me. That was nothing on earth.'

'You're getting the picture, old fella,' I said. Even after that experience, I could still get a twinge of pleasure out of being right.

'Is that what you meant by what you were saying?' Donald asked. He turned and looked into the searing black maw of the tunnel. No light came out. It was like the reverse of a torch. A black hole that sucked away the light.

'I'm sure I didn't imagine that,' said the old soldier. 'Those *things* in there. They were like . . . .' He looked at Paddy and stopped himself in mid-sentence.

'You're right,' he started off again. 'That was *wrong*. There is something not right at all here. I don't know what it is but you are truly right. Whatever can do that, it has got to be stopped.'

'Well thank God you've come round to our side,' I said drily. 'It'll save me having to stop and explain the facts of

399

life every ten minutes.'

'You just tell me what to do, laddie, and I'll be about it. I'm not too old to be taking orders, you know. Just you say the word.'

Donald was convinced. It had taken me weeks of pussy-footing to get to that stage.

I looked behind us, half expecting to see a row of maniacal faces leering down from the parapet, but there was no-one there. I took Paddy's hand again and waded her out of the stream with Donald and Colin behind us. We got to the flat bank and warily edged down the line of scrub and bramble that lined the stream, until we came to a sheltered spot in the lee of some bushes. I hunkered down and the rest followed suit. Donald leaned against his rifle and I used my walking stick as a rest. Paddy had an elbow on my knee and she seemed to have calmed down a bit. She was taking the horrors a lot better than you could expect any youngster, but I still was worried about what all this was doing to her. Having said that, my main worry was to stay alive and *do* something about this mess. What I had to do was still unclear, a memory that refused to resolve into focus.

Donald said he could use a cigarette, seeing as he'd left his pipe somewhere between McFall's farm and here. I reached into the pocket of my jacket and fumbled for my crumpled packet and lighter among the rest of the flotsam and jetsam. My lighter had slipped down amongst the collection, so I just hauled out everything from the big patch pocket and tumbled it on to the damp grass. I was about to fumble through it when Colin reached down past my hand and grabbed the smooth stone.

'You found it,' he said excitedly. 'You've found the stone. That's what we had and that's what we need.'

Donald looked at him, then down at the black pointed stone in Colin's hands.

'That's an old thing,' he said. 'An old spear-head, isn't it?'

I nodded. Colin was turning it over in his hand, studying it, *remembering*.

The major and I lit our cigarettes and though I've given them up now I can still taste that one. I needed it badly then. Paddy had long since given up wrinkling her nose. My smoking was the least of her immediate problems. She just sat close.

'I need a spear,' Colin said suddenly. 'Can you make me one, Nicky? Will you make me a spear with the stone? I've forgotten how to tie it.'

'Sure. If you think it will help.'

'We had one last time. We might need it again where we have to go.'

'And where's that?' Donald asked, blowing out a plume of smoke.

'Over there!' Colin said loudly, pointing through the bush towards the black hump of Ardhmor Rock that sat on a sea of grey mist. Above and around it there was a menacing black cloud that hung like a tight, powerful fist. Right above us, the sky was dark and threatening, although the storm seemed to have died while we were in the tunnel. But its menace was pale by comparison to that bleak obscene doom that swaddled Ardhmor.

'That's where it is. We saw it before, didn't we Nicky? But it hurt us. It hurt me. And we have to go there and see it again.'

Colin said this with a look of bleak determination on his face that almost won the battle with the dull fear written there. He was scared all right, and with good reason, but he was planning to face the fear and face the thing that had sent him to limbo for the past twenty years. When he said that, I could see the ten-year-old Colin, the fiery, adventurous one and only, and for an instant a wave of sadness washed through me when I thought of what he had missed. Yes, I was going down to Ardhmor to help him get his revenge.

Scared? I had got beyond that. I reckon I was in such a state of numbed horror that I'd come out the other side and become rational again. I just wished the memory mist would clear to prepare me for what was to come next.

401

Donald and I made the spear for Colin with a stout mountain ash sapling as the shaft. I cut a cleft in the top with my penknife, the old worn, horn-handled one that had been round the world with me, and I slotted in the stone until it wedged tight. Between us, Donald and I produced enough string to lash it securely until it looked just like a stone-age lance. I knew how to do it. I had seen it before in the hallucination that had been sent to me that sunny day down at the side of Strowan's clear water.

'Shouldn't you have a bow and arrow?' I asked Colin. He looked at my walking stick and shook his head.

'No. You take that. It's the right stuff.'

'What does that mean?'

'I don't know. The right wood maybe. We'll be fine with that.'

'I hope so.'

Beside me, Paddy said she was thirsty. I was about to suggest she took a drink from the stream, but it was grimy with the spate wash, then I remembered the bottle. I unhooked it from my shoulder and unscrewed the metal top and gave Paddy a drink, watching as she took a couple of big swallows before handing it back.

'Oooh. That is *good*,' she said, smacking her lips. Colin took a mouthful and I followed. As soon as I drank from the old bottle I felt good. It was as if the clear water had surged right down and hit the spot, spreading out, cleansing, and burning out the numbness. For an instant, I could see everything with bright clarity and Colin's grim expression had softened. He looked thoughtful, but almost at peace.

'It *is* good,' he said. 'We should save some for later. I know what we have to do now, but watch out. It will be waiting for us. It wants us to go there but it fears us too. From the last time. It remembers.'

'What makes you think that?' I asked.

'I don't know. It just *is*. It is getting clearer. I can't see it all yet, but I can *feel* it. I can feel *him*.'

'Cu Saeng?'

'I don't know his name. He doesn't have a name that we know. But he's old and he's bad. He wants to kill us, but I'm going to kill him because he *stole* me.'

'That he did,' I said under my breath, but Colin continued as if he hadn't heard.

'He's watching us, but he knows we're strong. The water has kept him back now and he is angry. He wanted out, but we've trapped him again and he's really mad.'

Colin stopped and seemed to converse with himself, then snapped out of his brief reverie.

'We have to be brave and careful, Nicky. Because he's going to come at us and he's going to try to kill us. We have to be ready for him.'

Donald coughed lightly at my side.

'I think we should be moving out of here while we've still got the light.'

'Right. I reckon we should. How do you feel Paddy?'

'I'm all right now.'

'Do you know where we're going?'

'Yes,' she said, resignedly. 'I know where.'

'Just keep a hold of my hand and stay very close. I'll be looking after you.'

'I know,' she said and looked up at me with a small smile on her pale face. I really hated the idea of taking her with us, but there was no way to avoid it. Nowhere was safe now in Arden, and no matter what I had to face, I wanted her close by where I could keep an eye on her.

Colin used the stout spear to haul himself to his feet, and as he did so, I got another glimpse of him. His four-day stubble was a black matt on his face and his dark eyes gleamed in the dim light. If he'd put on skins and let his hair grow long, he would have been the image of that long ago dream hunter who had followed the elk to the water.

This time, Colin led the way, with the major and his Armalite as rearguard. From behind I could see the white lines in the dark hair that had made him Badger. He was no longer that, as he stepped out firmly, maybe grimly, and we headed for the mist.

We got halfway to Swanson's farm when a shout halted us in our tracks. The major whirled just as a shotgun blast ripped the air and sent pellets rapping into the leaves of the hedge that lined the path.

Billy Ruine looked even madder than before. There was blood all over his face and there was something really odd about one of the other guys with him. I couldn't figure it out until I realised that he only had one eye and half his head seemed to have been battered to a pulp. How the man was still conscious, never mind walking, I couldn't imagine, but he was there with the rest of them, maybe a dozen or fifteen people, armed with shotguns and a whole array of blunt and sharp instruments. It was like a peasant uprising. One big man I recognised was carrying a garden fork for God's sake, and he was shambling along with the rest, staring straight ahead with a blank look that was more frightening than if it had been fury.

Donald shouted: 'Move. Quickly!'

We moved quickly in the direction we had been heading. There was another blast, and another rapping against the hedge as the shot tore out leaves and twigs. Whoever was firing had no aim. I hustled Paddy along the narrow path and risked a glance back. Donald was close to the hedge and down on one knee with the stock of his black rifle tucked right into his shoulder.

There was a sharp crack, not as loud as I would have imagined, and an immediate cry from far back behind us. We got to the stile and I lifted Paddy over. Colin followed me and I looked back again. The major was on his feet and running.

'Keep moving!' he bellowed. 'Fast as you can.'

He caught up with us on the other side and I got a whiff of the cordite from the barrel.

'Too exposed there,' he said. 'I need somewhere I can hold them off. I don't want to have to shoot them all.'

'Why not?' I asked, as we pounded along.

'Just the ones with guns,' he said. 'But there's too many of them. They could outflank me in the open.'

We got behind Swanson's farm and over the gate that led to the path to Ardhmor. The farmyard was deserted, which was good. I didn't fancy being stuck between two factions.

About a hundred yards down the track, with the cries of pursuit ringing in our ears, we came to the narrow space between two trees near where I had had my fright with the bramble vines (and that seemed like a pleasant daydream by comparison to what had happened since), when Donald tapped me on the shoulder.

Colin stopped when I did.

'This will do,' Donald said. 'I can hold them off from here.'

'Won't they get round you?' I asked.

The old soldier shook his head. 'No. I can see right and left and straight ahead. If they come at the side, they'll have to come through all that undergrowth. I'll hear them. You go on and I'll catch up with you. But hurry. Get moving now.'

I reached out and held Donald's arm. I would have much preferred that he came with us, but there was no way. He knew he would have to stay here and make a stand, and we *had* to get to Ardhmor and whatever awaited us there.

We didn't say anything. Donald and I just looked at each other, then he snapped: 'Go on, laddie. There's no time. Just watch out for those two.'

I let go of his arm and was about to move along, when Paddy stopped me. She reached up to Donald and he bent down, letting her wrap her arms around his neck to give him a warm, quick hug. He ruffled her hair, the way I was prone to do.

'You look after them both, my dear. Now be off with you. Scat!'

'Come *on*, Nicky,' Colin said, ahead of us, and we followed him down the path, leaving the major behind. In fifty yards, the grey mist swirled around us like thick smoke when we went through the wide gap in the old hawthorn hedge and into the territory of the thing that waited behind the walls.

The fog dulled everything and made strange shapes that writhed in front of our eyes and disappeared in wisps. Trees loomed out of the gloom and faded behind us, and even the noise of our passage seemed to be deadened, sucked away by the mist. Paddy gripped my hand more tightly, and I kept the pace up to ensure that I didn't lose Colin who was striding briskly ahead. Behind us, there was a muffled roar, followed almost instantly by a muted crack, like a damp squib. A faint cry diminished rapidly. I hoped that Donald was all right.

In the shadow of the big beech trees, the mist merged with that black cloud that loomed right over our heads like a solid mass that was getting ready to squash us. The wind was rising steadily and it seemed as if the air pressure had suddenly deepened, making it more *solid*, but the mist didn't move, except to writhe in ghostly shadows.

I made Colin and Paddy stop for breath beside a big tree. He was keen to get on, to face his enemy. I knew I had to but I was far from enthusiastic. Up close I could see Colin's face in the half light. There was a fury written all over it, a fierce, burning anger.

He stood there, leaning against his spear, like a warrior steeling himself for battle, psyching himself up for the greatest effort.

Paddy noticed the movement first, under her feet, and jumped so suddenly she nearly landed in my arms.

There was a groaning, ripping sound, and right in front of our eyes one of the great grey roots twisted and heaved itself out of the ground, sending leaf mould and compost scattering into the air. It looked like an elephant's trunk, ripping a pathway out of the soil.

I jumped back as the root tore free and seemed to slither towards us, thick as a man's thigh and covered in fine, dirt-coated rootlets. Lazily at first, it waved its tip in the air as the three of us edged backwards until we came hard up against a neighbouring tree trunk. It whipped around, like a tentacle, questing, then it coiled, quivered and unleashed its full length right at us, whipping down with such force the ground vibrated.

I lifted Paddy off the ground and jinked round the side of the tree, away from the lashing root, shoving Colin to the other side as I did so. Underneath my feet, I felt the ground heave again and another root started its flexing stroke. Then another, and another, until the boles of all the beech trees seemed to be squirming in the fog.

Colin didn't need me to tell him to move it out of there. I still had Paddy in my arms and the writhing of the ground under my feet gave me the impetus I needed to go from a standing start to a full sprint in the blink of an eye, with Colin right on my heels.

The stand of beech wasn't too wide, but it seemed like miles as we madly raced along, aware of the lashing, ripping sounds and movements all around. At one point, something looped out of the ground and caught me by the foot, wrenching me right off balance, and I fell heavily, twisting so that I didn't land on Paddy. I heard my breath whoosh right out and Paddy let out a little yelp. Something lashed at me and caught me as I lay sprawled on the dead leaves, sending a stinging pain right up my thigh, and I could feel small rootlets try to string themselves around my legs. Then I was back on my feet again with Colin's hand gripping the back of my jacket and almost jerking me straight upright. My breath came sucking right back in again and Colin shoved me forward, still with Paddy tight in my arms, both of us leaping like hurdlers over the tangle of writhing roots.

The forest floor was filled with the terrible raking and scuttling noises as the trees did their impossible dance, but it was like hearing something in the distance, for the sound was muted by the thick fog and the oppressive weight of the air.

Then, suddenly, we were out of it and on to the clearing that was blocked by the immense wall of basalt that loomed out of the deeper darkness ahead.

Ardhmor Rock's black face towered into the cloud.

'That's it,' Colin turned and almost snarled. 'Here's his place.'

'Where do we go now?' I yelled, striving to be heard above the tumult from under the trees.

Colin pointed to a scree of big rocks that had slipped at some time from the face.

'There. Where we were the last time when he . . . . '

Colin's words were lost as the ground heaved and buckled underneath our feet. Both of us were sent flying into the air and I landed right on the point of my backside with a thump that jarred my spine.

There was an immense cracking sound that seemed to rip into my head, as if suddenly a volcano had blown its top, and a rumble like a great train hurtling down a tunnel right towards me. The intense noise was a sudden, pressing pain in my ears and inside my skull and I felt as if the top of my head was going to lift off. Then from the cloud above there was a crash and a flash of lightning that forked down, almost in slow motion, and stabbed in at the face where the basalt merged with the short turf.

An after-image of purple and yellow fuzzed my eyes, and the ringing in my ears fogged my brain, but I still held on to Paddy and waited for it to clear. I also waited for the earth to open up and swallow us, or for the sky to send down another deadly fork and roast us into the grass, but for the moment I was paralysed and powerless to do anything.

Then Colin said: 'There. Look Nicky. That's where we have to go.'

His voice, over the telephone bell in my ears, sounded faint and scratchy, but I heard what he said.

Where his black-pointed spear was aimed, there was a deep dark triangle in the basalt that was denser than the surrounding pitch. There was a flicker of green light from above us, but without the deafening crash, and I suddenly saw what Colin meant.

Cu Saeng had opened his door.

There was nothing for it but to walk in.

TWENTY-NINE

The sound of the thrashing forest died as soon as we crossed the threshold of the hole in the rock and again I experienced the inside-out sensation of déjà vu when we walked through the sluggish time-stretching shadow and into the earth. Once past that dark curtain there was light of a sort, as if the very stone itself were giving off a glow that was just enough to see by, a dim, sickly luminescence. Ahead of us the hole in the volcanic plug widened and went straight for some distance and curved off to the left in a steep descent. I could make out the knotted twists of old lava. Cu Saeng's door was a natural fumarole, an ancient volcanic chimney where streams of white hot magma had flowed under the pressure of venting gases, leaving a snake-twist of tunnels. I have been in places like this before, in Iceland, but there was no eerie light in them.

Paddy was deathly quiet and I held her close by me. We made little sound, except for the tapping of my stick on the stones and the scuffle of our feet as we almost tiptoed into the fumarole. There was a gurgle from the water bottle that banged against Paddy's hip. We almost held our breaths, waiting for something horrible, something dreadful, to leap out from one of the vertical clefts that led off to right and left into pits of black. We rounded the bend on the slope and the tunnel entrance was out of sight.

Up ahead, in the phosphorescent dimness, the trail narrowed in on itself and the pathway became steeper so that I had to rely on my stick for balance. The rocks glistened with slime or water. I couldn't make it out, but the light made it look diseased.

'Shhh . . .' Colin hissed, and held out his hand for

silence. I felt Paddy tense against me as we both stopped.

We strained, and at first I heard nothing, then it came. A soft chittering noise, faint, like a half-heard whisper in the distance, like the sound of insects moving on a hard surface. It rose to a murmur, then faded, then there was a vibration through the rock, as if it flexed and trembled slightly. I had the sudden panicky dread that the walls of the fumarole were going to buckle and close together, slowly crushing the life out of us, but the tremor died away.

We steadily walked downward on the winding path and the tunnel widened again, arching high over us. The tapping of my stick and the butt of Colin's spear echoed away aloft to disappear in ringing murmurs far away.

Then all of a sudden there was a peal of hoarse laughter that scared the living daylights out of me. It was the kind of laughter you hear in the local mental hospital (before the orderlies move in with the hypos), deranged and guttural, wholly mindless. It did not even sound human. Paddy gave a little moan as the laughter rose in pitch and tailed off in an obscene gurgle. I could feel the backs of my knees start to shake uncontrollably, and I hoped the girl didn't sense it. Colin stood stock still, and if the maniacal laugh had scared him, he didn't show it. In the sick light, his face looked as green as mine felt, but his eyes were black, and his mouth was twisted down at the corners. We walked on and the cavern continued to widen and the slope levelled off until we were in the middle of a wide amphitheatre deep under Ardhmor. Colin stopped me again, and gestured with the stone end of his spear. There was a mass in the middle of the cathedral, a dark shape on the ground, right in the centre, but I couldn't make out what it was. I pushed Paddy behind me, keeping a grip of her shoulder, while with the other hand, I hefted the walking stick in an en-garde position. Colin was by my side with the sharp end pointing ahead as we both cautiously edged forward.

It was a boat. Sitting there in the middle of the cave, set

square down on the rock. I could see that the keel was either missing, or there was a keel-shaped hole in the stone so that it just sat there, as if it was in water, slightly proud at the prow. We inched forward some more, and then, as my eyes grew more accustomed to the light, I could make out more detail, and in an instant my heart gave one of those sickening lurches when I took it all in.

There were men in the boat. Or what had been men, for they were now dripping, rotted corpses, with unhinged, gaping jaws, and protruding bones through putrescent flesh. They sat on the slats of the lifeboat as they would have done in life, but their eye sockets were pits of black, and the bones which showed through the mouldering rot were green-tinged.

'It's the *Cassandra* lifeboat,' I whispered, still keeping Paddy behind me.

'What's that?' Colin hissed back.

'The boat that went missing. We couldn't find it. And no wonder.'

'They're all dead,' Colin said, still in a whisper.

'Thank God for that. Can we get past it without Paddy seeing?'

He nodded and pointed past the boat that sat in the centre like a seaman's tableau. I could see dense clumps of glistening bladder-wrack and kelp dripping over the gunwales. Beyond it, the cavern narrowed again to a cleft. That was the route we had to take.

We kept to the wall and skirted round the circumference of the big, high-roofed cave, keeping as much distance between us and the mouldering horror of the lost lifeboat crew. At the other side, when we were only ten yards or so from the cleft, Colin stiffened and the old piano fingers ran up and down my spine again. There was a faint noise, just a whisper, from over there by the boat. There was another soft slither and a movement that I caught in peripheral vision, followed by another, and a soft, smudged plopping sound.

I almost cricked my neck as I instinctively whirled, and

Paddy let out another, muted, cry of alarm.

Something moved on the boat. A hank of wrack slithered from where it had been caught on one of the rowlocks and slumped to the ground with a squashy thud. I almost moaned with relief. It was only seaweed.

Then I froze, almost screaming aloud in fright. For one of the rotting crew members slowly turned his skeletal profile and creaked his head round on an arm-thin, rutted neck to stare with vacant sockets right at me. The dark eye holes flickered with the reflection of the green light, then faded to a pale white, a cold pallor that seemed to beam out of the sockets and spear me to the spot. Below those white eyes (where had I seen them before? I couldn't recall) the slack jaw slowly hinged upwards, like a slow-motion trap, until it grinned at me.

Colin turned and caught the look on my face and darted a glance across to the lifeboat. Another skeletal head slowly turned, then another, and a bony, obscenely dripping, long-fingered hand raised itself off the gunwales. One of the dead crew members started to haul himself out over the side.

Inside my chest, my heart rose about three inches with every beat and was now trying to block off the supply of blood to my brain. It felt as if it was competing for space in my throat, and I felt I couldn't breathe.

We still had thirty feet to go and suddenly I wanted to be there, out of this cavern where dead crewmen did the impossible. Where mouldering bodies stared with white, sick eyes and grinned their disgusting glee. I almost wrenched Paddy's shoulder as I shoved her towards the cleft, still staring at the nightmare scene as the slow-moving corpses hauled themselves out of the lifeboat and on to the dripping weed fronds.

They walked like jerky puppets, but their white-filled sockets were fixed on us. I realised that we had to get to that cleft before they did, or we'd be trapped in the cave with a bunch of dead men. I shoved Paddy right ahead and made a break for it. We made it, Paddy keening a high-pitched expression of terror all the way, with yards to spare. I was about to run for it right up the narrow fumarole when Colin stopped me.

'We don't want them behind us. We have to stop them now,' he said firmly.

I really didn't want to hang about, for more than half of me wanted not to believe that this was happening at all, but Colin was right. Wherever we were going, we didn't want our footsteps dogged by something out of the *Evil Dead*. That's not quite what I thought at the time. I was so scared I couldn't swallow, but Colin still burned with the fury of his lost years. He stood at the entrance to the fumarole, then whirled with a hoarse yell and dived straight into the shambling crew. I saw his spear butt come up and swing round in a fast, sweeping arc, and heard it thud into soft dead flesh and bone. There was a splintering sound and for a moment I thought the stout ash stave had broken.

But it wasn't the spear butt. After the crack of the splinter, I saw two of the obscene walking corpses topple to the stone, smashed through their spines by the first blow. An arm flew into the air and hit the far wall with a sticky thud. Colin's shoulders flexed as he heaved the stave round for another blow and brought it high into the group. There was another crackling thud and I saw a skull bounce on the rock. Then to my horror I saw two of the things had slowly circled round and were coming for him from the back.

I forced Paddy hard up against the wall of the cleft and I remember shouting: 'Stay there!'

Then I let out my own war whoop. I don't know why. Maybe it was all the fear and horror and shock that had been bottled up getting uncorked right at that minute, but I remember jumping into that fray, shouting at the top of my lungs (it was a string of curses, and I'm sure I never repeated myself once), and lashed out with the heavy knobbed head of the walking stick.

Something crunched under the force and one of the

things dropped in a heap at my feet. Something reached for me with hugely long fingers and I grabbed it with my free hand, too mad with fear and fury to feel disgust at the cloying cold slime that I felt under my fingers, or the foul stench of putrefaction that suddenly filled the air. The hand twisted under mine, and came right away along with the forearm. I lashed out with the heavy end and a skull came off its shoulders, flipping back end over end while the dangling jaw fell right down on to the chest as the body tottered and fell. Then Colin and I were back to back, lunging and jabbing, hearing our spear and club smash into bare bones and sink into rotting flesh. Gobbets of foul, dripping stuff flicked into the air with every contact, and bits kept falling until there was nothing left to fight. Even then, we were carried along by the momentum. I couldn't stop myself battering and beating at the lumps of the dead that were scattered about in that chamber. I must have been wading in rotting flesh, flailing and battering until the whole floor was a sickening, revolting mess.

Then I just ran out of steam and I stood there panting for breath. Colin was gasping too, as we stood in the middle of that foul stench looking at the littered remains.

I sucked in a great breath of air, almost retching from the exertion and the thick stench of rotted and rotting human, when Colin really knocked the feet from under me.

'Where is she?' he said, still heaving for fresh air.

'The girl. Paddy. Where is she?'

I whirled around, almost slipping headlong into the charnel heap to face the narrow cleft where I'd pushed Paddy against the wall.

She wasn't there.

Summer 1961.
Colin was almost dragging Barbara behind us as we flew along the farm track, spurred by the cacophony behind us. There was no time to think. We went into the darkness of the trees where the gloom

414

descended within yards. We rebounded from trunks we couldn't see and crashed through undergrowth. There were other things that flew at us in the dark, like insects or moths, that we had to bat away, and then we were out and right at the face of the rock itself. There was a black shadow right before us, and we walked into a cave that had never been there before. Inside, there was a barely audible vibration, like the slow beating of a vast heart, so low it barely registered on the conscious. There was a light in the cave, a dim, greenish illumination that cast no shadow. Colin crawled on his hands and knees under the low overhang, then stood up. There was only one way to go.

We kept to the main passage, ignoring the side tunnels, keeping close enough to touch each other, until we came to a big cavern that arched above our heads in inky darkness.

Colin's breath hitched, as if he was about to say something, when a movement over beside the wall of the cave caught my eye. I whirled and strained into the dimness, but the movement had stopped.

'What is it?' Colin asked, turning to look in the same direction.

'I thought I saw something,' I whispered.

Both of us stared. Then Barbara said: 'Over there. Something.'

We both turned, and saw a brief, slow movement, low down. Then across to the right, there was another one. Then another, closer, on the ground.

Barbara shrank back against the wall.

'What is it?' Colin said.

There was a soft, slithery sound, right next to him, and we both spun and looked as a long, worm-like thing poked out from between the scattered stones.

Colin let out a muted cry of disgust and stepped back, right on to another of the white, maggoty things. It squelched under his foot. Right beside me, another of the creatures oozed itself out of the ground. It looked just like a big larva, like a dragonfly nymph, or a wasp grub. I felt myself shudder all over. Of all the things that gave me the creeps in the world it was grubs. Their sticky white, bloated bodies made me shiver with loathing, and these things were blown up to giant size. I felt my gorge rising as one of them looped itself about and nuzzled my boot. I kicked out hard and the thing

415

clung on with two curved pincers for a moment before flying off and landing with a squelch on a stone. Its insides spread out across the rock and it hung there limply.

From behind me Barbara let out a scream and Colin hit something off her leg and for a moment I was paralysed with loathing for the white, squashy things that humped themselves out of every nook and cranny. Then another probing grub reared itself up on its flat body and I stamped down hard on it and everything inside of it splashed out. I stamped on another, then another, and I started hitting out at others all around, doing what must have looked like a manic war-dance, smashing and pulping everything that moved, and all the time feeling as if I was going to be sick. Colin was beside and behind me, batting at the things with his bow. They weren't fast enough to dodge, and though their mandibles tried to bite us, there was no particular danger, but their very presence brought out in me the most primitive, gut-wrenching loathing that I just had to stamp and squash them all. I whirled and hit and battered and kicked, and every time I did so I could feel the splash of their disgusting liquid insides splatter all over me and the rocks, sending up waves of ammonia-like odour that added to my disgust.

Between Colin and me, we must have squashed hundred of the things, and then they just stopped crawling out of the grounds. All around us was a swampy puddle of crushed, pulped maggots and the smell of their juices was stinging our eyes.

'That's enough, Nicky,' Colin panted at my side. 'They're all gone.'

He clapped me on the shoulder and pulled me to him. 'They're away now,' he said.

I turned and vomited lustily on to the remains while he held on to my arm.

When I'd finished, he pulled me upright and said: 'Come on. Let's get out of here.'

He pulled me gently by the arm towards the wall. Underneath, the rocks were slippery with the glistening stuff that had come out of the crawling things and it was hard to keep our balance, but we got there anyway without mishap.

'Which way did we come in?' Colin asked.

'I don't know.'

I turned to look around the big chamber, trying to find our bearings.

'That way I think. We were going over there.' I pointed at the big fissure we had been heading for.

'Then where's Barbara?'

'She was standing just there . . .' I said, pointing at the basalt wall.

'Well, where's she gone?'

I looked at the big rocks that littered the edge of the cavern, and moved carefully towards them, expecting Barbara to be crouched behind them. She was a one and only, an equal member, but Colin and I didn't expect her to get involved with those things that we'd splattered all over the rocks.

We searched all the shadows and called out softly, but there was no reply.

We skirted the whole chambered cavern, but Barbara wasn't there.

While we'd been fighting those loathsome grubs, she'd disappeared.

'We have to find her,' Colin said. I nodded and he called out her name at the top of his voice. It echoed away through the caverns and fissures and came back in diminishing echoes from far away. He called out again, and I did too, but there was nothing. She was gone.

'What are we going to do?' I asked him.

He shook his head, and even in the dim light I could see the anguish on his face.

Then the two of us froze when we heard Barbara scream, long and high and terrible, a sound that sent shivers up and down my spine, a sound that was repeated as the stone walls bounced her terror back and forward at us until the cave was filled with her screams.

THIRTY

The scream of pure fear came echoing up from the cleft that led out of the cavern.

I was frozen with the shock of it, but Colin was quicker to recover. He was ten steps ahead of me by the time I started to move, and threw himself into the passageway, holding his spear ahead of him. I followed him through, my heart wrenched by the naked terror of Paddy's scream.

The fumarole twisted right and left, like the hole made by a giant earthworm, and the solidified lava on the walls looked like the sloughed skin of a crawling creature. In the dim green light we slithered and stumbled, but kept running, going deeper and deeper into the rock. The scream had stopped suddenly and my stomach had lurched hard when it did so. It sounded as if it had been cut off.

By what? Visions surged in front of my mind, visions worse than the dreams I'd had, worse than the roots that looped and twisted and grabbed at us. Worse than the horrible things that we'd fought as children, and that had suddenly swamped my memory in an overload of loathsome recall. Worse, too, than those dead men who had come to some sort of foul life in the cavern. Those were things from fantasy land. If necessary I would live with their images seared into my brain.

But what I couldn't live with was the knowledge that that bright little kid had suffered from my stupidity. She was in my care and I had to look after her.

And some instinct told me that she was very, very important to this whole nightmare.

Most of all I knew that if she was dead, I would never be able to live with myself.

Colin's feet thudded harder on the rocks and I

wondered at his ability to keep his balance. I kept up with him driven by the adrenalin that the scream had sent surging, like an electric shock, through my body.

Suddenly the passage widened and we came tumbling into a chamber that was even vaster than the one where we'd fought the dead crew. It was an immense amphitheatre, lit again by that greenish, unearthly light, where stalactites came down to meet the jagged teeth of stalagmites, and sharp, tumbled rocks littered the dank floor.

The scream came again, piercing and shattering in its intensity, from right in the middle of the cavern, spiralling upwards.

I remember letting out a gasp or a sob that was a mixture of anguish and relief. She was alive.

But what terror there was in that scream.

Colin and I skittered to a halt and stood in the middle of the chamber. Paddy was nowhere to be seen, but her scream had come right from the centre, right where we were standing. We swung right and left, peering into the darkness.

Then the scream came again, from right beside us, and I whirled.

Paddy was standing there, right behind a stalagmite, her face white with shock and her mouth agape in a huge circle.

I leapt towards her and suddenly I felt as if I was running through treacle. The air around her had become thick, like the entrance to the tunnel, where time seemed to be distorted. I pushed my way through, ramming into the thickness. Paddy screamed again, but I heard the sound inside my head, as if she was reaching out with her mind. I ran against the cloying barrier, feeling myself running in slow motion, powering forward. It took a long slow age, and the closer I got to her, the thicker seemed the warp that held us both. All around I could see flickering movement and hear sounds inside my skull as if the whole logic of time and space were turned inside out. Paddy was standing stock still, with that long, unfinished scream painted on her face, as if she had been frozen in time. It seemed, for a long time, that she got no nearer, although she had been only a few feet away when I started out towards her. I felt myself slowing down to a crawl, although I seemed to be travelling, subjectively, great distances with every stride.

I reached out a hand towards her, watching it recede from me, elongating into the distance, then it touched her, far away. There was a loud, snapping sound as the world gave a jolt, and Paddy and I were tumbling, in slow motion, through the air, getting faster and faster as we came towards the ground, and I hit with a jarring thump. Paddy landed on top of me and the scream that had been coming from her mind resumed from her wide-open mouth and was suddenly cut off as her breath gushed out with the force of the landing.

Instinctively, she put both arms around me and called my name, high and panicky, over and over again.

Colin called from the centre of the chamber.

'Nicky. Come here. Quick.'

I staggered to my feet, allowing Paddy to keep her grip of my neck, and using my old walking stick for balance.

'Look at that,' Colin said, and pointed his spear over to the wall.

There was a man standing in a patch of darkness.

Colin immediately went into a crouch, swinging the butt of the spear back, ready to stab forward with the obsidian point at the first movement. I held Paddy to the side, keeping myself and my stick between her and the man who stood in the shadows, and I wished Donald had been here with us with his big powerful rifle.

The figure did not move. It just stood. Colin eased himself out of the crouch and stood beside me, silent for a moment, then I felt Paddy stiffen against me and I turned my head. There was another figure standing against the wall. Then another. And another. The whole place was ringed with men. Motionless.

We stared all around in the half light. We were surrounded.

'Who are they?' Colin asked.

Then from out of memory I knew who they were.

And just at the same time, Colin whispered: 'The soldiers.'

We had seen them before.

Colin edged forward, keeping his spear pointed ahead, and I followed close behind. The nearest man was standing upright in a dark shadow, and as we walked towards him I felt the hairs on the back of my neck prickle a warning.

It was a soldier, in full armour. His breastplate glinted in a dull reflection of the green light, and he wore a helmet on his head. There was a short, straight sword in his hand, and his thick boots were laced right up his calves by thick thongs. One of his hands was up at his head and I could see the nails were dug right into the skin. One of his fingers was gouged into his eye, not just pressing against it, but dug right into the eyeball itself, and there was a look on his face, such an expression of agony, that it made my blood run cold. Beside him, there was another man who looked as if he had been frozen in the point of turning. He was holding a staff with a small banner on it topped by an eagle carved in wood over the Roman numerals IX. His left hand looked as if it had been caught halfway to his face, and his fingers were clawed like talons.

The hairs on the back of my head did their slow crawl upright and there was a nerve-pulse that shot up my spinal cord and sent shivers into my brain.

What was it? There was something I knew.

Then I *knew*. I remembered.

'It's the eagle of the ninth legion,' I whispered. 'It's the lost legion.'

'The who?'

'They're Romans. The ones who disappeared.'

I'd read the story as a teenager. The ninth Roman legion sent north and west by the commander on the garrison at the Antonine Wall to quell the Picts.

They had been sent through the pass at Dumbuck, marching on their hobnailed boots and carrying their eagle banner for the glory of the senate and the people of Rome to put down the insurrection and make their garrison a lot safer.

And this was where they had marched into legend. This explained the wall they'd built on top of the old dyke. They had come, not to put down a riot, but to investigate the strange reports that came from the terrified people around this place. They'd come to battle with Cu Saeng, who was already old when they came, not knowing what it was they fought.

There were Romans all round the chamber. Some in full battledress, and others in short togas, for it would have been summer then. And they weren't all Romans. There were people in skins and furs, there were warriors in leather and kilts. There was a man in the robes of a monk.

And, God help me, there were children, all frozen, as if in blocks of ice, and they all looked as if all the horrors of hell were paraded before their eyes.

Some of the figures had torn at their own faces, and their mouths were open in voiceless screams that told of the horror that had been in their minds at the moment of freezing. There were some who were crumpled heaps of skin, as if they had been sucked dry from the inside, and there were still older shadows where only fragments remained.

As I looked around at the catalogue of terror written on the faces of those damned souls, my mind made one of those intuitve leaps again, and I realised what this place was. A memory was stirring, way down in the deeps where it had been hidden, and it was powering its way to the surface of my consciousness.

But before it came, and I was afraid of its coming, came the realisation that these were not frozen corpses. I had seen these things before and not known why they were here. But now I knew.

This was a *storeroom*.

And these agonised men and terrorised children were still alive, caught in the unending horror of the collapsed-time snares that had caught Paddy. Like the entrance to the tunnel under Strowan's Bridge where the air was thick and dark this was how the Cu Saeng kept what it had to feed on. This was its larder. And it had been feeding off the horror of its victims for *thousands* of years.

With that sudden realisation, that these things were *alive*, and had been in agonised stasis for millenniums, came the creeping dread that it could have been Paddy or myself. Caught in slow time, seeing whatever Cu Saeng chose to show us, feeding off the ecstacy of our fear.

I couldn't draw my eyes away from those figures that lined the walls, shadowed all around by the light-sucking bubbles that were cages of time. Beside me, Colin was staring too in fascinated revulsion, the way the soldiers in the old newsreels did when they reached Auschwitz. Every face entrapped in those droplets of timelessness was agape with never-ending agony, an agony that would keep going for ever and ever as long as this obscenity that hunkered under Ardhmor remained.

As we watched, the glimmering darkness that shrouded the figures began to fuzz at the edges, dissipating into the shadows, and as it did, the prisoners' faces became even clearer.

Then, suddenly, with a displacement in the air that almost caused my ears to pop, whatever force it was that had made those cages let go, and first one, then another, grotesque prisoner slumped against the wall.

That was when the screaming started. The soldier with his finger gouged into his eye, a movement that had started maybe two thousand years ago, completed it in one jarring thrust that sent blood and viscous liquid pulsing out of the hole. Beside me I felt Paddy jerk suddenly with the shock of it. Another man, a big red-headed soldier, was freed from that terrible stasis with a start that was so violent, his head smacked hard off the solid rock, and he fell to his knees, seeming dazed. But no sooner had he got to that position than he brought his head forward in a fast, catapulting move, and smashed it straight on to a rock. There was a wet smack as his skull caved in, and an enormous pool of blood streamed out from under his eyes while his body shivered and twitched.

And all the time, the screaming of the tormented souls, the screams they had been crying for eons, were rending the air.

The figures jerked and danced in their agony, it seemed for ever, but could only have been seconds.

Then the screaming suddenly stopped. The sound faded in echoes high up in the cavern roof, until an eerie silence settled in the huge chamber.

We watched, in horrific fascination, our heads swivelling to take in the whole encircling panorama, and as we stared the faces turned to stare at us. Even the Roman who gouged himself swivelled his one eye on us as he pulled his finger from the socket which oozed. Almost as one, the figures started to walk towards us, very slowly, tottering, as if they had little control over their movements, but still they came. Beside me I heard Colin's breath hitch. I was finding it difficult to breathe, and Paddy was holding on to the fabric of my jeans so hard her fingers were gripped into my skin. I could feel her heartbeat, as fast as a mouse's, almost as fast as the pounding of my own.

Slowly, the figures came towards us, eyes fixed on the three of us as they staggered, and even as they came, I could see their expressions were still distorted with the suffering they were still, somehow, going through. At that moment, despite the fact they were walking, encircling us, I couldn't have said whether they were alive, or just being manipulated as the dead men from the boat had been.

I gripped my stick tightly, and sensed Colin bracing himself to get the spear into a defensive position. Implacably, stumbling, shambling, the prisoners of Cu Saeng tightened the circle around us. Closer and closer until I could have touched them with my walking stick.

The eyes stared out of skulls, wide and horrible, I thought, and then, I saw, with something more. In their depths I saw pity, and sadness, and pleading, and maybe that was the worst of it.

Almost as one, they stopped. There must have been a hundred or more. Romans, clansmen, tribesmen, and the

424

suffering children. All silent, and staring, with us right in the centre.

Ready for anything, I prepared to strike, feeling that I might be able to batter a way through, no matter what. Then there was a movement to my right that caused me to spin round. One of the soldiers had raised his sword. Slowly, as if fighting a force that wanted to prevent him, he managed to raise the hilt with one hand, and then with intense effort – and still with the most ecstatic agony etched on his face – he turned it until the blade that was black with blood from his last fight was pointing at his chest. He braced his legs as if against a tide, and threw himself forward. The sword went through him with a sound like leather ripping, and he hit the ground and rolled. He was only a few feet away and as his blood drenched the stone of the floor, ebbing out of him, I could see the agony ease from his face. It was as clear as anything could make it. Death was bliss by comparison to Cu Saeng's grip.

Another movement caught my eye, but this time it was more a twitch, rather than an action. It was on the face closest to me, a gnarled, wizened old face, scarred and pitted. I turned to stare, and there was another twitch, as if something had caved in, under the skin. One of the lines on that leathery seamed face seemed to grow longer, and wider, and then with a little spurting noise, it split. Another line appeared, edging down from under the hairline until it met a crease on a cheek, and that too lengthened to meet another seam coming up from the neck of the man's tunic. The skin started to warp and stretch, as the man's eyes locked on to mine. On the face next to that, the same thing was happening. The skin was splitting and crumbling, folding and distorting. It was as if it had been kept fresh for ages, and then been taken out of the pre-servative and allowed to fester in the air. All round us the faces writhed as their skin tightened and cracked, exposing flesh underneath that quickly dried and shrivelled. Just at the side of my vision, one of the Romans fell to the rock

with a clatter of his armour. Beside Colin there was a rending sound as a man's body seemed twisted into an impossible
position by the force of time that was dessicating his flesh.
Then the cave was filled with the sudden, twisting, jerking
movements as the process accelerated, and one by one, the
doomed prisoners fell to the rocks. The macabre dance
went on and on, until there was not one standing, and even
as they lay in huddled heaps, the tightening, tearing force
of decay warped and twisted the bodies, so that they still
shuddered as if clockwork springs were pulling internal
strings. Eventually even that movement started to subside.
The three of us stood there, fascinated, beyond shock.

The floor of the cave was littered with the finally dead.
The bodies were dried out husks, sucked dry by the very
fact that they had been freed from Cu Saeng's cages.

It was better for them.

I hugged Paddy tight and turned to Colin and said: . . .

Summer 1961.
'Come on. It's her.'

*Colin spun on his heel and followed me down the narrow crack
in the wall where the scream had come piercing through and into the
great chamber. We skittered and ran through the slick, wet tunnel
with that piercing screech still ringing in our ears and echoing off the
hard stone. It seemed as if we ran for miles down that twisting corridor
in the rock, going down deeper and deeper in a long slant into the
bowels under Ardhmor Rock.*

*It seemed to take for ever, but I knew where I was going. The
compass inside my head had locked on to the scream, and although
other cracks and tunnels branched off left and right, I kept plunging
ahead, slipping and sliding on the stones, in the direction; I could hear
the scream inside my head, bulling at my brain as Barbara called out in
an agony of fear.*

*Then we burst into the big chamber, almost falling over ourselves
from the headlong rush. I slipped and the knuckles in my right hand
that were holding my spear smacked off a sharp stone and the staff
slipped out of my hand and skittered away. Pain lanced across my
knuckles in a quick white burn and I had to scrabble around until I*

found the butt of the rowan staff.

Barbara's scream lanced through my brain again as she broadcast her fear on a wavelength that was finely tuned to mine. I reeled back with the force of it, and through watered eyes I saw Colin drop his bow and raise both hands to the sides of his head. Barbara's terror subsided and my head cleared.

I hit Colin on the shoulder to attract his attention.

'Over there,' I bawled. 'That's where she is.'

He picked up his bow that he'd carried all the way from our den in the valley and followed me past the pillars of the stalagmites.

The scream came again, piercing our heads, and more shattering for its closeness, and then I saw Barbara on a clear, flat piece of stony ground near the centre of the great cave. She was twisting and turning as if some invisible hands were grabbing her, and above her head there was a darkness in the air that was like a web, getting bigger and bigger, and descending down on the spot where she frantically struggled.

'What is it?' Colin yelled. 'What's doing that?'

'Just get her away,' I yelled back, and staggered through the force of Barbara's pain towards her.

Her pain was my pain, and it was Colin's too. We had to bear it to get to her and it was as if hot coals were inside my head, burning out everything, every thought. But there was some power in us that was greater than the pain, some binding force that was between Barbara and Colin and me that dredged up the determination to beat it. My eyes were streaming and my yell was hoarse in my throat, but Colin got there ahead of me to where Barbara squirmed against the unseen hands. Above her the black mass pulsed and danced, expanding from nowhere down towards both of them. Colin grabbed at her flailing hand and I reached them in time to get a grip of the other, and as we did so there was a blinding, searing flash of light that scoured the immense cavern into sharp relief and then the dark closed down on all of us, leaving us with after-images burned into the backs of our eyes. But the white-hot pain was gone.

Barbara sobbed in the darkness, hugging us both.

'Oh Colin. Nicky. I was hurting,' she moaned in the afterburn of the agony.

'Yeah, I know,' Colin said. 'But you're all right now. We've got you.'

She started crying then, from relief, maybe, or it could have been just shock.

And then she did something that she'd never, ever done before.

She pulled Colin's head towards her and kissed him hard and desperately, and then she turned and kissed me too, forcing her lips on mine so powerfully that I could feel the wet tears on her cheeks.

'I love you,' she said softly. 'I love you both. And I'll love you for ever.'

Colin and I just sat there, with Barbara between us, in the middle of the big cave, holding on to each other as if we could never let go.

Gradually, the after-images faded from our eyes and the dim green light cast shadows all around us.

Colin was the first to notice the soldiers. The hairs on the back of my neck began to prickle.

THIRTY-ONE

'This is where it was.'

'I know. I remember,' Colin said in a low voice that carried up into the shadows of the vast cave. How deep we were under that huge rock, I cannot say. I couldn't even tell you whether the time and space actually existed in the way that we know it, but even so, it was real to us then, as it had been before; a hole in the very fabric of rightness. The creaking, slithering sounds of bodies in rapid decay had died away. Around us lay the dry husks of the dead in their armour, their skins, and their rough woven rags. There was a stick-like rattle as a bone settled within dry skin, a metallic click as a helmet shifted on a decayed skull, and then silence. The kind of silence that is big and desolate and solid enough to feel.

The eerie green light showed the shadows of his face and limned the circle of sucked-out bodies that lay in concentration-camp heaps all around us. As we stared, wide eyed, the question arose in my mind. Was it time that caused the decay, or was it Cu Saeng sucking out the last drops from the souls he'd stored in his lair?

'It's coming,' Colin said, breaking off my thought. I nodded. I could feel it, deep inside me, where instinct crouches, seeing danger in the shadow, alert for the horror of night. Colin stood stock still, and I could see the emotions flick across his face, each fighting for control. He was scared, and so was I. After twenty years in the miasma that had been his life since the first time we'd been here, he had woken up, and he had good reason to be afraid. He had come alive, come to an instant manhood, making the transition from being a child without the benefits of sunny teenage years and hectic adolescence. He knew he was about to face what had robbed him of those years, and he was terrified.

But his teeth were clenched tight, making the muscles on his cheeks stand out; he was holding the fear within himself, and his knuckles, gripped on the rowan staff, would have been pure white if there had been enough light to see them by.

We stood in the silence, in the half light, feeling the change in the air, the charge in the air; a vibration that pulsed, almost imperceptibly, through the rock and through us.

From far in some distant place, the pulse came again, like a faint whisper of pretend life, like a creeping cold breath, like a black, sluggish heartbeat. Then again, a little louder, a little stronger. Then again. Closer. Bigger.

There was another jarring vibration under my feet, and I saw Colin shift his stance as the pulse shot through us. I touched his shoulder and motioned him away from the centre, across to the wall. Paddy clung tightly to me as we waded through the mound of bodies that crackled like sticks under our feet. There was no way to avoid it. They sagged like so many empty sacks.

The pulse echoed again through the chamber, a deep rumble that shook us again. It was a noise that came beating up from the depths of eternity, rushing towards us from across a vast distance of time, fleeting direct to the *now* that we were in. I felt Paddy stiffen against me, her hands still locked into the fabric of my jeans and my jacket. Colin raised his spear.

The roaring rushing noise got louder until it filled the cavern, pounding so deep and huge that it hurt deep inside our heads, and then there was a juddering roar that shook through the rocks, tilting the floor as if a wave of anger had passed through it like a seismic shock.

And it was there.

A black mass that was huge and ponderous, hunched in the basin of rock at the centre of the cavern close to where we had been standing. Around it the air crackled and

swirled in a maelstrom that was like the centre of a hurri-
cane that whipped around a hub with vast force. In that
storm I could make out the huge shape that had no form,
blacker than black.

And from it I could feel waves of hate and hunger that
drilled right through me.

Cu Saeng was there.

'Get back, Colin,' I urged again, shouting to make
myself heard over the terrible pounding and the shrieking
of riven air, and he nodded, almost to himself, eyes fixed
on that whirling air-pool where thunderclouds, compressed with immense force so that they were almost solid,
were hurled about in the maelstrom that was sucked in a
spiral right into the rock itself. There was a red-orange
glow at the edges of the basin, as if great heat were building up by the forces that caused the swirl, and a roaring
rumbling noise that shuddered the rock under our feet.

'What is it?' Paddy shrieked, and the wind took her
voice away and shattered it on the black walls.

All I could do was hold her tighter. The swirling dark
tornado screwed itself into the basalt, faster and faster.
Looking on to the storm was like looking into infinity, as if
everything was so compressed in there that if I looked
carefully I would see whole star systems, squeezed by
malignant force and tumbled about like toys in the hands
of some great power that should not ever be able to exist.

I felt myself drawn against my will towards the edge of
the pit, a compulsion to see further into the tortured air.
To see the thing that sat at the centre. I tried to stop
myself, but I took a step forward anyway. Then another.
The second step was an effort, because I tried to pull my
foot back, to will it to stay where it was, but it was impossible.

I felt myself being pulled towards that swirling mass,
and I almost screamed with pure fear, and with the exertion
of trying to prevent that third step, and I felt my muscles
and bones grind as they pulled against my volition.

In my head, a child's voice (and it was mine) was shouting:

No no *no*! as the terror of dream sequence became a reality. Panic screwed right into my spine and my crotch tightened in a muscular spasm as everything in my body tried to escape.

The forth step was a physical and mental agony as my mind screamed its fear at me. My survival instincts were overloaded to explosive point, and through my head ran pictures of the horrors I would suffer when it got me.

The pit had me. I was being forced into it.

The only movement I could make (of my own volition) was to grab Paddy by the hair – it was the only part of her my hand could reach in that split second – and peel her off me. I threw her down on to the ground, and while it did nothing to dilute the fear that was a runaway train inside my head, below all that, below the terror and strain of avoiding that pit, there was a little glimmer of satisfaction that it wasn't going to get her as well.

My right foot dragged over the stone. It made a scraping sound that I was strangely aware of, over and above all the roaring and screeching of the tortured air, and then I was at the edge of that pit which only moments ago had been only a few yards wide. Now it had stretched out like a great volcanic cauldron. Its edges were red where the rock bubbled without warmth, against which the great swirling galaxies of matter that looked like twisted clouds were screaming and tearing.

One more step and I was going to fall a million miles in one vast continuous scream, falling like Lucifer from heaven into the depths of hell. It was going to have me. It was going to . . .

. . . and then I was flat on my back, and the scream that had been building up under pressure in my tightened lungs came out as a groan as my breath was slammed out of me. Colin's hand was on my collar. He'd almost jerked me out of my shirt and jacket with the force of his desperate heave.

'Don't do that, Nicky. Don't go in there,' he said. From the look in his eyes, he must have thought I'd had a choice in the matter. In that moment, all I could think of was that I was alive, and that I wanted to hold him tight and tell him thanks.

Sweat had broken out on my forehead and was running into my eyes. I wiped them with the back of my hand, and let my clothes take care of the rest that had drenched my entire body. I had heard of cold sweat before. This was the first time I had ever really experienced it. I was clammy and I felt as if I wanted to be sick. Fear does that to you, and there is no fear greater than staring death in the face and knowing it has come for you.

Colin kept his hand on my collar and helped me across to the wall, away from the pit. On my other side I felt Paddy's hand on my shoulder, and I hoped I hadn't hurt her too much when I pulled her hair.

'Don't look at it,' I warned them. 'It pulls you in.'

'I won't,' Paddy said.

'What is it?' Colin asked, for with the swirling storm that raged over the edge of the rim, the bulk that hunkered in the depths couldn't be clearly seen. You could just feel the pressure of its hunger and its hate. Its evil was dead-alive.

'It's the . . . .'

The thick, swirling corkscrew of the storm blasted apart with a sonic boom of shattering intensity, like the scream of a thousand jet engines, like the rending of a mighty bomb. Rocks tumbled from high above. A stalactite broke off and lanced down like a missile to shatter on the rock below. The dry carcasses that sprawled on the floor were blown upwards and away, like rags in a high wind, crumping and crumbling against the walls. Everything flashed out in the red-hot pain that stabbed through my head, then flickered back again.

And I saw what we'd come for.

The hunched shape loomed from the centre of the cauldron, a twisted, angled blackness that seemed to grind as it moved. It was solid, yet not solid, crystalline, yet viscously liquid. It was a thing that didn't *belong*.

When I looked at it, sometimes I thought I could see it clearly, then there would be a flicker, and it would change. It was a huge bloated *dark*, an impossible, dizzying presence that had no real form, only a hunger and a hate and an anger that you could feel so hard with your mind that it was solid. It was as if the thick, warped air had congealed into a twisting, pulsing horror that had an intent that was not of this earth, and a mind that was so cold and evil it froze the air around it. The black shape contracted and expanded impossibly, shifting and warping on itself in incessant motion. Its geometries were hideously wrong and the impossibility of its existence hurt the eyes.

And it was vast, vaster than the space that it had created in this place to crouch in. It was as if the space around it had been twisted and distorted and ripped apart to allow this thing to be.

I could feel the focus of its will as it cast around in the cave. It turned around through itself and speared me with the appallingly repugnant alien-ness of its thought. It was as if a cold, scaly hand had reached through me into my heart and squeezed tight.

A shock of revulsion shook me from head to foot as the horror of that mind probed mine. I could feel it like icy claws scrabbling through the nooks and crannies of my brain. There was a shrieking pain right down my spine as the thing flexed and raked me, and then . . .

It changed. The icy claws pulled out of me, leaving me weak and gasping. There was a lurching sensation inside my head, and the black, amorphous mass in the pit roiled and humped and changed, crackling like cooling lava, elongating. It reared up high, and from the pinnacle a shape formed.

My grandfather stood there before me. Tall and gaunt, a shimmering figure of shadow outlined in greater black.

There was a creaking sound as his head – looming twenty, maybe thirty feet above mine – swivelled, and he leaned out of the mass of dimensionless black and stared into my eyes.

434

Then he smiled, a great wide smile, that chilled me as much as the dead-alive cold touch of Cu Saeng's mind had done.

My grandfather. Why?

Why did this beast keep putting my grandather up against me? I'd loved that old man, uncompromisingly, unquestioningly. He had been the great foundation stone of my childhood. He'd taught me and helped me and loved me in the same way that I'd loved him. He'd been the one who, with Kitty MacBeth, had dragged me out from under the rockfall down here all those years ago. He'd been the one who'd scoured the countryside and had organised the local farmers to help. He'd been the one who'd backed me and encouraged me and helped make me what I am.

I would have done anything for my grandfather, and when he'd died, when I was still in my early teens, I would have done anything to bring him back. Now he was back. But it wasn't him. It was the beast, the Cu Saeng, the ravener, who was bringing this shape back to mock him and terrorise me.

The smile widened, became a grimace, a yard wide, high over me.

'Ah, Nicky boy,' his voice came from a cavern of a mouth, rumbling up from a hideous depth, hoarse and flinty.

'You've come back again, have you? Back to the place I told you never to go!'

'What do you want?' I yelled, though no words came out. It was a shout straight from my mind that was still pinned in the grip of that vice.

'I want you, Nicky, my lad. I want you to come and join me. We can be together again. You and me. For ever.'

'No. It's not you. It's him. Go away.' This time, the words came out, and they sounded like the words of a child. High pitched and scared against authority.

'Yes, Nicky. Come to me. But throw it away,' the voice boomed inside my head.

435

'You're not my grandfather. You're it. Get out of my head. *Get out!*'

The thing that looked like a grotesque image of my grandfather leaned impossibly far out of the pit until it loomed over my head. The eyes changed from deepest black, shading grey then milky to maggoty white, like a blind snake's eyes. They rolled, the head swivelled, and they stared down into mine, sucking my will.

'Yes, Nicky. You have to throw it away. That's my walking stick, and we don't want that down here. We don't want that at all. You be a good boy and throw it away, because it's mine, and I don't want you to have it.'

'No. Get away from me. Leave me alone,' I cried.

'I'm old, Nicky boy. Old. And I need you to help me. But you don't want that old walking stick in here with me. It's a bad old hawthorn cromach. A bad old haw. We don't want that here. It's bad.'

I gripped the stick tighter. Somebody had said something about hawthorn. Was it Kitty MacBeth? And before, the time we were here before. What had happened?

The memory surged back to me then. It was Colin then. Colin with his bow and hawthorn arrows. He'd fired at the thing then, and hit it in the eye. And that had helped stop it then. The hawthorn. That's what was important. I needed it with me.

'No!' I shouted, probably aloud, although I'll never be sure.

'Throw it away now,' my grandfather roared in a voice that rose to a screeching crescendo that threatened to rip my head apart. I felt myself screaming, though I couldn't hear the words, and even as I did so, I felt another thought slipping into my head.

I don't know where it came from, or how it got past the iron talons that thing had hooked into my brain, but it came fleeting in and I heard the voice of Kitty MacBeth, Catriona O'MacConnor MacBeatha, old and wise, talk to me from within.

'A wall of hawthorn that was sacred because there is the

436

power in that wood, like the rowan tree. It is an earth power that is stronger in the earth-day born. A weapon to fight the Cu 'Saeng.'

And then I knew why it wanted me to throw away the hawthorn stick. The thing was afraid of its power. When that thought hit me, it came on a great wave of anger that washed up and over and through me. Anger at the destruction this thing had brought time and time again to Arden, anger at what it had done to Kitty MacBeth and to Barbara and Colin and all the rest. In my mind's eye, I saw Duncan Bennett's hideously swollen face. I saw that little shin with the black shoe on the foot that dangled from the pig's mouth and my anger swelled. I felt hot fury against its wanton mind-lust, the fear-hunger that fed the madness it spawned and sent out from the rock. I knew then that if we didn't manage to stop it, to kill it for ever, what had happened to Arden was only a starter for what it could do if it were free.

Suddenly my mind seemed to jink and twist out of the grasp that had pinned me to the rock and I jumped up and forwards towards that twisted thing that sometimes looked like my grandfather, and talked like a festering disease.

I raised the stick high over my head and swung it with all the strength I had, the strength of righteous fury, with the knobbly handle pointing forward. I smashed it right into that mad head that loomed above me.

There was a shock of impact that ran like fire up my arm, then a horrendous snap as reality twanged back and forth, and the thing at the centre of the pit let out a scream of pain and anger and hate that caused the walls to shake. I heard myself yelling like a berserker and battered at it with my stick as it shimmered and changed before me, resorbing back into the black mass in the pit.

From behind, I heard Colin roaring like the bull at McFall's farm. He darted in front of me with the spear raised, and the white lines on his head standing out like war plumes. His back bent as he coiled, then launched himself forward. His arm whipped past his head in a blur

437

of motion as he drove the point of his spear-head right at the great white eye that had re-positioned itself near the top of the black shape.

The spear crackled through that warped no-space membrane and seemed to travel in slow motion, centimetre by centimetre, until the obsidian point met the white orb that glistened wetly with obscene luminescence. The stone of power touched the horrid pupil-less eye with a rending sound. Pale viscous stuff bubbled out sickly, but Colin didn't stop there. He put his whole weight on the staff and shoved it further until the whole stone point was buried deep inside that eye, and half a yard of mountain ash with it.

The necrotic fluid dripped out and on to the stone where it hissed and bubbled, sending up a cloud of thick, choking fumes.

I pulled Colin back, forcing him to let go his grip on the spear, in case any of that stuff dripped on to him. I knew it would burn for ever.

Another mental blast, this time of anger and pain, came blistering out of the shape and almost knocked us sideways. The black thing seemed to go into a frenzy. It expanded up and out of the pit in a great shuddering motion that hurt the eyes to watch. The spear angled straight out of that jutting, pallid eye, and it seemed as if the thing were trying to shake it loose. Beside the spear, there was another eye that was half-closed and crumpled as if it had rotted away. There was a smaller shaft sticking out from the puckered lid and foetid stuff oozed from the wrinkled corner.

That was where Colin had fired his dart two decades ago, before the Cu Saeng had reached out and grabbed him and stolen his mind.

Another roar rent the air, and that huge, eyeless face twisted towards us, looming impossibly large, twisting and changing as if seen through frosted glass. I scrabbled backwards on the rock to get away and Colin tripped us on a stone. Behind us Paddy screamed.

I twisted towards her and she was pointing at the pit and I almost racked my back turning to face the other way again.

From the centre of the black bulk there was a movement and a scraping sound, like rocks being ground
together. The shape shifted and expanded as two masses
formed on each side, growing quickly out from the main
body. They literally grew, like black crystals rimmed with
sick green light, elongating, building on themselves from
the warped air.

My stomach lurched as I got an instant sensation of déjà
vu. It was coming for us, and I could not avoid it.

The final vision of what had happened down here at the
rock finally clicked into my head and suddenly I was a kid
again, terrified out of my wits, almost screaming with a
mad fear.

In a clarity of a memory that had never seen the light of
day before, I saw Colin's arrows streak towards that malignant eye, and then an arm snaked out across that terrible
distance and grabbed him. Great claws opened and
snapped shut on his head and lifted him slowly off the
ground. The claws tightened and Colin had started to
scream. But it was a mind-scream, a wave of pure agony
that had ripped through Barbara and me and had shaken us
to the core. His pain was so intense that he was broadcasting it to us soundlessly as the claw that had grown out of
the thing in the pit had squeezed and squeezed, and the
cold of the beast had lanced into his head. What Barbara
and I had felt were mere echoes of what Colin had suffered in those seconds as Cu Saeng took his revenge for
the hawthorn arrow, but it had been intense enough to
make my legs buckle and make me sink to the ground.

With that memory right in the forefront of my mind, I
realised what was happening in the pit. It was coming for
us again. It wanted its revenge.

We watched in fascination, like rabbits facing a stoat, as
the growths flickered in faceted lattices towards us. It happened quickly, but it was like being frozen, watching time-
lapse photography. The two elongated growths crackled
into being, building their way across the space towards us,
arms that reached out.

'Get back! Get away from it!' I bawled at Colin, trying to scrabble back from those reaching arms.

The thing was now blind, but it could sense us just as well without its eyes. At the sound of my voice, one of the extrusions shot straight across the intervening space, hissing through the web of compressed time, popping through into our space. It split at the end into a branch of claws that opened wide then snapped shut around my leg. Instantly a pain jolted right through my body in a cold, searing surge that was like electricity jolting right into raw nerves. The pain arched my back in a spasm that snapped me to the ground. My shoulder hit a sharp protrusion of rock with a thump, but that pain was lost in the roar of the agony express that was whistling through the main line inside me. I jerked like a galvanised frog and saw, impossibly, the crystalline growth spread from the claws, growing outward and into my flesh. I could feel the harsh rasp as the extra fingers popped into existence, binding me tight to that jointed arm. I could feel the stony texture gripping my knee, gripping right into my knee, and the surge of panic that ripped through me was so strong it killed the pain for a second. But that second was the only respite, the pain thundered back on a wavecrest, shooting through my body, blasting up my spine, exploding in my brain.

Pain.

I cannot adequately describe it. Red-hot irons do not come close. Sulphuric acid dripped on an open wound is only a starter. The pain surged in me and through me in such vast jolts that at that moment I would have done anything to make it stop.

The grip tightened as the growth spread up through my leg, eating into me, becoming part of me, and converting me to its own substance.

Beside me I heard Colin scream, and I saw him locked in the grip of those claws that had grown out of the thing. His pain was interfacing with mine, spanning the two decades since I'd seen him being sucked out of his head and losing his mind. The Cu Saeng had grabbed him and squeezed his brain until the blood ran out of his ears and it had eaten into him and discarded him.

But that was then. The screams I heard were not the agonised terror of a small boy. This was the hoarse shriek of a man in extremity. Colin was facing his own nightmare for the second time. I was whipped back to the present, and through the purple mist that had settled just behind my eyes, where the pressure of the pain threatened to make them pop straight out of their sockets, I saw Colin in that death grip. This time the claws on the end of those million-mile arms had locked around his chest and had spread out their fingers, burrowing into his ribs. Underneath the overlay of my own terror and agony, I was locked into what Colin was feeling. He was beaming it straight out at me, the way he had done before, and I cannot tell you which was worse. Feeling my own destruction, or sharing in his.

Cu Saeng had us in its grip. There was a rolling, coiling motion along those fast arms, as if something had flexed in the great bulk of the black thing that squatted – and still sent out its mental roar – in the pit. I was heaved up off the ground and high into the air. Beside me I was aware of Colin, struggling in a series of jerky spasms in the huge unearthly hand that gripped him. Up and up we were carried. Some internal eye in me was aware of the ground receding at a fantastic rate. Way down below, Paddy was a tiny figure. The ceiling raced towards us, it seemed for ever.

The arms that held us curled inwards and we were hauled in, like spent fish, over the pit. There was a shuddering sensation as we entered the roiling web of black that separated Cu Saeng in the twisted time membrane from the rest of the real world, the membrane that would shatter and rupture when all the walls were gone and there were no earth-day born to face him. And then we were through, into the place where the thing was.

There was a racking twist and we were in a vast hole, so big that the walls were way beyond our lines of sight, and the arms that held us were shrivelling down, de-forming but still gripping tight, as we were reeled towards the thing that seemed to grow from the bottom of the hole.

I was crying out at the pain, but there was no sound, except for the pulsing of the huge heart. Colin was broadcasting waves again that shook through me, but his screams were all from his mind. Down and down, twisting and turning, heading for the oblivion that awaited us. The arms shortened, became muscular, ropy extensions of the creature who sat in the depths. Brought us closer, and we were there.

Against the background of putrid luminescence the real shape of Cu Saeng came into view with an optical wrench that turned vision inside out.

It was a huge, warty thing with bulging eyes that were slitted and dripped a pus that smelled like dead swollen bodies. Here, in Cu Saeng's lair, the hawthorn dart that pierced the left eye, and the shaft that was lodged in the gaping tear in the other, shone with a clean fire. It was the only light that seemed natural in this place. It was more than natural. The light of the power burned forth from those horrible, puckered eyes, and through the pain that Colin was transmitting to me and through the agony that lanced with every heartbeat through my body, I could feel the suffering of this thing, and I knew that it could never get rid of that pain, if it lived for ever.

That thought sent a bolt of pleasure through me. Maybe pleasure is the wrong word, but it will do for now. At least I felt that it was right.

The thing brought us close to its face. It was covered in warts and nodules that swelled and burst and formed new sores on a hide that was continually in motion. I could smell its stink and feel the unclean emanations of its mind. This was something that should never have existed, on this earth or on any other. This was the dweller under the roots that had been called up by shamans who knew nothing of what they were summoning. This was the thing that had sent the madness into Arden time and time again since men lived in reed huts.

The very sight of it was offensive.

And now it had us down where it belonged. There was no going back.

I remember thinking, through the dismay that the feeling of being trapped for ever in anguish brought, that at least Paddy was safe. While it had its attention diverted, she could get away. Maybe we had hurt it enough to keep it from going back, no matter what it had in store for us.

Colin was pulled ahead of me, still writhing and twisting in the grip of that obscene claw. I watched as he was dragged towards the ridged, pulsating head that squatted on a wrinkled and wattled neck. Closer and closer. And then the grip seemed to tighten in a fast jerk, and I felt Colin's final agony as his body burst asunder. Blood flew in a cloud of red as every blood vessel seemed to rupture. It sprayed out of his ears (again, again) and in a great gout from his mouth. His jeans went from blue to red in an instant. And the grip kept tightening. There was a squeaky sound, and Colin's insides started coming out of his mouth. His eyes were black and popping out of his head. The ribs cracked in a short series of snapping sounds, and then his pain stopped coursing through me, leaving me only with my own. The clawed hand opened and Colin dropped. I watched him fall, down, down, into the darkness below, diminishing at speed until he was just a toy, just a dot, and then gone, as if he'd never existed.

Then it was just me and that thing, alone at the bottom of the hole, a million miles from anywhere.

The hand that had me in its multiplex of fingers pulled me in towards the face. By this time, I was beyond caring. The pain never lessened and I had reached the stage that I wanted only to die, to get it over with. In closer it dragged me, until I was right under the horny nose that was riddled with suppurating pores that dripped slimy ooze. From the eye closest to me, the one where Colin's spear had burst through, the putrescent viscid excretion was running in a nauseating rivulet down a horny cheek. Inside the turbid flow, there were things wriggling, like worms or maggots,

443

feeding off it, like bacteria that had been living inside the thing, and now had come out to graze. The smell was that of a week-old corpse that had been lying in hot sun.

I wanted to shout and scream at the thing to get on with it; to finish me off. The sight of it up close was worse than any nightmare. I wanted to wake up, even if I woke up dead.

The other hand, the one that had dropped Colin's mangled body into the black depths, clenched once, then opened, as the creature brought it up. It held me, like a mouse, and brought the other claw right up to my face. One long, gnarled finger poked out from the rest, then stabbed down, right into my eye, right into my brain, and the pain I had suffered before, on the way down as the acid grip burned its way into me, was like a soothing balm by comparison. Something lanced right into the back of my head and pulled me right out through the hole in my eye and took me away with it. I was hauled out, right out of me, and away. Down, into blackness, down below the bottom of the pit; slung for ever away into infinity.

I passed myself on the way, seeing me writhing and screaming, beside Colin in the grip of those hands. I saw myself watching the flow of Strowan's Well the second time, when we'd breached the stoppage, and the first time, when we'd burst the dam. I saw me lying in a crumpled heap under the rockfall, and my old grandfather scrabbling with the other men to free me. I saw my mother in her bed, giving birth to the slippery squalling thing that was me. And back, and back, to Kitty MacBeth on the foreshore, dressed in long black skirts, her hair golden and her face strong and beautiful – and so much like Barbara – watching the rock from the foreshore. And back, and back, to the horrors that had visited Arden down through the years. I saw fathers do horrible things to their children, to their daughters, in the dark, mad hours. I saw priests pray to the Devil. I saw a mother cut out the heart of her husband and feed it to her sons. I saw sacrifices at high tide, full moon, that sent rivers of blood along the runnels in the ring stones. I watched as the Roman soldiers fought shadows, thinking they were demons. I went back, and back, and watched as men in rough clothes and skins on their backs and antlers on their heads shook their bones and shrivelled hands on the rock and I saw it split asunder and the black cloud roll out, as though from the pits of hell, with lightning crackling all around it, and I saw the evil that was Cu Saeng being born into this world.

And before that, Arden was clean. I could see it, as my mind – or my soul or my spirit or whatever the essential me was – soared down that time tunnel.

Then I was drawn back, saw the cause and then the effect in sequence, all down that line of time, whipped back to the now, where my eye and brain were gouged out in that pit at the bottom of the world, and there was a great screaming and crying, and a blinding light and then I was in the cave again, and I could see, with both eyes. Colin was beside me. He was struggling and kicking, in the grip of the hand, but he was alive. And his pain was gone, disappeared, startlingly, suddenly, as mine had. I could no longer feel his mind-blast, the mental scream of one earth-day born, one one and only, to another.

There was a golden light that sent sparkles of pure brilliance high up into the rocky roof of the great cavern, a light that should have burned my eyes (my two *good* eyes) but merely washed them with a balm. It was coming from way down on the floor, a pinpoint of radiance that was like the brightest light at the end of the deepest tunnel.

There was a high-pitched screaming that was coming from far away, and it got louder as the hands that held us faltered, loosening their grip, and the arms that held us aloft seemed to lose some of their power, lowering us down from the arched roof. Cu Saeng's mind was diverted. He was not all-powerful, he couldn't concentrate his mind-force in every direction at once.

Colin and I had been jerked back through the time-web into reality, or what passed for reality in the middle of a waking nightmare.

THIRTY-TWO

In front of us, the humped shape shimmered, behind its membrane that looked like frosted glass. The surface crackled with black lightning, then part of it changed again, forming out of the surface as the arms had done, building obscene crystal on crystal, solidifying into a shape that took on human proportions. There was a flicker and the shape suddenly sprang into focus.

Barbara looked down at Paddy who was standing on a rock screeching her anger and pain.

She had called him up; ordered him to come back again. She had called him out. Suddenly the screaming I had heard, as if from a great distance, had tumbled around inside my head and formed into the words that had rebounded from the stony walls. Paddy had demanded that Cu Saeng come back and face her.

He had come back, bringing us with him, and he had sent her own mother to face her.

The things that looked like Barbara bent her head to the child, and said in a soft voice: 'It's all right my dear. Everything is fine now.'

The voice was like Barbara's on the surface, but underneath the soft tones was a hollow, rumbling growl that made it all the more numbingly horrible.

'I'm here now, and you're safe. Come to mummy now,' it said, leaning towards the girl. As it did, I saw it screw up its eyes, flinching from the light.

'No, Paddy!' I called out at the top of my voice. 'Get back. Run away from it. It's not your mother.'

Paddy's screech cut off abruptly. She just stopped and stared.

'Mommy?' Her voice high and incredulous. 'Mommy, is

that you?'

Colin's voice cut in desperately: 'No Paddy! It's the thing. It wants to kill you.'

'Come to mummy,' Barbara's image said, urgently. The rumbling undertone was a hiss. 'I'll take care of you. Just take that thing off your neck. It's a bad thing.'

Paddy's hand flew to her neck and touched the torc that had been the gift of Kitty MacBeth.

There's power in that, Kitty had said. And there was. The light that dazzled the eyes of the creature that protruded from the pit was coming from the simple band of gold; a pure white light that fought the shadows. And as Paddy's hand flew to her neck, it touched the torc, and her hand was bathed in a white flickering energy that was the exact converse of the black force that had skittered obscenely over the surface of the monstrosity in the pit.

'No!' Paddy yelled back. 'You're not my mother. She's in hospital.' She stamped a small foot on the rock in anger. 'And it was you that put her there. It was you that hurt my friends and made everything go bad. I hate you. I hate you for what you did.'

The thing that looked like Paddy's mother raised her arms towards the child, in a welcoming gesture. Under the skin I saw things twitch and squirm. Paddy stood her ground, and I couldn't force the warning out of my throat. The girl touched the torc again and there was a flash of brilliance, and the thing drew back with a hiss.

'You stay away from me!' Paddy shouted in a voice that was nearly a scream. 'I don't want you. I want you to die.'

The light flared more brightly, and the thing recoiled again. I felt the grip of the black growth on my leg slacken momentarily. On the other side, Colin was struggling frantically to get free, and I was scrambling for the hawthorn stick where it had fallen amongst the rocks. It was two feet from the furthest I could reach.

The thing that looked like Barbara started to waver and pulse. The face elongated as if it were being pulled from the centre into a mantis-like mask. Then the whole front

447

of it stretched out, became pointed, became a beak, like that of one of the birds Donald and I had seen spearing the fishermen out in the bay. The beak was hard and long and viciously pointed.

It opened in an impossibly wide gape until it could have swallowed us all whole, then the beak snapped shut. The neck uncoiled like a snake, rearing backwards, and I managed to call a warning to Paddy, who stood on the rock, staring as if mesmerised, just before it slashed down with a whip-like crack, stabbing at her with immense force.

Paddy seemed to start out of her trance, and just at the last moment she jinked to the side and spun as the beak hit off the rock where she'd been standing. The neck arched back for another strike. The mouth gaped open again and Barbara's laugh came out of it, and that was worse than the hissing cackle it turned into. On my leg, the hard grip slackened again as the thing concentrated its mind on the child, and I twisted to get free, turning to see Paddy back on the flat rock, staring up at the thing.

The great beak swivelled from side to side, as if in indecision, as Paddy yelled at it in her loudest voice, taunting it, challenging.

The apparition with the beak shrank back, away from the light, and started to merge itself back on to the black bulk that now heaved itself ponderously forward.

There was a split second of unearthly silence, a frozen moment of time, and then the air suddenly seemed to be charged with a wild force. The grip on my leg gave up completely, and I hauled myself to my feet, just as there was a crackling noise like an electrical discharge rupturing the air. I looked up to see the outline of the horror in the pit covered in a weird green sparkle that flickered like tiny arcs of lightning gathering together. It was drawing power from down there, gathering itself together for an assault. I could feel it tense, ready to surge, and every nerve in my body squirmed as the charges built up like a sparkling green fire, and then, without warning, the fire pulsed out in a lancing green bolt, pure, raw evilness that pulsed out straight towards Paddy, ripping through the no-time barrier right at her head.

My breath caught in my throat, and I heard Colin's gasp as that screaming surge of raw, mad power surged out . . . and then stopped dead, as if it had hit an invisible barrier.

Only a foot from her face, there was another light that seemed to surround the girl, sending off sparkling shafts from her golden hair. The torc was a blaze of real power, white and blinding. On her neck it was a line of fire and it radiated its pure energy, pure *clean* energy outwards. It diffused through her body in a radiance that was stunning in its purity. It danced along her arms and down her legs, sparkling into the ground.

The weird green power hissed and crackled as one force met another. There was a smell of ozone, as if a mighty charge had jumped from one contact to another. Paddy and the thing were locked in a vast power struggle that left Colin and me helpless. We couldn't even move.

Paddy stood there, eyes locked firmly on the shadowy bulk that was hidden behind the web. She was standing with her hands at her side and she radiated power. She was tiny and defiant and she was magnificent.

For a moment in time she was the power of the prophecy. Whatever was locked in that golden torc, whatever magic had been forged into its making, was now in her. The two combined in something that was greater than both. Maybe it was her fear, but I think it was her anger that finally unlocked the key to the gift of Kitty MacBeth. And I reckon Paddy was the only one who could have opened that door and become the power.

It seemed that the two forces battled each other for ever. The blinding, brilliant white that pulsed out from Paddy, and the evil, sick, crackling power that rammed out from the monstrosity.

But Paddy's power was not just of the torc. It was in her, and it *was* her. The prophecy that Kitty MacBeth had told me down on the shore was manifest in that child, and she *knew*, with an instinct that had been passed down to her through the ages, what real power was.

I watched as her shoulder gave a twitch, and the strap of the water bottle that she'd carried since we left the nightmare of the tunnel under the road slid down her arm. She swung it loosely and caught it in her free hand. Her eyes were still locked in the strange mind-to-mind duel with the creature. I saw her twist the top and it came free.

'You hurt everything,' I heard her say. No screaming, no screeching. No fear. 'You hurt my mother, and my friends, and you make everything dark.'

Her voice seemed to deepen and smooth out. There was less of an American accent. It sounded more like the voice of someone who might live down on the foreshore, at one with the firth and the birds and the winds.

'You tried to kill us, but you can't kill us, because you don't belong here. You're nothing now. You made everything wrong, but we have been here since forever.'

Her voice, calm and matter of fact, deadly cool, hitched up an octave.

'All of this is your fault. All of the killing.'

She paused, as if for breath, and then she screamed, high and clear, in a battle cry.

'Now I'm going to kill *you*!'

She bent her slim body and swung the water bottle round her head.

In a flickering picture I saw the image of the old priest who dipped his thumb in the water and put a drop on my forehead. He gave me the bottle of Strowan's Well water, cold and clear from the stream that had been the powerful barrier against the worst ravages of Cu Saeng. What prophetic power had been in that old man?

Like a sling-shot, once, twice, three times it swung. Then Paddy let it go. It spun out of her hand, tumbling up through the green crackling line of roiling fire, twisting in the air, and sending out a curve of droplets that caught the fire that radiated out from Paddy and the shining torc on her neck.

The water bottle whipped across the edge of the pit and

travelled in a high parabola, slicing through the timeless web, directly at the black thing. It hit with a thud and the water splashed out in a shimmering spray and splashed all over the black mass. There was an instant, shuddering recoil and an immense tearing sound of pure, unearthly agony. The thing convulsed as if an explosion had erupted within.

In the pit, the monstrous being writhed and swelled. Through the rent in the barrier I watched it collapse in on itself, the horrendous wailing rising to a crescendo. It looked as if it had been burned with acid that was eating away at it as it wriggled. A green-black noxious vapour belched up from where the water had struck.

The obscene tearing scream got higher and higher, louder and louder, and the foul fumes got thicker, filling the cavern with a choking, acrid cloud. There was a bubbling, smacking sound as the thing swelled and burst, dripping like molten plastic in a hole. The earth shook as if a huge explosion had been set off deep in the bowels of the world.

Then the wailing died away into a burbling moan, and then there was silence. The thing started to shrivel, like the corpses of the victims had when they were loosed from their no-time cages. The strange barrier that had surrounded Cu Saeng ripped apart and I got another brief glimpse of the obscenity. But this time, the power and the evil were diminishing.

There was another cracking sound as the shadow in the pit contracted in on itself, folding and warping, losing whatever shape it had. It got smaller and smaller, as if it were falling down a deep hole into hell. Then there was a sudden, strangely soft pop, like a tension being loosened, as it dwindled to a pinpoint. It seemed to shoot away at speed into another space, and it was gone.

Paddy stood on the rock, staring into the hole, and Colin and I stared at her, watching as the radiance flickered around her fingers, pulsed at her neck. But now the thing was gone, it was a softer radiance, fading to a warm glow.

Paddy's face was serene, composed. The radiance died to a mere glimmer.

We stood there for long moments, frozen.

Then came a rumbling noise from the pit. My eyes caught a movement, thinking the thing had returned, but no, Cu Saeng was gone from this world. It was the void he had left, filling itself in. Forces were gathering and compressing to re-adjust the very earthspace that he had pushed aside to exist here. The pit was being filled in.

Colin jumped up and grabbed Paddy before I could get to her, and swung her off her feet and into his arms.

'Quick, Nicky. We have to get out of here.'

Just as he said that, the walls shook with a deep sonic shock as the ground readjusted itself. Another stalactite fell from the vaulted arch and crashed on to the spot where rock was being compressed and heaved to cancel the vacuum.

Colin was ahead of me. We ran for it. Another spear of rock shot down and shattered in fragments that ricocheted off walls, sending tiny sharp fragments spattering on our backs. We raced into the cleft and skittered up that narrow passageway, Colin carrying Paddy as I had carried him, battered and bleeding, the first time.

We never broke our stride, although the walls of the fumarole juddered and heaved as the dying spasms of Cu Saeng's passing twisted the earth all around us out of true.

It seemed we ran for an age, through the twisting tunnels, then at last we saw light ahead of us. True light. Daylight. I had taken Paddy from Colin on the last stretch, again without breaking stride, and her arms were tight around my neck as I sprinted for that light triangle, with Colin's footsteps thudding hard behind me.

Just feet from the cave mouth, there was a last, final, cataclysmic shudder that rippled right through the rock and almost knocked me off my feet.

But I remembered the rockfall from the last time, and I just knew it would happen again. I kept going, retaining my balance just at the last moment. All around us, rocks started peeling off the walls and crashing down like bombs. I put an arm up to protect our heads, and maybe it was luck or maybe the residue of the power that Paddy had displayed down in that hellish arena that got us through unscathed while behind us the tunnel was filled with the roaring of falling stone as if the whole twisting cavern was imploding.

We streaked out of the dark and into the day just as the rock erupted in that final heave and great shards of stone came off the cliff face in an avalanche that brought down tons of basalt. The earth shook under our feet with the force of that massive landslip, but we were well past it and heading for the trees before the big rocks landed, sealing that cave mouth for ever under half a mountain of stone.

Just at the trees, I slipped and went down, instinctively twisting to avoid crushing the child, who, it seemed, I'd carried non-stop for the last couple of days. My breath went out of me for a moment, and I lay there still, with Paddy locked in my arms, looking up at a clear blue sky. Colin stopped and hunkered down close to me as I got my breath back.

Behind us, the rumble of falling rock was diminishing, and a cloud of dust was billowing out from where the cave mouth used to be. I rose to watch the last of it, dimly aware that my backside was covered in what I'd landed in and not caring less. A light wind soon dispersed the dust.

Paddy loosened my arm, then threw her arms around my neck and planted a big kiss on my lips. Then she reached for Colin and did the same. She held on to both of us, just a wisp of a girl, tiny and slender, and looked earnestly from me to Colin.

'I love you, Nick. I love you, Colin,' she said. Then she hugged us again.

And in that moment the memory of her standing on the rock and facing down the monstrosity came back. I knew Colin was also seeing the picture. And we loved her too. For ever.

I hauled myself to my feet and Colin stood beside me, with Paddy between us. She put her hands in ours and we walked through the now-quiet forest where the sunlight lanced through the trees as the light breeze sent dust motes dancing prettily in the beams.

Behind us loomed the bulk of Ardhmor Rock. Strangely, it held no threat. It was just another lump of rock on the firth, the worn-down remains of a long-dormant volcanic plug.

Paddy and Colin and I walked towards the edge of the forest where the fields opened up at the silver fork of Strowan's Well, and the path would take us up to Arden in the sunlight.

It took Arden a whole long time to settle down again. In fact the process of healing takes a long time. The scars are raw, but they are healing, slowly. Painfully.

The council's roadworkers breached the landslip blockage on the Kilcreggan Road west of town just about the time that Paddy and Colin and myself were tumbling out of the fumarole and into the light. Things started to get better from then on. That was the start of the aftermath.

The road crew squeezed through the gap they'd cleared and trundled into a town that was still in the shaky grip of the nightmare. Nobody had had any idea of what had been going on. It was as if Arden had slipped out of real time for a spell and had suddenly been brought back again. Maybe that's just what happened.

Then came emergency teams. Oh, and newspapers and television crews by the score, who buzzed in like flies round a fresh kill. They must have knocked on every door in the parish, and panned every view that was worth swinging a wide angle on, and they drank the Chandler dry.

The TV crews drove their units slowly along the house fronts where curtains stayed firmly closed against the light of day. They took shots of dead animals and crashed cars, and the rare inhabitant they managed to catch out in the open, slowly walking the pavement slack eyed, numbed. Arden made prime time. The headlines screamed *nightmare* and *madness*. Names were named, gory deeds were charted and in detail. There were inquiries, investigations. Teams of scientists mingled among the swarm of reporters, each only too ready to get their face on TV and their names in print with as many theories as there were dead bodies, and that was plenty.

When the medical and scientific teams eventually got down to serious business, it was the ergot, that stray fungus spore, that got the blame for the whole sorry mess. It has happened before, in other places in other times, when the powerful hallucinogenic wheat fungus has caused mass hysteria, mass *madness*. It was convenient enough, and realistic enough, to let the brains trust indulge in a mutual back-slap and wrap up the mystery. Arden, dazed and shambling, knew better than that. Maybe it didn't know the full story, but the people of the town *knew* that it wasn't just the ergot, knew there was something deep dark and old that had woken up and fed and was now gone. By some unspoken intuition, Arden kept its mouth shut about such matters.

Officialdom totted up the bodies and the missing (never to be found again in all but a few cases) and there were fifty-two.

At the seminary, twenty priests had died on their knees in the chapel, praying for who knows what, burned as they prayed, oblivious to the fire that raged through the seminary. They never found a cause for that fire. Old A.J. was one of them, that good old man with the face of fury and a heart bursting with humour. I wish I'd got to know him better. I won't forget, not *ever*, that without him, and his special gift, we would never have made it out of that festering hole. The nightmare would still be going on, and I reckon it wouldn't have stopped at our little parish boundary. The old monsignor gave us the gift of water that allowed Paddy to complete the prophecy that was made long before the old priest's God came out of the desert.

Billy Ruine was dead. Donald shot him through the head at a hundred yards, and the old man took a shotgun blast through the leg that took a long time to heal. We found him at the path to the farm, where he'd set up his last stand, patching up the mess on his leg with pieces of his shirt. He'd lost a lot of blood, but he's a tough old guy. Without him at our backs we'd never have made it.

Alan Scott they found a week later, in his car, or what was left after the bluebottles had done a fair job of stripping everything clean. He was the only Milligs boy I ever heard of who made it to Upper Arden, and it's a damn shame. His wife didn't stay long in town. I reckon she cut the price by a fair chunk just to get rid of it and fled to God knows where. Some others did too.

Jimmy Allison died of a broken neck. That was just put down as an accident, and while it could have been, I don't believe it. I stopped believing in coincidences some time back.

They found Mary Baker blown up like a blimp, and they took Tom Muir away, along with other bits and pieces from his butcher shop. He's still in the local mental hospital without limit of time, and there's no way he's getting out again. There's another couple of folk who joined him because they just didn't make it back from where they'd been flipped over by that thing under the rock. Brian from the arty crafty shop was one of them. He makes baskets when he's lucid. I'm told the sight of a candle lands him in the rubber room.

John McFall hanged himself, and his other young son was found wandering in the Kilmalid glen scared of anything that moved. They dug out what was left of his little brother from that mean old pig that Duncan shot.

They fixed up the old bridge on the east side at Milligs end and, with the official opening of the ring road, traffic came in decreasing numbers. The flood of pressmen trickled away as other catastrophies hit other places and Arden became a kind of sleepy hollow, which was good. It gave us all time to start pulling ourselves together. As I've said, Arden has been around a long time. It's survived before. The town just wanted to be left alone to start the slow process of recovery.

Now you may think, like so many other people, that all this *can* be put down to the chance mishap of the ergot spores landing in just the right place for it to grow without the threat of chemical pest control at the seminary's green acres. A freak mass psychedelic trip into hell.

Well, you can think that if you like. Maybe I imagined it all.

But remember, not everybody ate the bread at the festival. I know for a fact that neither Paddy nor Barbara had any. Donald has had coeliac disease most of his life and can't eat anything with gluten in it. I didn't have any that day.

And ergot doesn't have the effect on animals that it has on humans, but bees, pigs, horses, dogs, they all went crazy at the same time.

Then there was those birds; the gannets that Donald and I saw down at the bay. Oh, they found the poor fisherman's body five miles down the coast on the foreshore at the Kilcreggan peninsula. Yes, the body was full of holes. There were three birds *still* attached to it.

Cu Saeng? Well, there are only a couple of people who know the full story. I wish old Kitty MacBeth was still around to tell me the full history. Old Catriona O'MacConnor MacBeatha, the Daughter of Heroes and the Sons of Life. She may have been dead, but she was with us all the way. And she gave me that golden torc for Paddy. That was her gift of life to us, her bequest. The fulfilment of her years of watching.

Only a couple of people know exactly what it was all about. The rest of the town have an instinct. They smile at me and Paddy and Colin and treat us with gentle respect. I can't explain why, but it's as if they *know* we were there, at the finish. They don't ask questions. They just seem to accept.

I'm willing to concede that some of the foregoing was all in our minds – like the roots, and those monstrous insects, the maggots in the cave. But if they were in our minds, then they were put there by something that had the power

457

to manipulate our thoughts. I know that force was real. I saw what I saw, we did what we did, and that's what happened.

As for me, I'm writing now. I've got a million ideas for stories and novels, all bubbling under the surface, just waiting to spill out. I'll get there yet, and when I start to write, then I'll do it without the handicap of writer's block. I can feel that those mental shackles have been struck off. But I've had to write this first.

My big Silver Reed has hummed and stuttered under my fingers.

I don't expect this story to sell, and frankly I don't give a damn. I just had to get this out. To burst the dam. To start fresh.

Sure. I still get nightmares. I wake up in a sweat and Barbara soothes my shoulders and holds me until the shivers pass, but those nightmares are fading. I'll live with them.

Barbara? She's in great shape now. She was in hospital for twelve weeks and spent a long slow time recovering, then another longer, more painful time in therapy, but she worked at that with a determination that I don't think I have. She was a bit unsteady on her legs when she got home, but she insisted on climbing those front stairs on her own, and the smile of triumph and joy on her face when she reached the top, lit up by the morning sun, is imprinted on my mind for ever. She came out of her coma, as near as I can estimate, just about the time her gutsy little heroine of a daughter was battling with that thing in the black pit. Barbara spent some time recuperating at home under the watchful eye of her father, and then she just came down to my place to stay with me, and that's the way it is.

I suppose I was falling in love with her before the crash, and there was certainly no question, once she got home, that the two of us were to be together. There's something special that binds us, and I think it's more than just the love between a man and a woman. It is something that was maybe *meant*, and from long ago. The old stone, down at the point, told something of that centuries ago, and I don't question it. We are very happy.

Paddy is certain to become the stunner her mother is. She came out of the whole thing better than any of us, and maybe that's because she had more power, or whatever it was that had brought the old prophecy to a focus. There was no trauma for her. No nightmares.

Most of the time, she is a normal kid, playing ordinary kid's games. But there are times when I look at her as she sits quietly, and I feel the serenity that is in her heart. She is the distillation of what made the one and onlies special.

Oh, and another thing. That golden torc around her neck never comes off. Unless it is cut in two, it never will. Whatever happened down in that hole under the rock, when Paddy and that thing were battling for the final outcome, the force of that fight fused the two golden balls together, welding them for ever, completing the final circle.

And Colin. Badger Blackwood.

And some people still call him that, and he doesn't mind. I occasionally use the nickname and there's no hurt in it. His hair is still the same, but his eyes flash bright fire, and he's one of the best people I have ever known.

Colin had a lot of catching up to do. He went out of the town and down to Strowan's Well a child, and came back a man. He went down to the rock to face the thing that had robbed him of his growing years and had stolen his youth, and he knew what he was doing. That speaks for itself.

Now he's all fire and high humour, as sharp as he was in those long ago days when he was the third one and only. He devours books at the library and has gone through all of mine and the stack that old Jimmy Allison left to me. He's been talking about going back to school to pick up where he left off. Before our episode at the sleeping rock, Colin's horizons reached no further than the parish boundary. Now they are boundless.

You can often find him down at old Kitty's shack, sitting on the step reading a book, and just occasionally staring across at the rock where it all began and where it all ended. He's taken over the job of watcher, although we both know he doesn't have to do it, because we killed it. He just does it, and that's that. He is working quietly on translating the whole of the message on the standing stone using the old book Kitty left behind, and he's promised to write it all down for us. Nobody else knows about that.

Colin keeps his hair cropped short and the white lines still show where the claws burned into his head way back at the start. But he's a good-looking guy and now gets a lot of sidelong glances in the street, where previously there was only pity. Linda, down at Holly's bar, seems to have a thing for him and both of them could do a lot worse. I keep hoping, because I love him a lot.

And then there's me. What can I tell you?

Kitty MacBeth told me I would have a long life, and while there were one or two times I would have reckoned she was dead wrong, maybe she was right after all. That old lady had some power, and it worked through long after that thing under the rock killed her, so, barring accidents, I am looking forward to a long and hopefully peaceful time, with the people that mean most to me.

The old woman said I would write, and I'm writing this to get the monkey off my back. After that, I've no fears. Donald limps a bit when he and I go fishing or birdwatching, or drinking up at the Chandler. (It took me six months to go back to Holly's to face John's wife, but Helen never said a thing, and from the look in her eye there was nothing to say. She's forgotten all about *that*.) Donald has taken the place of Jimmy Allison and my grandfather. He keeps my feet on the ground and he looks like he'll last for ever.

As you may have gathered, I live in Arden and probably always will. I remember, when I started this, driving along the Kilcreggan Road and wondering which way really was home. Now I know. This is it.

Arden is an old place, and with the ring road it's a quieter, more secluded spot than before, and maybe that's not a bad thing. It has some bad memories, but the cause is gone now, so we'll recover. We'll live to fight another day. The nightmare is over.

So maybe sometimes I wake up in the dark, hurtled out of a dream that has sent me back to both times when I saw Cu Saeng in his chamber, but I can live with that.

And as far as the story is concerned, I can only tell you that it happened.

Look out for
Joe Donnelly's
spellbinding new novel,
STILL LIFE,
published in Century hardback
January 1993.

THE SHEE

Joe Donnelly

Kilgallan – a small, quiet community on Ireland's west coast. Things at Donovan's Bar get a little raucous sometimes, and the people carry their share of Ireland's tragic history, but in Kilgallan, the fights are happy, the songs are sad, and the days are as rich as slow-poured, peaty beer.

It happens first to the children.

To little Mikey Boyle, whose auntie takes off all her clothes, takes off his too, and persuades him into the river . . .

To sweet Marie Lally, barely sixteen, when Mike O'Hara ties the cord around her neck and slides up her nightgown . . .

Village tragedies. Casual eruptions of horror . . .

But at the heart of a nearby hill, something turns in its sleep.

Breathes . . .

Awakes . . .

The Shee will put her fingers into your dreams, and leave you crying for more.

ROOFWORLD

Christopher Fowler

'A major new chiller writer takes a chair halfway between J. G. Ballard and Stephen King' – *Newsday*

High above London, on the rooftops of the city, lives a secret society of misfits governed by a bizarre code of honour. It is a world known to only a few people on the streets below – until the murderous battle for its leadership breaks out.

As the Roofworld fights to keep the powerfully evil Chymes and his occult worshipping followers at bay, Robert Linden and Rose Leonard, two innocent outsiders, are drawn into a twilight, dangerous world.

They face far greater terrors than they could have imagined. And the battle is on for the ultimate prize – London itself.

RUNE

Christopher Fowler

THERE ARE A MILLION WAYS TO DIE
THE DEVIL KNOWS THEM ALL

London is in the grip of an epidemic. Corpses with strips of paper bearing hieroglyphics are found across the capital. To his horror, advertising executive, Harry Buckingham is linked with these victims. Dodging the police he follows his own investigation to uncover the terrifying truth.

A multinational company has combined sophisticated technology with ancient mythology. They call it confrontational marketing. Harry calls it pure evil. The devil is loose in London. Who can stop the most hostile takeover bid of all time . . .?

CITY OF THE DEAD

Herbert Lieberman

**'I became afraid – literally afraid to turn the page'
– *New York Times***

Paul Konig is Chief Medical Examiner, New York City. Each day's grisly workload of strangled whores, battered babies and dismembered corpses is just routine to him. Contemptuous of the police, the public and his fellow doctors, he presides over the morgue like a monarch. But things can go wrong, even for Konig . . .

Suddenly a piercing, wrenching scream, followed by a lewd giggle in the background. 'Dr Konig . . . that was your daughter.' Another loud, wrenching scream. Then the phone is slammed down.

Not only has Konig's daughter been kidnapped, but he's up against a dead-end in the most gruesome multiple murder case of his career.

TOTAL RECALL

Piers Anthony

Based on a screenplay by Ronald Shusett & Dan O'Bannon and Gary Goldman

'It's like a movie, and you're the star. By the time it's over, you'll have got the girl, killed the bad guys and saved the planet.'

Obsessed by dreams of Mars that he can't afford to realise, Doug Quaid, a construction worker, settles for the Rekall Incorporated Ego Trip mind-travel package.

But when the treatment dislodges some *true* memories, Quaid suddenly finds he is playing the fantasy for real . . .

Fast-moving, all action, this is totally compulsive entertainment which you won't forget.

Total Recall, is a major new film from Carolco directed by Paul Verhoeven and starring Arnold Schwarzenegger. Based on an original short story by Philip K. Dick. Screenplay by Dan O'Bannon.

THE ABYSS

Orson Scott Card

NOW A MAJOR FILM FROM TWENTIETH CENTURY FOX

Far beneath the blue Caribbean sea lies Deepcore, the world's most advanced high-technology drilling station. When a mysterious force sends the submarine *USS Montana* spinning out of control, Deepcore is commandeered as the base for a naval rescue operation.

Lindsay Brigman, designer of Deepcore, insists on joining the team. When the operation gets underway, she witnesses something astonishing, activity she can only define as non-terrestrial intelligence. Nobody takes her seriously – there are far more pressing concerns. For up above, the world is spinning towards nuclear war . . .

From Orson Scott Card, one of science fiction's most heralded authors, comes an extraordinary adventure of wonder and terror.

ANCIENT IMAGES

Ramsey Campbell

'Ramsey Campbell is better than just good'
– Stephen King

British film editor Sandy Allan is searching for the print of a film made fifty years ago starring Karloff and Lugosi. It seems all those who have worked on it, or owned a print, have either died nastily, including her friend, or fled the film industry. Her quest takes her to Redfield, an idyllic rural town. It is there, surrounded by green fields and beauty, that she begins to understand.

Woven into the frames of 'Tower of Fear' was an evil so ancient, so powerful, so monstrous that nothing can survive its malevolence . . .

THE HUNGRY MOON

Ramsey Campbell

'A gripping, terrifying novel' – James Herbert

On the black moors of northern England in the shadow of a modern missile base, a band of Druids enact their pagan rites . . .

Rites which unleash a nightmare vision of two unspeakable horrors – ancient supernatural evil and nuclear catastrophe.

'He uses the Lovecraftian themes of survival, the occult and the things which may live at the rim of the Universe in a way that rings true for our time' – Stephen King

A SELECTION OF LEGEND TITLES

☐	Eon	Greg Bear	£4.99
☐	Eternity	Greg Bear	£4.99
☐	Forge of God	Greg Bear	£4.99
☐	Heads	Greg Bear	£4.99
☐	Queen of Angels	Greg Bear	£4.99
☐	Sharra's Exile	Marion Zimmer Bradley	£3.50
☐	The Influence	Ramsey Campbell	£3.50
☐	Ender's Game	Orson Scott Card	£3.99
☐	Seventh Son	Orson Scott Card	£3.99
☐	Songmaster	Orson Scott Card	£4.99
☐	Speaker for the Dead	Orson Scott Card	£4.99
☐	The Worthing Saga	Orson Scott Card	£4.99
☐	Wyrms	Orson Scott Card	£3.50
☐	Knights of Dark Renown	David Gemmell	£4.99
☐	Lion of Macedon	David Gemmell	£4.99
☐	This is the Way the World Ends	James Morrow	£3.50
☐	Unquenchable Fire	Rachel Pollack	£3.99

Prices and other details are liable to change

ARROW BOOKS, BOOKSERVICE BY POST, PO BOX 29, DOUGLAS, ISLE OF MAN, BRITISH ISLES

NAME...

ADDRESS ....

....

....

Please enclose a cheque or postal order made out to Arrow Books Ltd, for the amount due and allow for the following for postage and packing.

U.K. CUSTOMERS: Please allow 75p per book to a maximum of £7.50

B.F.P.O. & EIRE: Please allow 75p per book to a maximum of £7.50

OVERSEAS CUSTOMERS: please allow £1.00 per book.

Whilst every effort is made to keep prices low it is sometimes necessary to increase cover prices at short notice. Arrow Books reserve the right to show new retail prices on covers which may differ from those previously advertised in the text or elsewhere.

BESTSELLING SF/HORROR

☐ Total Recall	Piers Anthony	£3.99
☐ Eon	Greg Bear	£4.99
☐ Forge of God	Greg Bear	£4.99
☐ The Abyss	Orsen Scott Card	£4.99
☐ Ancient Images	Ramsey Campbell	£3.50
☐ The Hungry Moon	Ramsey Campbell	£3.50
☐ The Influence	Ramsey Campbell	£3.50
☐ Red Prophet	Orson Scott Card	£4.50
☐ Seventh Son	Orson Scott Card	£3.99
☐ Child Across the Sky	Jonathan Carroll	£3.99
☐ The Shee	Joe Donnelly	£4.99
☐ Stone	Joe Donnelly	£4.99
☐ Roofworld	Christopher Fowler	£3.99
☐ Rune	Christopher Fowler	£3.99
☐ City of the Dead	Herbert Lieberman	£4.50

Prices and other details are liable to change

ARROW BOOKS, BOOKSERVICE BY POST, PO BOX 29, DOUGLAS, ISLE OF MAN, BRITISH ISLES

NAME...

ADDRESS ....

....

....

Please enclose a cheque or postal order made out to Arrow Books Ltd, for the amount due and allow for the following for postage and packing.

U.K. CUSTOMERS: Please allow 75p per book to a maximum of £7.50

B.F.P.O. & EIRE: Please allow 75p per book to a maximum of £7.50

OVERSEAS CUSTOMERS: please allow £1.00 per book.

Whilst every effort is made to keep prices low it is sometimes necessary to increase cover prices at short notice. Arrow Books reserve the right to show new retail prices on covers which may differ from those previously advertised in the text or elsewhere.